D0850265

JACK
ABSOLUTE

Also by C. C. Humphreys

NOVELS:
The French Executioner
Blood Ties

PLAYS:
A Cage Without Bars
Glimpses Of The Moon
Touching Wood

SCREENPLAY:
The French Executioner

JACK ABSOLUTE

C. C. HUMPHREYS

BCA

To Philip Grout, director and actor,
who cast me as Jack Absolute
and has been both friend and mentor ever since

'Delivered from a neighbour [France] *they have always feared, your other colonies will soon discover that they stand no longer in need of your protection. You will call on them to contribute toward supporting the burden which they have helped to bring on you; they will answer by shaking off all dependence.*'

COUNT VERGENNES

'*Of all the means I know to lead men, the most effectual is a concealed mystery.*'

ADAM WEISHAUPT, Founder of the Illuminati

'*There is one thing that I dread and that is . . . their spies!*'

GEORGE WASHINGTON

JACK'S JOURNEYS MAY to NOVEMBER 1777

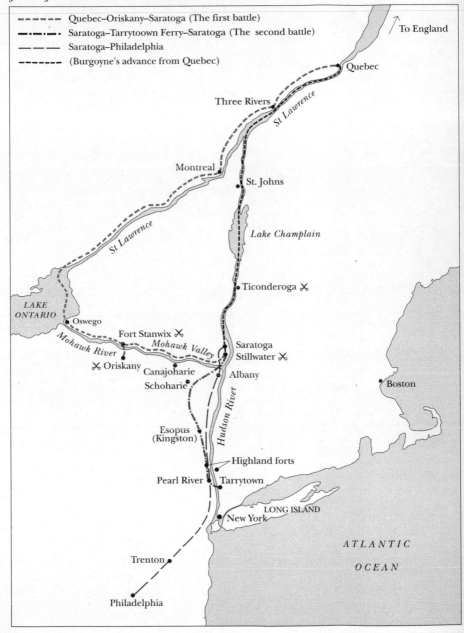

- - - - - Quebec–Oriskany–Saratoga (The first battle)
-·-·-·- Saratoga–Tarrytown Ferry–Saratoga (The second battle)
— — — Saratoga–Philadelphia
- - - - - (Burgoyne's advance from Quebec)

To England

Quebec

Three Rivers

St Lawrence

Montreal

St. Johns

St Lawrence

Lake Champlain

LAKE ONTARIO

Ticonderoga ✗

Oswego

Fort Stanwix ✗

Mohawk River

Mohawk Valley

✗ Oriskany

Canajoharie

Schoharie

Saratoga

Stillwater ✗

Albany

Boston

Hudson River

Esopus (Kingston)

Highland forts

Pearl River

Tarrytown

LONG ISLAND

New York

ATLANTIC

OCEAN

Trenton

Philadelphia

– ONE –
An Affair of Honour

The snow lay deep over Hounslow Heath and the light was failing fast. They were already late, a double annoyance to Jack Absolute; not only was it considered ungentlemanly to keep people waiting for such an affair, it also meant that by the time the ground had been reached, the Seconds introduced, the area marked out and the formalities dealt with as to wills and burials, it would be too dark for pistols. It would have to be swords; and by the look of him, his opponent was in fighting trim. If he wasn't twenty years younger than Jack he wasn't far off and, as a serving cavalry officer, would be fencing daily; while it was five years at the least since Jack had fought in such a manner. With a variety of other weapons, to be sure. But a tomahawk or a Mysore punch dagger had a very different feel to them than the delicate touch required for the small sword. Of course, one could only be killed with the point, it had no cutting edge. But the point, as Jack knew all too well, was all that was required.

As his feet slipped yet again on the icy bootprints of those that had preceded him, Jack cursed. *How large will the damned crowd be?* The affair could hardly have been announced more publicly, and many would choose to attend such a fashionable fight. Money would already have been staked. He wondered at the odds. Like an older racehorse, Jack had form. He had 'killed his man' – in fact, in the plural, several more than these

1

gentlemen of London could know about. But his opponent was certainly younger, probably stronger, and above all, in-flamed with the passion of wronged ardour. He fought for a cause. For love.

And Jack? Jack fought only because he'd been too stupid to avoid the challenge.

He sniffed. To top it all, he suspected he was getting a cold. He wanted to be warm in the snug at King's Coffee House, a pot of mulled ale in his hand. Not slip-sliding his way across a frozen common to maiming or a possible death.

'Is it five or six duels you have fought, Daganoweda?'

Jack, whose eyes had been fixed on the placing of his own feet, now glanced at the speaker's. Their nakedness seemed like vanity, especially as Jack knew his companion had a fine pair of fleece-lined boots back in their rooms in St Giles. However Até would never pass up such an opportunity to display the superior toughness of the Iroquois Indian. The rest of him would probably have been naked too had Jack not warned him that ladies might attend. The concession had been fawn-skin leggings, beaded and tasselled, and a Chinese silk vest that scarcely concealed his huge chest, nor obscured the tattoos wreathed around his muscles. Midnight black hair fell in waves to his almost bare shoulders. Just looking at him made Jack shiver all the more and he pulled his cloak even tighter around him.

'Six duels, Atédawenete. As I am sure you well remember. Including the one against you.'

'Oh,' Até turned to him, his brown eyes afire, 'you count a fight against a "savage", do you? I am honoured.'

The Indian made the slightest of bows. Iroquois was a language made for irony. Jack had had too much cognac the night before – the first error in an evening of them – and a duel of wits was one conflict he could live without today. So he reverted to English.

'What is it, Até? Homesick again?'

'I was thinking, brother, that if this young brave kills you – as is very likely since he is half your age and looks twice as vigorous – how then will I buy passage to return to my home across the water, which you have kept me from these eleven years?'

'Don't concern yourself with that, brother. Our friend here will give you the money. It's the least he can do. He owes me after all, don't you, Sherry?'

This last was addressed over his shoulder to the gentleman acting as his First-Second, as the hierarchy of duels had it. The dark-haired young man was struggling to keep pace with his taller companions, his face alternately green and the palest of yellows. The previous evening, Richard Brinsley Sheridan had drunk even more cognac than Jack.

'Ah, money, Jack, yes. Always a wee bit of a problem there.' Though he had left Ireland as a boy, a slight native brogue still crept in, especially in moments of exertion. 'But, of course, you'll be triumphant today, so the need will not arise. And in the meantime, can you and your fine-looking friend speak more of that marvellous language? I may understand not a word, but the cadences are exquisite.'

Jack pulled a large, soiled square of linen from his pocket and blew his nose hard. 'Careful, Até, you'll be in one of his plays next. And we all know where that can lead.'

The playwright wiped an edge of his cloak across a slick brow, sweating despite the chill. 'How many more times can I apologize? As I said, you were thought dead and thus your mellifluous name was free to appropriate.'

'Well, I may be dead soon enough. So your conscience may not be a bother too much longer,' Jack muttered. He had caught sight of movement through a screen of trees ahead.

If the crowd's big enough, he thought, *perhaps even the incompetent Watch might have heard of it and turn up to prevent this illegality.* Once he would have objected vigorously to any attempt by the authorities to restrict his right to fight. Once . . . when he was as young as his adversary, perhaps. Now he could only hope that the Magistrates' intelligence had improved.

But no reassuring Watchmen greeted Jack, just two dozen

3

gentlemen in cloaks of brown or green, a few redcoated army officers and, in the centre of the party, wearing just a shirt, the man who had challenged him – Banastre Tarleton. Jack was again startled by his face. The youth – he could be no more than eighteen – was possessed of an almost feminine beauty, with thickly lashed eyes and chestnut curls failing to be constrained by a pink ribbon. But there was no hint of a lady's fragility in his movements, laughing as he lunged forward with an imaginary sword.

He looks as if he is on a green about to play a game of cricket, Jack thought, and wondered if it was the cold that made him shrug ever deeper into his cloak. He glanced around the circle of excited faces that turned to him. No women, at least. Not even the cause of this whole affair, that little minx, Elizabeth Farren. The hour was too close to the lighting of the footlights at Drury Lane and her show must go on. Yet how she would have loved playing this scene. The sighs, the sobs wrenched from her troubled – and artfully revealed, carefully highlighted – bosom, as she watched two lovers do battle for her. She would be terribly brave one moment, close to fainting the next.

An actress. He was going to be killed over an actress. It was like one of Sheridan's bloody comedies, not dissimilar to the one in which the playwright had made him the unwitting star. It was an irony perhaps only an Iroquois could fully appreciate. For if Sheridan hadn't used his name in *The Rivals*, if Jack hadn't then felt it necessary to watch some posturing actor play 'him', if he hadn't succumbed, yet again, to the effects of brandy and the actress playing the maid, and if she wasn't already beloved by this brash, stupid, handsome, young officer . . .

Até and Sheridan had moved across to commence the business, and Jack noted the two men with whom his companions were discussing terms. One, an ensign in the resplendent, gold-laced uniform of the Coldstream Guards, was talking loudly and waving his arms about. Yet it was the other, Tarleton's Second-Second, who held Jack's attention.

4

He was standing behind and slightly to the side, his will seemingly focused, not on the details of the duel, but entirely forward on to Jack, just as it had been the previous night, when his soft whispers had urged Tarleton on. This man had the sober but expensive dress of a rich cleric, the long, pale face of a scholar. And looking now at the man he'd heard named the Count von Schlaben, even in the poor light of a winter sunset, Jack could see that this man desired his death as much as the youth who had challenged him; perhaps even more. And in that moment of recognition, Jack knew that there was more than actresses involved and that honour was only a small part of this affair.

If I am about to die, he thought, looking away and up into the cloud-racked March sky, *the least I can do is to understand why.*

Something had occurred the previous night at the theatre, aside from the play and the challenge. Something that had brought them all here to this snowy common. So it was back to Drury Lane that Jack's mind went, in the few moments before the formalities were settled, and the dying began.

— TWO —
Theatre Royal

Captain Jack Absolute marched forward, his eyes reflecting the flames of a hundred candles.

'There will be light enough; there will, as Sir Lucius says, "be very pretty small-sword light, though it won't do for a long shot."' He raised an imaginary pistol, 'fired' it with a loud vocal 'boom', then added, 'Confound his long shots!'

This last, delivered in an exaggerated Irish brogue, conjured a huge roar of laughter from the pit and a smattering of applause from the galleries. The bold Captain had a way with him!

Or was that just the actor playing him?

In the pit, the real Jack Absolute had suffered more than enough. He rose and squeezed through the tiny gap between knees and the backs of benches, trying to obscure as little of the stage as possible, though his kindly efforts were rewarded with cries of, 'Sit down, sirrah,' and 'Unmannerly dog! Woodward is speaking!' From above, the actors glared down at him before continuing the scene.

The evening had been a nightmare. Only one week back in London, his legs still moving as if the deck of the East India Company sloop and fifty fathoms of water were beneath him, he had been forced to sit and watch this parody of his past. Jack had learned of his new notoriety when, on his first day back, he'd taken a chair from the City to Covent Garden and the chairmen, on discovering his identity from the banker

6

who'd handed Jack in, had called out to all they passed that they had the 'real' Jack Absolute inside. A crowd had followed, calling out his name. Thereafter, every clerk, innkeeper and trader he'd been introduced to had inevitably said, 'You're not *that* Jack Absolute, are you?' And when, in a fury, he'd tracked his old friend Sheridan down, the rogue had barely blinked at his misappropriation of Jack's name and history.

'But you was gone seven years, Jack. We all thought you was dead. You was lucky, actually. I beat poor Ollie Goldsmith – God bless his memory! – to the name by a hair. He would have used it in *She Stoops to Conquer*. Then you'd have been that st-st-stuttering booby Marlow, rather than the dashing, handsome Captain of my *Rivals*.'

Dashing? Handsome? The ever-popular Mr Woodward, who personated Jack, was sixty if he was a day, and no amount of face paint and kindly, low-level candlelight could conceal the wrinkles. As for the play itself, Jack had to concede that Sheridan had a sharp memory and sharper eye. Jack's youthful escapade had been captured in almost every detail. His on-stage father, Sir Anthony Absolute – at least the playwright had had the minor decency to alter his name from James – was a perfect study of the tyranny, humour, and incipient insanity of the original. The object of desire, Lydia Languish, was modelled on just such a mix of beauty and romantic imbecility. However, Jack knew he needn't stay till the epilogue. This story would resolve in universal reconciliation and joy. Unlike the original. Perhaps that was what galled Jack the most, propelled him now from the auditorium; that Sheridan had usurped his youthful folly for a romantic comedy, when the reality was more of a farce and, in the end, almost a tragedy. The then nineteen-year-old Jack had *not* ended up with the lady – as his stage incarnation undoubtedly would this night – indeed, he had nearly died in his attempt to carry her off. And, having failed, he had begun the first of his many extended exiles from England.

Fortunately, he had good reason not to remain and witness further banality – for another exile would commence tonight.

A coach stayed for him at his inn, as a boat stayed for the tide in Portsmouth. After seven years away, he had been in the realm for as many days, long enough to deal with the affairs that now took him hence again, with a line of credit from Coutts Bank to transform the sugar plantation on Nevis in the Antilles, which his recent skill, acumen, and simple bloody-mindedness in India had won him. He just had two matters to attend to first. Two people to see. A man and a woman.

He gained the side aisle and advanced to the stairs. The first of those people had a box. All that was required was a brief, courteous refusal of that man's offer, followed by a visit backstage for an equally swift, if potentially more passionate, farewell.

Could it have been only one week? In that short time, had one of the most powerful men in the realm sought a favour and one of its most desired ladies sought to seduce him? And now, in the space of five minutes, was he to refuse them both? He could not wait to return to the sea. Life was so much simpler aboard a ship.

A ticket collector tried to halt his progress upstairs, but a coin gained him passage. There was an officer at the box door, wearing the uniform that Jack himself had once worn – ensign of the 16th Light Dragoons, the smartest regiment in the Cavalry. But the young man recognized Jack, and his Commander had obviously left word that he was to be shown in promptly.

Jack would have preferred a moment to ready himself. To refuse the man inside was no light thing. But the heavy-brocade curtain was immediately slid back. Hearty applause seemed to greet his entrance, though, in truth, it was paying farewell to his stage incarnation's exit Stage Left and the end of Act Four. The Theatre Royal immediately filled with the cries of hawkers selling refreshments, while the orchestra struck up an air for the entr'acte, an Italian acrobat team called the Zucchini Brothers, just now making their entrance, Stage Right.

'Faith! There's the finest piece of stage trickery I've seen all night. Jack Absolute's coat-tails are still visible in the wings . . . and here the man stands in my box!'

8

'General.'

Out of long habit Jack nearly saluted but remembered in the nick that he was no longer in the regiment and was there to refuse that honour again. So the arm gesture transformed into a rather awkward half-bow, which the General would not have failed to miss. John Burgoyne missed nothing.

'Cognac?' A glass was tendered, accepted, gulped. The liquor was even finer than Sheridan's.

Burgoyne had absorbed the years far more kindly than the actor Mr Woodward. Though his hair was as white as the snow on the ground outside, it was a drift not a scattering. Black sideburns emerged from its banks like curled highlights for the strong, straight jaw; while equally dark, full eyebrows sheltered and set off the deep-set, grey eyes. Eyes that showed the intelligence of a man recently appointed to one of the highest commands in the army, who could also pen a play, *Maid of the Oaks*, which had enjoyed even more success than Sheridan's *Rivals*. Those eyes sparkled now with the joy of the joke, which he was all too eager to share with a figure Jack could barely make out in the corner of the box.

'This is the fellow of whom I was telling you,' Burgoyne spoke to the shadows there, 'whose history has been so diverting us tonight. My dear, allow me to present the real Jack Absolute. Jack, Miss Louisa Reardon.'

The shadow shifted, a face came into the light, and Jack took a moment – for it was worth the study. Eyes the colour and pattern of eastern jade, a delicate nose surmounting an 'O' of a mouth, gold and russet-red hair falling in waves, framing skin that, wanting any touch of make-up, wanted nothing. The voice, deep in timbre yet light in delivery, was as velvet as the skin.

'This the heroic Captain? The ardent lover?'

Jack bowed over the hand offered, his lips brushing it before he spoke. 'I am sorry to disappoint, madam. A captain no longer, heroic or otherwise. And as for the ardent lover . . . well, surely, that is not for me to say?'

'But have the ladies of London been given the opportunity to discover it for themselves?'

9

It was said matter-of-factly, with a lack of flirtation that made it all the more beguiling. And there was something intriguing in the accent, a memory. While he sought it out, Jack replied, 'Perhaps fortunately for everyone, that sort of exploration requires time, which is not available.'

'A pity. I am certain there are . . . some ladies who would find the true Jack Absolute more compelling than his onstage counterpart.'

'Compelling codswallop! Younger and more handsome is what you would say, is it not?' A smile had come to Burgoyne's face as he witnessed the exchange. 'I tell you, Jack, here have I been at my most gallant and charming all evening, and the most I have got in return is genteel civility. Yet the moment you walk in—'

'It was mere observation, General,' said Louisa Reardon, laughing. 'With so many gallant officers abroad in the service of their King, the Captain would have made a welcome addition to the society of the town. And,' she leaned forward, tapping her fan into her hand, 'I have only behaved with such reserve towards you, because we are nearly alone in this box . . .' She gestured to a rotund maid who sat in the far corner, soundly snoring, '. . . and I was concerned that if I admitted merely one of your addresses I should not be able to resist any of them.'

Burgoyne gave out a sharp bark of laughter. 'Ah, Jack. You may now guess how my poor wits have been addled in our exchanges of fire tonight. If I did not know you was coming as reinforcement, I should have fled this field long ago. And as to the time needed for "exploration", how does at least five weeks at sea suit? For Miss Reardon is to sail with us on HMS *Ariadne*. She returns to her family in New York.'

Ah! That was the memory, the accent. He would have liked to converse more with her, for he had often found the women of the Colonies to have an openness, a lack of guile that was most attractive. But the General had returned to business. So, sighing, Jack did too.

'Sir, that news makes what I must say all the more regrettable.'

He watched the smile vanish from Burgoyne's face and pressed on before any other expression could replace it. They had been through much together over the years and he hated to disappoint him.

'I am aware of the immense honour you do me, sir, in offering to reappoint me to the Dragoons. And it is with a heavy heart that I must refuse you.'

'What's that? Refuse?' Burgoyne's warmth had been replaced by a dangerous coolness. 'It would not be me you refused. It would be your King. Your country.'

'I am aware that is how it could be perceived.'

Burgoyne snorted. 'Could be? *Will* be! England is at war with damn'd Rebels in a land you know better than almost any man in the realm. And you would refuse to go to her aid? There's no "could" about it.'

Jack tried to keep the colour from his voice, though he was aware it had flushed his face. 'With respect, sir, there are many here who also refuse. Many, even, whose sympathies are with those Rebels.'

'Yes, and I well remember how often your own sympathies have sided with so-called freedom's cause. That Irish mother of yours, God bless the memory of her beauty! But this is different, sir. You are an officer of the Crown. Dammit, you are an officer of my own regiment.'

'Was, sir. I resigned my commission eleven years ago, as you well know, since you struggled long to dissuade me from doing so. And I have since been with the East India Company and about my family's business.'

'Family be damned! This is the King's business. Have you forgotten your oath?'

Burgoyne had stood to face Jack, his voice rising in volume as it had deepened in tone. It could have carried across a parade ground. Many in the surrounding boxes had left watching the leaping Italians to stare.

It was Louisa who calmed them. 'Captain . . . Mr Absolute. May an American speak? One who does not side with these "damn'd rebels"?'

Both men nodded, giving ground slightly.

'The General has confided a little of how he intends to subdue these traitors. Just as much as he thinks a simple girl can understand. But I was raised in a family that has fought for the Crown for three decades. As we speak, my father commands a Loyalist regiment in the field.'

'A damned fine one too!' Burgoyne growled. 'And he pays for their uniforms and powder out of his own pocket.'

Jack looked again at Miss Reardon. He had never found an attractive woman less attractive for being rich.

'Thank you, General,' she said. She turned again to Jack. 'He tells me that His Majesty's Native Subjects are the key to winning the war.'

Jack smiled slightly. He was glad Até was not there. 'If the General is referring to the Six Nations of the Iroquois, they are not "subjects", Miss Reardon. They have never been subject to the Crown. They are His Majesty's Native *Allies*.'

'The General also tells me that you know these . . . allies, better than any man alive.'

'I would not say that, necessarily, Miss—'

'Don't dissemble, Absolute.' Burgoyne had lowered his voice under the lady's influence but the anger had not left it. Turning to her, he said, 'The man lived as one of them for several years. He speaks their tongue as a native. Under that silk shirt and embroidered jacket his chest is covered with their skin paintings. You should see them!'

'Indeed. That would be most . . . educational.' She allowed the faintest of smiles before she went on. 'But do you agree with the General? Are they essential to winning this war?'

'I have no idea of the Crown's specific plans—'

'But speaking generally. Can the war be won without them?'

Jack sighed. This beauty was boxing him in. 'If the war is to be fought in the north, from Canada down, then . . . probably not. I am sure you are aware of the wildernesses where any campaign will be conducted. Vast tracts of forest with hardly a road fit for the name. My brothers – excuse me, the Iroquois Nations – know that land, can forage, scout, and skirmish where marching regiments cannot. And they provide the information necessary for those regiments to bring all their force to bear when appropriate. No, Miss Reardon, in truth, the war cannot be won without them.'

He forestalled her next point. 'But I . . . I have no real influence with these people. I have been gone eleven years and new leaders will have arisen whom I do not know. I can speak the language, yes, and I know their ways. I am indeed useful to the General. But I am not essential. And I have spent seven years in India trying to rebuild the fortune my father lost on the turn of one card. If I do not get to our new estates in Nevis in the West Indies, with the profits I have laboured long for, the Absolute fortunes may be lost again. And many people will suffer, not just my family.'

He turned to Burgoyne. The anger had left the General's face and it now bore the look that Jack had feared more than any other – disappointment. Nevertheless, he kept his voice steady. 'And so, sir, I have, most reluctantly, to refuse your gracious offer.'

'And if duty to your sovereign and your country cannot move you, what of your loyalty to me?' His voice softened and he looked direct into Jack's eyes, though his words appeared to be for Louisa. 'For it is not only his native connections I need, Louisa. The man before you is the finest field intelligence officer I have ever known. He could discover information in the deserts of Araby, simply by talking to the camels. He has a way with codes and ciphers that perplexes a mere horse-trooper such as I. And wars are won by information more than by powder and shot. Absolute here can sniff it out swifter than my hound can start a hare.' He paused and his hand reached out to rest on Jack's shoulder. 'You know how I need you. Will you not come?'

This appeal, so gently spoken, was far harder to counter than any cross word and Jack winced. He owed this man many times over; for his first commission at the age of sixteen, for countless opportunities since. They had fought together in Portugal and Spain. In 1762, in the mad attack at Valencia de Alcantara, he had saved this man's life – and amongst the

13

Iroquois that meant he owed a far greater debt than if his life had been saved by the General. In so many ways, Burgoyne was the father that Jack had lost when Sir James Absolute went mad because the card he'd turned over at the Pharo table had been a queen and not a king.

Yet there was no choice. Possible ruin lay in a change of heart.

'I am so sorry. General. Miss Reardon. A safe voyage to you both, I trust.'

He bowed, turned to go. Burgoyne's voice came, still more softly. 'You have a night and a day to change your mind, Mr Absolute. But a word of advice, whether you accept my commission or no. Watch your back. Or get that savage, your shadow, to watch it for you. I was so certain you'd accept that I told everyone that you already had. And as you pointed out, London is full of those . . . sympathetic to the Rebel cause.'

Jack frowned, then nodded, left the box, made his way down the stairs and towards the street. Gaining it, he paused, looked up and down. Now that Burgoyne had drawn attention to it, he realized his 'back' had felt strange for some days, as if someone was indeed eyeing it, him. He'd put it down to the mobbed streets of London, so very different from India. Now, as he studied the people swaying back and forth, the audience taking the air, hawkers and whores selling their respective wares, he knew it would be impossible to tell if anyone was interested in him as anything other than a customer.

In a doorway opposite, Até stood where he had all evening, startling the passers-by. He hated the theatre – unless they were playing Shakespeare; and even then he was a purist. The happy endings appended to *Lear* or, especially, *Hamlet*, infuriated him. And despite his mission school education, Até still felt that by portraying Jack in a drama they were somehow stealing his soul.

At the slight shake of Jack's head, the Mohawk slipped back into the darkness. Now he would wait for Jack to pass and follow him at a distance, to see if his friend was being stalked. Such caution had saved their lives a score of times.

14

Jack turned into an alley. It was the swiftest way to get backstage so he took it despite the fetid darkness. The second of his interviews awaited him there.

Surely, he thought, *it cannot be any harder than the first.*

The necessity for this encounter was Sheridan's fault. When Jack had learned of his fame and, in a rage, sought the Irishman out at King's Coffee House, the playwright had placated him, initially with three pints of porter – a nectar Jack had not tasted in seven years – then persuaded him to come to the theatre, where *The Rivals* was in rehearsal for its remounting.

'There's someone I would like you to meet,' he'd said, taking Jack's arm.

That someone was Elizabeth Farren. Dressed as Lucy, the mischievous maid of the play, she was the epitome of all Jack had missed in his years away, the embodiment of many a youthful passion. Though small in height, she was perfectly formed – 'A pocket Venus,' Sheridan commented in a whisper, as they watched her rehearse. She was dressed and made-up as she would appear that night, breasts thrust up and forward, dusted in a light vermilion powder, speckled with gold. A lace attempted to hold in the front of the bodice, artfully half undone. It made a man instantly desirous of completing the task.

It certainly made Jack feel so. No matter that it was all artifice, that Lizzie merely feigned the wide-eyed country maid. Jack fell.

And later, as they were introduced in the cramped wing dressing-room, it seemed that Lizzie did too.

When the blushing actress had returned to her acting, Jack, somewhat flustered also, had told his friend that it must be the introductions that lured her – for the Irishman had told her that Jack had once written for the stage, rather than any quality he possessed. This had set Sheridan on a roar.

'P'shaw, Jack! I despise modesty in a man as much as vanity. Have you looked in a mirror lately? Here. Here!' He pulled Jack round to face the cracked glass before which lay the potions and creams of transformation. 'Four months on a sunlit sea, the winds buffeting your face? You glow, sir! Look at any winter-pale Londoner, lord or baker, for comparison. And if you were always a dark-skinned Cornishman, your years in India have turned you into a positive native! You could pass as the brother of that Iroquois who follows you around.'

Jack grinned. He often had.

'And that smile. Those blue eyes that seem all the bluer in their dark setting. And if your nose is slightly larger than is perfect for proportion, and your hell-black hair somewhat longer than the fashion and lacking in style,' he flicked his own trained locks, 'what of it? I doubt there is a woman in the realm who could resist you. And you wonder that poor Lizzie fell? Sure now, if she had not been called to the stage, she'd have had you on the spot, whether I'd been there or no!'

Sheridan had led Jack to a tavern with a slap and a guffaw, and their friendship was further restored amidst more pots of ale. By the end of an evening Jack barely remembered the next morning, he had forgiven his friend everything; indeed, he had a memory of begging the Irishman to write him into a sequel. And Sheridan had confessed that by pursuing Lizzie Farren, Jack would be doing him a favour. He was now the manager at Drury Lane as well as its premier playwright, and John Rich, manager at Covent Garden, was trying to lure Lizzie away. Nothing would distract her so much as a love affair – at least until she signed her new contract.

Distracting it may have been. Fulfilling it was not. Between her hours in the theatre and Jack's chasing of money about the town, they could snatch only moments from his fast-diminishing store of time. It heightened their passion. But it left no opportunity to take them from that height.

'*And that is where it should be left,*' Jack had decided in a more sensible hour.

Yet pausing now between the piles of refuse in the court behind the theatre, he took another good pull at his flask of Sheridan's cognac, his heart as dark as his surroundings because of that sensible decision. The *Isis* stayed for a tide in Portsmouth and then it would be gone to the West Indies. He had to be on it. But he had grown fond of Lizzie, her youth, her ardour, even her actorly ways. He was flattered by her attentions but he was no longer the Cornish Romeo of his youth, to steal a moment's satisfaction from a pretty girl and then be gone with the dawn.

Such was his resolution as he walked into the wings at Drury Lane. Yet it did not stop him pausing before a mirror near which the two Italian acrobats were conducting a furious, sotto voce argument, their gestures indicating that something had gone horribly wrong on-stage. He flicked at his black hair, dishevelled by the wind and falling snow outside.

May as well leave her with a good memory, he thought, smoothing the thick locks. He remembered how well actresses loved their final scene. Grinning, he stuck his tongue out at his reflection.

Lizzie awaited him in the same dressing-room where they'd met. She was alone, and through the half-open drape that gave on to Stage Right, he could see the other actors taking their positions. The orchestra struck up. Act Five, the conclusion of the play, was about to begin.

'Leave? Tonight?' The back of the hand went to the brow, the lower lip trembled, water came to the kohl-lined eyes. 'Oh, Jack, my Jack, say it isn't true!'

It was a damned fine performance. She wanted this scene and he was still playwright enough to give it to her. But the scene would require a touch of jealousy on his part, to show her how much he cared. Glancing around, he spotted the prop he needed, a necklace of rubies that lay on a velvet glove. They had to be paste, yet they were exquisitely done.

'Will you miss me that much, Elizabeth, when you have admirers who send you such gifts? Do you play *The Rivals* then, for real?'

'Oh him!' She ran her fingers down the links. 'He is a mere boy! And . . . that is not all he gave me, look . . .' She rolled up her sleeve. Her wrist was coloured with bruises. 'He is a brute. When I told him I could not see him again, that I loved another, he . . .' She stifled a sob, more genuine this time, and rubbed her wrist.

Jack felt a tug of real anger, now rapidly displaced by a sudden thought. 'You did not tell him my name?'

'I . . . may have mentioned it.'

Excellent! All he needed was some incensed lover stalking him through London on his last night. Was that the regard he'd felt upon his back? All the more reason to be gone – and swiftly. He would have to gabble his lines.

'Elizabeth, this is farewell. Adieu, my dearest. I will carry you in my heart to the Indies.'

It was far from his best. But as he swept up from his bow, he saw that Lizzie had stepped near. Very near.

'Nay, sir,' she said, 'you do not intend to leave me without a kiss?'

'But are you not on soon?'

She turned her head. They listened to the dialogue. 'Oh no. It is the Faulkland and Julia scene. It goes on and on and on. Especially the way Mistress Bulkley drags out her lines.'

She mimed a yawn, turned back, smiled. 'So kiss me, Jack Absolute. Kiss me for the very last time.'

So he did. Pulled her tight and kissed her as if the kiss could last for ever. The scent of her, some French fragrance rising from her warm body. That lace, half-undone, at her uplifted breasts. Her hand caught between the velvet of her dress and his tight, black breeches.

She pressed her fingers into him and, in a voice suddenly more Deptford than Drury Lane, said, 'Ooh, Jack!'

Planned exits and good intentions. Gone in a moment. He pushed her back, or she pulled him, the table behind swept clear of its potions and bottles, glass breaking, creams leaking, powder rising through the air. She was lifting her dress, parting her undergarments. He fumbled at the buttons of his breeches, heard two rip.

'Jack!' she sighed. 'Here. Let me help. Here. Oh . . . *oh*! Yes. Yes! *There!*'

Four months at sea. Seven years away from England. Apparently he was still a Cornish Romeo after all.

She was as ready as he. The whalebone of her stays beneath the dress bent under his pressure, then snapped like bullet shot, a splinter thrusting into his hip. Jack scarcely noticed – for he was inside her.

There was brief, delightful resistance and then he was moving slowly deeper. She shuddered, squeezed him tighter to her, making it hard to force his head down. But he persevered. His teeth fastened on the lace of her bodice and he jerked free the tormenting half-knot.

'God,' he cried, 'I've been wanting to do that all week.'

'And I've been wanting you to do it.' She giggled and, as his head rose bit his ear.

Tongue and teeth, fingers rubbing, lifting, rolling. Her breasts were as beautiful as their promise. He bent to kiss them, to tease them with his tongue, then his mouth found hers and she bit him again, his lip, they tasted his blood together. Her head banged into the mirror, she groaned, but not in pain. A part of him was aware of the noise they were making, of the voices on stage grown suddenly louder. And he didn't care. He saw his face in the mirror, his hair dishevelled again . . . something else he didn't care about.

The scent of their lovemaking mingled with spilled creams and French fragrance. She was moaning, a single note, and he joined her in counterpoint, somehow a fifth below. Their notes rose, as did the volume from the stage; but that was another world, beyond them now. Inseparable, their voices entwined, along with every other part of them, and when they could not be any closer, they reached their height as one.

She turned her head aside then, with a diminishing sigh of ecstasy. Jack opened his eyes, looked again into the cracked mirror, saw again a contorted face . . . and realized, suddenly, that this time it was not his own.

Banastre Tarleton clutched a long, hot house rose in one hand, which was slowly drooping towards the floor. His expression was of greeting, tempered with shock, rapidly escalating to fury, mirroring Jack's anger, surprised in such an intimate act. But the expression of the man who held the dressing-room curtain aside for Tarleton was quite different. Indeed, the face of the Count von Schlaben displayed nothing but the purest joy.

The tableau held for a moment. Then Jack was up, taking a step towards the intruders, his eyes locking with Tarleton's, his hands busy at the fastenings of his breeches. Behind him, Lizzie hopped off the table, began smoothing and adjusting.

The shock on the younger man's face had now been entirely displaced by rage. Lifting the rose, he slashed it, like a cavalry sabre, across Jack's face. Thorns raked him, the bloom snapped off and the thick stem was drawn back for a straight thrust toward his eye. To prevent this Jack stepped forward and grasped Tarleton by the lapels of his jacket. Their faces were almost touching.

'Enough,' Jack said. 'Calm yourself, sir.'

The words had the opposite effect. Tarleton went berserk.

'Dog!' he yelled, grabbing Jack's hands, bending his knees, thrusting up. Jack's feet lifted and he was rushed backwards. Bracing himself to collide with Lizzie, or the dressing-table, he encountered neither. A drape was brushed aside, there was a sudden, intense brightness, and a vast space opening behind his propelled body. A woman screamed, there were shouts, and Jack, sailing backwards, instinctively dropped into a move that he'd rarely practised since his youthful wrestling with the village lads in Zennor, let his weight drop down and back-wards and, as Tarleton fell towards him, brought his legs up. When his back reached the floor, he planted his feet in his assailant's chest and used the man's rush to launch him over his head.

There was a huge crash. Jack felt the reverberations shudder through the wooden floor beneath him. There were further gasps, some shouts of 'Shame!' one of 'Bravo!' and then a face loomed above him. It was painted, eyes shadowed and highlighted, cheek bones sculpted in powder.

'What do you do here, sir?' hissed the actor.

Jack turned his head and looked out at a host of upturned faces. And the audience of the Theatre Royal, Drury Lane, looked back.

In an instant he was on his feet. His first thought was of his opponent but the fall had winded Tarleton, who was now struggling to rise, Stage Left. Meanwhile, making her entrance, was Lizzie. She rushed across to him with well-supported cries of, 'Jack! Oh Jack!' A pace behind her was the Count von Schlaben.

There was a silent moment, time slowing. Lizzie came into his arms. The two other actors retired upstage to stare. His head turned again to the auditorium. The audience had settled back, to enjoy this fresh sub-plot and all these new actors. Jack felt his hand rise slowly to his face. There was blood there, from the rose's thorns and Lizzie's bites. An inner voice spoke. *Sheridan*, it said, somewhat bitterly, *I know you will write this.*

Then noise returned along with time's normal pace. Von Schlaben helped the winded Tarleton to his feet.

The youth croaked, 'You cur! You will give me satisfaction.'

It was spoken in barely a whisper. From the footman's gallery, someone yelled, 'Speak up!'

Jack whispered to Lizzie, who was now staring frozenly into the auditorium, 'Come. Let us leave.'

He managed to turn her. They even took a step. Then Tarleton's hand closed on his arm.

'Did you not hear me, sir? You have come between me and my love. And you will suffer for it.'

This carried to the back of the pit. 'Ooh,' went the audience.

Jack let Lizzie take a step before him. He turned, took Tarleton's hand, bent it back at the wrist.

'You have now touched me twice, sir. Do not make the mistake of doing it a third time.'

'Aaah,' sighed the house.

He pushed the younger man away.

'And your answer, sir? You have wronged my friend. He has demanded satisfaction.'

This was softly spoken, yet still carried. Von Schlaben did not have to speak loudly to be heard.

'Go on, fight him,' someone yelled from a box.

Another voice countered, 'For shame, sir.'

Jack's gaze moved over the enthralled faces below before settling on the Count's. 'This gentleman had no prior claim to the lady's affections. She is free to choose and chose me. That is all. I will not fight for a boy's petulance.'

'That's good,' someone cried, 'awfully good.' There was a patter of applause.

'Perhaps you do not understand, Captain. My young friend will have redress for his injuries. As an officer of the King, are you not unable to refuse him?'

Jack smiled. Duelling was illegal, yet soldiers found it hard to turn down a challenge, the disgrace to their uniform. Some had been cashiered for doing so.

'But I am not an officer, sir. I resigned my commission eleven years ago.'

He had half-turned away. The absurdity of the situation was becoming too clear to him. He needed to get away from this public arena.

He wasn't halfway there before Tarleton spoke again. 'Then you put aside your courage when you put off your uniform. You, sir, are a coward.'

The word sailed up into the flies of the Theatre Royal, hung there like a backcloth waiting to drop for a change of scene. Two thousand pairs of eyes fixed upon him as Jack turned back.

'Now that,' he said, 'is a very different matter.'

'Aaah,' was the sound released from two thousand mouths. Then there was loud and universal applause. Stage managers appeared in the wings and took this chance to rush on to the stage and sweep the non-professional actors off it.

They gathered. Lizzie was swooning, comforted by a dresser who had appeared with a bottle of sal volatile for her to sniff. Von Schlaben had taken charge of the formalities.

'My card, Captain Absolute. Do you have a friend with whom I can arrange the affair?'

'I'd be happy to act for him.'

Jack turned to the voice, hearing the Irish lilt in it. 'Sheridan. Thought you wouldn't miss this drama. Been taking notes?'

'Indeed, Jack. It is lodged in here.' The playwright tapped the side of his head. 'Wonderful line, by the way – "Now that is a very different matter." Beautifully delivered. You missed your vocation.' He turned back to the Count. 'Sheridan is my name. I do not have a card. But I will be acting for the Captain.'

'Will you all stop referring to me as "the Captain"? I'm no longer a damned captain!'

Von Schlaben smiled at him. It was the second time Jack had seen him do so and it remained a thoroughly unpleasant sight. 'So, Mr Sheridan,' he said, 'where and when?'

The two men moved away to discuss terms. Jack looked to Lizzie where she seemed to be recovering under the attentions of her dresser. She raised a 'brave' face to him; then, looking across to his rival, seemed to swoon again.

Jack also looked to Tarleton. He was rubbing the wrist Jack had twisted. It was his left wrist, which was disappointing, for he was obviously right-handed – his sword straps hung on the left side. Just as well he'd left his sword in the cloakroom, as audience members were encouraged to do; though Jack knew he'd be seeing a sword in the man's hand soon enough.

Jack began to curse himself – for not sending a note to Lizzie with his farewells, for not already being on the road to Portsmouth, for being tricked into this cursed fight. He suspected trickery from the triumph he'd noted in the Count's grey eyes. He hoped to discover the reason and soon. He did not want to die in ignorance.

Sighing, he headed for the world. He needed more cognac and some paper. He had a will to make. And it would take no time at all.

— THREE —
The Duel

My young friend will have redress for his injuries. As an officer of the King, are you not unable to refuse him?

Jack stared across the duelling ground at the Count von Schlaben, the man's words, spoken so softly the previous night, echoing in his head. That the German wanted him to fight and, presumably, die was clear. But why? Why? Because he was an officer of the King? He wasn't. And yet . . . hadn't Burgoyne made it known that Jack had already agreed to re-join his regiment as the General's Intelligence?

Jack shook his head. The remains of the cognac he'd drunk the night before still muffled his reasoning while the cold was beginning to numb other parts. And he suddenly realized that such musing would clarify nothing. The reason might not matter anyway, as he could be dead very shortly. The best – the only – way to avoid that was to get this fight over with as soon as possible. There would be time enough for 'why' later.

Or not.

Jack had been content to hang back with his thoughts and leave the formalities to others. But it was clear, by the increasing volume of the voices, that a resolution was far from being reached. Blowing his nose again, he went over.

'Gentlemen, if we do not commence soon, I'll freeze before I fight. What is the problem?'

A babble arose. Sheridan's voice, used to the demands of the theatre, won through. 'Jack, they wish to make it to the death. And to ensure such a result they wish to fight with these.' He gestured to a servant standing behind the squabblers. The man held two 'hangers', the cavalryman's main weapon. The wounds this heavy, curved sword could deliver, in capable hands, were hideous. His opponent's hands looked more than capable.

'As a tribute to our branch of the army, sir. Do you not think it fitting?'

Tarleton's almost pretty face twisted with emotions he could barely suppress.

He is a man for whom control is difficult, Jack thought. *Something to remember in the fight ahead.*

'Fitting?' he said. 'I have no desire to kill or be killed as a tribute to anything.' Before anyone could speak again, he added, 'Furthermore, gentlemen, as the challenged party, I believe my Seconds have the right to decide. They act for me.'

Sheridan stepped forward. 'My friend is correct. And, as I have said, we choose small swords, since the light is poor for pistols. And the matter to be honourably settled at the sight of First Blood.'

Muttering began at that through the gallery of spectators. People had come to see a death, not a wounding.

'Never mind.' Tarleton stepped forward, his eyes holding Jack's, his voice quavering, though there was no fear in it. 'First Blood can be last blood too.'

The promise hung in the air until Tarleton's First-Second, the Ensign from the Coldstreams, spoke, his voice unpleasantly thin and nasal. 'Your Seconds? An *Irishman* and . . . what is this fellow exactly? We know that the Absolute name has fallen low. Your father bays at the moon, does he not? But could you not get better than an Irish playwright and a *savage* who does not even comprehend our language?'

The emphasis was contemptuous in the extreme. Jack felt Até stir beside him. The Mohawk had little concern for the etiquette of a duel. He'd stove this man's head in and not think twice about it. Quickly, Jack said, 'Do you refer to Até here? He does indeed speak English.'

The Ensign turned to the semi-circle of men who had gathered closer to listen. 'My betrothed, Lady Augusta, keeps a parrot who can talk. Any animal can be taught tricks.'

Guffaws rippled through the gathered gentlemen.

'Shall I spill his brains on to the ground, Daganoweda?' Até had stepped back to give himself room to swing, his hand resting on the tomahawk at his waist. He'd spoken in Iroquois and Jack answered in the same.

'I doubt you'd find any to spill, Até. Could not you quote him some of your infernal *Hamlet* instead?'

The Mohawk's gaze flicked to Jack. 'Could not Lady Augusta's parrot do as much?'

Jack sighed, looked heavenward for a moment. He really needed to get his friend back across the ocean. So-called civilization was sapping his reserves of irony. Then, in that moment, Jack recognized the Ensign. Savingdon was his name, a Viscount, and Jack had been at Westminster School with the man's elder and equally bovine brother.

'Até here can trace his family back for seven generations and every ancestor royalty of the tribe. Wasn't your grandfather, Savingdon, the coal merchant who bought his title?'

It was true and all there knew it. The laughter made the Viscount's already florid face flush a deeper red. He stepped forward, hand reaching for his sword.

'You dog, Absolute! If my friend here doesn't kill you, I will.'

Tarleton said, 'You will not get that chance.'

A hubbub arose from the gallery. The president, a colonel of the Foot Guards, tried to lift his voice above it and restore calm. He failed.

'Enough.'

The word was spoken quietly. Yet the speaker's command was such that there was an almost instant hush.

'Is this how such matters are conducted in this realm? Are we here to talk or to fight?'

26

Once more Jack looked at Tarleton's Second-Second; into the grey eyes, so mild in that long face framed with white-blond hair. Once more he was puzzled. Everything else concerning this affair reminded him of episodes from his youth, the English gentleman and his prickly honour. But this man, this German, was out of place in such a scene.

Before Jack could consider any further, Savingdon was braying, 'Enough, indeed. Let us begin,' and Jack was being pulled away by his friends.

'My lawyer, Phillpott's of the Inner Temple, has all the details should anything befall me,' Jack said in answer to Sheridan's entreaty. 'There's precious little left in the Absolute coffers, we're mortgaged to the last button, hence the importance of my journey to the Indies. Enough to keep Sir James supplied with wine in his cell at Bedlam for a time. But it's a pauper's grave for me and nothing for you, I'm afraid, Até.'

'Then may I suggest you win this fight so we can complete your business and I can return to my people, as befits my status, with rich gifts for all.'

'Is that what concerns you?' Jack looked at his friend. 'Your status? I might be dead in a moment. Have you nothing to say of that?'

'I will say just two things, Daganoweda. Firstly, this man who talked of parrots will die moments after you do. Secondly, concerning your death, remember this.'

He drew himself up to his full height, arms extended before him, as if he was about to speak in the meeting lodge of his tribe and, in sonorous Iroquoian, declaimed, ' "If it be now, 'tis not to come. If it be not to come, it will be now. If it be not now, yet it will come. The readiness is all".'

'Zounds,' Jack muttered, '*Hamlet* again! I wish I'd never introduced you to that bloody play.'

'He is the Wise One. Wiser than you, Daganoweda. For when he was to die, he knew why. He had accepted it, like a warrior. Yet you still think you are to die for a woman. And I think you are wrong.'

Jack had little time to consider his friend's words. Tarleton had taken his position at one end of the rectangle of snow, tamped down by those who'd come early to enjoy the fight. He stood there, swishing his sword, still clad only in his linen shirt.

'Your coat, Jack?' Sheridan already held his cloak.

'No,' Jack sniffed. 'I don't mind being killed – but I'll be damned if I'm going to catch a cold.'

He stepped up to his mark. They saluted the President, their opponent's Seconds, each other. Then their two swords rose, ends meeting with the faintest of chimes. It was like the toll of some far-away bell, a stirring of consciousness, and it instantly cleared the very last effects of cognac from Jack's head.

His plan was simple. He assumed, from their previous dealings, that his opponent would be mad in assault, contemptuous of defence, that he would fall like a storm upon Jack's artfully casual resistance. Fire and fury was what was expected from youth; coolness and calm the prerogative of age and experience.

Yet in the opening exchanges, the younger man refused to conform to Jack's prejudice; was not tempted into an extended lunge, did not respond to the first of Jack's feints when he left his weapon slightly out of true, in tierce. He parried and riposted and parried again in the least exerting of ways.

Damn him, thought Jack, taking a breath, *the bastard's come to fence.*

Tarleton was obviously conscientious in his attendance at Master Angelo's Academy in the Haymarket. Though Jack had himself been one of the Italian's foremost pupils, it had been fifteen years since he'd last ascended those steep stairs – and the small sword required a subtlety of mind, a strength and nimbleness of wrist, and continual practice. The last thing he wanted was a fencing bout.

The fighters separated, sword tips an inch apart, the preliminaries ended. Each had a sense of the other. Jack breathed, tried to focus on his plan. A glimpse of blood was all that was needed for honour to be satisfied, to enable him to walk away.

28

If Tarleton would not be drawn into rashness, there were other ways to attain this end. A good scratch would do it. He just had to set about inflicting one.

Yet as Jack considered, his opponent began on stratagems of his own. A dozen rapid passes, a flank temptingly exposed; Jack lured, over-lunging. His rear ankle bent instead of staying sole-flat to the ground, requiring an extra second to restore his balance; and in that small moment, Tarleton circular parried hard to the right. Jack's thigh was stretched out, exposed, his weapon too extended for protection; and the spectators who knew their sword-work, waiting for the swift strike at thigh that would at least wound but could kill if the artery were pierced, caught their breath.

The moment passed. Tarleton did not move; Jack regained his balance, dropped his point, and slashed. Since the small sword has no cutting edge, all knew that was mere desperation on Jack's part. They also knew that a chance for Tarleton to end the fight had not been taken; most realized, then, that for him, a glimpse of blood would not be enough.

Recovering, Jack returned once more to guard. His breath plumed the air before him, dissipating before it could join with his opponent's negligible exhalation. He was hot and now wished he *had* taken off his jacket. Yet to do so at this stage would be an acknowledgement he would not give his enemy. That last desperate slash had spent enough of his credit for coolness.

'Agitated, Absolute?' Tarleton's voice was calm, seemingly unaffected by the exercise. 'You're as red as you were when I caught you astride that whore last night.'

Recognizing the goad to anger, disdaining it, Jack took a deeper breath and smiled. 'You malign a lady, sir, whose only wrong is preferring a man to a boy. Though, if the story be true, her rejection of you was more to do with the, uh, length of your sword. Quill-trimmer was the term used, I believe.'

He heard Sheridan mutter, 'For God's sake, Absolute.' Indeed, the jibe was barely worthy of the playing field at

Westminster. Yet it seemed to have such a startling effect that it left Jack speculating it must indeed have been true.

'My sword? You shall feel the length of my sword, you dog!'

Jack had but a moment to marvel at the change in Tarleton's colour. Roaring, the youth disengaged his blade and hurled himself wide, thrusting for Jack's right flank. Retiring a step, parrying with point down, Jack riposted to the man's breast, under his arm. Stuck at the full length of his lunge, Tarleton went to parry hard . . . but encountered no blade there; for Jack had merely feinted, disengaged again and thrust to Tarleton's left shoulder. The younger man was forced to pivot off his front foot to make the parry, his back leg spinning out and round. Jack followed, keeping his blade bound tight to his opponent's, moving him around. He could have struck again but decided to savour this first little victory – and let Tarleton savour it too. Finally he stepped away.

Oaths were uttered, in approval or condemnation depending on the support. Suddenly, a one-sided fight had become a contest. Tarleton, smarting from conceding even a point, immediately began another assault. Jack had only a heartbeat to congratulate himself on the success of his provocation before he was protecting himself from the result of it.

A lunge in carte, one in seconde, the next in tierce. Jack contented himself with parrying and nothing more, but refusing to give any ground. This was forcing Tarleton to 'thrust at the wall', an academy exercise to make sure parries were true . . . and almost an insult to a good swordsman. For Jack had discovered that, once the river of Tarleton's anger had flooded, it would not recover its banks with any rapidity.

Another thrust came, another step to the right taken, parrying with point down. Jack's weight was on his back foot and, still in his fury, Tarleton slashed diagonally up at Jack's face. Yet Jack had seen the preparation for that, the slight withdrawal of steel that indicated it. He ducked low, back over his bent right leg. The slash had taken the younger man off-balance, and now Jack lunged, stretching from the crouch to his full length. Desperately, Tarleton threw himself to his right, his sword point down, just preventing Jack's from puncturing him. Their hands were almost touching, their bodies close, and the youth tried to pummel his sword-fist into Jack's face. Withdrawing his blade and swinging his back leg away, Jack used his left hand to slap down the blow.

They separated again. Two equal clouds of breath met and mingled in the frigid air.

A voice called out, English, but with an Iroquois accent. 'You can finish him now, Daganoweda. Your name says what you are and his says nothing.'

'And what does that name mean, Até? I always meant to ask,' said Sheridan.

' "Inexhaustible".' He turned to the Irishman and winked. 'His first wife gave it to him.'

Jack, meanwhile, simply breathed. He was not as inexhaustible as once he'd been. And his younger opponent would recover quicker.

So he began to attack. He'd noticed that a patch of mud and grass had appeared beneath the snow, scraped up by their endeavours. All he had to do was draw Tarleton into an extended lunge . . .

Yet it was he who was drawn. Instead of parrying, Tarleton avoided the blade with a volte, a leap and a thrust to the left side. Jack had to step hard right to parry it . . . and his foot landed square in the churned earth and melting snow.

He slipped down to one knee, his sword arm halting his fall. With a grunt, Tarleton drew his weapon back and thrust down with a blow meant to puncture flesh and snap bone.

With a part of his mind Jack watched the weapon come, aimed straight into his watching eye. With another he let the hand, still holding his sword that pressed into the snow, slip. So sure was Tarleton of his triumph that his blade didn't waver, didn't follow the slight movement of the head. So he was as surprised as Jack when the point met cloth, not flesh, and plunged through the collar of Jack's jacket, the one he'd wished he was no longer wearing, ripping half of it away.

The force of the blow pushed the torn shred of wool down,

impaling it into the frozen ground. The weapon shivered with the blow, then snapped.

'Hold, sir, hold,' cried the man acting as President. Tarleton would not be halted. Pulling back the half-sword, now with its jagged end, he made to thrust again. Yet his target had shifted, Jack had rolled on to his back. His own weapon, lifted from the snow, came round. The broken blade descended but Jack swiped it aside with the outside of his left hand. At the same time he jabbed up with his right.

He didn't have to jab far. Tarleton was falling. Jack's point pierced his ear in its centre, went through, and held it like a piece of meat prepared for an open fire. Blood, for the second time in twenty-four hours, spattered Jack.

'First Blood . . . sir,' Jack said.

A howl from Tarleton, a cry from the onlookers. And another sound, unheard till then – a horn, then another, a third from their proximity minutes only from the duelling ground.

The combatants were pulled apart. The President came forward.

'Fielding's men. The Runners are come! Here's First Blood drawn and honour satisfied, eh? Shake hands and let's be gone. None of us wants to spend time in the Clink, do we, gentlemen?'

'Come, Jack, to Drury Lane.' Sheridan's face was flushed. 'I'll dress you as Harlequin in a pantomime and hide you on-stage. And, by God, if you don't put this into a new play, I will!'

The horns were drawing closer, and the yelping of dogs was added to them. The hunt was on. At the far side of the trampled square of snow, Viscount Savingdon had withdrawn Jack's sword and was trying to stem the blood flowing from Tarleton's ear while Von Schlaben whispered urgently into the other.

'No!' screamed Banastre Tarleton. Suddenly he leaped to his left, where his valet still held the weapons that had been rejected for the duel. Pulling one of the cavalry sabres from its sheath, he ran across the square toward Jack.

Jack, shrugging into his cloak, turned at the scream, but not in time. The heavy blade was rising and, in that instant, both he and Tarleton knew that there would be no second miss, no collar to save him now.

Something else did. Something that flew from the edge of the clearing and struck the shrieking man on his temple, just before the sabre could begin its descent. Tarleton dropped to the ground as if he'd been shot. The sword sank into the snow beside him while, on his other side, another weapon fell as if from the sky.

'God?' yelled Sheridan, looking up, as if searching for the source of such divine deliverance.

'Até,' said Jack, and bent to pick up the tomahawk. 'Good throw, brother.'

The Mohawk thrust the weapon back into his belt and shrugged. 'I do not understand all the rules of these contests. But as your Second, was I not meant to stop such a thing?'

Savingdon had rushed to the fallen man. 'Your savage has killed him!' he cried.

'If my *savage* had meant to kill him, then he'd be dead.' Jack smiled. 'Is that not right, Até? You struck him with the top of the weapon, not the cutting edge, eh?'

For the first time, Até looked a little disconcerted. 'Actually, brother, maybe it was just not such a good throw.'

The horn blasts sounded again, much nearer now. Shouts too, seemingly from all sides.

'Come, gentlemen,' said Sheridan, 'time to make our exit.'

The crowd had scattered swiftly, for anyone arrested at the scene of a duel could be prosecuted. The largest body, counting on the strength of their numbers, headed for the most direct route back to the road – which was, of course, the direction in which the constables were approaching. Others broke, in singles and pairs, in all directions.

'This way,' called Sheridan.

They burst through a screen of trees cresting a small bank. The snow had drifted here, rising to their thighs, making it hard going. To their left came an excited shout, a blast of horn.

33

Looking there, Jack saw three men in grey greatcoats. Each was armed and one now unleashed two hounds.

'To the right, lads,' Jack cried, and began to straddle the snow, seeming to go where it was thickest. It was exhausting work but looking back, Jack saw his choice had been correct; for the dogs were finding the drifts too deep, leaping like porpoises in a white sea only to be swallowed and having to leap again. Their handlers were not faring any better.

They had gained some advantage when they reached a drover's path where the snow had been beaten down with hooves. Immediately, they began to run, stumbling at first, used as they were to the sensation of resistance. Soon, however, they picked up a good pace, though by the sounds of the yelps behind them, it would not be long before the dogs were moving swifter than they on the packed snow.

Ahead, through the gloom and falling snow, they saw a light. A shepherd's hut stood on the edge of the common there.

'The Windsor Road, I think. Means our landau is round the other side, dammit.' Sheridan was breathing more heavily than the others, unused to this outdoor work.

'It would have been secured by the Runners anyway.' Jack led them around the side of the hut. In its lee they paused for a moment, squatted down. Sheep in a pen regarded them incuriously. 'If Windsor's that way then so's the river. We can lose the dogs in the reeds on the bank. Come on.'

Jack rose, Até beside him. Sheridan struggled up but, red-faced, fell back.

'No, me boys, this hare has run his last. I think I'll converse with the owner of this fine establishment. Always useful to hear how the simple folk are talking these days. And when the Runners find me here, I can entertain them for a while.'

Jack began to protest but Sheridan interrupted him. 'Go and Godspeed. They will not incarcerate me long. We play my new comedy, *The School for Scandal* for the King next week, and he will not like to be disappointed. Go!'

Two swift handshakes, and Jack and Até turned, began to

run. Behind them Sheridan called out, 'Write me, dearest Jack, of your exploits, if you please. You always provide such thundering good plots!'

Jack snorted. He knew how this plot had to end. They needed to buy – or steal – horses in Windsor and ride south. The Portsmouth road was not far. He had to beat the news of this action to the coast. With the right tide, he could be a-ship and on his way to Nevis ahead of any pursuit.

They were a few hundred paces along the road when they heard the dogs again. Glancing back, they saw lanterns and shapes moving before the shepherd's hut. Some lingered, but a significant body set off in immediate pursuit.

They ran faster, looking to the left for a gap in the hedgerows, a path through the fields and down to the river. Behind them, the horns blew again, dogs bayed. And then another sound came under it all, a rolling, crunching noise, joined by the clear snap of a whip. Half-turning, Jack saw the huge shape of a coach and six, moving at speed through the pursuing pack. He was close enough to hear the curses heaped upon the coachman.

The vehicle drew alongside, slowing slightly to match their stride. A blind went up.

'Care for a ride, Jack?'

John Burgoyne leaned in the window, a pipe in one hand, silver flask in the other. Jack didn't hesitate.

'Much obliged, General,' he said, swinging a foot up on to the running board. The door of the carriage opened and he threw himself inside while Até, a pace behind, scrambled up the rear of the coach to its roof. As he was joined, the coachman cracked his whip again and the six horses surged forward.

'Strange . . . that you should just . . . happen by, sir,' Jack gasped.

'Strange indeed. And fortuitous, it seems.' Burgoyne smiled at him. 'Cognac?'

'A moment . . . to catch my breath, sir . . . if you please.'

He leaned out of the window, looked back. Darkness had

enveloped the sight of pursuit. The sounds of horns, frustrated men, and yelping dogs retreated into the night.

Jack sat back, then became aware of a presence beside him. He turned. 'Ah, Miss Reardon. Please excuse the intrusion.'

She smiled. 'Mr Absolute, how glad I am to see you again.' Then her smile vanished. 'But you are wounded, sir! Quickly, may I help you? I have some knowledge of these matters.'

'Wounded?' He glanced down. 'Oh, the blood is not mine.'

And he laughed. It suddenly felt rather good to do so, so he carried on for a little while, until Burgoyne, a broad grin on his own face, said, 'So, did you kill your man, Jack?'

'I did not, sir. I had hoped to avoid it. I merely pricked him.'

Burgoyne shook his head. 'You might come to regret that. This Tarleton has built up a brutish reputation. Scarce eighteen, and he has already dispatched three fellows. He's not the sort to consider honour satisfied if he loses. And he keeps some strange company.'

Jack now took the flask and drank. The cognac tasted even better than it had the previous night.

'Are you referring to his Second, this German Count? I did wonder about him.'

'And so you should.'

Louisa added, 'The General believes he is aiding the Rebels in my poor country.'

'In what way?'

'Have you heard of the Illuminati, Jack?'

'I have not.'

Burgoyne took the flask back, drank, then continued. 'Of course, you've been away. And even if you'd been here, you might not have . . . you do not move within the Mystery, do you?'

The General was referring to the Freemasons. Jack had always avoided the Brotherhood, even though it might have aided him in his business ventures. He felt there was more than enough secrecy in his life, enough obligation. But he knew Burgoyne to be high up in the order.

'I do not, sir. Are these Illuminati a lodge then?'

'Of a kind. A new one, formed in Munich only last year by a man called Adam Weishaupt. A professor of religious law, apparently, and many of his followers are of the same ilk. Lawyers!' Burgoyne gave the title a soldier's contemptuous emphasis, drew on his pipe. 'Yet these fellows have formed a secret society *within* a secret society. No one is quite sure what they want, though they have tried to infiltrate every lodge in the realm, succeeded with many. This Von Schlaben even approached me.' Burgoyne exhaled a gout of smoke toward the carriage window. 'I now regret not leading the Count on a little to discover more. But a contact who did said this Weishaupt's motives are shrouded in Jesuitical casuistry. He was educated by Jesuits, apparently, and rejected them later as not *extreme* enough, too tied to a Catholic orthodoxy. Thus my friend did not learn much; but he got the impression that these Illuminati seek, in all societies, disorder, disruption—'

'Revolution?'

'Indeed. To build an "illuminated" new order out of the chaos of the old. With them in control, presumably.'

Now that Jack's heart had calmed, his mind was engaged. And there were questions here that puzzled him.

'So why his interest in me? He seemed very set on my extinction.'

As he asked the question, he recalled again part of their conversation at Drury Lane, Burgoyne's parting words, and, remembering it, he had the beginnings of an answer.

'Did you not let it be known, sir, that I had already accepted your offer to rouse the Iroquois for the King?'

Burgoyne smiled. 'I'm rather afraid I may have given out that impression.'

'So if Von Schlaben understands the importance of the Iroquois to the British cause, he might perceive me as a serious threat to the Revolution? To the disorder he seeks?'

'You know, Jack, I'm rather afraid he might.'

Jack looked out of the window at the roadway speeding by.

The fields were giving way to more houses. They were entering the outskirts of Windsor.

Of course. There always had been more to it than a dispute over a pretty player.

'Well, General, I think you have enmeshed me here.'

It was said with a little heat but Burgoyne merely smiled still. 'Alas, Jack, I fear you are right. How ever can I make amends?'

'You are bound for Portsmouth?' He received a nod. 'Then a ride there would quit your obligation. My boat, as yours, awaits. If you will but take me to the docks—'

'And you will be arrested the moment you set foot upon them. My boy, you were called out in the most public setting possible. In accepting Tarleton's challenge, you in turn challenged the Authorities . . . and they seem very serious about restricting a gentleman's prerogative of honour. Examples must be made and you will make a fine one. Not too wealthy to cause a fuss but still well known. Your estates will be forfeit, your neck may well be stretched, you will at the least be thrown into the Clink and nothing can save you.' Burgoyne smiled again. 'Well, almost nothing.'

' "Almost nothing", General?' Louisa leaned in. 'Oh, do say there is something that can be done for the gallant Captain!'

They seemed to be sharing a private joke. Jack, looking from one to the other, suddenly realized what it was. And that it was on him.

'As usual, my dear, you have hit upon the very heart of it. If you were indeed "Captain" Jack Absolute again, entrusted by a commander of one of His Majesty's armies – odds life, I suppose someone very much like myself! – entrusted, as I say, with a mission vital to your country's cause . . . why then, my boy, no civil power on earth could touch you.'

Enmeshed indeed. There was no escaping from the snare. Instead of further anger, though, Jack could only tip back his head and laugh.

'It really is a very good plot,' he said, looking at each in turn, 'I must write Sheridan with it.'

'You will have plenty of time on our voyage to America.' Louisa smiled, laying her hand on Jack's arm, squeezing it gently.

He looked from her fingers up into her steady green eyes and seemed suddenly to see in their pattern something of the land from which she came. It appeared he had no choice now but to return to that land, to North America, eleven years after he'd left it. Até, facing into the wind atop the carriage, would be delighted. And Jack, now he had no other option, was strangely pleased too. His business in Nevis could, with very careful handling, wait a short while. And as for the Colonies, he had had another life there, other causes; it would be a homecoming, of sorts. Once more, to be Daganoweda, the 'Inexhaustible' of the Mohawk. Once more to be a captain of the 16th Light Dragoons. Once more to be a secret agent of the Crown.

Leaning back into the cushions of the carriage, Jack Absolute faced the inevitable with a smile. Até's words on the duelling ground came back to him.

The readiness is all.

He took the flask again, raised it first to the lady and then to the General. Taking a long pull of the exquisite cognac, Jack realized that he was, indeed, ready.

— FOUR —
Ghosts

Jack Absolute leaned on the taffrail of HMS *Ariadne* at dusk, staring at the skyline of Quebec. It looked very different from the first time he'd seen it, eighteen years before. Then it was undergoing a siege, had been reduced by artillery for a month. In the lower town, roofs had tumbled in, walls had crumbled, and the docks had been turned into a profusion of splinters and spars; in the upper town the French held on, protected by their unassailable cliffs, certain that winter's approach would force the besiegers to withdraw before the ice of the St Lawrence trapped and crushed their ships. The old enemy looked down upon a starving English army, wasted by the bloody flux, mutinous. Falling apart. Until . . .

Jack searched for and found a slice of shadow in the granite rockface.

In 1759, control of that slice, that narrowest of roads, had allowed General Wolfe to move his forces up onto the Plains of Abraham before the City. But seizing the track had required an advanced party to scramble up the cliffs in the pre-dawn dark and dispose of the French piquets before they could sound the alarm. And since half the officers already there were sick, and the majority afraid and since he was newly arrived from England and as foolhardy and expendable as only a sixteen-year old Lieutenant of Dragoons could be, he had been one of the first to volunteer for the assault. With muffled swords and powderless pistols, the advanced guard, Jack near the front, had killed the sentries on the cliff-top then guided the rest of General Wolfe's army into position. The Marquis de Montcalm, awaiting his enemy further up the river, had discovered them suddenly before Quebec's weaker landward walls; he'd marched his men down to confront them. For glory. For France. And had been one of the first to die in the perfect volley the British had delivered that day.

Distant thunder underscored his thoughts, and Jack shivered in a way that had nothing to do with the chill May wind. That track had not been the first place he'd hazarded mortality even then; but it was where he'd received his first battle scar, now just one of many. And here he was, a lifetime on, back where his Colonial adventures had begun. He wondered briefly if the fate he'd only just escaped then awaited him now.

Not here though. Not in Quebec. The battle at the end of that track, atop the Plains of Abraham, had won a continent for the Crown. Even if the townsfolk still spoke French, that enemy had been vanquished. The English returned now to fight someone different. Someone that had, until very recently, been on the same side in the overthrow of that ancient foe.

Jack sighed, wondering how many old allies he would now squint at along the barrel of his musket, men he'd called friends, whom he must now call Rebels and traitors. His secret hope was that Burgoyne meant to keep him at his side. In the five-week voyage from Portsmouth, the General had been large with questions, niggardly with answers, not very specific as to Jack's duties. '*Help rouse the Iroquois.*' Yes, but they were a disparate people scattered over a vast wilderness. '*Gain a true knowledge of the enemy.*' Yes, but was he to seek it out, or decipher it when it arrived?

They had dropped anchor only that morning. Messengers had come and gone all day, bearing information that Burgoyne would be using to refine the plans he'd hitherto kept to himself. His key officers had been summoned to a special supper that night. No doubt Jack and all the others would get their answers and their orders then. And find out exactly how the man the American Rebels contemptuously called 'Gentleman Johnny' planned to defeat their Revolution.

As always, Jack hadn't heard him come, until the words were spoken.

'Shall we dive in, Daganoweda, and see who is first to the shore?'

Jack squinted ahead. 'It's far.'

'We've swum further.'

'Not when we weren't being chased.'

He turned to Até. The Mohawk's gaze remained fixed ahead. As usual he was wearing the little that passed for his clothes, so Jack continued, 'And even you might find it cold, Até. The ice is not long gone.'

Até grunted. 'Colder than the high Ganges the day the Thugees chased us to the cliffs?'

Jack smiled and winced at the same time. Another land, another scar. 'No, not as cold. And probably not as far.'

'Well then. I am ready if you are.'

Neither man moved, just stared at the shore, at the sweep of woods above the town just gaining its spring shrouding. The forests here were so different from England, from India and the Caribbean; silver maple and spruce, white cedar, hemlock. Both men breathed deeply, held the scent in their nostrils.

'It is good to be back.'

Jack said nothing.

Até turned to him. To his silence. 'Do you fear what we are to do here?'

'I fear what we may find. Friends who are now foes. All wars are civil wars in some way, Até. This one more than most. Eleven years we have been away. A world changes in eleven years.'

The Mohawk thumped his chest with a closed fist. 'It does not change here.'

Jack studied the shoreline. 'I think it changes there most of all.'

Até's voice came then, a little softer. It was not the Iroquois way to dwell on past sadness. But he had lived in Jack's world long enough to know that the Iroquois way was not universal, more was the pity.

'We buried her, Daganoweda. Your woman dwells in the village of the dead. And those who killed her, they burn in hell.'

'I know this.'

'And now you believe love ends in death. This land, our land, makes you think this.'

'No,' he said, more sharply than he wished, 'it doesn't.' Contrary to what his friend believed, he didn't live in that past. He had mourned, moved on.

And yet? A secret path to a cliff top, the scent of white cedar, an echo of a woman's laugh on the breeze? Ghosts, gathering.

Até studied him for a moment, then said, 'Be careful? About what?' Até sighed. 'I have seen you before. Many, many times. You are as fast as any member as of the Wolf clan, as good in a fight with gun or tomahawk. But you are unlike us only in this – you are a fool with women. In this one thing, you are a fool.'

Jack felt anger again, bit back on it. This was an old argument between them.

He did not hear Até go as he had not heard him come. He heard the next footfall though, knew it from its soft determination, the way the heels struck upon the deck. He had learned to listen for it, in the five-week voyage from England. More of what Até would call his foolishness.

'The General's compliments, Captain Absolute. The company is assembling.'

He faced her. Louisa was wearing something new, obviously saved for this last, most special supper. Nancy, her maid, had gentled her thick, red-gold hair into ringlets that corkscrewed down over the bare shoulders and forward to her décolletage. The silk dress was a shade of green that amplified that of her eyes.

He reached to her, crimped a piece of the material in his fingers. 'This is beautiful.'

'Why, thank you.'

She twirled slightly, let the lower folds float outwards, sink back.

'As if your eyes needed any help.'

'Truly? You think this colour suits with my eyes?'

She opened them wide and they both laughed. In the first week of the voyage they had established that each despised what passed for conventional intercourse between man and woman; the endless complimenting, the simpering response. That sort of thing was the subject of the sentimental comedies that brought audiences to the theatres, silver to the novelists. Yet rejecting one game left them uncertain which one they should play. Jack had been delighted to discover that his favourite was also hers, even if the eventual endgame was impossible to reach in the cramped conditions of a ship. There could be no checkmate, not with ears a thin plank away.

He was still holding the sleeve of the dress. With the slightest pressure, he pulled. She resisted, but not enough to dislodge his fingers. Slowly, she began to move towards him.

'You'll tear it,' she breathed.

'I'd like to,' he whispered.

She leaned into him, but for a moment, till a movement above distracted. A sailor was edging along a spar, towards a stay come loose in the wind.

She pulled away, began drumming her fan rapidly before her face.

But, as the feel of silk between Jack's fingers lingered, he took in the significance of the colour she wore.

Louisa saw his frown. 'Something distresses you, Jack?'

'No. Yes.' He turned to look again at the trees above the town. 'I was in a reverie here. This,' he gestured to the shore, 'world.' He sighed. 'Até found me. He has a way of knowing my mind and that was running on . . . old memories.'

'Good memories?'

'Yes. No. Both. It depends how you choose to regard them. Até would quote you *Hamlet*: "For there is nothing either good or bad but thinking makes it so."'

'Wise words. How did you choose to think on these memories?'

'Badly, I fear.'

Should he tell her? Did any woman truly care to hear of a man's previous loves?

She saw his hesitation. 'Tell me.'

'I . . . there was . . . someone here, once. Tonesaha, of the Mohawk.'

'Tonesaha? A beautiful name.'

'As was she. After the events you saw so selectively depicted by that scoundrel Sheridan in *The Rivals* I returned here in sixty-three. Met her. She . . .'

'Died?'

'Was murdered.'

'Oh.' Red came to the skin that she could not restrain. 'Oh, I am so sorry.'

'As was I. But it was fourteen years ago, I had not forgotten, however,' he looked to the shore, 'returning here, it made me think of her. Of death.' He turned back to her now, urgently. 'The dress. Take it off.'

'Why, sir—' she began, unfolding her fan.

'No. Listen to me. We have an expression in Cornwall: "She who buys a green dress will soon wear a black one."'

The splayed fan was telescoped, lowered. 'We have a similar expression in New York. It is one of the reasons I wear the colour.'

'Defiance?'

'Always. I am a woman of this age, Jack. I will not be governed by nursery fears. Your tale is a tragic one but . . .' She shrugged. 'Death is the only certainty for us all. It will not be cheated by superstition.'

He looked at her for a moment. Finally, he nodded. 'Then take care,' he said softly, as the sailor above began whistling to accompany his work. A shanty, gloriously off-key.

'I am not the one disembarking to danger on the morrow.'

'You are. You have chosen to join your father, and the regiment he commands. We are going to war.'

'And I will be back at the camp, knitting socks, gossiping with the wives. I often wish it could be otherwise. That I could

45

trade blows with these . . . Rebels.' She sighed. 'There will be no danger for me.'

Her jaw was set, pointed to the lights just now appearing in the windows of Quebec. In the dusk, they looked like fireflies beginning their nightly dance.

'Endless supper parties, young gallants fawning before you, and me, perhaps, away. No, you are right – I *am* the one in true peril.'

He had reverted to their game. But now it was she who would not play.

'In that sense, you are in no peril at all, sir. And, at war's end . . .' She paused.

They had never finally settled on what peace would mean, for much depended on which side was victorious. If the Rebels won, those who had remained loyal to the Crown would be perceived as traitors, driven away. Many whose lands lay in Rebel control had already sacrificed them. But if the Crown triumphed . . . could there be a future for them?

The sailor dropped from the mast above, preventing any clarification. He landed with a thump that made them both start, tugged his forelock to them, and went whistling ever more tunelessly on his way. As he moved off, they laughed and eight bells sounded.

'Supper?'

'Aye.' Something in him was reluctant, something of their conversation still clinging to him. He remembered something else now about green dresses. Lizzie Farren would never wear one on stage. For the same reason as the Cornish or the New Yorkers.

He shivered. She took his arm in an instant. 'Cold, Jack?'

'A little.'

'Then let us get warm together.'

The aft cabin of the *Ariadne*, which Burgoyne had commandeered from its Captain, was bright with light. Lanterns perched on every surface not filled with food or drink, dangled from hooks in the ceiling, yellow beams reflecting off cut glass decanters, crystal bumpers, and the silver trenchers that held the best Meissen china.

On the morrow, John Burgoyne would step ashore and take command of the Army of the North. So the end of the voyage and the eve of a glorious enterprise demanded only the finest in all things. It also was an opportunity for the General to gather his commanders, to make or renew acquaintance with the men who would serve throughout the coming campaign. He intended to feast them well, to test their mettle and know their minds by loosening their tongues with the miracles his personal chef had conjured from the ship's galley and with special selections from his famous wine cellar. 'Gentleman Johnny' was said to dine as well on campaign as King George did in his palace. Better, many maintained, for the General had better taste.

Jack, as befitted his lowlier rank, sat at the table's far end, away from his Commander. Yet there were barely a dozen people in the cramped cabin and he was able to hear any conversation he chose. Indeed, one of his particular talents was an ability to keep two in mind at once while conducting a third. A practical skill for a spy and Jack had been asked to use it, to study and note the men gathered there that night, and to report his observations to Burgoyne later.

The difficulty with any mission of espionage lay in its geography. The terrain Jack had to cover here presented no obstacles of bog or leaf-choked trail; there were no impenetrable codes to crack. Here he merely had to negotiate bumper after bumper of Burgoyne's fine liquors. Sipping discreetly was only allowed between toasts and it was a rare five minutes when someone did not have something or someone to huzzah. Honour demanded that when a king, a general, a lady, a regiment, or any other of several dozen excuses was called upon, a whole glass must be drained. Upon which some hearty would nearly always cry, 'Aye, that's right, fellows, always wet both eyes,' and a second would immediately follow. If Jack had been in a tavern or even his regiment's mess, he'd make sure that every second glass, at the least, was thrown over his shoulder but the floor of the cabin was not a suitable receptacle. And even if the glass he'd managed to choose was smaller than most, too many full ones had still found their way into him.

Then there was the heat produced by the lamps, by the dozen bodies in their finest clothes, by the richness of the food consumed after weeks at sea on a simpler diet. The cook had not resisted this first chance to shine and had used the fresh provisions brought from the shore to create rare treats: fish baked in herbs and sweet wine, beef wrapped in pastry and flamed with brandy, a dish from India called salmagundi, which consisted of the hot spices of that land enflaming a *mélange* of minced meat, anchovies and eggs . . . well, sweat seeped from every man there while the two ladies – Louisa Reardon and one Mrs Skene glowed and dabbed their perfumed handkerchiefs to their brows and breasts.

At that moment, this was distracting Jack the most. He knew he should be listening to the conversations nearest him, the discussions between the officers on whom Burgoyne would be relying. But his attention kept being pulled to Louisa, sat on the General's left, the way she kept fanning the silk handkerchief across the rise and fall of her glowing décolletage, how the General kept watching her do it as he made her laugh with tales of his London life, his twin arenas of Drury Lane and Parliament. The old rogue had long since conceded Louisa to Jack's attentions. 'Miss Reardon is not mistress material,' he'd declaimed; unlike the wife of the commissary agent, who had already come from shore and awaited Burgoyne in another cabin below. But Jack had drunk enough now to still feel jealous at every laugh.

Fortunately, as Louisa laughed again, that musical run of notes that came from somewhere in her depths, the laugh he wanted reserved only for himself, his attention was demanded by a toast proposed by the man to his left, lower both in age and rank than Jack, and a fellow Cornishman, Midshipman Edward Pellew.

Like Jack, Pellew had the black hair typical of their county.

It was pulled back into the queue that most junior naval officers sported, though the wine and the heat had pulled strands from their restraint. These were plastered to the young, flushed face that now thrust towards Jack, a bumper raised before it.

''ere, Jack. Let's you and me pledge to an allegiance as great as we hold to England. And even older.' He raised his glass. '*Kernow!*'

Jack smiled. He liked Pellew, beyond a countryman's affinity. When they'd boarded the ship, and the crew had stood to attention to greet Burgoyne on every mast and ratline, one man was at variance with his shipmates. Midshipman Pellew was standing, gloriously alone, on the highest yardarm. On his head. Burgoyne had kept him close ever since.

'*Gwary whek yu gwary tek!*' Jack drained his bumper of Bishop, the heated, spiced liquid firing his throat and chest, and raised the empty vessel.

The loudly expressed toast had halted conversations up and down the table. To the General's right, Baron von Riedesel, Commander of the German component of the Allied army, leaned into his interpreter and muttered a question. The portly General spoke no English and the attempt for the company to respect that and speak French had degenerated on the third bumper.

The interpreter, a lean Hessian named Von Spartzehn, listened then looked at Jack. 'Excuse me, Kapitan Absolute. I speak English, as you see, quite excellently. But what you say, it eludes me.'

'That's because it is not English, Kapitan, but Cornish, the ancient tongue of Cornwall, now, alas, spoken very little even there.'

'And what did this mean?'

'My esteemed young friend proposed the name of our land. Kernow is Cornwall. And I replied with an oath, sworn by two wrestlers before they begin a contest: Good play is fair play.'

'Cornish wrastlers are the best in the world, see.' Pellew's

Penryn brogue was becoming more pronounced the redder he got.

'Is that what you were practising on the foredeck on the voyage across?'

It was Alexander Lindsay, Earl of Balcarras who had spoken. Tall, so pale his skin appeared untroubled by his prodigious consumption, seemingly effete, with an accent bred at Harrow and Oxford, Jack had discovered that the man entrusted with Burgoyne's Light Infantry had a core of metal. 'Sandy' was also a fine fast bowler and had taken Jack's wicket in the annual Westminster versus Harrow Old Boys cricket match seven years before. Despite that, Jack liked him.

'It was indeed. Though my young friend here is somewhat more agile than myself.'

Pellew said, 'Tosh, Jack,' but his argument was interrupted by a voice Jack had already learned to loathe. Its tone was whining, high-pitched, eerily at variance with a corpulent body.

'Cornwall, eh?' said Philip Skene. Turning to Burgoyne, rudely leaning right across the vole-like Mrs Skene, he shouted, 'General, did you read Johnson's latest satire on the Rebels and the legitimacy of their revolt? He wrote that the Cornish have as great, nay, a greater claim to self-government than these . . . *Americans*.'

The tone the fat Loyalist gave the last word made Jack colour, and he saw Louisa's smile vanish. Her family might be Loyalist too, colonists who supported the Crown against the Revolution. But she was an American as well and proud to be so. Whereas Skene was one of those men who became more English the longer he lived away, the more he profited from the New World he plundered. He owned vast tracts of the Hudson Valley, the very land the British army must march through to wage their campaign. He had boasted of the thousands of Loyalists there who would rise up at his command, to Burgoyne's aid.

Jack looked at Skene, at the roll of fat that spilled over his too-tight collar, the heat in the porcine eyes. He also had the taste shared by many Americans of wearing a wig, long deemed unfashionable in England. Skene's was old and wispy, two powdered rolls lodged above the ears. It had worn away in places to reveal patches of flaring pink skin. Rich *and* miserly, Jack noted, a not uncommon combination. He suddenly remembered a story he'd heard of the man – that when his mother died he'd kept her corpse on a table because so long as she remained 'above ground' he could collect her pension.

Jack was there to observe, not comment, let alone debate. But the man irked, not least because he represented all that the Rebels were right to oppose. Feeling the latest bumper to an old allegiance inspire him, Jack spoke.

'What Johnson failed to address, Colonel Skene, was that my countrymen of Cornwall can make their grievances known in Parliament through their elected MPs. The Colonists cannot.'

' "No taxation without representation!" ' Skene brayed. 'The Rebel cry! I hardly expected to hear that treason repeated at the General's table. But then I ask you, Captain, do children in Cornwall have the vote? Hmm? Do women? Eh? Do the illiterate miners in their holes? Eh? Eh? For that is what these Americans are, sir. Dependants. Nothing more!' He jeered, 'The Declaration of *Dependence*, that's what they came up with. That's what must be crushed, this . . . Children's Crusade! Do you not agree, sir?'

Jack glanced around the table. The Germans looked bemused; Pellew was already bored and rooting for more Bishop; Louisa's face was composed, but her eyes glowed still at Skene's gibe at all Americans; Burgoyne's face held a slight smile, knowing Jack's beliefs, relishing his predicament.

He returned his gaze to the flushed face before him. 'I do not, sir. I believe each American wants only what their brothers in England already have: the freedom to decide their own destiny. And they want it unrestrained by a political process in which they have no voice.'

'You speak like a follower of John Wilkes, man. Are you, then, a . . . uh, Democrat?' Balcarras gave the last word an especially Harrovian shudder.

51

'I am . . . not sure what I am, my Lord.'

'You sound like a damn Rebel, that's what. Is this the sort of officer you will rely on, Burgoyne?' Skene once more shouted up the table.

The smile on the General's face broadened. 'Oh yes, I know I can rely on Captain Absolute. I have had a number of proofs of his loyalty over the years.'

'Even when he proclaims damned traitor sentiments?' Skene's heated face had coloured even more dangerously.

'Especially then. When he stops proclaiming them, I may begin to watch my back.'

Thwarted, Skene muttered, 'Well, you appear like a damned traitor to me.'

'No traitor, sir. Just a true born Englishman who breathes liberty as he breathes air and would not deny that same air to others.' He paused but only for breath. 'It is just fourteen years since all Englishmen, on both continents, put an end to the threat of France and their tyranny in these lands. We could not have done it without the men we now call traitors. Together we can keep ourselves free of that tyranny. Together we can have what every man desires – the liberty to pursue his own course, unhindered by the restraint of obligation. Many of our American brethren feel, with some cause, that they are unequal partners in that enterprise. So let's beat them, but not humiliate them. Let's beat them, then welcome them back as brothers – good play is fair play – and, together, we can conquer the world.'

It was a failing of his, this venting of passion. He could no more contain it than he could catch the wind in cupped hands. The hot Bishop, the hot room, the hot eyes of Louisa were all goads. But he'd have probably spoken the same way alone in the Arctic.

Skene seemed as if he were about to choke. He pulled at his collar, grabbed a glass, and drained it, set it down with a determination that spoke to a renewal of the fight. But it was a woman's voice that prevented him.

'I've always maintained,' Louisa said calmly, 'that Jack is an "absolute-skein" of contradiction.'

It was a little joke, the kind of pun they all revelled in. The company exhaled their laugh as one, saving Skene and his timid spouse. The tension punctured, Jack looked to Louisa, joined in the laugh. He had broken cover, revealed his position. Now perhaps he could sink back and resume his watch. He had to report to the General, after all.

The General was not going to give him the chance. 'Since Captain Absolute has raised the subject of a fight – and given us some indication of the contrary opinions we are likely to encounter – perhaps the time has come to reveal to you all, esteemed allies and officers, how I intend to carry that fight to my opponents. How I intend to pin them to the floor of the wrestling ring and make them plead for terms. You there!' At his raised voice, servants came into the cabin, at his gesture, the remnants of food were cleared swiftly, leaving only glasses and decanters of port and cognac. Most of the men reached within pouches for tobacco. As the hubbub swirled around him, Burgoyne stood calmly filling his pipe, his eyes unfocused, as if he were staring through the wood of the table and on through a continent.

Louisa and Mrs Skene rose to leave, but the General waved them down. 'I have a feeling you will both be sharing the hazards of this campaign,' he said. 'You should share the knowledge of it too.'

When the last of the servants withdrew, when all glasses were charged, Burgoyne picked up a lamp, held it so that his face was lit from below.

'St John's, north of Lake Champlain,' he said, placing the flickering glass on the table before him. 'The advance guard of my army gathers there, organized by my dear General Phillips, whose skill with artillery you will all acknowledge.' There was a muttering around the table, glasses raised. 'We march to join him with our main forces: our German allies under dear Baron von Riedesel here,' the General, with his interpreter whispering in his ear, inclined his head, 'the British regiments of the line, each carrying banners that denote a hundred triumphs. The Canadian and Native contingents will rally to us there and

53

along the way. I vouchsafe I will command a force of some ten thousand men and have them mustered by the first of June.'

More murmurs, more draughts taken. Ten thousand men was surely a force no Colonial general could oppose!

'A wee question, sir, if I mae?' A Scottish voice ventured from Jack's side of the table. It was General Simon Fraser who spoke. He sat to Burgoyne's right, the perfect place for the man Burgoyne called 'his rock'. Old for his years, he had been promoted on sheer ability; for his family were said to be Jacobite rebels to a man and could spend no money, exert no influence, to speed him through the ranks. His skills on campaign were legendary, his loyalty to the Crown, and especially to Burgoyne, unwavering.

At his Commander's nod, he continued. 'The Americans make much of their ability to fight an irregular war, to harry us from forest and mountain, to obstruct our route to our objectives. Do we no hae muckle plans to counter tha'?'

Jack recognized a planted question when he saw one. If strategy had not been discussed, there had been many conversations on tactics during the voyage. The answer was aimed at others, at the Loyalist Skene and the Germans.

'I'm so glad you raised that point, Simon.' Burgoyne's theatrical skills were not limited to writing. 'It gives me great pleasure to inform you, and the company, that I have decided your own command will be of our Advance Corps. The grenadier and light companies from each regiment will be formed under you, brigaded with your own, inestimable, 24th Foot. Also a select corps of marksmen will be drawn from the best shots of all ranks. Together with the Canadians and our savages – oh, excuse me, Captain Absolute . . . our "Native Allies" – we will have an irregular force, capable of taking on and countering anything the American Woodsman can muster.'

Fraser, not an actor, was doing his best to feign surprise. Balcarras, designated to serve as the Scotsman's second in this brigade, proposed a toast of congratulations. Bumpers were downed.

Then Burgoyne took Louisa's glass and placed it a foot in front of the decanter of 'St John's'.

'Lake Champlain,' he announced. 'Feel free to sip of the lake's waters, my dear.' Over the laughter, he continued. 'Let the Rebel cut trees in our path on the water. If they muster a fleet, we will destroy it, as we did last October. We will move most of our army and our supplies by barge. By the middle of June we will be here, at the lake's end.'

He moved down the table, placed another decanter, stood regarding it for a long moment, pipe in mouth. Then he gently exhaled, expertly ensnaring the vessel's spout in a ring of smoke, which hovered and dissipated on his next words.

'Fort Ticonderoga, gentlemen. The key to a continent.'

Von Riedesel waved his interpreter away, muttering, 'Das Schloss,' and leaned in, as did every man at the table. Ticonderoga needed no translation, the name a legend from the French wars. The fortress squatted over the southern route, a bulwark to invasion north or south.

'I have . . . ideas for how we will deal with it. And deal with it we will, before we move on, sweeping aside any army they dare send against us. We will move both along and parallel to the Hudson River, which is the second key, the most proper part of the whole continent for vigorous operations. Along it, we will transport our grain, our baggage and powder, even our wine.' He smiled and took a sip. 'I sense that, after Ticonderoga, they will try to stop us here,' a glass placed, 'at Fort Ann, near the home of our dear friend, Colonel Skene,' the Loyalist acknowledged the attention with a small rotation of his fat wrist, 'or here, near Fort Edward, or even here, at Saratoga.' The General looked up, meeting the gaze of every man there, one after the other. 'But rest assured, gentleman, wherever they choose to stand and fight, they will be beaten, and beaten soundly.' He glanced at Jack. 'Fairly, of course, dear Captain. We will seek to instruct, to correct, not to humiliate. But we will beat them nonetheless. And then we will seize the prize.'

Since the attention was on him anyway, and recognizing a

cue when he saw one, Jack ventured, 'Which is, sir? Can you now tell us the final goal of all these endeavours?'

A knock prevented Burgoyne's immediate reply. A servant entered, one of the Baron's; he spoke softly in the German's ear, who then passed the message on to his interpreter.

'A cousin of the General seeks permission to join us. His ship has just arrived.'

Burgoyne looked less than pleased, the playwright in him upset at the interruption to the flow of dialogue and the suspense he'd created. Nevertheless, he nodded and the servant withdrew.

'Now, what matter were we discussing? Ah yes, something minor like crushing a revolution, wasn't it?' Having seized back attention with a laugh, Burgoyne gestured to Jack. 'Would you be so good, Captain Absolute? That decanter of port, about a dagger's length below Saratoga.'

Jack placed the decanter as instructed, kept his fingers on it as he spoke. 'And this is, General?'

He already knew, as did most of the men there. But no one would deny Burgoyne his moment. He returned slowly to the head of the table, laid his pipe carefully down, placed his palms on to the wood, leaned forward so that lamplight played on his face.

'Albany. The heart of the country. When General Howe and I rendezvous there, New England will be split in two. Washington's armies will scatter or starve. We will have won back the Colonies for the Crown.'

There was a short silence, only just long enough for the words to be absorbed. Not quite long enough for anyone to huzzah, or declare a toast, because another knock came and the door opened. Jack, his back to it, his hand still on the port decanter that was Albany, did not turn at first. Instead he looked at Kapitan von Spartzehn, rising to his General's right.

'Gentlemen, ladies. May I have the honour to present the Baron's cousin – Adolphus Maximillian Gerhardt, the Count von Schlaben.'

Jack's hand slipped. The decanter fell forward. Somehow it

56

didn't break, but its neck, pointed at Burgoyne, coursed red liquid up the line of glasses and vessels that delineated the Northern Campaign. Like a river of blood it flowed to the table top, straight between the General's hands, and began to drip there, fat drop after drop, on to the floor. For the moment, it was the only sound in the room.

Jack turned. In the doorway stood the man he'd last seen on a snowy Hounslow Heath. The Count von Schlaben's grey eyes returned his gaze. Jack couldn't read them. He didn't need to. He knew what was written there: the same sense of foreboding caught earlier on the deck, in memories, in the scent of familiar trees, in the light green of a dress.

— FIVE —
Reunion

Jack's first thought was of a weapon. Swords had been left in cabins, cutlery cleared away. So he righted the decanter he'd upset and stepped away from the table, clutching it by the neck. It was of lead crystal, heavy. He didn't think it would shatter well and give him a fistful of glass to thrust. But it was eminently throwable.

Jack's pick-up was not obvious, his move away from the table covered by the general squeak of chairs slid back, of men rising from their places to be introduced. But he saw the man in the doorway glance briefly down at his now full hand. Jack was beginning to learn that the Count von Schlaben missed nothing.

'General Burgoyne, a thousand apologies for this late intrusion. A boatmen's dispute on the dockside left me stranded. These Canadians seem very prickly about their prerogatives.'

Von Schlaben's English was near accentless, far better than the Interpreter's.

'My dear Count.' Burgoyne came forward, hand outstretched. The German took it, bowed over it. 'Alas, we have finished the eating part of our meal. But can I get my cook to bring you a plate?'

'Indeed, General, I would be grateful only for . . . is that Bishop I smell? Yet another thing we Germans have to envy the English – their limitless invention when it comes to drinks.

Who but they would have thought to roast an orange and drop it into port?'

At a nod from Burgoyne, Pellew filled a spare bumper. The German raised it. 'To the enduring amity between our nations.'

Glasses were raised, drained, Jack drinking left-handed, still keeping the decanter in his right. Only when the toast was finished did he place it, deliberately, on the table before Von Schlaben. The grey eyes swivelled to him.

'Ah, Captain Absolute, delighted to see you again. And under somewhat more pleasant circumstances.'

'Oh, I don't know, Count. I rather enjoyed our last encounter.'

The German smiled faintly, then trod around the table, introduced by his host as he went. Once he'd shaken hands, Simon Fraser moved to Jack's side.

'Is that the man, Absolute?' The tale of Drury Lane and Hounslow Heath had been re-told by Burgoyne many times on the voyage across, gilded and transformed into an epic, sparing neither detail nor Jack's blushes – even if the suspected motives for the duel were left out.

'It is, sir.'

'We have a wee saying in the Highlands: "Fiddlers, dogs, and flies come to a feast uncalled."' Fraser pointed his chin to where Von Schlaben was bending over Mrs Skene's hand. 'And he doenae look like he can play a fiddle.'

Jack suppressed a snort of laughter, turning it into a cough. A servant entered discreetly to clear up the spilled port. Noticing him moving among the 'map' of his campaign, Burgoyne raised his voice above the continuing pleasantries.

'May I suggest some air while the servants make all ready for the entertainment?' He turned to the Count. 'You may have missed supper, dear sir, but you will be able to sit in on the theatricals. I venture you will be impressed. To alleviate our boredom we have been indulging ourselves all the way across the Atlantic. We have attained, I may say, a standard that would not disgrace many a stage in England. But five weeks is a long time and we know each other's better tricks by now. Perhaps you have something new that the company would enjoy?'

Von Schlaben shook his head. 'I fear I am no actor, sir.'

Burgoyne's reply was almost inaudible. Almost.

'Not what I heard.' Then he went on, more loudly, 'Ladies, gentlemen, to the deck and let us rendezvous back here in . . . half an hour?' As the company began to file out, he added, 'Captain Absolute, a word?'

Von Schlaben was just passing Jack when he spoke. 'By the way, Captain, I bring greetings to you from our young friend, Tarleton.'

'I am surprised he is not with you. I thought you inseparable.'

'Alas, your Native friend's blow had him confined to a bed for a time and my ship awaited. But he wishes you to know that he looks forward to renewing your acquaintance.'

'Will he serve in this campaign?'

'He is bound for New York, I believe, and General Howe's command. Still,' the German gave what passed for his smile, 'I am certain your paths will cross again.'

Jack nodded. 'Can't wait.' Then he gestured to the doorway, and the Count, with the slightest of bows, went through it.

The room was empty at last. Burgoyne came to stand beside Jack and together they listened to the laughter, as the gentlemen helped the ladies climb the steep stairs. When the last voice had faded into the night, Burgoyne murmured, ' "Yon'd Cassius has a lean and hungry look . . ." '

'. . . "Such men are dangerous".' Completing the couplet, Jack stepped back into the cabin, reached for a decanter, poured two glasses. Handing one to Burgoyne, he continued, 'Is he a danger you would have me remove?'

The older man sipped, smiled. 'Why, Captain Absolute! Are you proposing, perhaps, a dagger in an alley? How does that square with the Cornish sense of a fair fight?'

'I'd kill a mad dog in Cornwall, same as anywhere. Especially one that has already tried to kill me.'

'The Count, mad? I think not. Dangerous, I will concede. We already have the proof of that with his design upon you in London.'

Burgoyne moved back to his place at the head of the table. There, he reached into a leathern case that hung from the back of his chair, withdrew some small object. He continued, 'But are we certain – certain now, Jack, not just assuming – that the Count sought to eliminate you because of my proclaimed patronage and need of you? No, we are not. You were caught, in flagrante, and the Count was young Tarleton's friend before I even knew of your return to London.'

'But, sir—'

Burgoyne held up a hand. 'Furthermore, we still do not understand why these Illuminati concern themselves with our affairs. We believe that they seek to profit from the disorder in this land, the chance to build on ashes. But what is it they seek to build? And why? That's what we must discover. And until we do we shall follow the advice of the Hebrew: Keep mine friend close and mine enemy closer. Agreed?'

'Sir.' Jack could see that his Commander would not be moved. Were it a private matter – and he knew Burgoyne did not believe the affair in London to be merely about the love of an actress any more than he did – Jack would not hesitate to strike before he was struck again. But he had to grudgingly admit that to kill Von Schlaben now would be a mistake. The Illuminati, like any secret society, would have as many heads as the Hydra. To cut off this visible one would merely leave them exposed to another they could not see.

Burgoyne now lobbed what he'd been passing between his hands across the cabin. It sparkled as it flew through the lamplight. Jack let it drop into one palm, then raised it to his gaze.

It was a musket ball. Yet its dull surface had been scored across and a brighter hue shone through.

Jack tossed it into the air, caught it again. 'Silver. And light. Hollow.'

'Yes.' Burgoyne was reaching once more into his case. 'The

ball was found on – or should I say "in" – a merchant from Connecticut, a proclaimed Loyalist, come to trade in Quebec. He was observed in some dubious company and, when taken, was seen to swallow that ball. He then had it disgorged from his guts with a dose of emetic tartar so severe that it cost the unfortunate fellow his life – it's all right, Jack, it's been thoroughly cleaned – and this was found within.'

Burgoyne was carefully spreading a small piece of paper out on the table before him. 'Governor Carleton only received this intelligence a few days since. So far, none of his officers here in Quebec have been able to decipher it. So we were wondering, Jack, if you . . .'

Jack moved a lamp closer. The page held five lines of numbers, cramped yet legible enough. It was gobbledegook; but even a swift glance told him it was gobbledegook with a pattern.

'Can you give me answer me this riddle, Jack?'

'It will take me a little time, sir. Longer if it is in French.'

'Which you speak even better than I do. But then you have French blood, do you not?'

Jack shook his head. 'A long way back, General. Yet it's a tradition in the Absolute family that the sons always have the same French middle name.'

'And that is?'

'Rombaud. There's a legend connected with it too. Fanciful beyond belief.'

Burgoyne smiled. 'I love legends. You must recount it when we have more time.'

'Certainly, sir.' Jack squinted at the tiny piece of paper. 'Do you know if there is a list of the merchant's possessions?'

Burgoyne pushed across a page. Jack studied it. 'No books or notebooks, I see.'

'Do you think Washington would be so kind as to send his spies out with both his secret messages and the means to decode them?'

Jack smiled. 'It's been known. It could be an innocuous novel that sender and recipient both possess and the numbers

62

here could correspond to the words on a single page. That would be the crib. Without the book, the message would be hard to discover.'

'Is this a code of that sort?'

'I think not. I can see patterns here, repeated numbers. Do we know who this was meant for?'

Burgoyne shook his head. 'Sadly not. The fatal consequence of the disgorging deprived us of any further information. But . . .' He hesitated, then reached into another bag. 'I do not wish you to read too much into this. But something else was found among the merchant's possessions. Don't look for it on the list, it's not there.'

He pulled out a set of keys on a hoop. They were standard ones for various-sized locks. There was also a metal fob, about the size of a thumb. It was in the shape of a pyramid. Just beneath its apex was an eye.

'Yes, I grant,' the General sighed when Jack looked up at him, 'it is Masonic. Unusual – but my own lodge uses similar symbols as do lodges here in the Colonies. Masons fight on both sides of this cause. I know of seven for certain among Washington's commanders. So this,' he took the fob and dangled it in the lamplight, 'need not imply anything sinister. The recipient, though a spy, could just be an ordinary member of an ordinary lodge. He need not be—'

'Illuminati?'

'No.' The General looked as discomfited as Jack had ever seen him. Jack had always refused any offers, Burgoyne's amongst them, to be initiated into the Brotherhood of Freemasonry. 'The bad apple of these Illuminati does not taint the barrel of the whole Order, Captain. Remember that. And we cannot presume that the ball was destined for the Count, for example.'

'We should presume nothing, sir.' He handed the keys back. 'Would you like me to begin on this now?'

'Indeed not. We have our theatricals to perform. The morning will be quite soon enough.'

63

Jack carefully folded up the paper and placed it into his waistcoat pocket. 'Shall I fetch the players?'

'Do. And on the way, send in the servants to prepare the stage.'

When Jack reached the doorway, he paused, looked back. 'Sir, I am not boasting of my skill. But if Von Schlaben *was* the intended recipient, this seems an odd sort of cipher to send to a man of his intellect. Not as complicated as I am sure he would want it to be. That could, of course, mean that the sender was not as gifted. Or—'

'Or that it was destined for someone else. As I said.' Burgoyne smiled. 'No, the good Count cannot be our only suspect. He may, perhaps, lead us to another though, eh? So . . . no dagger in the alley for the moment, Captain Absolute.'

'General.'

Jack walked slowly up the stairs, the patterns of numbers he'd briefly studied swirling before his eyes. These patterns so held him that when he reached the deck, it took a moment for them to clear. A moment to realize that the figures a dozen foot from him, silhouetted against the night sky of Quebec Town, were Louisa and the Count. A moment more to focus on the way his hand was gripped on to her elbow. Even as he watched, she jerked it away and moved to the railing. Then Balcarras and Pellew approached and, taking an arm each, walked Louisa up the deck, out of sight. As their laughter was caught and lost in the wind, Jack looked back for the Count. But the German had gone.

Jack loathed acting. In his brief dalliance with the theatre crowd in London seven years before, he had always preferred the writer's role, seeing his imaginings rendered into flesh by others. But that was in the profession. In private company, a gentleman was expected to perform.

The audience cheered and applauded each good line and piece of business as if they were at Drury Lane. Balcarras declaimed, with great feeling, Gray's 'Elegy'. Pellew attempted, rather less successfully, some sonnets by Pope, his tongue thickened by further bouts with the Bishop. General Fraser, to the delight of the company, displayed a surprisingly light and pleasant baritone to render, 'My Dear Hieland Laddie' and Burgoyne had been flattered into producing extracts from his own dramatic works. He, Jack and Louisa took the main roles in these. And when the General spoke the closing words from his London success *Maid of the Oaks*, 'I love an old oak at my heart and can't sit under its shade till I dream of Crecy and Agincourt,' the company rose as one with a toast to those glorious victories of the past, huzzahs to the glorious ones to come.

The cabin was packed. More had joined after dinner and included fourteen officers, some wives, the Skenes, and two other prominent Loyalists. In the swirl, Jack lost sight of Louisa. It took him half a dozen turns about the room, a number of brief conversations, before he realized she was no longer there.

He leaped the stairs three at a time. On the deck, his eyes took a moment to adjust to the darkness after the brightness of the cabin-stage. When they did, he saw her straight away. She was poised at the top of the ship's ladder, watching her maid, Nancy, descend.

'Eloping, Louisa? Doesn't that take two?'

She started, turned at his voice. 'Jack.'

'You did not tell me you were leaving this night.'

'My father has arranged lodgings in the town. After five weeks cramped at sea . . .' Her voice trailed off.

'Were you not going to say farewell?'

'I hate farewells, Jack. Detest them. Nancy spent much time in the shading of my eyes for the play and promised she would punish me if I let them run. Besides, I do not leave to join my father and his regiment at St John's for a few days. I will see you in the town, without the weight of a shipboard goodbye upon us.'

'I hope there will be the time. I believe the General plans to keep me busy.'

'I am certain he does. But I accompany the campaign, remember. We will have much time together. You will grow sick at the sight of me.'

There was a falseness to her tone, as if she were still in the play.

Suddenly Jack realised why.

'Von Schlaben upset you, didn't he? I saw you here . . . before. His hand on you. I have reasons aplenty to loathe him already, but if he has caused you a moment's unease—'

'Nay, Jack. Pay him no mind. I . . .' She hesitated, then sighed. 'Yes, I will admit it. He did fluster me. I knew him a little in London, and—'

Jack frowned. 'I recall you said you'd met him. You never said your acquaintance had gone so far as to allow him to touch you.' Jack did not like his tone of voice, but her silence made him continue with it. 'I find it strange that you did not talk of him before now, Louisa. Considering what passed between he and I.'

'Why strange?' Her face flushed. 'After all, it was only this evening that you chose to tell me of To . . . ne . . .'

'Tonesaha?' Jack shook his head, bemused. 'How . . . how is that the same?

Her jaw was pointed at him like an accusation. 'You chose not to once mention this love on the voyage bringing us to the land where you loved her.'

'Why on earth would I have done?'

'Exactly, Jack. Exactly. And neither have you once mentioned the supposed reason for the duel.' At his blank look, she added, 'The actress?' When he flinched, her tone softened and she stepped closer. 'I apologize, Jack. I . . . I do not tax you with this. I merely observe that when one is . . . paying and receiving addresses, it is not customary to talk of previous loves.'

Chill replaced his heat. 'Von Schlaben was your lover?'

'Of course not! The very idea!' She shuddered. 'I found him loathsome before I ever heard either of his designs upon you or the little the General has told me of his Illuminati's designs

66

upon my country.' She laid a gloved hand on his arm. 'But we cannot always be understood the way we intend. In his imagination, it seems he took my coolest politeness as encouragement. Perhaps that is how the women woo their men in Germany.'

She laughed, briefly, but Jack did not join her, his mind still full of this new reason to hate the Count.

She saw the look on his face. 'I am sorry, Jack. It was why I was so poor in the play tonight, why I am so hasty in my departure. I do not wish to be in his company any longer. And as for you and I . . . we will see each other tomorrow, or the day after, in the town. So do not look so glum.'

Below them, on the water, Nancy had settled into the bow of the little wherry. The boatman, a stockinged wool hat pulled well down over a swarthy face, called up. His accent was rough, of the town.

Louisa half-turned. 'What did he say?'

'He asked that you hurry as he has a young wife warming a bed. Do you not speak French?'

'Hardly a word. Heigh-ho for an American education!'

The boatman called up again, a string of oaths.

'I will see you on shore, Jack Absolute. And on the march. We will have our time again, I know.'

She reached up and their lips collided, something desperate in the kiss, and before he knew it he was handing her down the ladder. The boatman was there, guiding her feet to the rungs. Then she was in the boat, settled in the stern, oars were in the water and the craft pulled swiftly away, aimed at the docks.

Jack watched her, the set of her shoulders. She did not once look back. But half way to the wharf, one hand was raised in sudden farewell.

The gloom of night took the boat. Still he stared, going through the words he had not spoken, that perhaps would remain unspoken now.

When at last he returned to his cabin, he was looking forward to the distraction from his thoughts that the code would furnish. Pellew's snores provided a varied musical backdrop.

With a newly sharpened pencil he copied the numbers on to the top half of a clean sheet of paper. Then he bent over the page, focusing first on the blank area, then letting his eyes drift up till they were full of the numbers laid out in six lines:

716854596563555455569642
52646369765269527452766964597
656953765351
62765272745959626551526566
5560577561595165
123

Assuming each letter would be represented by a number, he knew a single numeral would be too easy, three per letter too complex. It was probably a pair per letter – though this left an uneven number on the first two lines and the last.

He would come back to that. Swiftly he used a pencil to mark off pairs, leaving the ends of those first two lines as threesomes. There were clusters, flows of linked numbers – 555455 in the first line. That could be a consonant, bonded with vowels, he thought – 'ini' for example, as in 'dining.'

He looked for the lowest number of the pairs, found it in the third, fourth, and fifth lines – 51. If 51 was 'A', then 52 was 'B' and so on.

He swiftly wrote out a crib on a separate page. Then taking the third line, he matched each paired number to its letters and wrote out the result: Osczca.

A code within a code? A name? Acronym? Even an anagram? For half an hour he tried to make one, first in English, then in French. He tried the other lines and got equal nonsense – though these yielded up some surprising, useless (and two quite rude) anagrams. Nothing worked.

Throwing down his pencil, he rose and went for a turn around the deck. When he came back he stood above the page, looked again at the lines of numbers . . . and suddenly saw what he might have missed. Perhaps, as a further concealment, the code writer had altered the starting letter for each line? If there *had* been a '51' on the first line it would have been 'A'. On the second line, '51' would then have been 'B'. Thus on the third line, where '51' actually did appear, it would be the third letter, 'C'. Scratching swiftly, he made a new crib for the third line: 51 was 'C', 52 was 'D' and so on. When he got to 'Z' at 74, 'A' became 75, 'B' 76. He then substituted the numbers for this new order of letters and wrote out a different version of line three.

It was a single word: Quebec.

Excited now, a new crib for each line was the matter of moments. Soon almost the entire message was laid out before him. After a struggle he concluded that the threesomes at the end of the first two lines – 642 and 597 – were just that – numbers, codes for agents' names, to be used in future communications.

There was only the last little scribble that took Jack another ten minutes to figure out and when he did he could only laugh. He'd been looking for concealment and it was the one unencoded part of the message. And the only part in French.

1–2–3, it read, the '1' with a line through it. Un-deux-trois. Un-de-trois. One of three.

All spymasters would send multiple messages as so many were intercepted. This, recovered from a silver bullet and a man's guts, was the first of three.

Jack threw down his pencil and rubbed his eyes. Through the porthole, a faint light was glowing in the east. He would sleep for two hours and then he would report.

He lay down, tired now, thinking that, despite the droning from Pellew's bunk, he would fall asleep fast. But it wasn't his fellow Cornishman's snores that kept him awake. It was the memory of a boat rowing away from him, bearing Louisa, their last conversation full of his suspicion and jealousy. He'd been foolish. On the morrow, ashore in Quebec, he would make amends.

*

His firm knock at Burgoyne's cabin door the next morning was answered with an equally firm, 'Enter!' The General was standing at the table's end, a steaming mug in one hand, a long fork in the other. Before him was a plate of what could only be kidneys. In their campaign together in Spain in 1762, the General had conceived an enormous appetite for them in 'the Spanish Style'. The acrid smell of offal, masked by the sweetness of sherry, filled the room, causing Jack's stomach to give a warning leap. He was not over fond of mornings. And the indulgence of the night before, coupled with his lack of sleep, now sat heavily upon him.

'Grab a fork, Jack. These arrived by the first rowboat, compliments of the Governor.' Burgoyne stabbed down and waved pinkish flesh at him. 'Quite delicious. D'ye know, I am as hungry as a hunter this morning. Can't think why.'

A loud giggle was heard from the corner of the cabin. The screen that had concealed actors the previous night now concealed something else. Burgoyne gave him a pronounced wink.

Jack tried a smile. 'Just some of that coffee, if I may, sir.'

At Burgoyne's nod, Jack filled a cup from the jug. The General, who was merely in shirt and stockings, now reached for his breeches.

'Shall I call your servant, sir?'

'Have you unravelled the mystery?'

'I have.'

'Then I think I can dress myself while you explain it.'

Jack raised his eyebrows toward the screen. Burgoyne shook his head. 'Impeccable source, Absolute. Do not concern yourself there.'

Jack sighed. One thing that made his trade more difficult was the wilful disregard by senior commanders of secrecy. Still, he laid the piece of paper he carried on the table's end, and tried not to inhale too much of the kidneys' rich steam.

Beneath each numerical puzzle-line was its solution and Burgoyne slowly read each one out.

U R DIOMEDES 642

CONTACT BY CATO 597

QUEBEC

OBEY ALL ORDERS

INK COMES

Burgoyne's finger rested on the name. 'Diomedes?'

'Wouldn't surprise me if it was our late guest last night, sir. This supplies him with his agent name. The three numbers at the end of the line – 642 – will be his number code.'

Burgoyne tapped the butt of his fork on the paper. 'And Cato, 597?'

'I would suggest he is Diomedes's immediate superior. "Ink Comes" means they are moving from pure codes to codes in invisible ink.'

'As will we, no doubt?'

'Indeed.' Jack hesitated. But he felt he must try one last time. 'Sir, I am convinced Von Schlaben is at the heart of all this. Do you still wish him to remain . . . unmolested?'

'Oh, I think so. You forget another thing, Jack. The Count is Baron von Riedesel's cousin. We are going to have enough trouble merging with our German allies without knocking off their commander's kin.' Burgoyne laughed. 'No, my boy. You leave the Count to me. I'll keep him on a tight leash, believe me. And when I have learned all I need to from him, when we have discovered all there is to know of these Illuminati, why then, my boy,' Burgoyne stabbed his fork down, impaling the last glistening kidney, '*I* will deal with him.'

Burgoyne chewed, swallowed, sighed with joy, and dropped the fork on to the plate; then he reached for his black stock. Jack took it, moved behind.

'Thank you, Jack.' He began to tie the cloth around the General's neck and Burgoyne leaned forward, pulling a map towards him. 'You have demonstrated once again, dear Jack, how valuable you are to me as an agent. I would keep you by my side throughout the campaign if I could and I hate to part with you. But, much as I need you here, I have something even more important for you to do, which will suit another of your peculiar talents. I decided not to expand on it last night in, uh, mixed company.' The General jabbed down at a spot on the map. 'Know it?'

His finger rested just on the edge of a large expanse of water.

'Lake Ontario. More specifically, I believe you are pointing at Oswego.'

'Exactly. Oswego. A good rallying point, wouldn't you say? Word will go out to the Six Nations of the Iroquois – and any other savage who cares to gather there – "Come to the biggest party you've ever seen. Come for powder, presents, and plenty of rum." Should prove irresistible, what?'

Jack knew it would, and the knowledge saddened him. His Mohawk brethren, every other tribe, Iroquois or not, were now dependent on these handouts from the Great White Father, King George. It didn't mean they would fight, necessarily. But impressive gifts and substantial supplies of rum were powerful persuaders.

Jack looked at the map again. The Mohawk River flowed inland, down the valley of the same name, the heartland of his adopted people, through rich farmlands of settlers, both Loyal and Rebel, and on to a place the General had talked of the night before, where a continent could be won.

'You've seen it, ain't ye?'

'I believe so, sir. A third force, striking along the Mohawk. To rendezvous with you and General Howe at Albany.'

'Ah, Jack! You should have stayed in the army, my boy, not run off to India to make money. You'd have been a General yourself by now.'

'I couldn't have afforded the purchases.' Jack still stared down at the map. 'And the size of the expedition?'

'A small force of Regulars. Perhaps some Germans. Can't spare many from the main thrust. But there'll be two Loyalist regiments at least and our friend Skene assures me that the Mohawk Valley is filled with others waiting to rally to our standards. But the main threat will come from your Indians.' Burgoyne, his stock finished, rose and laid a hand on Jack's shoulder. 'Dazzled by our generosity, they'll sign up in droves. I've already sent to that Iroquois leader, Joseph Brant. You know him, don't you?'

'A little. He and Até are both Mohawk and Wolf Clan, and also both graduates of Moor's Indian Charity School.'

'Good friends, then?'

'Can't stand each other.' Jack laughed. 'But they'll work together nonetheless.'

'Good. Well, you and Até and his schoolfellow Brant will drink with the tribes, smoke with them, speak their blessed lingo with them. Rally them, Jack. And then, set them loose in their thousands. I wager you'll depopulate the Mohawk Valley of Rebels inside a month.'

While the General was occupied with the buttons of his waistcoat, Jack stared at the map. He had already voiced his doubts as to the size of the Native contingent that could be expected, as well as their enthusiasm. 'Who is to lead us?'

'Wish it were you, my boy. Alas, not even I have the dispensation to raise a Captain to Brevet-Brigadier in an instant. No, it will be Colonel Barry St Leger. Know him?'

'A little. Experienced. Is he still . . . ?' Jack cocked a hand toward his mouth.

'Apparently not. Found temperance and God, they say.' Burgoyne shuddered. 'Still, better for our purposes to have him sober, eh?' He laid his finger again upon the map. 'Do you remember what's here?'

Jack looked at the point indicated. 'Fort Stanwix, is it not?'

'Aye, Jack. Apparently it's close to a ruin and defended by half-trained Militiamen, at best. They'll probably run off; but if they do fight, just encourage St Leger to end it with all dispatch. A week at the most, eh? The swifter you move inland,' Burgoyne's finger traced along the Mohawk Valley, 'the swifter the Americans will have to detach men to oppose you, while half the Militia will desert to protect their own farms. The weakened forces they put up against me I'll sweep aside,' his finger drew down the line of the Hudson from Canada, 'while General Howe will be scattering Washington's forces to the south and marching to join us here.' His finger climbed from New York then stabbed down on a black circle. 'Albany, Jack. We'll see what the kidneys are like in Albany at the end of August. Three months! Why, it will be like a stroll around Vauxhall Gardens!'

Jack decided merely to nod. There was so much he could say as to the hazards that lay ahead and no point in saying them. The General would counter anything he brought up. He was that most dangerous of military men – an optimist.

'When do I leave, sir?'

'Immediately. I have your papers here – orders, requisitions for horses and equipment, some gold so's you can do some bribing. No doubt you and Até will prefer to travel as civilians so you can leave your uniform with me. Then you and your savage can go where you think fit, urging all the warriors you meet to the fight. You know the country better than anyone. Just be at Oswego for the gathering of the tribes in the last week of July.'

'Must I leave immediately, sir? There was a personal matter I wished to attend to in the town.'

Burgoyne smiled, somewhat sadly, then reached for his scarlet coat. Even in the dawn light the gold thread dazzled. It was exquisite, as were all his clothes, the facings the deep blue of his own and Jack's regiment, the 16th Dragoons. 'I would give you the time, dear Jack, but you would find it fruitless. The boat that brought the kidneys brought this as well.' He picked up another note and passed it to him.

It was in Louisa's strong hand and asked the General to convey to Jack her deepest regrets; but her father had made arrangements for her to travel to Montreal with the dawn sailing.

His face must have betrayed his disappointment. Burgoyne laughed. 'Damn me, Jack, but I fear you have become a sentimental dog. When you were younger such a letter would have given you joy. You've had five weeks of her charms. As a youth, that would have been an eternity. Sheridan had you to perfection in his play as a rogue and a schemer. What's happened to you?'

'Age, General.'

Burgoyne glanced at the screen and smiled. 'Don't know what you are talking about. Well, never mind, my boy. The lovely Miss Reardon travels with the army. I will watch over her as a second father and you will see her in Albany, if not before. Should goad you to keep St Leger pushing swiftly forward, eh?'

'Aye, sir.'

Briskly, his sash was tied, his gorget affixed, his high black leathern boots slipped on. Burgoyne paused briefly to whisper behind the screen, then he strapped on his sword, picked up his gloves and hat, and beckoned Jack toward the door.

'Follow me, Captain Absolute. Let us take the first step together on to the land we shall soon rule completely once more.'

He swept out. Jack hesitated a moment, then turned back to the table, gathering up the maps there, putting them into their case. He suspected the woman behind the screen was Hannah Foy, wife of a commissary officer, Burgoyne's mistress from the previous year's campaign and too dim to be a danger. Or the reverse, dim enough to blurt out all she had heard in the cabin that morning to some willing ear. There was no need to leave her with maps as well.

Jack paused in the doorway, listening to this woman's light breathing, thinking of another. The General had judged the Captain by his own standards and, he had to admit, some examples from Jack's youth. He assumed that Jack had been taking the same pleasure from Miss Reardon as he just had from Mrs Foy. It may just have been possible, despite the restrictions of shipboard life. There was indeed a time when such obstacles would have held him up not a jot. But Jack had wanted something less transient, and Louisa had seemed to want that too. It was one of the things that intrigued, this holding off. Quite unlike Lizzie Farren in London and a host of other liaisons he could name – along with many he could not.

Suddenly, with the scent of a woman in a cabin in his

nostrils, Jack began to wish away those wasted weeks. He was going to war and there were dozens of ways he could die in it. Burgoyne was right, he *had* become a sentimental dog. As he climbed the stairs, to the music of ship's whistles and the percussion of Quebec's cannons saluting the new Commander-in-Chief, Jack knew that in the months ahead, he would spend many nights cursing this change in his character.

– SIX –
The Fort

'*Fire!*'

The order was roared with a martial ardour of which Jack could only approve. If the young ensign's vocal enthusiasm at his first command of an artillery battery had been enough, the log walls of Fort Stanwix would long ago have sundered and split, Grenadiers would even now be forcing the breach, the Rebels choosing to yield or die. And the strange new flag that floated over the ramparts – unseen till that day, concocted of stars and stripes obviously ripped from spare cloaks and petticoats – would soon be replaced by the Union Standard of Great Britain.

Unfortunately for the besiegers, the officer's command was the loudest noise made. Jack didn't even bother to plug his ears as the British artillery whispered its shot toward the walls. The small balls from the two six-pounders, the two three-pounders, and the four coehorns went the same way as all the previous ones. They either bounced off the solid pine trunks leaving barely a mark, or buried themselves with harmless thuds in the sod and earth piled around the fort.

Ignoring the jeers of the defenders, the ensign commanded his troops to swab down and reload. He would keep firing until ordered to stop, despite the negligible results. Shaking his head, Jack began to step through the ranks of Indians gathered there for the show. He could at least try to get the order to desist, though he doubted his success. So far, Colonel Barry St Leger, Commander of the British forces at the siege, had neither sought Jack's advice nor paid attention to any tendered.

'Apples thrown by children at a garden fence.' Até had risen from the rear rank of Natives to join him. He was as disgusted as Jack, not least because he had persuaded a goodly number of his relatives and clan members to join the expeditionary force on the promise of watching the vaunted British army in action.

'I know. I'm going to try to persuade St Leger to get it stopped.'

'And then what, Daganoweda?'

Jack sighed. 'I wish I knew.'

And he also now wished that, at the outset, he had made clearer to Burgoyne the obstacles that lay ahead of them. Like all optimists, the General had only foreseen the progress he desired. And indeed, initially, Jack had found the optimism justified, his orders easy to obey.

He and Até had left Quebec on the first day of June, with two pack horses, amply provisioned, and loaded with all the goods and presents his native brothers could desire. It was vital for Até's prestige that when he returned to his people, he returned as if from the most successful of trading trips and as befitted his status as a member of one of the 'royal' families of the Mohawk. Indeed, Jack knew that if Até had remained in his homeland, and not followed his white brother to India in 1766, he would be a senior sachem by now. By bringing gifts, he re-established his status and drew warriors to him as a 'Pine Tree Chief' – unelected, but able to lead men to the war path.

And men did rally. Many had promised to join them at the meeting of the tribes at Oswego in the third week of July. Most would come – few Iroquois would miss such a party. Some talked with excitement of the coming war. This generation of young men had not had a fight in which to prove themselves and they did not fully consider themselves men until they did.

But despite the sunshine on their progress, as they had

moved out of Canada and into the forest fastnesses of the northern American colonies, there were hints of darkness along the way. They had met others of the Six Nations of the Iroquois, especially Oneida and Tuscarora, the tribes who lived closest to the Americans and were most influenced by them, who were sullen, even hostile. They learned that the Supreme Council of the Iroquois League, made up of the chief sachems of all the tribes, had been unable to decide unanimously on which side to take in the war. In that Council, if unanimity wasn't agreed, no action could be taken. Thus, neutrality was declared. This was unacceptable to many warriors who sought the glory and spoils of war, and to honour their old allegiance to the English. The Iroquois League was split.

The meeting at Oswego, however, had been a qualified success. The British Commander, St Leger, with his Loyalist subordinates, had brought enough rum and gifts to buy allies. Many had joined when his force marched from Oswego en route to the Mohawk River. Ominously, many of the undecided had come to share in the continuing handouts of presents and rum, and to observe the promised easy victory at Fort Stanwix.

How had Burgoyne described it? *Close to a ruin and defended by half-trained Militiamen, at best.* Jack wished the General was there to see the sturdy bastion, the well-armed and obviously well-trained troops. But Jack had not spoken out, and he had not warned that once the meeting at Oswego was called, their intended target would be clear to the Rebels. The Americans he'd fought beside against the French all those years ago were intelligent enough to recognize the strategic threat posed by a third British force striking down the Mohawk Valley and would have prepared accordingly. As, indeed, they had.

Now, as he and Até walked through the rudimentary siege lines, his despair increased. The King's army was a shambles – and they'd only been there three days! Emplacements had been half-dug then abandoned, as the Colonel thought first of one point of attack, then another. Men lay about the holes and little caves, smoking pipes, some playing cards or dice, all swigging ceaselessly from canteens. The early August heat lay heavy on the land. It was hard to tell Native from Loyalist, as all were wearing as little as possible – tattered shirts, aprons, or leggings, feet bare. Some flapped caps in futile attempts to ward off the clouds of tiny black insects that tormented. Others slapped and cursed, as the bigger horse flies or mosquitoes savaged them.

In many ways the Regulars' lines were as bad. There was order to be sure – tents set up in even rows, latrines dug, a cook tent gushing smoke – but the soldiers drilling were in full campaign uniform, an insect head-dress around each, unable to break ranks and swat them away, sweat turning their scarlet almost to black. Those who had fainted lay to the side, a growing number, while the officers and sergeants controlling the drills were becoming more and more irritable, striking out with stick and boot. Jack could sense fury building like an electrical storm within the persecuted ranks.

Yet it was not the soldiers of the 8th or the 34th regiment that concerned Jack. When the time came, they would rally and fight and kill and die as they always had, as Jack had witnessed them do on many occasions and marvelled. It was not even the two green-coated Loyalist battalions under Butler and Johnson who were exchanging insults and shot with their former neighbours, friends, even brothers, within the fort. It was rather those warriors who made up the slight majority of the allied army that worried him, their situation that the Colonel must now address: His Majesty's Native Allies.

He approached the tent through crowds of them. They sat – some swaying, others chanting. One group was vying with another to create ever more elaborate paintings on their bodies, for war paint was highly prized and St Leger had obtained a panoply of colours for them. A small number had formed a circle, each man playing a Jew's Harp. Many Natives delighted in the instrument, its strange humming a rival for the buzz of insects. Most had flagons of rum, swiftly passed, swiftly drained, this 'darling water' the most prized gift of all – and the most dangerous. Jack had seen it happen before: rival tribes, too much liquor, too little space.

The Iroquois kept to their tribal groups: Seneca with Seneca, Mohawks with other Mohawks, the Cayugas, Onondagas equally separated. Try as he might, Jack could never convince his superiors that they could not deal with the Iroquois as one body, just more individual regiments for their forces. And that didn't even account for the other tribes – Delawares, Shawnees, Missausauga Algonquin, and many others – who had gathered to partake of British hospitality. Even if they were uncommitted to the fight, as the Senecas were, for instance, they knew they would still receive their share of gifts. Especially the rum. If the British turned them away, the enemy would not.

All these dark thoughts swirled through Jack's head as he approached the Commander's tent. Standing near its entrance, sucking hard on a pipe, was St Leger's adjutant, Captain Ancrum.

'A word with the Colonel, Ancrum?'

His fellow officer winced, then tamped out his tobacco on his boot heel. 'I'll try, Absolute. You'll, uh, wait here, yes?'

He twitched the flap, went in. Why Jack had to wait outside had been made very clear to him at his most recent meeting with St Leger. Men chose different methods to ward off the near-constant biting of insects. Some stayed near fires, despite the already ferocious summer heat. Others, like Ancrum, buttoned their uniforms tight and smoked continuously, thus keeping their faces relatively unbitten at least. Jack and Até had chosen to revert to Native ways. On their first day in camp at Oswego they had tracked and killed a bear. They had not eaten of it, for a rutting bear's flesh is bitter. But its grease covered them now, the most effective ward against bites; no creature would choose to come near them – either winged or two-legged. It sometimes amused Jack to think how his friends at Boodles Club or the Turk's Head Tavern would react if he came, thus fragrant, into their company. Much as St Leger had

81

reacted, probably, when Jack had entered his tent for the first and only time.

'Egad! You reek, sir. Out. *Out!*'

So now Jack awaited him outside, Até squatting behind him. The tent flaps parted again, the Colonel emerged, and Jack reflected on yet one more option for keeping away the insects.

Pickling. Barry St Leger, despite the early hour, and the necessities of command, was inordinately and utterly drunk.

'Absholute!' The Colonel stepped very carefully out of his tent, his eyes seeking a point on Jack's right shoulder. He was a tall man, forty years old, though the effects of his drinking made him seem closer to sixty. He halted about six paces away, swayed, steadied. 'Close enough, I think, what?' he declaimed, glancing back with a smirk at Captain Ancrum, who had relit his pipe in the tent's entrance. He smiled weakly, then shook his head slightly as he caught Jack's eye. Though he was obviously being warned off, Jack felt he had to try.

'I was wondering, sir, if just this once . . .' He gestured to the privacy of the tent.

'Certainly not. Took me three days to clear the stench at Oswego. Well, man, something to report?'

Jack sighed. If it had to be in public, then so be it. 'Yes, Colonel. I was wondering about the guns.'

'Guns?' St Leger's face took on a parody of concentration. 'I am aware of many aspects of your . . . remarkable career. Dragoon. Sepoy. Tree fighter.' The last was delivered with an unmistakable sneer. 'Never knew you for a gunner though.'

'I am not, sir. I was merely observing that we seem to be expending a lot of powder to little effect. We are under-powered, sir, in that branch of the service.'

St Leger swayed, spluttered. 'False information. Your damn savages, Absholute. Told us the damn fort was virtually a ruin. Otherwise, would have brought bloody bigger guns. Never trust a bloody native, what?'

Behind him, Até stirred and muttered under his breath. Other tribesmen drew closer. Many found the Colonel's love of his 'milk' amusing.

To speak more quietly, Jack took a step forward, but the Colonel took an equal one back, stumbling slightly as he settled.

'Then I was wondering, sir, since we cannot hope to penetrate the walls—'

'Not being a gunner, Absholute, you wouldn't know the effect shot has on an enemy. It demoralizes him, sir. And it impresses the savage.' St Leger waved a limp wrist at the gathering Natives.

Jack knew the cannonade was making the reverse impression, but he could see no words of his would halt the paltry bombardment. Yet he could at least attempt to remove part of the unimpressed audience.

'Another point then, sir. If I may return to the suggestion I made yesterday?'

'Eh?' St. Leger looked as if yesterday had been the year before.

'A reconnaissance in strength, sir. Take the Mohawks, at least, up their valley to see what the enemy is about.'

'Set them loose on the population, you mean. Let them indulge in every type of barbarity.' Phlegm was flying from the Colonel's mouth and he was swaying alarmingly with drink and passion. Ancrum took a cautionary step toward him, arms outstretched. 'When we know that thousands of Loyalists in that valley are ready to rise up and meet with us, you wish to set these bloody heathens upon them, to ravish, butcher . . . scalp?' He was virtually screaming now. 'No, by all that's holy. God and England would never forgive me.' He looked to the heavens, sighed deeply. 'And God and England would be right!'

Passion expended, he did slip then. Ancrum's arms supported him, guided him back toward the tent. At its entrance, St Leger turned again. 'I will not split my forces. We shall deal with Stanwix and only then will we begin our march to Albany. But you, Captain, since the sound of cannon so displeases you, may return to your watch in the woods.'

The Colonel disappeared inside. Jack stared after him. Até rose at his side.

' "As a dog returneth to his vomit, so a fool returneth to his folly." '

'*Hamlet*, I suppose.'

Até smiled. 'Proverbs. Chapter Twenty-Six, Verse Eleven. You are the greatest heathen here.'

Jack laughed, feeling the tension within him ease. He had done his best. And now, at least, he had received some kind of order.

'And you had Christianity crammed down your throat at that charity school of yours. It was the main advantage of a Westminster education. We were all bloody heathens there.'

It was an old debate between them. Até grunted. 'Well, Daganoweda. Shall we continue the argument at the camp?'

'Aye.' They had set up an observation post an hour's march down the valley. There they could fend for themselves, clear of the tensions of the siege.

As they were moving away, Jack felt a tug on his elbow. 'A word, Captain Absolute, if I may?'

The Mohawk who now stood beside Jack was as tall and as old as he. Like many of his people, centuries of contact with the Whites had sharpened the flatter Native features. Even with the copper of his skin, he would have passed nearly unnoticed amongst the darker denizens of Cornwall. This was emphasized by his European style of dress, his shirt, breeches, and waistcoat. An officer's gorget swung at his neck, and beneath it dangled a medal. Presented, Jack now recalled, by King George himself when this man, Joseph Brant, had visited London the previous year. It was said that he had refused to bow to the sovereign because he was an ally, not a subject. His English, as befitted one educated at the same school as Até, was excellent, although his accent differed. Society had befriended him on his English tour. Romney had painted his portrait, he had moved among the court and now sought to emulate their tones in his speech.

The man turned to Até. 'James,' he said, drawing out the word as if he were at tea on Piccadilly.

'Joseph.' Até, colouring slightly, nodded. Though they had

been part of the same force travelling down from Lake Ontario, Até had been thus far able to avoid his old school-fellow, for Brant was the one man in the army who would call Até by his baptismal name. They were of the same tribe of the Iroquois, the same clan of the Wolf. But Jack knew Até felt, like many others, that Brant was trying to become a white man . . . and despised him for it.

Jack had no such concerns. Brant may have affected all things English but he was still a tough Mohawk warrior, the well-dinted tomahawk at his waist testifying to that. And he was tireless in his devotion to the King's cause. Jack also knew that Brant commanded a good following among his tribe, warriors, who like himself, were not content with the neutrality the Council was trying to impose.

Brant turned to Jack. 'I heard what you were saying to our drinking leader. You are right, and he is wrong.'

'Can you and the other sachems not get him to agree?'

'When we cannot agree amongst ourselves?' Brant swept his arm around the dispersing tribesmen. 'Your Colonel said to the Senecas at Oswego, "Come and watch us smash the Rebels. You do not even have to fight. And we will give you equal shares of gifts, of rum." Equal! To the Mohawk who raises his war club for King George! And since the Senecas are without honour they accepted this spectator's role. As if they were in a box at Drury Lane. But at least the Seneca are Iroquois.' He pointed at another group. 'All these others . . . Shawnee, Delaware, Missausauga Algonquin with their filthy tongue – how can we get them to unite under the Union Jack?'

Though this tirade had been pronounced in almost Oxfordian tones, Brant now turned and hawked very loudly in the direction of the Senecas, some of whom muttered and fingered their tomahawks. Jack took Brant by the elbow, led him slightly apart.

'I know how you feel, Taiyendanaygeh.' Jack had reverted to Iroquois, feeling Ancrum's gaze upon him, newly emerged from the Colonel's tent. 'But these divisions will only make the Rebel enemy glad. Is there nothing we can do to unite us?'

'Fight.' It was Até who spoke. 'Throw them into battle. They will all want glory if the bullets begin to storm.'

'My brother is right,' Jack said. 'This siege, these toothless cannon, this is not the tribes' way of war. But we are going out now to our camp. We will have first news of any enemy who march to relieve the Fort, as I think they will do. If I send back to the camp, will you come?'

Brant smiled for the first time. 'I will. And you are right. They may lack the honour of the Mohawk. But even these others will fight.'

Jack squeezed Brant's elbow. 'Then let us go. And may we send word soon.'

'Amen,' said Brant.

They went to the Quartermaster's tent where they had left their own weapons. Stripping off the shirt, breeches, and boots he felt obliged to wear when in conversation with fellow officers, Jack was soon dressed – or undressed – like Até; a hide apron around his waist, reaching to mid-thigh, moccasins on his feet. Até was painted in red stripes right up to the scalp lock, the single bunched tail of hair that ran from his crown down his back. Jack had decided that the tattoos he'd acquired as a young man were sufficient painting and that his hair had better remain uncut since he had his dual role to think of. A shaved British officer would not be invited to sit down, even at Burgoyne's table. But he gathered the thick hair back, tied it with rawhide. It reached down his spine nearly as far as Até's.

Cross straps held three pistols apiece. They dropped their powder horns over their shoulders, the pouches that contained ball and grain to eat on the trail. There would be plenty of water and game in the woods. Finally, they picked up their fusils. Point 65 calibre, they had been taken from the French years before, much lighter than the Land Pattern Firelock issued to British soldiers, far better constructed and with shortened barrels. Among the trees, one needed accuracy and speed rather than distance, and a shorter barrel was easier to wield.

'Ready?' Até was grinning at him from the tent entrance.

'Oh yes,' said Jack. 'Let's see if we can start some trouble.'

– SEVEN –
Hunters

Within the silence of the trees, the wolf howl pierced like musket shot. Roosting pigeons exploded from branches, careless of the canopy, wings hammering the leaves aside in panicked flight. A squirrel, which Jack had been studying with the idle curiosity of the slightly hungry, disappeared into the higher reaches of a black walnut with a flick of his tail.

Jack looked to Até and his friend peered back at him through his spectacles. He had acquired a new pair in London, delighted with an improvement that had occurred in their time in India; these were called 'bi-focals' and had a reading lens occupying the lower half of the glass. The contrast between these and the shaved head and war paint had given Jack much amusement, though Até had not seen the humour. A copy of *Clarissa* by Samuel Richardson lay on his tattooed chest. He did not usually read novels, preferring philosophy or Shakespeare, but Burgoyne had thrust it at him on the voyage over and he felt obliged to the General to finish it. After two days in the forest, he was nearly done.

They waited for the chorus that should follow the single cry. But it was not long before the one voice cried once more, from a little nearer, a longer ululation ending in a series of sharp yelps.

There was something strange in it. Jack tipped his head. 'Lone wolf?'

Até was folding his spectacles, putting them and the book to the rear of their birch bark, half-moon lean-to. 'Yes,' he said, reaching for his gun, 'but not an animal one.'

Jack had heard it too. Someone was moving through the woods towards them. Their shelter was set back from the main path, hidden by a thicket of young birch. Priming their fusils with a sprinkle of powder in the pan – they were already loaded – they moved swiftly down to the trail. Jack's raised eyebrows drew the slightest of nods from Até, who swung himself into the lower branches of a beech. Jack lay just off the path, squinting along the barrel down the path that led to the Rebel lands.

It was not a long wait. Within moments, they heard the sound of feet slapping the earth. Or rather one foot, then a dragging sound accompanied by a harsh exhalation. And there were other sounds beyond these. Straining, Jack could make out at least three other footfalls, maybe more, coming fast. Faster certainly than the one they obviously pursued.

The first man to appear looked as though he had run for miles. He was dressed, much as Jack and Até themselves, in breech cloth, moccasins, and little else. But the black and gold paint that striped him from crown of head to knees was smeared and, Jack instantly saw, run through with red. This was not done in the formal patterns of the paint. This was blood. It spread across the body in a spider's web, streaming from beneath the hand the man ineffectually clutched to his side. And Jack saw that the leg, the one that dragged, had another wound, also pulsing red.

They saw him and a moment later he was upon them. Laying aside his gun, Jack stuck out a leg.

The wounded warrior had been glancing back so he went down hard. But he rolled twice and came up to his knees, a knife in his hands. Jack followed, tomahawk drawn, but the blade halted him. Besides there were friends as well as foes in this forest.

There was a moment of near silence; only a moment, because both men heard, above the desperate breathing of the kneeling one, the rapid approach of those other feet. Maybe two hundred paces through the brush. Maybe less.

'Mohawk?' whispered Jack. He said it in English and the man's eyes widened.

'Cayuga. I seek the forces of the King.'

'You've found them. Some, at least. Those who follow?'

'They serve the Rebel. They seek to stop my mouth.'

'How many?'

'Five. I think five.'

Jack had a moment to believe or not. When he did, he pursed his lips and whistled. First, just the once and like a spruce partridge, the best of the eating birds, indicating to Até that they had found a friend. The second time, five quick bursts with the aid of his fingers (a quail rising in alarm from a nest) gave the number of the enemy. Then he stepped off the path and reached down for his musket.

The first of the pursuers crested the slight rise and yelped in triumph when he saw the fallen Cayuga, an Ironwood war club lifting as he ran. He was just about to throw it when Jack fired, the buck-and-ball load taking him in the chest, spinning him back. A second warrior hurdled the falling man, came on without a pause, shrieking, his own weapon rising, then spinning from his grasp as a hole opened in his side, the sound of Até's shot coming almost simultaneously. He cried out, staggered, tried to run on, fell slithering toward them.

Behind, three other warriors appeared, hesitated. In that still moment, Até dropped from the tree straight into their midst. His tomahawk rose, fell; another blocked it. Wood cracked on wood, metal on metal, as the metal heads slid towards each other, clashed together. Another blade sliced down toward Até's back, but the warrior was aiming where Até had been. He'd used the interlocked heads to pull himself and his opponent off the path.

Jack now had a target. Drawing his own tomahawk again, he threw, spinning it fast through the air. Somehow, the man saw it come, raised his own to deflect it, skittering it into the woods. Jack only had a moment to curse his choice to throw

89

before he was dealing with its consequences – a screaming warrior running at him, tomahawk raised high up to that point where the killing strokes begin.

He'd held on to his fusil in his left hand. Now he snapped the butt up into his right, raised the weapon square across his head, just in time. The tomahawk blade drove into the gunstock an inch from Jack's fingers. He pulled his right arm down sharply, twisting his body aside. The running attack, the slight slope, Jack's sudden movement, all caused the warrior to slip past, fall to one knee. But he wrenched the weapon from the stock and sweeping around, cut at Jack's extended knee. Jack leapt back, using the fusil almost as a sword, sweeping the barrel down. The tomahawk, the better balanced of the two weapons, knocked the musket from Jack's grasp. He staggered back and the warrior, with a shout of triumph, raised his blade high and stepped forward to deliver the death stroke.

Jack reached his left arm across his body and drew his dirk from the sheath at his right side. In the same movement he threw it underhand, though it was not truly designed to be thrown, and he was aware, even in that instant, of the poor results he'd obtained from the far more airworthy tomahawk. But the blade flew effectively enough, taking the warrior in the throat just as he was about to strike. It halted him in mid-blow, a look of surprise, even reproach taking over his face. Then he sat down very suddenly, legs thrust out before him. A gurgle, it might have been a curse, and he lay back.

It had taken no time at all. Jack turned to see Até still entwined with his opponent, spinning around as each tried to loosen the other's grip on their tomahawk. Even as he watched, his friend leaned back, then suddenly forward, his head cracking down on the opponent's nose. With a cry the man lost his hold on his own weapon, and, with it, his life.

The last of the pursuers had not moved from where the fight had begun. Now, he looked quite slowly at the bodies of his friends, at Jack, at Até. Then he nodded once, turned, and ran.

'Yours.' Jack indicated the path. Até paused only to jerk his tomahawk's head from his victim's body and he was gone. Twin footfalls faded.

Jack turned to the Cayuga brave. The man had fainted and, looking at his wounds, Jack could see why. Both chest and leg must have bled extensively and a terrible pallor underlay the dark skin. Jack bent and lifted the man, carrying him the few paces to the shelter. There, he swiftly ripped apart a shirt reserved for cooler nights and wrapped the swathes of cloth around the wounds. The leg injury was deep but would heal with time. The other, in the side of the chest, was more serious; Jack felt the ball might still be in there. The man needed a surgeon and swiftly.

As Jack bound the more serious wound, the man stirred then started.

'Easy, friend. My name is Jack Absolute. You are safe now. Rest.'

The man shook his head as if to clear it. 'I cannot. My name is Samuel. Water?' When Jack had fetched it and he had drunk deep – though it caused him pain – he said, 'I have *wampum* for the King's Army.' He nodded to the pouch that Jack had removed from his shoulder. Jack opened it, pulled out the belt of beads. The majority were purple, though white ones were spaced along it in rectangles the size of a thumb.

'I am not gifted in the reading of *wampum*. I know this means danger, and that it is incomplete.'

'There was not time to finish it. I bring the news . . . here.' the man touched his mouth. 'But Molly Brant sent this so that my words would be believed. I speak what she would make into *wampum*.'

'Molly Brant? Joseph's sister?'

The man nodded. 'She lives still in Canajoharie, down the Valley. It is full of Rebels. She listens and sees them gather. They are coming here, their soldiers.'

'Regulars?' Jack would be surprised to see Washington's regular army, the 'Continentals' as they were called, this far west. Not with Burgoyne marching down from the north and Howe from the south.

The man shook his head. 'Tryon County Militia. But many. They come to fight for the fort.'

Jack frowned. The Militias varied in quality and training, summoned as they were only for short bursts of service. But the best of them were doughty fighters. 'We had heard this Militia was fearful, that they would not fight.'

'A girl was killed. White girl. By tribesmen allied to King George, it is said. It makes them angry.'

'How long?'

The man looked east. 'Soon. Maybe even tomorrow. They set out after me but it is not far. They . . .'

They both felt the faint vibration on the earth. Jack picked up a pistol, but, a moment later, Até was before them. He threw something down in front of Samuel – a long black braid attached to a piece of skin.

'The last of your pursuers.' Até toed the scalp a little forward. 'Oneida, I think.'

'Yes. Oneidas love the Rebelmen. As do the Tuscaroras.'

Jack looked up. 'Two of the Six Nations. That confirms what we heard on the way to the gathering, Até – we are not the only ones fighting our own.'

'Did you not say, Daganoweda, that all wars are civil wars?'

'I did.' He looked down at Samuel. 'If I help you, can you make it to Fort Stanwix? It is about an hour's march, maybe a little more with your wounds. I think the Colonel will need to hear it from you. He doesn't value my opinions.'

Samuel raised himself on one elbow. 'I must.'

Até reached into the shelter. In a moment, all his possessions were across his shoulders.

'I will . . .' He nodded down the path in the direction the enemy would come.

'I'll be back by dawn.' Jack was helping Samuel to stand. Once on two feet the Cayuga warrior shrugged off the supporting hands. 'And hopefully I'll bring an army. At the creek?'

'Oriskany?'

'Aye. Oriskany.'

With a flick of two fingers at his brow, Até loped off down the path. Samuel had already begun to limp the opposite way, through shafts of late afternoon sunlight slanting through the canopy. Before he followed, Jack went to seek his thrown tomahawk. Rooting among the undergrowth, he finally found it, straightened . . . and was struck by how peaceful everything was, all the colours of the forest in harmony. Then, turning to follow, he looked down, saw the one colour that was out of place, because the season for it had not yet come. Red. Their victim's blood, on the bodies they would have to leave, on the forest's floor. Jack knew, that if Samuel's message was heeded, the hue would soon be spread much wider under the canopy.

This time there was no question. The urgency of the matter demanded that Jack was part of the war council within their leader's pavilion – though St Leger, drunk as a lord, made much play, before his crimson nose, of a large stained hand-kerchief that he regularly anointed from a flask of perfume. The scent was of the very cheapest, cloying and more noxious, to Jack, than anything that could come from a bear. And it combined unfortunately with both the grease sported by several of the Native councillors and the pipe smoke many others were using to ward off the stench. The approach of evening had barely tempered the heat of the day. Within minutes of the council commencing, the tent smelled like a combination of bordello, sweat lodge, and abattoir.

Yet to Jack, the nasal assaults were as nothing to the main irritation under the canvas. There, right next to the swaying, sweating Colonel, and as apparently in favour as Jack was out, stood a man in the dark green uniform of a major of Jaegers, the Light Infantry from Hesse-Hanau. He was a senior officer with the final reinforcements, newly arrived from Lake Ontario. But on Hounslow Heath he'd been Banastre Tarleton's Second-Second, and in a secret message in Quebec he was, Jack felt certain, 'Diomedes' of the Illuminati. Here though he was, once again, the Count von Schlaben.

As soon as he'd seen him, Jack had cursed Burgoyne silently.

The General had promised to keep this dangerous man tight to him. In the chaos of campaign Von Schlaben had obviously contrived to slip away. Burgoyne would not know where he had gone and if he'd finally found out, any warning sent would almost certainly be far behind the German. And Jack could see, by the way St Leger already deferred to the Count, that speaking out against him would have no effect, could only hurt Jack's standing in this company further.

And, once again, Von Schlaben opposed Jack on everything that mattered. His position as a leader of the German contingent gave him a voice. His was as soft and persuasive as ever as he counselled caution, consolidation, even withdrawal in the face of the approaching foe. Surely better to preserve these forces and return them to Burgoyne if the Fort could not be taken quickly and was soon to be relieved? Even St Leger demurred at this. He did not want a return to a subordinate position where both his incompetence and his drinking could not help but be noticed. But he agreed that his forces should not be split – his regular forces anyway.

'They shall maintain the siege,' he had drawled. 'I am convinced the defenders are soon to falter. Since my esteemed ally Joseph Brant here and, uh, *Captain* Absolute are so convinced of the prowess of their tribesmen, let them show it. Let them to prove their vaunted forest fighting skills. Let them do it alone.'

Jack had no need to raise his voice in the counter-arguments that followed. The two Loyalist leaders, John Butler and John Johnson, commanded troops who were nearly all farmers and landowners, like themselves, in the Mohawk Valley they were due to march through. It was their farms that had been appropriated by the Rebels, their neighbours, former friends and, in many cases, even brothers and fathers who formed the Militia that marched to relieve the Fort. This was the personal war they had come to fight. They would go with the Mohawks and their allies and join in the ambush. And, much to Joseph Brant's disgust, a Seneca sachem declared that his people, as had been promised them, would come along and watch.

It was far from perfect. But it could be enough. From Samuel's report, the Militia numbered about six hundred men and the Allies were mustering about the same – four hundred Native, two hundred Loyalist – with the advantage of surprise and of choosing the terrain. Both he and Joseph knew the valley and, like Até, had spotted the ravine at Oriskany, about six miles from Fort Stanwix, as a likely site. Yet when Jack saw the swiftest of smiles appear on Von Schlaben's lips, he suddenly felt less than sure.

The meeting broke up, participants gratefully fleeing the fug to go and ready their men. They were to march in one hour. Joseph immediately set off for the Mohawk camp. Von Schlaben had preceded them and Jack saw his green coat disappearing down a side trail toward the German lines. They had set up in a small clearing just away from the main encampment. On a whim, Jack followed.

He caught up with him down a dip, in a small stand of fir. Their dense needles screened the two men from sight and the rallying trumpets were muted there. Von Schlaben had stopped, was staring ahead. Drawing nearer, Jack saw the reason.

A rattlesnake lay curled up, slap in the centre of the path. It was a large one, several years old, its rattle at least seven ligaments long. It raised this as it confronted the Count, shook its warning at him, its tongue slipping in and out, head weaving from side to side.

'Communing with a cousin, Count?'

The German half-turned toward Jack, endeavouring to keep his eyes in both directions, that faint smile as ever on his lips.

'Captain Absolute. My, such deadly forest creatures both fore and aft. What is a poor townsman to do?'

'I am flattered you consider me deadly,' Jack left the slightest of pauses before adding, 'Diomedes.'

If he hoped the name would provoke a reaction he was disappointed.

'My first name is Adolphus, not . . . whatever it was you just said. Though I hardly think we know each other well enough to be on such terms.'

'Oh, I don't know.' Jack had stopped about four paces away. 'I think one should always be on easy terms with a man who has tried to have one killed.'

'I?' There was no real denial in the tone. His gaze swung back to the snake, which had begun to move. Certain of its precedence on the path, it uncoiled and, with a final warning rattle, slithered off into the brush.

Von Schlaben shook his head. 'A nasty way to die, I am told.'

'Very. You should try it.'

The German's pallid eyes moved back to Jack. In a voice devoid of inflection, he said, 'You wish something from me, Captain Absolute?'

Jack took a moment to look the dark green uniform of the Jaeger officer up and down. 'Do you qualify for this role?'

'We all play many roles, Captain. I have seen some military service, yes.' He gestured with his chin to Jack's encampment garb of green wool shirt and buckskin leggings. 'Do you qualify for yours?'

There was a moment's appraising silence between them. Jack broke it. 'I know why you set that young lunatic on me in London. You would try to prevent me in the duty I perform now – rousing the Natives to fight for the King.'

'I would?' Again, it was barely a question.

'I am curious. What do you consider your duty?'

The smile left the eyes but not the lips. 'I think it might be beyond your comprehension, Captain.'

'Oh, I know I am but a simple soldier, Count. But you could speak slowly and try me.'

Von Schlaben looked around. The trees were very dark but above them the high summer sky still glowed in evening light.

'Very well. Since we are alone here. You may have more imagination than I credited you for. You may even . . .' He brought a hand up before him, thumb and middle finger pinched together, and described a small circle before his heart.

Jack knew the response even if he did not hold with the Masonic creed. He delineated his own circle in the air, filled it with a hint of a 'rosy' cross.

'Well.' For the first time Jack saw something other than amusement or calculation in the German's eyes. 'If I had known that, we might have spared ourselves some unpleasantness.' He sighed. 'You talk of duty to a King. My duty is to something beyond kings. Beyond countries. My duty . . . is to humanity itself.'

'A higher cause, then.'

Von Schlaben took a step closer now, his voice lowered. 'The highest. "To make of the human race, without any distinction of nation, condition or profession, one good and happy family".'

'Interesting words. Your own?'

'My sentiments. The words themselves were written by a friend. A colleague. A leader.'

'His name?'

The German stepped closer. 'There's no harm in you knowing it. Very soon the greatest in every land will praise it. The name is Adam Weishaupt.'

'Ah, the Bavarian professor.'

For the first time, Jack had taken the German by surprise. 'You know of him?'

'The founder of the Illuminati. Even a simple soldier hears tales.' Jack stepped in. They were now just a pace apart, and he lowered his voice to match the other's. 'And so, this American Revolution . . .'

'A necessary beginning. So long as the right people end up in charge. People who are sympathetic.'

'Illuminated?'

The smile came back. 'Why, Captain Absolute, you are not such a simple soldier, after all. This is the duty beyond all duties, the supreme loyalty. Men of all nations, of all ranks of society from kings to innkeepers are beginning to understand this. And there is a special place for men with skills such as yours. An "elevated" place I might say. It would be an honour to lead you into that brightness. For our Leader says to all, "Let there be light and there shall be light".'

Jack thought for a moment. In the distance he heard the

drums begin, summoning the warriors of his adopted people to war, summoning him. One of Até's quotes nearly came then, hovering in his head, just beyond recall. He looked up to the treetops, into the evening sky; then he had it. Not *Hamlet,* for once. *Othello.*

'Speaking of which, do you know this one? "Put out the light and then put out the light".' As Jack said it, he closed the gap between them. They were standing toe to toe.

Von Schlaben's eyes widened. 'Captain Absolute. You are not offering me violence? Are you not an English Gentleman?'

'I am,' said Jack. 'When in England.'

He placed one foot on one of the Count's. Then he hit him, sweeping the uppercut from waist to chin. Fear, fanaticism and questions, all put out, along with that light in Von Schlaben's eyes.

He didn't know exactly why he did it. The memory of an unwanted hand on Louisa's arm? The part the German had played at Drury Lane and Hounslow Heath? Not wanting such a snake at his back in the conflict that lay ahead?

He wasn't sure exactly why he did it. He just knew how good it felt.

He took his foot off the German's who fell back, hitting the ground hard and lay still.

Bending, Jack rolled him over, raised an eyelid. It was hard to gauge how long the man would be out. A few hours, with luck. Long enough to prevent him interfering again in what lay ahead, perhaps.

Dragging the Count under a pine, Jack heard Burgoyne's voice forbidding him a dagger in an alley.

'Oh well,' he said aloud, wiping pine needles from his shirt, 'he never said anything about a punch on a path.'

As Jack made for the Mohawk camp, under the sound of war drums he heard the faintest of rattles. He wondered if the snake might return, find the unconscious German . . .

He shuddered. He had been bitten once himself. It was an agony that haunted him still. Much as he disliked Von Schlaben, he would not wish that fate even on him.

EIGHT

The Ravine

Beneath the canopy of leaf, the air was thick with insects and the promise of rain. Heads throbbed from the pressure, the yearning for relief. In the hour since dawn, thunder was heard again and again in the distance but would not come near. Jack felt it like a bearskin robe pressing down, him a fever victim, too weak to throw it aside. From the valley floor, traces of marsh gas broke the spongy surface, tendrils drifting upwards bearing mould spores, the scent of corruption. Above, the clouds loured, so low they seemed tethered to the crowns of beech and elm by strings of smoke.

He shifted, the parched brush crackling below him, cursing again that he had not brought more water. The contents of his canteen had been part consumed on the two-hour march to this position at Oriskany, the rest long since divided with the Mohawks on either side of him. Though he did not know them personally, they were of his clan, the Wolf. They would have shared their last drop as he had shared his.

He squinted across the narrow ravine, to the equal point on the other side. The gloom made discerning difficult and, anyway, Até could conceal himself in a cornfield with a single stalk. But Jack thought that perhaps there was a glint there, where spectacles reflected the faintest of light. Até did not need water so long as he had a book.

Those behind Jack, up the slope, were not so hard to spot,

although he was sure they'd be invisible from the ravine's floor. The Seneca were sat there in rows, hands folded in their laps where they clutched club and tomahawk. They had assumed the role offered of spectator; yet they were still armed, dressed, and painted for battle – for they, as well as any other Iroquois, knew that neutrality needed two sides to respect it.

The Wolf to Jack's right, Otetian, touched his arm lightly, flicked fingers towards the east. Jack strained, heard nothing . . . then it came. Faint but sharp, the ascending notes of a fife. Under it, he was soon able to discern other sounds. A single drum. The murmuring of voices. The Rebels were coming.

They had decided to use only hand signals for fear that bird calls would be recognized as something else. He waved his hand above his head, made a fist, splayed the fingers three times. He saw slight shifts in the ground opposite, a flash of glass as spectacles were put away. All around him, men reached for priming powder, pouring a little into the pan. Frizzle covers were removed, the metal plates were lowered. As ordered, the muskets were then laid down again. It had been made clear that they were to wait till the very last of the enemy column had entered the ravine before anyone fired. The only way to guarantee that, among four hundred excited warriors, was to remove the weapons from their hands.

The air, so thick before, had turned electric, hair rising on heads. It was that mix of fear and blood hunger, a compound Jack recognized of old, swelled by the approach of thunder. Jack knew that, for most of the young men there, this would be their first real fight, one they had yearned for, trained for all their lives. The siege of Fort Stanwix was an alien, European-style battle. This was ambush, the Native way of war, how their fathers had fought – man against man, with musket, club, and tomahawk.

The music drew nearer, the voices suddenly distinguishable. The Rebels had obviously reached that stage in their march where the more jaunty of the songs had been sung and sung again. Someone had struck up a ballad and the vanguard were singing it lustily.

> Me oh my, I loved him so,
> Broke my heart to see him go,
> And only time can heal my woe,
> Johnnie has gone for a soldier.

Jack was sure he was not the only one looking down into the valley soon to be filled with death, who joined in the next verse under his breath. The same songs, he'd found, belonged to both sides in any war.

> I'll sell my clock, I'll sell my reel,
> Likewise I'll sell my spinning wheel;
> To buy my love a sword of steel,
> Johnnie has gone for a soldier.

As the chorus swelled again, something luminous entered the ravine, its brightness startling in that grey world. It was a horse, huge, magnificently white. Astride it sat quite an old man, upright and strong-looking, in the uniform of a general. The high-spirited stallion skittered sideways down a stretch of soft path, as if it sensed what lay ahead. The General effortlessly brought him back into control with a flick of rein, a hand reaching out to caress, to calm.

Behind the horse, the fifer and single drummer kept up their music. Behind them, an ensign carried the Militia's standard at the head of the main body of men. These straggled, but because the path dictated it rather than from a lack of discipline. They came in twos and threes, sang as they came, and looked more than capable of using the muskets and swords slung around their bodies. Interspersed among them were groups of Natives, war-painted, scalp-locked, breech-clothed like most of the men watching. Oneidas. Another of the Six Nations of the Iroquois.

As the ranks marched past him, Jack sighed. In moments he

would be trying to kill these men whose song he'd joined, just as they would be trying to kill him. Neither side now had a choice. But they fought for a cause with which he did not entirely disagree. And eighteen years before, he had fought beside them, Native and White, under the Union Standard, each helping the other to defeat the French and win a continent for the Crown.

Samuel, the messenger whose wounds had nearly killed him after the message was delivered and might still, had told of maybe six hundred men marching to the relief of Fort Stanwix. Jack reckoned perhaps half that number had passed his position when what he and Joseph feared would happen, did. The pressure from the thunderous heavens and the sight of the enemy before their guns proved too much.

'AH-ah-ah-ah-AH!' It was the rise and fall of the Iroquois war whoop, a single voice, young sounding. It clung in the air like mist to a tree, and then it was lost in a storm of voices, which panicked the men on the valley floor, crying out as they scrabbled for weapons. Then all human sound was engulfed by the crack of musketry that rolled down the length of the ravine like a wave running down a shoreline.

Jack aimed at an Oneida warrior, fired, smoke immediately obscuring the view of his aim's success. He turned, paper cartridge already to hand, bit the end off, poured the powder into the barrel, a little saved for the pan, ball and wadding crammed into the muzzle, his ramrod grabbed from beside him, thrust down. A glance to the left showed him a rearing white horse, an old man falling. Turning back, he searched through the smoke for another target.

Though they'd had the advantage of surprise, their unanswered first volley was now being countered with steady fire. A bullet snapped the bark of the elm before him, some splinters sharding into his face. He closed his eyes, wiped the debris away, opened them again. Otetian to his right, cried out, fell back, blood running down his shoulder. And suddenly there was Joseph Brant sprinting between the trees to fall beside Jack.

'There!' He was pointing back down the valley in the

direction the Americans had come. The head of the column, thrust into the trap, had no choice but to fight or die. Those who had been warned by the premature attack, had an another option. Even as Jack looked, he could see the rearguard hesitate, falter, break. He heard a cry of, 'Run, boys, run, or we shall all be killed.' He saw most there discharge their shot wildly in the air, turn, and flee.

'We have them pinned here,' Jack shouted above the gunfire, gesturing to the ravine, 'so—'

'So we should rout these cowards!' Joseph nodded, a fierce grin coming to his face. Then he was up and waving his musket above his head, careless of the shots he drew, pointing it down the valley to the American backs. His own men, Mohawk and that handful of white Loyalists who followed only him, were all around. They rose in an instant and set off behind their leader, chasing the fleeing Rebels.

Jack rose too, shouted, 'Até!' across the valley, although he did not really hope to be heard. However, his friend was as experienced in this sort of combat as Brant. He too would have seen the advantage to be gained from attacking those who fled. And he had gathered family about him who would support him.

Jack, running just behind the main body of Brant's men, saw some of the enemy crawling into bushes, trying to hide, then being dragged out and struck down with club and tomahawk. He saw knives falling swiftly, rise nearly as fast, bloodied patches of hair and skin shaken aloft in triumph. However much he considered himself one with the Iroquois, he had never been able to share this part of their warfare. And despite what Von Schlaben had discovered to the contrary, he had an English gentleman's restraint that prevented him striking at backs. Fortunately, there were some among the enemy who were trying to rally. So he sought these as targets for his new sword, unblooded as yet, for he had bought it on his second-to-last day in London from his old sword-maker, Bibb of Newport Street, who had sent it ahead to Portsmouth. It was a heavy cavalry sabre, the type Tarleton had wanted to duel with. Jack had demurred then, remembering the savage cuts the beautifully balanced weapon could inflict – in the right hands.

A huge captain of Militia, well over six and a half foot tall, stood cursing and striking at his own men as they ran by him. 'Sneck-draws! D'ye foryet the bairn McRea?' he cried, his Scots accent so thick Jack only understood the name, one unfamiliar to him, though not, apparently, to some of the fleers. A few paused, then a few more, looked longingly at their comrades' retreating backs, turned to their Captain. They were rallying.

Have to put a stop to that, thought Jack, and discharged his musket to the man's left, where an ensign was desperately waving his company standard. He went down with a cry and Jack, slinging the musket strap over his shoulder, drawing his sword, charged at the Captain. A huge claymore, weapon of the Highlands, rose in defence.

Jack was running, his opponent stationary, so Jack used his speed as if he were making the leaping attack of a fleche in a fencing salle, bringing his sword down in a sharp cut to the head. The Scot parried it nearly square, staggering back, and Jack slid his blade down his opponent's, cutting at his side. Again the man parried, a desperate shove to the side, too far, taking him off balance. But before Jack could take advantage of the slip, he felt, rather than saw, the bayonet thrust at his back. Spinning away, he sliced down, knocking the bayonet aside. The man who thrust it screamed, drew the musket back to strike again. Jack stepped inside the point, wrist cocked, then sharply ripped his sabre across the man's throat. The Militiaman dropped his gun, fell back, blood pumping between his hands.

A glint was falling fast towards him from the sky. The Captain had recovered his balance and was striking down. Jack just managed to parry the first blow, feeling the shock run through his wrist as the weapons clashed. The last thing he needed was his new sabre to be broken so he deflected the frenzy that followed, letting each cut slide down his blade. The man was strong, taller than Jack, bringing the sword down from his great height so Jack had to dart and weave to avoid the blows. Seven fell as Jack moved him around, keeping the huge body between him and his rallying men. He saw the Scot was tiring so he took the eighth blow on the guard, reaching up his left hand to join his right. With the strength of two arms, he flicked hard in a tight circle and, to keep hold of his sword, the Captain had to lean far out to the left. Two-handed still, Jack stepped through, slashing across the man's chest. The heavy blade split the Scotsman's coat like silk, and a button flew off, hitting Jack in the nose. Then he felt, through his edge, the solidity of flesh, parting. The giant screamed, tumbled back.

The move had taken him past. Suddenly he was standing in the midst of those who had rallied. Though many were facing outwards, frantically loading and firing at the screaming Mohawks who circled them, four had turned inwards at their Captain's fall. Two with swords, two with bayonets.

He could not hesitate. Safety, for the moment, lay within those points rather than without. Spinning, he moved into the space between the muskets, snapping an elbow into the face of one man who reeled back. Another, though, swung the butt, the wooden edge driving into Jack's side, just above the kidneys.

The pain was extraordinary. Jack slipped down to a knee, knowing he mustn't go over, and the slip saved him, as one of the swordsmen thrust over-excitedly to the place Jack had been, the blade passing over his head and making the other swordsman stagger back to avoid it. Jack reached up to the wrist, twisted it, forced the sword out of the grasp, though the strength it took shot agony through his bruised back. The man immediately reached down and a dagger was in his hands in a moment.

Shit, Jack thought distinctly, forcing himself up, throwing his blade out before him. One man was down, but three still held weapons and were advancing on him. And his back was aflame.

He parried, struck, tried to keep his weapon circling. Suddenly, hands gripped his legs and he swayed.

'Rabble the callant,' bellowed the Captain, his huge hands wrapping around Jack's ankles. The men seemed to understand their leader if Jack could not, for as he tottered, his sword waving before his face, fighting for balance, he saw the bayonet point driving toward his belly . . .

The tomahawk took the man with the bayonet in the side of the head. One moment he was there, the next gone. The dagger had been reversed in the other soldier's hands, raised high for a downstrike. A blur of arms reached up, checked the weapon brought it hard down into the man's own body. This left the last swordsman, who, confronted by a huge Mohawk even now reaching to jerk his tomahawk from a body, decided his rallying time was over. He dropped his sword and fled.

Jack lost the struggle with gravity. He fell, landing heavily on the big Captain, who cried out some strange profanity and fainted away. Jack rolled off him, ending up on his knees.

'Took your time,' he grunted, looking up at Até.

'Been busy,' the Mohawk replied. Jack wasn't sure, as his vision was a little blurry, but it looked like there were at least three more scalps dangling from his friend's hide belt.

He felt another surge of pain in his back and groaned.

'Wounded?' There was at least some concern on Até's face.

'No.' Jack pulled up his shirt, looked at the red mark spreading there. 'Just struck.'

'You are getting old and slow. Four would have been no problem for you once.'

'Well . . .' Jack muttered, rubbing at his back and looking about. The main struggle seemed to be further on down the valley. And it appeared that most of the resistance was now being led by the Oneidas. Jack saw Brant charge a tall warrior, striped from crown to toe in yellow paint. War club met war club and the two men locked and spun into the mêlée.

'I think your old schoolfellow can handle this. We should see how the main ambush goes. I am not so assured of the courage of our Loyalist friends.'

'Then let us join them.' A hand was offered and Jack used it to pull himself up, restraining another groan.

Até smiled. 'And remember, Daganoweda. That is now seven to six.' He ran ahead.

Jack watched his friend's back moving away, then cursed silently as he began to follow. He never could remember how many times each had saved the other's life. There was always dispute about some of the actions anyway, whether intervention was actually needed. Até was especially disputatious about such points. Jack knew he could have no argument about what had just happened, but hoped he would get a chance to even the score before the battle's end. Otherwise the gloating around their next camp fire would be intolerable.

As he took his first painful step back down the valley, he felt the first raindrop. It ran down his face, soon joined in its trail by dozens more. A relief to some, but bad timing for the ambushers. Like everyone else on the battlefield not directly engaged in action, Jack tucked his powder horn and cartridge pouch under his shirt.

By the time Jack and Até had returned to the main site of the ambush, the rain was falling in walls of water. The approaching thunder, lost till then in the roar of musketry, now crashed overhead, following sharp stabs of lightning. Here and there, these illuminated for the briefest of moments a struggle between combatants too entwined to notice the deluge. A club would fall, or a blade find flesh, and a body would slide away. Only then would the victor look up, startled, to wipe raindrops and sweat from blurred eyes, then stagger off to his own lines.

Most had already withdrawn. Everywhere was the carnage of the sudden attack. Bodies in groups, some still moving, hands reaching in supplication to their comrades safe behind tree stump or in any slight dip. Steam rose from all, joining the miasma of marsh and men's exuded fear.

While the rain fell – twenty minutes, perhaps a little more – that was all the movement on the field. Then, as suddenly as it had come, it ceased. The 'thunderbirds,' as the myth of the Iroquois named them, moved away to the east, lightning striking the slopes further down the valley. The drops shrank in size and a last line of them rode through the ravine, like a curtain being drawn across a stage. The Second Act of the drama was about to begin.

It took only a moment. The ends of paper cartridges, kept scrupulously dry, were bitten off, contents tipped into barrels, powder poured into pans.

'For the King!' a bass American voice shouted down.

'For shit!' came the reply from the valley floor. 'I see you, John Chisholm. Got a nice crop of beet planted on your land, you traitorous arse.'

'You're the fucking traitor, James Dingham,' the Loyalist's deep voice sounded again, 'and a thief. And *I'll* plant *you* where you can see those beets grow, real close to.'

Laughter rose, from both sides, from both came the distinct click of hammers being cocked. 'Ah-ah-ah-ah-Ah!' was the cry from hundreds of Iroquois mouths. On the final ascending note, musketry exploded again down the length of the valley.

Jack lay beside Até and the two men became automatons – biting, pouring, ramming, cocking, firing. Gunsmoke pooled in the ravine bottom, though a slight wind had arisen that pulled and tore at the cloud. Through the shreds, grey figures moved, brief targets for their fusils, though the effect of any shot was hard to tell. The two men kept loading and firing anyway.

A bullet bit into the tree trunk Jack sheltered behind. It came from the side and, squinting, Jack perceived that some of the Rebels had forced their way up the slope and seized a hillock of land. In their midst lay the old general, last seen falling off a white stallion. He lay propped against a tree, obviously wounded, though the wound did not seem to affect his ability to fire off his musket while coolly puffing on a long pipe.

Jack suddenly noticed something else. The hillock was up the slope, close to the ranks of hitherto silent, spectating Seneca. Even as he watched, he saw some Militiamen pushing further up the hillside, and that the chiefs were having difficulty restraining the younger warriors. And watching, Jack knew what was to come. The Seneca were like any other

Iroquois nation, glorying in war, in the acts of courage required.

He did not see the moment that provoked it, hothead brave or encroaching Rebel, but suddenly the Seneca lines rose as one and charged down the slopes.

'Até!' Jack gestured to the attack.

The Mohawk looked, grunted. 'So, the Great Hill People have found their courage. About time.' Then he turned his gun barrel again to the valley floor.

Jack watched the charge. A ragged volley halted the first of them, but the others came on, crying out their war whoop. When they got close enough, the warriors almost offered their painted chests as targets. As soon as the musket was discharged though, and if the brave remained unhurt, he would charge the soldier now frantically trying to reload. A hatchet would fall – once, twice – and a red hand would be raised in triumph, something bloody clutched in it.

Someone on the American side had noted the weakness. Perhaps it was the general still prone and puffing tobacco beneath his tree. Jack could see orders being shouted out. Men formed into pairs and when one fired and bent to reload, the other stepped forward to discharge his weapon at the charging Seneca.

The tactic wreaked havoc. Painted bodies soon lay scattered on the ground before the slight rise occupied by the Rebels. The Senecas kept coming. They had some success. But Jack knew this was not the Native way to fight. It was becoming a pitch battle and that was the last thing the King's ragtag army needed.

'Where are the rest of the fucking Loyalists?' Jack shouted at Até. Only two companies of Johnson's regiment and some of Butler's men were engaged. The majority, under Major Watts, as they had been throughout the campaign, were tardy.

'My gun is too hot and I tire of this.' Até waved down the slope where targets had become hard to find. 'Shall we go look for help?'

At a nod, the two men ran in a crouch up the slope. Bullets

slapped and winged around them but they made the line of trees where some of the Seneca chiefs still sat, watching and muttering. Running behind them, they soon came to a little path that paralleled the valley below. Jack found that his sore back eased with movement. They began to run faster.

They did not have far to go. Below them, where the valley widened out, the movement of a body of soldiers could be discerned. Instantly, Jack and Até cut down the slope toward them, vaulting the low scrub and young trees in their way. They emerged in front of a column of green-coated men. A portly officer was at their head.

'Leaving so soon, Absolute?' the officer drawled. Major Stephen Watts, of the Royal Greens, had a way of speaking that complemented the slowness of his movements. He seemed to be in a perpetual yawn.

Jack felt a sudden anger. Good men were dying up ahead, Loyalist and Native, and this officer strolled. But he was Jack's superior, albeit an American.

'Looking for you, sir. The action is quite hot ahead.'

'Yes?' The syllable stretched out. As swiftly as he could, Jack précised the situation.

'Really?' Watts yawned again at the report's conclusion. Jack wondered if the man had been at the laudanum. 'Well, no doubt the Rebel will be hoping for a sally from the Fort to their aid. Let's feed that hope.' He waved his hand at a man beside him. 'Captain! Turn coats.'

'Aye, Major.' The officer faced the ranks behind, then yelled, 'Turn coats!'

The cry was passed back down the lines. Men gave their muskets to the man next to them and reversed their coats. From the green of a Loyalist they were transformed into something similar to the men back in the valley, the buff uniforms of the Tryon County Militia.

When his ranks were once more organized – an agonizingly long process to Jack – Watts lifted his tricorn hat and waved it above his head.

'Strike me up one of those damn Rebel songs,' he cried, and

his fife and whistle players commenced a snail-like version of 'Yankee Doodle'.

Gradually, though, the regiment advanced to the action. As they entered the ravine, Jack could see that the hillock had become a Rebel rallying point, Seneca dead and dying scattered before it.

'There, Major. There's the centre of resistance. Break them and the field is ours.'

'I can see that perfectly well, Captain.' Watts's tone was frosty, the emphasis on Jack's rank deliberate. He lifted his tricorn again from his head, waved it, and shouted, 'For the Colonies! Freedom!' His cry was echoed by his men as they marched cheering toward the hill, deploying in a line as they came.

For a moment, the sight of the regiment brought near silence to the field. Men on each side squinted through the gunsmoke at what they hoped were friends or feared were a new enemy. Hopes soared or sank as to their conclusions. Then a voice pierced the near silence. It came from the centre of the Rebel-held hill.

'Bollocks, lads! It's a trick. Look in the front rank there – that's Isaiah Herkimer, the General's traitor brother!'

Jack sighed. It was always a poor plan, he'd felt. Too many connections in a civil war. Knowing what was coming, he moved away from the main body of the troops, Até following. Behind them the advancing ranks halted.

'And there's my bloody cousin, Frank, Aunt Mary's boy.' Another voice came. 'Always was a little bastard. Give 'em hell, boys.'

More recognitions, more voices rising, soon lost in ragged gunfire. It was not much of a volley; two men dropped in the front rank. The rest prepared to return fire. But Watts was staring at his hat, until a moment before aloft above his head. He put two fingers through two holes and it seemed to decide him.

'Retreat, lads,' he cried, clamping the hat on his head. 'Regroup at two hundred paces.'

Then, with an alacrity he'd failed so far to display, he fled

111

the field. Jeers and more bullets followed the buff backs. Jack knew that they would not halt at two hundred or two thousand paces. They would halt back at their camps.

'I think this fight is over, Daganoweda.' Até jutted his chin toward the battleground. They watched as the Seneca withdrew back up the slopes. To the left, the rest of Johnson's Loyalist regiment were imitating their comrades and streaming back toward Fort Stanwix.

'They hold the field, Até. But we have stopped them, hurt them. They will not relieve the Fort, at least.' Jack shook his head. 'But it could have been so much more. Shall we see if we can find our Wolves?'

On the higher path, Joseph Brant was leading his warriors back. Scattered amongst them, and roughly handled, were various Rebel prisoners. Jack noted that the huge Scots Captain he'd duelled with was being dragged along, clutching his bloodied side, cursing his captors continuously – and unintelligibly. Jack was surprised but, strangely, not altogether displeased to see him alive.

Brant grunted in frustration when he heard Jack's tale. 'Our White Father across the water is served by some poor sons this side of it,' he muttered.

'But not his Native Sons.' Até pointed to the slopes where the Iroquois – Seneca and Mohawk – were kneeling among the wounded and the dead. Lamentations were being uttered, voices raised in anguish. The Condoling Time, the Iroquois way of mourning, was beginning.

'They fought like a marvel,' said Jack, 'in a way that was unfamiliar to them.'

'And paid in blood,' Brant said. The three men stood for a moment, as the agonized cries became more general, turning into one song of despair. 'The white man can afford to lose this many. His supply is like your name, Daganoweda – inexhaustible. We . . .'

He did not need to go on, his gesturing hand falling slowly to his side. In their journey to Oswego, Jack and Até had already noted how scattered were the nations of the Iroquois, how thinly spread its people. This loss of its manhood was an horrendous blow.

'Come,' said Jack, 'let us return to the camp. Maybe there'll be some comfort for us there.'

They knew something was wrong long before they reached Fort Stanwix; they could smell it on the wind. A breeze, blowing from the west, bore into their nostrils the taint of smoke. At first it gave them hope that somehow the inefficient artillery had managed to set the Fort alight. But cresting the last rise, they saw that the black-grey columns spiralled up, not from the wood and earthen structure but away to the east and south of it. From the Indian camps.

Jack, Até, and Brant began to run. Soon, other sounds added to their dismay. Not only the staccato crackling of flames but the wails of men and women.

They sprinted into horror. The camp of the Iroquois was burning. Cedar-bark shelters and deer-hide tents were topped by crimson, those that had not already collapsed. Some warriors, newly returned from the fight, were rushing about desperately, seeking, calling. Bodies lay everywhere.

Jack bent to one. A young woman's, curled up as if in sleep. Yet her deer-skin dress was not singed. It was neither flame nor smoke that had killed her but the deep gash in her back.

Jack rose. His voice croaked and he had to clear it to speak. 'Bayonet,' he said, wiping blood on to his shirt.

An old man sat near, knees drawn up to chest, long white hair falling to his shoulders, and Brant knelt swiftly beside him. 'What happened here, Sagehjowah?'

'Soldiers came. From the Fort. They brought their fire and the knives on their guns.'

'The Fort?' Jack squinted through the smoke to where the tops of Stanwix's palisades were just visible. Above them still floated that strange banner of stars and stripes. 'But they are under siege. How did they sally out? Weren't the Regulars here to protect you?'

Coughing racked the old man and Até bent down, gave him

water from a canteen. When he had recovered, they had to lean in closer, for he could only whisper. 'The Green Ones guarded us, those who speak the language in the throat we cannot understand. One came, made them move to the other side of the Fort. The door opened, the Yankee soldiers came out to our camp.'

Another fit of coughing took him and he slipped on to his side. Jack was staring again, this time toward the Regulars' encampment.

'German is a language of the throat. And the Jaegers wear green.'

Brant was only giving voice to Jack's thoughts. With Até at his side, Jack began running again, towards the Union Standard.

A table had been set up outside St Leger's tent. The Colonel sat behind it, red-faced and sweating. Before him stood the two Loyalist commanders, Johnson and Butler, arguing furiously with each other, with him. Behind him were grouped his own officers, including, leaning on a cane and sporting a livid red bruise on his chin, the Count von Schlaben.

Jack strode straight into the centre of the group. 'Who ordered the guard withdrawn from the Indian camps?'

'Captain Absolute, how dare—' St Leger was struggling to rise from his chair.

'Who ordered the guard withdrawn?'

'For shame, sir.' Ancrum stepped forward, laying an arm on Jack's. 'You will not address your Commander in such a manner.'

Jack threw the arm off. 'I care not a fig for that. Our allies' camps are in flames, women and children lie massacred there, families of men who just sacrificed themselves for our cause in that damned ravine. And you wish me to be concerned about etiquette?'

A hubbub arose – the shocked Loyalists, the blustering St Leger, the reprimanding Ancrum. But it was a German voice, as ever, that cut through it all.

'I ordered my Jaegers into a new position, Captain Absolute,

114

to cover the withdrawal from the battle in the ravine.' Von Schlaben stroked his jaw as if he could get it to function better. 'I thought it the proper course to take.'

'You thought it . . . proper?' Jack rubbed his fingers together. They were still tacky with a young woman's blood. 'You allowed these people to be slaughtered, you . . .'

He ran out of words, anger choking them in his throat. As he tried to regain breath, as he took a step toward the German, St Leger finally managed to stand.

'Your superior's orders are not yours to question, Absholute,' he slurred. 'It was sound tactical thinking on the Count's part. It may have had somewhat unfortunate results but—'

'Unfortunate? Colonel, this tactic . . . that man . . . may have cost you more than half your army. If the Natives stay—'

A hand at his elbow halted him. Até jerked his head back the way they had come. Jack listened. A drum had begun a frenzied beat. Within the keening of loss, the wails of lamentation, an uglier noise was building.

'Oh no,' Jack murmured, 'no.' He turned and began to run, ignoring the immediate cries of 'Captain Absolute' that pursued him.

They arrived back at the smoking camp too late – and just in time. A gauntlet had been formed, two lines of warriors of all the Iroquois nations and others beside, men and women, united at last – in vengeance. They clutched war clubs, knives, brands snatched from the flames of their ruined shelters. They used these and their fists and feet to strike at white men, prisoners from the battle, and some Oneidas too, forcing them to run between the lines. Many had not made it, lay broken to the side where they'd been dragged. Those who did were knocked down at the gauntlet's end, their heads pulled back, throats slit. A group was bottlenecked at the start, waiting their turn, some on their knees praying loudly, some crying, most just standing there staring, disbelieving.

One was roaring. The Scots Captain was leaning on a smaller comrade, still clutching at the jacket that Jack had shredded with his sabre. As warriors ran to spit at him, to curse, he spat and cursed back. He was a few men away from the run to death.

Jack did not hesitate. Their earlier duel bound the Scot to him, somehow. 'Mine!' he yelled. Plunging straight in, he grabbed the huge man's jacket, began to pull him from the crowd. The man he'd leaned on clung to him, two others saw the gap and followed in the wake.

Two furious warriors leaped before them. 'Ours! Ours!' they screamed, ripping Jack's guiding hand away, trying to shove the men back. More warriors started to push nearer, anxious not to be deprived of their prey. The four white men were bunched into a group, Native hands grabbing, jerking.

Jack stepped away to give himself room. Then he drew his sabre, waved it above their heads if not straight at them.

'See where my sword has cut him.' He gestured to the slash still oozing in the huge man's jacket. 'I marked him for death. Only I can claim him.' Reaching down, he stuck his fingers into the Scotsman's wound.

The man groaned, cried out, 'Gan awa, ya loon.'

He tried to swing at Jack but the blow was weak and Jack ducked it. Swiftly, he used the blood to mark the faces of the four men.

'Mine. They bear my mark. I will take them and only I will kill them or make them slaves. I am Daganoweda of the Mohawk and it is my right.'

With that, he raised his sword again, let all see it, then rested it on his shoulder. With his other hand he grabbed the Militia Captain, then elbowed the biggest, most argumentative warrior out of his way. Screams from behind drew the attention of the others. Turning, they saw that there were still plenty of white men to kill, revenge easier to take. With a final glare and a spit, they let Jack and Até pass.

They did not turn back, did not stop until they were in the shelter of the woods. There the prisoners fell, three of them sobbing, to the forest floor. The trees were a screen to the sights only, some trick of sound making it seem as if they were still in the very midst of the shrieks of agony, the death wails, the cries of cruel triumph. In one of the lower reaches of hell.

Jack looked down at the Militiamen, two little more than boys, weeping for their mothers, the third older, near toothless, hands clasped before him in prayer. The fourth, the Scotsman whose life he'd tried to take and now had saved, because of some strange sense of honour was clutching at his side, fresh blood once more running down to join a huge stain on his breeches. Despite his size and obvious strength, he looked as if he was about to faint.

'Come on,' said Jack, raising his voice above the din. 'There's something useful the king's army can do. At least they can stitch a prisoner's wounds.'

He bent, put his arms under the big man's, helped him to rise. The effort made him suddenly realize how tired he was, how his back, forgotten this while, ached where he'd been struck.

The Scotsman leaned on Jack. He truly was enormous, and bulky with it, his hair as red as his blood, his eyes loch blue.

'MacTavish,' he bowed. 'Ye are a buckie, ken.'

'Friend,' said Jack, 'I haven't understood a single bloody word you've said.'

Até was, none too gently, kicking the prone men to their feet. Brant had disappeared. Knowing his Christian principles, Jack felt he would be trying to do what Jack had just done, save a few lives. But Jack knew he'd just been very lucky with these four and only just in time; for the sounds gradually fading behind them had changed. Before, there'd been distinct voices raised in individual cries of horror, of fury. Now the voices had merged into one, and a single note alone could be heard – the dull and ugly chant for vengeance, exacted as cruelly as possible. As Jack limped away, he knew that note would echo loud through the weeks ahead.

— NINE —
The Idiot

'Three weeks,' Jack cursed under his breath, as he helplessly watched the antics before him. 'Three damn, bloody weeks – and this could destroy that work in a moment.'

In those three weeks since the battle at Oriskany, he, Brant, and Até had, by ceaseless argument, bribery and prayer, just kept the tribes together. Despite their hatred of the static warfare of the increasingly ineffectual siege, despite their terrible losses in battle that almost forced them to return to their villages to condole with relations, despite the rations getting shorter and the rum running low, somehow, the Natives had been persuaded to remain true to the British cause.

And now all their success was being undone by one man, an idiot.

He swayed in the centre of the circle, his arms spread wide, lifting the tails of his long blue frock coat. From Jack's angle, it looked as though a score of stars were shining from the heaven of the coat's dark lining.

'A whole regiment! *Ke-poo*! *Ke-poo*! *Ke-whee*! All takin' aim at poor Hans-Yost Schuyler. But they missed me, every mother's son! *Wheesh*! *Wheesh*! *Wheesh*!'

He dodged from side to side, his coat-tails flying up, then stopped to thrust fingers through the bullet holes. 'Poor coat. Holey coat. Won't be keepin' me warm this winter. Be needin' some straw to plug the gaps in this barn, 'fore then.'

He broke into a loud shriek of laughter and all the Indians joined in. Their eyes never left his strange personage – his corn-blond hair sprouting out in thick sheaves under a hat as holed as the jacket; his pock-marked face on which hair clung in unconvincing patches; his mouth, an overabundance of teeth crowding each other to the extent that one thrust through the upper gum. He dribbled constantly, a line of drool running down his chin on to his lapel.

As the laughter built, Jack looked around. On the far side of the circle was Samuel, the message-bearing Cayuga, whose wounds were now nearly healed. Jack crossed to crouch beside him.

'Blessed by the Gods,' Samuel was rocking with glee. 'Brings news of Rebelmen who shoot him – and all miss. Look!' He hooted, pointing at Hans-Yost, now jumping up and down on his hat.

Jack sighed. In England, if men behaved in this manner they would be locked away in Bedlam. His own father, Sir James Absolute, had discovered that. Among the Indian, however, such lunatics were honoured as sages of special vision. When he'd returned from a hunt and heard the rumour that a fool, newly arrived from Tryon County, was in the tribal camps, talking to groups of Natives about the war, he'd suspected something was amiss. When he'd first pushed his way through the circles of the idiot's latest audience, he'd seen the danger immediately, had tried to grab Hans-Yost and drag him away. But three huge Senecas, their eyes glazed with a surfeit of rum, had pulled his hands off, thrown him back, pulled knives from their belts. With Até elsewhere, Jack had had no choice but to stand back and watch the performance.

The idiot had finally stopped his jumping. Now he was looking sadly down at his hat, a line of drool seeming to still connect it in some way to his head. 'But they're goin' to get another chance at poor Hans-Yost.' His tone was mournful. 'Chasin' him all this way. Comin' fast too.'

The laughter ceased as if by signal. A Seneca sachem rose up, stepped forward. 'How many of these come?'

Hans-Yost just kept staring down, mumbling to himself. The Sachem stepped closer, poked the man in the chest. He tottered backwards. 'How many Rebelmen come?'

The idiot finally raised his pale blue eyes. They seemed to seek different points high above the Chief's head. A hand rose up, wiping drool from the chin, transferring it to his jacket. When he finally spoke, it was in a whisper that carried to the farthest reaches of the circles. It made Jack suddenly think of Drury Lane. 'Cover the wheat fields like locusts, eating as they come.'

'How long?' When the Chief received no reply, he grabbed the tattered coat's front. Hans-Yost sagged in his grasp. 'How long till they come?'

This reply was muttered, only audible to the Chief. But he released the man as if he was tainted, letting him fall to the ground. He sat there, legs splayed and immediately began to sing.

The Seneca looked around to the expectant faces. 'Half a day. Maybe less.' As murmuring broke out, he shouted above it. 'I have had enough of this stupid fight. I go to my village now to mourn my dead.'

At that, he strode away, leaving mayhem behind him. Tribesmen ran back and forth, shouting, gesturing. Jack briefly glimpsed Brant clutching the buckskin shirt front of a huge Mohawk warrior. As he watched, the man swept Brant's hand aside, spat, and marched away.

Everywhere, the Natives were running to their shelters, knocking them down, rolling up the birch-bark strips that served as wall and roof. Goods were pulled out, hide straps swiftly tied around them.

To try to stop it would be like shouting into the wind. So he went to the centre of what had been the circle, where Hans-Yost sang softly to himself.

Jerking the idiot to his feet, Jack said, 'You are coming with me.'

If he expected that the man's supposed news would get a

different reception from the commander of His Majesty's forces he was mistaken. Idiots and drunks, it seemed, had a special bond.

'Merciful God! How many? How far?' The Colonel had learned that from the middle of the day he should not attempt to stand. But he clutched the arms of his chair, his neck tendons bulging as he stretched toward Hans-Yost, his face a dangerous slough of colours.

The slurred question had been rhetorical. All had heard: three thousand men, most of them Regulars, Washington's 'Continentals', under the command of that firebrand, Benedict Arnold. Less than half a day's march away.

'Outnumbered, begod! Three to one!' St Leger slumped back.

'That is if we believe him, sir.' Jack stepped forward, tried to draw his superior's wandering gaze.

The eyes focused. 'Absolute. Always questioning, what? Why shouldn't we believe him?'

'Because the fellow's patently an idiot!' Jack was trying to rein in the frustration in his voice, failing. 'And his last name is Schuyler.'

'Schuyler? Schuyler? What signifies Schuyler?'

'Philip Schuyler is one of the enemy's foremost generals. He commands the army opposed to General Burgoyne. This man is his cousin.'

'We all have cousins on the other side, Captain.' It was the Loyalist Major, Watts, who spoke. Since his precipitous retreat at Oriskany, he had lost his sloth, become increasingly skittish.

'Aye, sir.' Jack replied. 'I just feel that his word should not be taken as Holy Writ.'

'You blaspheme, Absolute!' St Leger, whose love of the bottle constantly warred with his love of the Bible, was leaning forward at a dangerous angle. Another moment and he'd be off the chair, joining Hans-Yost in the mud before his tent.

He was spared the ignominy by the arrival of Captain Ancrum. 'The savages, sir. The savages! They desert, every heathen dog of them!'

Jack closed his eyes. His plan had been to calm St Leger and dispatch scouts to verify Hans-Yost's story, before this tale reached the Colonel. There was no hope of that now – especially as the report was swiftly reinforced by the evidence of sight. From the slight rise of the Commander's pavilion, all turned to see columns of Indians heading back in the direction of Lake Ontario.

'Then may I suggest, Colonel, that the time has come for us to raise the siege?' The voice was, as ever, equally soft and commanding.

Jack opened his eyes to look at Von Schlaben. The man's Jaeger uniform was as immaculate as ever, unlike the somewhat ragged British around him. He could rival Burgoyne in his tailoring. Also, Jack was displeased to note, the discolouration from the punch had entirely faded.

Should have hit him harder, Jack thought. The legacy of that blow still puzzled him – for it had obviously not been reported to St Leger. It would have been if the Count saw any advantage in the revelation. Von Schlaben must have a reason for his silence – which worried Jack a little.

Still, now was not the time for that concern. 'And may *I* suggest, Colonel, that to retreat now, on the word of an idiot and the advice of,' he just couldn't help himself, 'a German, would be both premature and dishonourable.'

'No, sir! You would have me stand and fight, pinned between Arnold and the Fort!' St Leger was upright now, with the aid of Ancrum's arm.

'I would have you stand until we know that Arnold is coming for sure. Until Até and myself have scouted and reported back.' As St Leger stared stupidly at him, Jack felt his anger, the curse of his Cornish childhood, surge. 'General Burgoyne expects you to fulfil your mission, Colonel. To do your duty.'

It was too much. Even Até sighed. But St Leger roared.

'My duty? You dare . . . dare . . .' He swayed against his adjutant. 'I will listen no more to your insolence and rudeness to our gallant ally,' he nodded toward Von Schlaben, 'whose advice is always of the highest order. My *duty* is to preserve my command. My *duty* is to survive to fight another day.' He shook Ancrum off, staggered a little, then stood straight-ish. 'Give all orders necessary for a calm withdrawal. We will march back to Lake Ontario and sail for Montreal.'

Instantly, with the enthusiasm of much-relieved men, officers scattered toward their companies, already standing-to in their encampments. Calmness was nowhere to be seen.

Jack followed St Leger into his tent. 'Sir,' he said, pressing on despite the hand flapped at him as if he were a black fly, 'Montreal is four weeks away. And it would take another four at the least to reach General Burgoyne, who is moving south along the Hudson. It is the most indirect route. This campaign will have been decided by then.'

'What would you have me do, Absolute?' St Leger was drinking rum straight from the flask, as Ancrum scurried around, throwing papers randomly into a valise. 'March through Arnold to join him?'

Somehow Jack kept his temper. 'No, sir. But I, at least, would try to support my General.'

St Leger lowered the flask and fixed Jack with a liquid stare. 'You have been under my command but never a part of it. You have been insubordinate, disloyal, and rude. You gall me, sirrah, and always have. I have never seen the point of you. So you may go, Captain, to your General or to the devil. I suspect it will be to the latter.'

Then, with a loud hiccough, St Leger lay down on his bed. Jack needed no second bidding. He finally had a command from the Colonel he was eager to obey.

Até awaited him outside the tent. 'Do we leave with this rabble, Daganoweda?'

'No, my friend. We'll march to Burgoyne, even if this drunken sot will not.'

'Good.' Até smiled, a rare thing. 'In three dawns, we shall come to Canajoharie. I heard that some of my family might still be there.'

'Then let us go and greet them.'

Jack took a pace toward the Quartermaster's tent but Até stopped him. 'Brant sent word. He thinks some of the other Mohawks would do what we do. But he needs help to persuade those who waver. And to keep them on the path.'

Jack hesitated. He didn't like to travel without Até. But Burgoyne would need every tomahawk he could get and Jack needed to prove the myth of the Rebel reinforcements immediately. Maybe there would yet be time to halt this withdrawal.

'Then, if I do not return here in the next hours, let us rendezvous at Canajoharie. In three dawns, I will see you, and your schoolfellow Joseph, there.'

Até nodded, squeezed Jack's shoulder, and was gone.

As Jack watched the retreating back, that voice he'd grown to loathe spoke from behind him. 'Not joining us, Captain Absolute?'

Jack took his time in turning. Von Schlaben was standing with his back to the encampments where the results of his interference were manifest. Soldiers and Natives were running everywhere, dithering by tents they could not fold quickly enough, scattering them and many other goods upon the ground. The few Rebel prisoners were being herded, now this way, now that; Jack could just make out the recovered MacTavish roaring unintelligibly at all around him. Women left camp fires burning, pots of stew still cooking, meat smoking on skewers, potatoes roasting in the ashes, all abandoned so they could join the masses assembling for the retreat toward Lake Ontario.

It was clear Von Schlaben had made the wise choice never to be alone with Jack again. Beside him, in the uniform of a sergeant of Jaegers, stood a huge-chested man with cropped black hair, who looked as if he needed to shave four times a day. Squatting near the Germans' feet were three Native warriors, their hair not in a single scalp lock but falling in straight shanks from the crown, their heads bald from there forward and painted in orange down to their noses. All three stared at Jack, lips parted hungrily, as if he were prey.

Abenaki, thought Jack, and grasped the tomahawk at his waist in reflex. They were among the oldest of Iroquois enemies, feared and hated in equal measure. Von Schlaben had obviously learned the way of the land. He had acquired himself some Native allies.

'You really shouldn't listen at keyholes, Count.' Jack took a step back to give himself throwing room. 'People might mistake you for a spy.'

Von Schlaben smiled. 'I am desolate that I will not have such . . . amusing company on the tedious voyage to Montreal.'

'Oh, we'll meet again, Von Schlaben. You may be sure of that.'

Jack began to walk backwards, away, his eyes on his enemy, his hand on his tomahawk. When he was far enough, he turned. Not far enough, though, to escape that soft, insinuating voice.

'Oh, I am, Captain Absolute. Quite sure.'

In the chaos of the Quartermaster's tent, Jack was able to take the best of the supplies he would need. Some grains, maple sugar, bacon, powder for his guns, that was all. He would travel unencumbered, as usual. What took longer was the letter he wrote to Burgoyne, to send with Captain Ancrum. He did not know if he would survive what lay ahead and the General must hear, eventually, the true tale of this debacle at Fort Stanwix. Especially Von Schlaben's continuing part in it.

So he set out later than he'd hoped. Yet the further he went into the forest, the lighter his spirits became. Like his Mohawk brethren, he had rapidly wearied of the siege, the too-slow creeping of the siege lines towards the stockade, the frustration at St Leger's ineptitude. The defenders of the Fort had seemed well supplied with food and water and if these ever ran out, it would not be until the crisis of Burgoyne's campaign had come and gone. The artillery had continued its ineffectual popping at the sturdy timber and sod walls. Jack had spent as little time as necessary in the British camp, where the officers followed their leader's example in drunkenness each and every night. There may have been a lack of resolution but, until very recently, there was none of wine, brandy, and rum. This applied equally to the Indian camps where the few leaders such as Joseph who opposed the 'darling water' were overwhelmed by the many that craved. The results were familiar, predictable. More tribesmen died in midnight brawls than fell to Rebel bullets.

At last, thought Jack. *At last. Clear of it all.*

It was fragrant beneath the swathes of tree, so different from the rancid fug of the siege lines. With August nearly over, there was even the slightest hint here of the season to come, a finger of coolness in the caress of the breeze that flowed through the beech and walnut, the hornbeam and elm. He felt a sudden desire to have that touch over all of him and acted on that desire on the instant. His buckskin shirt and breeches were stowed swiftly in his knapsack, his hair released from its deer hide strap to drop on to his bare shoulders. He ran his hands through it . . . and suddenly recalled standing in the wings at Drury Lane, flicking at his ungoverned locks in a mirror just prior to that last, wonderful, fateful encounter with Lizzie Farren. What would she think of him now, standing near naked in a forest? Jack grinned. Just what she'd thought of him then, the minx! And with the same response as in that crammed dressing-room with Act Five of *The Rivals* beginning just a few feet away.

Memories brought sensations, shifted to another woman, a more recent time, the glorious agony of five weeks aboard, five weeks of unfulfilled desire. He wondered, as he did almost daily, where exactly Louisa was now. How far had Burgoyne progressed? They had received the glorious news that Fort Ticonderoga, the American's strongest bastion against invasion, had fallen with scarcely a shot, on the 5th July. Rebel deserters and Indians had brought reports and rumours in the succeeding weeks – most concluding that Burgoyne was advancing swiftly southwards. By this time in late August, Jack surmised he might even be close to the prize of Albany, about sixty miles east of where Jack stood. And if Generals Howe or Clinton were sweeping up from New York as the plan dictated, the Rebels would probably be powerless by now to prevent the juncture of the two British armies. The war could almost be over, despite the ignominy and failure of this third thrust under St Leger.

He sighed. All he could know for certain was that Louisa was there, up ahead of him somewhere, awaiting, he hoped, their reunion. And there was nothing he could do now with these sensations, these memories and longings. Except run. So he did, bursting through the late August sunbeams, which hung like panes of glass between the trees.

He did not know how long he ran, loving the freedom of it. Finally, he recognized where he was, paused at the top of a rise within the forest, just before the descent into the ravine of Oriskany. Closing his eyes, he let his breathing steady, used his other senses. The forest creatures that had started at his approach now settled again; a flying squirrel resumed its leap from branch to branch. He heard the snicker of a pine marten, its high-pitched call seeking mate or prey. There were wolves here too, drawn as ever to the feast that human conflict always leaves behind. They would be ahead of him, down in the ravine, for though the tribes and the British had returned to collect their dead, the Militia had not paused in its flight to do the same.

Was that one he heard now, the guttural grunt, the snapping of a dry branch upon the ground?

He opened his eyes . . . and saw the thrown club a moment before it struck. That moment gave him time to twist his head, the ball of Ironwood striking his shoulder, glancing off, instant agony if not a crippling one. Dropping, the musket came off his shoulder as the thrower drew a tomahawk from his belt and began to run down the path toward him, screaming as he came.

At ten paces, Jack had the cover off the frizzle. At five, he pulled the hammer back. The blast happened at three when there was no time to aim, when the tomahawk had risen to its ultimate height. Buck and ball caught the Abenaki warrior in the centre of the chest and he flew back down the path as if a horse had kicked him.

The second Abenaki didn't scream but Jack heard him nonetheless, heard the knife clear leather and flash down to Jack's shoulder. He rose to meet it halfway, one arm thrust up to block, forearm to forearm, his free hand yanking his dirk from its sheath. His grip was reversed so he could thrust straight up, but as he seized the warrior's weaponed hand so his opponent seized his. He twisted Jack around, and the two of them fell, rolled twice. From his wrestling days in Cornwall Jack knew the one important law – end up on top. So he did, twisting hard to achieve it, his enemy's dagger pushed out to the side, his own bearing down steadily toward the black-circled eyes within the orange mask. Then he saw those eyes flick to Jack's side and he remembered that there had been three Abenaki squatting at Von Schlaben's feet. And it was the last thing he remembered because of the sudden pain at the back of his head, the world going white.

Voices raised in dispute woke him, but it was pain that kept him awake, not only the relentless throbbing at the base of his skull but the agony of the too-tight deer-hide straps that held his wrists behind him, his fingers bent and ground into the rough bark of the cedar to which he'd been tied. He tried to stretch them, to shift position and alleviate the strain in his body, without opening his eyes and thus drawing attention. But the shift caused another surge of pain and he could not stop his groan.

The voices ceased. There was no profit in pretending further so Jack tried to open his eyes. Something sticky held them, blood, he presumed. When he'd succeeded, it took a while to focus. And when he had, he wished he had not bothered. For the Count von Schlaben stood a few feet before him, a delighted smile on his face.

'Captain Absolute! You are with us again. I was so concerned that my friends had been over zealous in their capture of you. I had given strict orders, but as you know, these children are hard to rule. And because you killed one of them, they were most anxious to take their revenge. It is only because my dear Tosselbach here is so persuasive that you still have your hair.'

Jack looked beyond Von Schlaben. On the ground squatted the two Abenaki by the body of the third, whose arms were folded across the ravages of his chest. They glared both at Jack and at the man who stood above them. The huge Jaeger Sergeant had obviously neglected his toilet that hour for a beard was fast developing. Folded in his arms, looking small, was a huge blunderbuss.

It took Jack several tries before his voice would work. 'Do you expect me to reveal secrets to you, Von Schlaben?'

'No, Captain Absolute,' the German sounded surprised, 'I expect you to die.' He came closer, leaned down. 'However, I did not want you to die oblivious. I wanted you to know, at the last, who was responsible for your death. These savages,' he gestured to the glowering Abenaki, 'are rumoured to eat the heart of an especially spirited enemy. I would not go that far but . . .' He smiled, straightened. 'You were an interesting opponent for a while, Captain, but I cannot let you interfere in my work any further. You caused me some inconvenience and some pain,' he stroked his jaw, 'and that cannot be tolerated. I might have told the amiable Colonel St Leger of our last encounter. I think he would have believed me. But then, what? Sent back to Burgoyne in disgrace? I know you would have appeared again to oppose me. And really, I did not wish to deprive myself of a sweet moment I was so certain would come at the last.'

He moved away. On the other side of the small clearing, the German and Abenaki possessions were stacked. From their midst, Von Schlaben pulled a Hessian sack. He held it slightly away from his body. As he walked slowly back toward him, Jack saw one brown side bulge suddenly out.

'So uncivilized, this scalping, do you not think? I do not mean because of the blood, the pain involved – if the victim, as so often is the case, is still alive. No, because it is indiscriminate, each enemy receiving only the same punishment, no matter what their crime. *That* is uncivilized.'

Von Schlaben stopped a few feet away. Inside the sack, a wriggling continued. Suddenly Jack realized what made the sacking move and all his defiance fled. If he could have gotten his mouth to work again, he might have screamed. But there was not time even for that because the Count had loosened the string at the sack's mouth, was grabbing the sack's end . . .

The rattlesnake landed in the centre of Jack's stomach, curled up in an instant, its head raised. It was huge, bigger even than that other one on the path. Jack couldn't hold back the scream, couldn't help jerking his face away from the horror. The creature, maddened by its imprisonment, followed the movement and struck – once at Jack's shoulder, again at his neck. Then it rolled off and slithered into the undergrowth.

The horrors were upon him. Jack barely saw the Count crouching down before him, staring intently. His words seemed to come from very far away, terror distorting their volume and sound.

'They say that, especially if the victim is strong, it can take many hours for one to die this way. And that every minute increases the agony. It would be educational to stay and watch but, alas,' he rose, stepped away, 'I must be gone, and swiftly, so that I arrive at Burgoyne's camp in time. He *will* be surprised that I have been involved in this part of his campaign. My cousin, dear Baron von Riedesel, arranged a pass to allow me to indulge a passion of mine – to hunt.' He smiled again. 'I did not specify the quarry I sought, naturally. And he did not bother the Commander with such a petty detail since I am, of course, merely a civilian, an observer. And yet a uniform,' he stroked the green of his Jaeger jacket, 'so becoming. So useful. Along with the correct papers, of course.'

He smiled again. 'Now, as you so accurately observed to the Colonel, this campaign is approaching its climax. There are always so many opportunities for mischief in the final acts of any war. It can take such a little push to alter the balance.' He signalled to his men, who swiftly gathered their supplies. When they were ready, Von Schlaben bent once more. A cloth gag was produced and tied around Jack's mouth.

'I do not think that anyone will come near but . . . a precaution.' He finished tying, stepped back. 'I only have one regret – how annoyed my young friend Tarleton will be. I promised you to him. Ah well.' He turned, nodded. The Abenaki, and the hirsute Sergeant began to move off. Von Schlaben took a step after them, paused, looked back. 'You were good enough to quote Shakespeare to me a little while ago. May I quote a young German writer I am very fond of. Goethe is his name. Your countrymen will all know him one day. You will not. I am sure it sounds better in German but . . . let me see . . . yes . . . "You must either conquer and rule or lose and serve, suffer or triumph, and be the anvil or the hammer." So. You die knowing you have served and lost. Goodbye, for the last time, Captain Absolute.'

A brief salute and he was gone. Sounds faded into the forest swiftly enough, even if the Germans weren't woodsmen. Their departure disturbed the wolves still scavenging in the ravine who set up an immediate howl.

Jack began to shake. His skin felt slick, sweat breaking out, coursing down. Yet he felt cold, colder than he'd ever been in his life. He tried to keep his eyes open. But he was struggling, and soon they would not budge despite his efforts. He let his head roll down on to his chest. Suddenly, sleep seemed the only option. Just a little before the pain came. He knew, from past experience, that he would be awake then, long enough.

— TEN —

Resurrection

So this is death, Jack Absolute thought. The undiscovered country. Different than he'd imagined. Being an atheist from earliest childhood, he'd always felt it would be mere oblivion, a great nothing. Yet this was undoubtedly . . . something. There was sensation in the void – pain, no, more than pain, agony. This thought – *so there is consciousness, too* – gave him a pang. For with thought came fear, thus proving in that moment that *feelings* also existed. And just because he was an enlightened man of his time and did not believe in an afterlife did not necessarily mean that an afterlife did not exist. *Heaven and—*

Of course. *Hell.* He was in hell, the place to which countless teachers, commanders, former lovers, and present enemies had often condemned him. He had only to listen – *another sense* – to the voices that surrounded him, voices that could only come from demons about their hideous work. Guttural grunts, expectoral explosions, curses in tongues long dead. *So all the tales were true.* And if his ears now worked so, presumably, would his eyes. If he could force them open no doubt he would see what these satanic imps were about, what further horrors they prepared for him to add to the steady crushing of his lungs, the bands of metal squeezing his head, the jagged pain at his neck and shoulder . . .

Someone – something – grabbed him there, squeezed. He

had no true desire to add sight to the terrible sounds he was witnessing. He was sure the torments would come to him whether he looked or no. But the sudden surge of agony caused his eyes to fly open, to focus on the demon's face before him. It was huge, flat, as red as anything that could be expected in Hades, broken blood vessels and curling rust hair rippling across the expanse. And yet . . . hadn't he seen it before? Confusion temporarily displaced fear. *He recognized the face.* If hell existed, this man was as likely a candidate for it as any, but Jack was confused as to why he should have preceded him there.

'MacTavish?' he croaked.

'Aye. Some Dogone has leeft thee in this unco sair state, nae right?'

Jack, of course, had no idea what the man had just said. Furthermore, he could not understand how he, whom he'd last seen being herded toward the lake with the other prisoners, was before him now. Yet these rapidly became secondary considerations to more pressing realizations. Not least, that he was alive. This became clear when he discovered his hands were free and he made use of them now to raise one toward his injuries. His throat was grotesquely swollen, yet he managed to squeeze one further word through it.

'Snake.'

The Scotsman nodded. 'Timber rattlesnake. *Corachulus Majores*, tha' ken. Thy neck's ower pluffy, but if th'art chancy, there's plantain in this scrog. My boumen seek it oot. Ah . . .' As he spoke, two young men came through the undergrowth. Jack recognized them as those others he had also saved from the native vengeance, as scrawny as MacTavish was vast, yet equally rubicund. They dropped bundles of a broad-leafed plant before their leader. He picked up a handful, shook it. Dirt fell from the roots.

'Plantain. So th'art chancy, reet enough. If we found thee in the nick.'

For the first time in an age, Jack felt a little hope. He didn't know the word 'plantain' but the Iroquois called this plant '*mahtawehaseh*'. He had seen it used on snake bites before. Some survived, some didn't. He had, once before. Much depended on how quickly it was administered to the victim after the attack, how weak they were. When a man was bitten, his skin would blacken, and blood would flow that no amount of staunching could stop. Shoulder and chest were already soaked in his. But he watched MacTavish spit on two stones, begin to pound the leaves between them, saw the sap bursting forth, and his hope continued to rise.

At a nod, one of the other men used some water from a canteen to wash some of the blood away, then this same man began to squeeze first the shoulder wound, then the one at the neck. Torment, blood, and a foul-smelling yellow discharge flowed at each touch. Jack felt an urge to strike out, to push this demon away. But he bore it, near silently, then watched MacTavish approach. He had wrapped the mash in two of the leaves and these he now pressed to Jack's wounds. Strips of cloth were bound around and a shirt was taken from his knapsack, pulled over him, buttoned up. Then he was lowered till his head rested on a pile of leaves swept up for the purpose. Instantly, though the pain appeared not to diminish, a desperate urge to sleep took him again.

He struggled against it. 'MacTavish . . .'

The huge face loomed over him. 'Wheesht, man. Naw tha' must thole. Either tha'll live or nae. But tha'art bucksturdie, ah can tell. Weel watch thee till the morn. Wheesht!'

'MacTavish,' Jack muttered, as his eyelids closed, 'I wish you'd speak bloody English.'

Jack was watched 'till the morn' and well past it. The sun was already above the trees when arguing voices woke him. The same guttural sound had awoken him the day before, yet they filled him with no fear now. He knew he was not dead. Indeed, he could feel that the poison that had brought him to the very brink had now largely left his body. He felt weak, but he was most definitely alive.

His stirrings caused the argument to cease. When he opened

his eyes, that huge red face was once more before him, studying his intently.

'Aye,' MacTavish nodded, 'th'art as yellow as a potatoe-bogle and twice as ugly, but I ken th'all live. And th'all be wishin' soomat to slocken thy thirst.'

Water was produced, fresh from the nearby stream. Jack drained a canteen of it; then some more was splashed into a wooden bowl that contained oats.

'Drammach,' MacTavish said, pointing. ''cos we'll no light a fire to make parritch. There's reepons mean us harm in these woods, ye ken?'

Though Jack was still not understanding all the words directed at him, he could now make out most of what was being said, partly because the huge Scotsman was speaking slowly, as if to a child or simpleton. While Jack consumed a second bowl of the drammach – he'd discovered his hunger was as fierce as his thirst – MacTavish squatted beside him, explaining that when Jack awoke, he and his two men, Alisdair and Gregor, had been arguing as to what to do with him. They had set out for the disaster at Oriskany three weeks before and God only knew what havoc war was wreaking on their homes, their kin. The others were for abandoning him, pressing on.

'But Angus MacTavish is nae one for inhonestie.' He was scratching shapes into the mud before them with a hefty walking stick, carved from the same Ironwood that the Iroquois used for their war clubs. 'Yon man saved oure lives, I seid. I'll stay by him till I'm sartin the favour has been returned.' He rose. 'Ochone! We canna bide mere. We must be tenty, flit and flit fast. The Heathen are fighting each other the noo and we can never ken which we'll meet. But what to do with thee, eh? Th'art still the enemy, officer of the tyrant we fight, life-saver or nae. Th'art oor prisoner noo, as I once was thine. But can thee e'en walk, laddie?'

The Scot reached down an arm and Jack grasped it, pulled himself up. He tottered a step, another. He was weak, there was no doubt. He had lost a lot of blood.

'I can walk, if I can borrow that shillelagh of yours, and perhaps an arm over rougher ground.'

MacTavish handed over the heavy piece of wood. Its solid ball-head fitted Jack's palm perfectly. 'And, as my prisoner, wilt thou gie me a gentleman's word that thou'll not try to fly?'

Jack squinted up into the broad face. 'Did you not give such a word at Stanwix?' He received a grudging nod. 'Yet here you are.'

For the first time, Jack saw the Scotsman's face transformed by a smile. 'Ah did. But then again, ah never laid any claim to being a gentleman. And the circumstances changed a muckle.'

Jack returned the smile. 'Well, there are many who do not consider me a gentleman either – including the man who left me to this fate. A man I desire greatly to meet again.' Jack glanced at the cedar to which he'd been bound, the bloodied cords lying at its base, and shuddered. 'But I have no desire to be left in these woods. And I presume you are bound up the valley, to Tryon County?'

'To Tryon, aye. To oor homes.'

The direction he needed to travel. Up the Mohawk, to Canajoharie, his rendezvous with Até and on to the Hudson, to Burgoyne. 'Then I will rest your contented prisoner at least till we have reached them. And until circumstances change – *a muckle.*'

There was a moment's study before the smile came again and a huge hand reached out to pump Jack's with reckless vigour. 'A deal made, till Tryon at the least. I'm relieved, I tell thee. T'would seem a dour act to save thee then pike thee with my dirk straight after.' Finally releasing Jack's hand – to his great joy – MacTavish turned to his men and yelled, 'Let us link!'

While they gathered what little they had managed to grab from the rout at Stanwix, Jack, with the support of the stout stick, tested his legs. Maybe it was the relief of being alive. Maybe the thought that the man who had left him thus to die was ahead, seeking to wreak further mischief upon Burgoyne's campaign. But they seemed a little stronger with every step.

As they walked, they talked. First Jack asked by what luck he'd been discovered. MacTavish informed him it was luck indeed because, having escaped the British in the chaos of the march from Fort Stanwix to Lake Ontario, they'd just come up to the place of Jack's ambush when the Germans set out from it.

'And them callants are nae woodsmen, ken. The noise they made through the scrog! We went to bide off the path . . . and there ye were.'

They talked more and through the day. MacTavish was of 'auld Jacobite stock', English haters to a man, his clan driven from their homes in the aftermath of the '45. Fifteen when he reached the Colonies, his family had immediately pushed to the farthest boundaries, clearing the Frontier land, planting corn, raising cattle as they had done in the Highlands, yet here free of the threat of the despised Redcoats and the control of the Crown.

'Until seventy-five, ye ken.' MacTavish had dropped the formal 'thou' and 'thee' now he had shaken Jack's hand and each had acknowledged that they owed the other a life. 'Dod! I'd no come so far, and strived so hard, to submit again to dowie tyranny.' He spat expansively off the path, then continued. 'I rallied with the first, marched with that great looby Benedict Arnold, and nearly died with him before the walls of Quebec.'

It was near dusk of their second night's march before Jack had regained enough strength to interject occasionally into MacTavish's monologues.

'And you believe that your way lies only in total separation from England? Many would have the rights you claim but still remain loyal to the Crown.'

MacTavish snorted. 'The only King I might acknowledge is the one across the water.' The Scotsman circled a fist before him, as Jack had seen many a Jacobite do over beer mugs in taverns from London to Boston when the King's health was pledged. 'But braw Charlie had his fling and lost the jing-bang at Culloden. And there's muckle Palatine Germans, Dutch,

Swedes, and Poles here who have nae knowledge of the Bonnie Prince.' MacTavish sighed and spat again. 'He'll come no more.'

Further nostalgia was prevented by a cry from Gregor who had loped ahead. He appeared a moment later, pulling at the nose ring of a reluctant, bellowing cow. Jack took the chance to fall on to the ground, his back to a black walnut, while a swift and hot conversation was conducted, of which he understood maybe every tenth word. Some nuts from the tree lay scattered about him and he was endeavouring to crack one of these – the endless diet of oats and cold water had long since wearied him – when MacTavish squatted down.

'A coo in a forest, alone. S'not a good sign, ken. And we are only half a day's march from our own lands.' He sighed. 'Too far to gang tonight, in the gloaming, on empty stomachs.' He reached down, put two nuts into his palm, cracked them with an easy squeeze and handed half the proceeds to Jack. His face brightened. 'Still now. We'll feed oor bellies with nuts . . . and some meat!' He nodded toward the cow.

'You'll slaughter her in the forest?' Jack had lain fully back, relieved that his day's march was over.

'Slaughter a milch coo? You're no farmer, Mr Absolute!' MacTavish smiled. 'Nae, look there.'

Gregor had been busy sharpening his dirk. Now, he crouched by the cow's foreleg, muttering gentle words while the other young man, Alisdair, held the cow's nose ring. Then the knife was jabbed swiftly in. So sharp was the point, so swift its insertion, that the cow barely flinched. But blood flowed, caught by Gregor in a wooden bowl. When he had enough, he smeared some spit and mud on to the wound and moved to his sack where four further bowls were filled with oats and the blood poured evenly on top of them. Two were borne across to Jack and MacTavish.

Jack grimaced. 'You jest.'

MacTavish hooted. 'Would'na the fine Sassenach gentleman eat a blood sausage?'

'Heartily. But a sausage is cooked.'

'Weel, it was oft too wet to cook on the droves to market in Edinburgh or Aberdeen. This is how we survived. If I had disdained the blood in my drammach, I'd have ended up a scrawny wee thing like ye.'

Jack laughed. And despite another lurch of his stomach, hunger overcame his scruples. He ate, gagged, then ate on.

The Scot nodded approvingly. 'Aye. Eat hearty, Captain. For the morn will bring us to Tryon County and our farms. And let us hope yon coo is just a stray and not a portent of something disemal.'

It was not only farms that lay ahead. Canajoharie, the village appointed as his rendezvous with Até, was also there. Realizing his waxing strength needed still more support, Jack took the advice and tipped back the bowl.

They were on the path with the earliest glimmer of light. And an hour's walking brought them the first sign that the wandering cow was indeed the harbinger of hard times.

The farmhouse was smashed like an egg, burnt walls stoved in, the huge, solid logs once so laboriously raised into place now mere charcoal ghosts. Singed cedar shingles lay scattered where the flames had flung them. Their cow, now chewing at one of the few patches of grass not blackened, had been lucky; for four of her sisters lay around, bellies swelling in the muggy heat, clouded by flies, legs stiffened and pointing straight out.

At their first sight, the lad, Gregor, had run forward with yelps of anguish despite Angus's shouted caution. Indeed, as soon as he entered the still-smoking ruin, the one wall left standing cracked ominously and swiftly collapsed, sending up a pall of dust, smoke, and sparks. They had each started forward at that, but Gregor emerged almost immediately, a black version of himself, sooted from crown to toe. In his left hand he clutched a rag poppet, a sister's plaything, and as he muttered what he'd seen inside to Angus, he twisted the little doll's head back and forth between his fingers till it finally detached. Seeing this, a tear carved a channel down his blackened cheek. Angus patted him on the shoulder and moved over to Jack.

'A dreigh sight, sure. But nae bodies in there, at the least.' Angus bit his lip. 'There's hope then that Gregor's kin have taken shelter up ahead, in the Native village. They were always friendly to us, the Oneidas there.'

He was talking of Canajoharie. Though a Mohawk, the wanderings of Até's family had led many of them to live among their brother tribe.

'Shall we check on them then?' Jack said.

'Aye. And my own farm lies not an hour beyond, on the edge of Herkimer township.' He looked again at the ruins. 'Dod! I pray my eyes do not see such blae things there.'

But the sights they encountered at the Native village were beyond the Scotsman's worst fears. Here the corpses were not only animal but all too human, both Iroquois and white, their differences eradicated now in the uniformity of death. The attackers had not bothered with flame here; they had slaughtered, with gun, tomahawk, and club.

Gregor had fallen, weeping, by a pile of bodies, a family clustered around a man's corpse still clutching a shovel, his remains, like all the others, violated with the removal of his scalp. Before them, two other bodies lay, stripes of war paint running in bands around their chests, their heads smashed, in what must have been the dead farmer's last desperate defence.

As Alisdair led the sobbing boy away, Angus poked at one warrior's body with his toe. 'Mohawk,' he said, flatly, as if any colouring of the word would release too much emotion.

'Yes.' Jack, his voice as toneless, nodded, turned away. These dead warriors could be the Mohawk who lived among the Oneida, could even be Até's relatives. They could also have come from another village. Either way, his brothers had taken to the war path and this was the way they fought their wars, in raids, in slaughter. And though some of the bodies lying about were white, like Gregor's family, the majority were Native. The promised civil war that Jack had foreseen when he saw the

Oneida warriors leading the Tryon County Militia into the ravine at Oriskany was upon them. The Hodensaunee, the People of the Long House, were divided now as they had not been in two centuries, their confederacy shattered. Iroquois fought Iroquois and the result would be a ravaged land and many sights as horrible as the one before him now.

He turned back, something nagging at him. The Mohawks had not been scalped but that wasn't it. Then he realized.

'This war party was disturbed. They'd have taken these bodies with them otherwise, for burial in their own villages. Who stopped this slaughter?'

He had the answer in a heartbeat. 'Lay down your weapons, easy now. Or you'll die where you stand.'

The voice had called from the tongue of forest that still reached down to the village. And it was from there that the single shot was fired, the ball passing close enough to make MacTavish duck. The Scot's first instinct had appeared to be defiance but the shot's passing and the sight of the still-weeping Gregor, changed his mind. Laying his rifle on the ground, he raised his arms.

In an instant, men on horses sallied from the woods. They circled, forcing MacTavish's band to cluster tight. Finally, reining in, the horses jerked their heads up and down while their riders regarded the captives silently – a silence broken by the same voice that had called out before.

'Zook! If I don't see the world's most insubordinate Scot before me.'

MacTavish's face lightened when he heard the words, then darkened almost instantly. 'Colonel Benedict Arnold,' he muttered, 'is't thee that mouches aboot to greet an old comrade, with shoots and shouts.'

Jack studied the horseman. Unlike the rest of his men, who were dressed in a ragtag assortment of uniform and civilian clothing, this Arnold wore a fine blue coat with a gold epaulette on his right shoulder and brilliant gold buttons down the front. It parted over a buff waistcoat, again gold-trimmed, with a lawn shirt poking from its top, a black stock spilling out. His tricorn hat split his face at a jaunty angle, perched atop hair as black as Jack's and that, unlike with most American officers, seemed to be entirely his own. He was taller by a good head than his subordinates and wider too, though not fat. A prominent beak of a nose dominated the swarthy face, grizzled with a half-beard.

The face flushed at MacTavish's words. 'That's *General* Arnold, as I am sure you are aware. Are you here to scavenge?'

It was MacTavish's turn to colour. 'As I'm sure you are aware, *Arnold*,' the name was laden with a dose of venom a rattlesnake could have envied, 'nae MacTavish has e'er been a scavenger. Ah've escaped my English captors at Fort Stanwix, and noo am bound to my hame. If it yet stands!'

'It does. We stopped those raiding heathen here. Everything further down the valley, both your lands and mine, are safe.' While he was speaking, the General had flung his reins to the man beside him and descended his horse. 'But tell me, man,' he said, excitedly, 'how did my subterfuge work? Did the idiot do his work? Has my little Hans-Yost put fear into the Royal Army?'

'Aye, that looby did. So much so that Benedict Arnold's name alone has driven the enemy to flight.' Jack could hear the sarcasm in the Scot's voice even if its intended target could not.

'What? The siege is lifted?'

'Indeed. Colonel St Leger is now engaged in running all the way to Montreal.'

A great cheer went up from the mounted men and many huzzahed their General. Arnold tried to look modest and failed.

'The devil you say! The devil! That pays them for Oriskany and then some. And I can now get back to the real war. I can ride to . . .'

It was only then that Arnold's wandering eyes finally focused on the other man standing before him. Jack had remained perfectly still and silent amidst all the ballyhoo. He was thus the most conspicuous person present.

'Who's this, MacTavish?' the General barked. 'Another

kinsman? He's black-browed enough to be a Celt. And with their insolence in his eyes.'

The Scot grunted at the insult but breathed deeply and then laid a hand on Jack's forearm. ''Tis a bonny lad, a fine swordsman, and a true gentleman. He felled me once, then saved my life after Oriskany and gave me the honour of letting me save his soon after. Ochone, his one clear fault is that he is an English officer.'

All cheering stopped. Arnold took a pace back and looked at Jack from toe to crown. 'He's not dressed like an officer nor as a gentleman.' The dark face darkened further. 'He looks like a damn spy to me.'

There were mutterings from his men at that. There was a constant watch for spies on both sides. And a universal method of dealing with them – a rope slung over a branch. It was time Jack spoke.

'I regret, General Arnold, that I cannot be presented to you in the uniform of my regiment. For it was stolen from me by the scoundrels who left me for dead in the forest.'

'Your name, sir? Your rank and regiment?'

Jack had already spoken in the voice of a class somewhat above his own, his friend, 'Sandy' Lindsay, the Earl of Balcarras, as his model. It was pure instinct, for he suddenly saw that in anything close to the truth there was no safety. Also some detail about the man interrogating him was lurking in his memory.

'Lord John Absolute, General Arnold. And I have the honour of being a Captain of His Majesty's 24th Regiment of Foot, seconded to the staff of Colonel St Leger.'

He was aware of Angus looking at him in some surprise, but he kept his attention fixed on his interrogator. For he had suddenly remembered what it was that nagged him about the man, why his instinct had led him to declare himself thus. Arnold's fierceness in the Rebel cause, his bravery that was akin to madness, were subjects well known to both sides. But he was also reputed to be a great admirer of all things English – especially rank and class.

143

Indeed, the grey eyes did almost instantly soften in their regard. 'General Benedict Arnold, Captain . . . my lord . . . sir!' He flushed again as he struggled with titles to maintain his status yet not diminish Jack's. 'And will you now consider yourself my prisoner as you were once MacTavish's? I am sure I'll be able to entertain you somewhat more lavishly than he. He's probably been feeding you blood and oats, what?' He turned to a soldier mounted nearby. 'Sergeant, provide his lordship with my spare mount. MacTavish, you may check on your homestead and family then join us if you choose. We ride to verify this information of St Leger's defeat.'

Instantly, there were shouted commands, horses snorting as they wheeled, men calling out. Not least of the noise was the Scotch invective, unintelligible to most there, aimed squarely at the retreating blue coat of Benedict Arnold.

Jack, who had learned to decipher some in their short acquaintance, turned and whispered in the huge and hairy ear. 'Wheesht, Angus. It's what must be. Dinna fash.'

The words, thus delivered, pierced the wind of outrage. MacTavish laughed and spat a moment later.

'Tha' bumfy rides roughshod over all o'us, as usual. He and I have a history, ye may have been able to tell. We've been neighbours five years and I was with him to Quebec in seventy-five. Aye, and carried him back most of the way when that British ball broke his leg. Had to harken to his dreadful whinin' and moanin' and carryin' on. I dinna think he's ever pardoned me for being a witness to his blubbin'. But he's a brave lunatic for all tha' and as changeable as the wind. So be canny round him, ken.'

'You understand why I told him I was a lord?'

'To secure better treatment?' Jack nodded. 'Aye, y'ere no dunce, Jack Absolute. For nothin' will fetch ye into that callant's esteem like a title. I dinna know why he doesnae fight for t'other side, he worships the English nobility so much.'

The Sergeant had led a roan mare to where they stood. Just before he mounted, Jack made to give the shillelagh back to Angus. But the Scotsman just shook his head.

'Ye may be needing it mair than me.' Then with a wink, he added, 'I do so hope to meet you again, *my lord*.'

'So do I, MacTavish. And thank you. I owe you.'

'Och, the owin's mutual. Awa'!' Angus slapped a huge hand on the horse's haunch and the animal gave a leap forward then settled into a slow canter. It was small yet biddable, though Jack doubted it would provide much pace. Not enough to outrun the Sergeant astride his own spirited and far bigger gelding. It brought him up beside Arnold though, soon enough.

'Ah, Lord John.' The General, like Jack, was attempting to speak in an accent and tone different from the one he'd used in addressing MacTavish. 'These scoundrels who abandoned you for dead in the wood? Savages?'

Jack had already heard the American declaim one prejudice, against the Scots. He presumed on another.

'Worse in my estimation, General. Germans.'

The reaction was all Jack could have hoped for. Arnold shuddered and rolled his eyes. 'Worse, indeed! If you have their names and their route, I would be delighted to set a watch for the scum.'

Jack considered. It was tempting to let Arnold and his forces loose on Von Schlaben. But instantly he decided against it – for two reasons. The first that there was much more to be learned from his enemy should Jack have the fortune to catch up with him. And the second was for the same reason the Count had not told St Leger about the punch. Vengeance was indeed a personal affair.

'I wish I knew either, General. And I am inexpressively grateful for the kind thought. But they were unknown to me, deserters from our army.'

'Deserters and Germans. They will get their punishment then, I am certain. But now, my lord, as is customary, I take it I have your word as a nobleman that you will not try to escape? This prevents the encumbrance of too close a watch upon you.'

Jack smiled. 'As a *nobleman*, sir, I give you my most earnest pledge.'

The General nodded. 'And perchance I will not have the pleasure of your company for long. We can seek to exchange you, of course but there may not be time even for that. We ride to the crisis of this campaign, sir. Burgoyne is hedged in. Our forces are gathering around him. The endgame is upon us.'

'And may I ask where this hedge is being woven, General Arnold?'

Once more the man smiled. It was not a pleasant sight, its distastefulness having little to do with the crooked and discoloured condition of the teeth. 'No harm in telling you, my lord. You will have heard it in the camp by nightfall anyway – for how these Militiamen will gossip. Burgoyne will be brought to bay near a settlement called Stillwater, just to the south of Saratoga. Now, first we must check that these tales of MacTavish's are quite true – never trust a Caledonian, sir, is a motto one lives by in these parts – and then we must make with all haste for Saratoga.'

Affecting a need to lengthen his reins, Jack let the blue coat surge ahead, while the Sergeant slowed beside him. He had no desire to return to Fort Stanwix but it would be less than a day's ride away. By his calculations, Saratoga would then be around ten days' march, assuming Arnold travelled at the pace of his infantry. There would be no point in slipping away before then, still somewhat weakened as he was, on a slow horse through hostile country. Not when he was being escorted where he wanted to go, to Burgoyne.

As he rode, he considered further. His first mission for his General had ended in failure. Fort Stanwix had not fallen, the third force had not struck along the Mohawk, Natives and Loyalists had not rallied in their thousands to the Union Standard. It was not his fault but it was frustrating. Yet time spent with one of the Rebel's foremost generals would be time *well* spent. There was much to be learned in Arnold's camp concerning men, morale, the logistics of campaign. Food and drink for a man used to listening and observing. And perhaps Arnold would get careless and leave some invisible ink or a code-crib lying around. Or even more importantly, confirmation that Von Schlaben was indeed Diomedes, the spy at the centre of the King's army.

With the campaign reaching its climax, Jack had no need to risk his life, for the moment, to hurry to his General. Burgoyne was the master of that phase in chess and in war. He could serve his Commander better where he was.

Easing into the gentle canter that seemed to be the roan's natural gait, Jack eased also into the skin of Lord John Absolute. That man had given his word not to escape. That man would not. But at the sound of the guns, Captain Jack Absolute must. And would.

ELEVEN

Saratoga – 19 September 1777

Jack Absolute lay concealed in the decaying trunk of a fallen cedar, musing on death.

Strange how my mind runs so on that subject lately, he thought. Not, he hastened to point out to himself, in a philosophical 'Prince of Denmark' way. No, indeed, Até would not discover him in the mood to receive one of his infernal theoretical diatribes about the Dane. On the contrary, Jack's mind focused only on the mundane and myriad ways death had tried to take him in the last six months; they could certainly be counted on his fingers – if he even had that much room in his cramped quarters to extend them.

In March, in London, a man named Banastre Tarleton had sought to impale him on a small sword and, frustrated in this, had tried to finish the job with a sabre. Another sword, a claymore, swung by an unintelligible Scotsman, had attempted to remove his head while the Highlander's confederates sought to stick him with bayonets and bludgeon him with gun butts. He had been extensively shot at by Rebels in the forests of Oriskany where, later, one Abenaki had hurled a war club at him, another had attempted to extrude his brains with a tomahawk, and a third had cudgelled him. A German Count had dropped a viper on him, which had stung him twice. To top it all, he half-believed that same Scotchman, Angus MacTavish, had made a second attempt on his life by feeding him oats and cow's blood, a combination from which his guts had yet to recover and which had rendered his afternoon's stay in the cedar tree additionally uncomfortable.

Though maybe their stirrings now were more to do with what lay ahead than behind. For in the next hour, he had an equal chance of being shot by his own side *or* the enemy, depending on who spotted him first, the British pickets or the Rebel.

Jack sighed. He was sure he had left a few out. The temptation was to stay in the log, perhaps for the duration of the war. But he couldn't do that for two main reasons and one minor: he was hungry; he had learned the war was going badly for the Royal Army so he had to resume his position at Burgoyne's right hand; and some creature had slipped inside his trouser cuff and was engaged in biting its way up his leg.

He had to lessen the odds against him if he were to survive the next sixty minutes. He felt proud that he had already taken a deal more care by hiding in this tree while a battle was fought in the valley below him. He had been in enough such fights to know that men on either side would shoot precipitously and not query his allegiances till later, especially dressed as he was, as neither friend nor foe but in the gaudy civilian suit Arnold had lent him.

Benedict Arnold. Two and half weeks he'd spent in that braggart's company, from Stanwix to Saratoga, encouraging him to talk, though in truth the man needed little prodding. Jack had made himself the perfect audience – reticent himself but 'noble'. He had learned much of how the Rebel army worked, and too much of Arnold's several loves and even more numerous hates – for, it seemed, he was the only capable general the Colonists possessed and grievously overlooked for the highest commands. He had not gained enough knowledge about American spy rings, however. A boaster he may have been but Arnold was not so foolish as to parade his deepest secrets before an English officer. So when Arnold had told him as much as Jack felt he ever would and when he had brought

149

Jack to within running distance of the British lines, Jack had made his escape.

And now, another man seeks my death, Jack thought, trying in vain to thrust his hand down the narrow log and scratch his leg. *For a peaceable fellow, I seem to make an inordinate number of enemies.*

Fortunately, the General had been so concerned about the forthcoming combat he'd barely had time to yell, 'Return or die, you dog!' as Jack sprinted for the cover of the trees, balls snapping branches above his head as he entered them. Once in the forest, Jack knew the odds were on his side against any but the most thorough search. He had reverted to his Mohawk nature and men had passed within feet of his concealment.

Jack sighed, though taking care that the sigh produced no sound. All he had to do now was cross a battlefield full of the Rebel dead and wounded and the parties that sought to bury or save them; then repeat the trick through the British soldiers embarked on the same tasks, and further unnerved by constant American sniping. All? And the only true odds-lessening plan he had come up with was to await the inevitable thunderstorm when men would be forced to ward their powder. Much less chance of being shot, then. But presumably there would be the usual array of bladed weaponry ready to be thrust, thrown, or swung at him.

Jack sighed again, not as silently, then felt two things – the bite of the creature, which had now reached his upper thigh, and the log drumming with the first drops of rain.

With a mixture of relief and terror, Jack crawled from his lair. He took time only to reach in and dig out his assailant – a grotesquely large centipede – then began to move, as cautiously as he could, down the night-darkening slope of the valley. Lying in the log he had overheard various conversations. Knew that the fighting had been especially heavy, and that each side, as usual, was claiming victory.

The rain consisted of thick and constant drops, stinging the eyes and making the features of the terrain, ill-lit enough by the twilight, still harder to discern. By the way the land sloped,

Jack guessed there was a stream somewhere nearby; he soon hit upon it and, keeping it on his right side, moved parallel to it down the valley.

Streams drew soldiers. Many of the Rebel army were clustered now on its banks, seeking sparse shelter under the overhanging branches of maples, their foliage just beginning the turn to the red of autumn. Jack sought not to meet anyone's gaze but, glancing up briefly, he saw men recovering from what, for many, would have been their first full battle. Most eyes were filmed over, staring ahead. Some wept. Others had a euphoric gleam, as if they had suddenly discovered joy in every sensation. They looked to the fat raindrops, or pawed at the dripping leaves, hugged themselves in pleasure, talked incessantly.

It was in the fourth group he passed that Jack, in the quickest of perusals, encountered something else – a challenge. He looked away swiftly, too late.

'You there. Yeh, you, in the dandy duds. Where you goin'?'

Jack cursed, yet again, Benedict Arnold's taste in clothes. That particular Yankee could indeed stick a feather in his cap and be called a Macaroni! The frilled shirt and elaborately gold-stitched jacket were hardly battle attire.

'You'll pardon me. I bear a message to Colonel Morgan.'

He had not bothered to disguise his accent. There were probably more Englishmen in the numerically superior Rebel army than in the Royal. But the tall man who now stepped into his path and placed a hand against Jack's chest had the broad vowels and drawling speech of an American frontiers-man. A tasselled buck-skin jacket confirmed the impression.

'And who might this message be from?'

Jack had attempted to slide past, but the hand that had stopped now grasped his lapel. 'General Learned,' he muttered, reluctantly.

''sat a fact!' The American whistled. 'Interestin' Learned should be sending messages. Considerin' the Colonel be havin' a meetin' with him right now.'

The man's companions, buck-skinned as he, stirred beneath

their tree. Jack felt the grip tighten at his chest, more gaudy material grasped. The man was taller than Jack by a head and wider too.

Wonder if he's done any wrestling? Jack thought briefly, before dropping his left hand on the wrist before him. The man might well have had an advantage in height and strength but his wrist, when twisted the wrong way and with sufficient pressure, would break as any other. As Jack jerked sharply, the man gave a cry and bent away to save himself further injury. Whipping him to the side, Jack stepped past and ran.

Instantly, the men under the tree began to shout, 'Stop him!' Jack was still close enough to hear the distinct sound of guns cocking, despite the rain. Judging that these men knew what they were about, Jack counted to three then threw his feet out before him and slid along the ground. The deluge took care of four of the guns for he heard the distinct 'puff' of wet powder. The fifth fired and a ball flew over his head at the place where his hips would have been. He rolled up in a moment and was running near flat out in another.

Near flat out. The path was slick with rain and the first fallen leaves of autumn, while twisted tree roots reached across it to snag his toes. He had half his vision fixed on his footfalls, half on the group of Rebel Regulars crouched on the ground ahead, rising at the hallooing and the single rifle shot.

A blue uniform was almost in his road. 'Quickly!' Jack yelled as he came level, slapping the soldier on the back. 'A British spy! There! Do you see him? There!'

The man turned as Jack ran by him. He could hear the distinct tones of the frontiersman he'd felled urging pursuit. Jack fancied himself in any footrace but not if he had to slow up every ten paces. Other groups were visible ahead. Reluctantly, he dodged off the path and began to forge through the low scrub between the trees.

They still had him in view. Another rifle surpassed the rain and a bullet thunked into a maple beside him. Twice, he nearly fell, just keeping his feet, slithering and stumbling to steady himself against a tree, running on. Then the rain slackened noticeably and, as suddenly, ceased. It made his task a little easier; at least he could see somewhat more clearly through the dusklight. But it made him a clearer target too; and the powder would stay dry.

The steepness of the slope was diminishing, the trees thinning. He felt he was reaching the valley's floor, an impression confirmed in a moment by a sudden increase in the numbers of Rebels standing before him, for the valley bottom would be the front line. He could see they were at the edge of the woods, that a clearing lay beyond. He even glimpsed a structure within it and remembered one of the voices he'd overheard while lying in the log – the battle that day had mainly been fought around a farmhouse. Was this it?

There was no way around the men before him. He had to go through them. Behind him, he could hear that the pursuit was closing. He ran straight.

'Look! To your fronts, boys. A British spy.'

He could not really expect it to work a second time. It didn't. The man he'd chosen to run at stood square.

'You'll just be holdin' it there, me lad,' he said, his Irish brogue thick.

But Jack had the advantage of the slight slope, his momentum, and his desperation.

Beyond the man, the trees stopped, there was a field, open ground. It had to be the space between the opposing armies. So he dipped his shoulder and took the Irishman in the chest, knocking him aside. A flailing hand grasped at him as he went by and he almost fell, while one of the boots that Arnold had lent him with the clothes, which were a size too big, slipped off easily.

He was through, in the open, and felt both hope and a hurtling fear. It was a hundred yards at the least to the shelter of the building he now saw was a barn. The clearing was, in fact, a field that must, until recently, have held corn. Stalks snagged at his ankles as he sprinted. But it was the first body that saved him, as he misjudged his jump, catching it with a toe, and plunging, as a ragged volley crackled out behind. He slid along the churned ground face first, his progress halted sharply when his forehead encountered something soft. Spitting mud, he looked up to see he had slid into another corpse. A swift glance from side to side showed that the field was filled with them. Terrible slaughter had been done there that day.

'We got him, boys! He's down. Let's grab the bastard.' The voice of that first frontiersman, still dogged in his pursuit, came from behind. It spurred Jack to rise, to stumble on. Suddenly, he was as tired as he could ever remember being, but he forced himself forward.

The next shot came from in front of him, and passed through the embroidered epaulette of Arnold's coat.

'Hold!' Jack cried. 'I'm English, damn ye.'

'Steady! Hold Fire! On my word!' There was something familiar to the sound, beyond that of regimental command. He altered direction and sprinted toward the voice.

It spoke again. 'You there! Down!'

Jack had no doubt he was being addressed. He flung himself flat, simultaneous with the next words. 'Company, present your firelocks.' A moment's pause. 'Fire!'

Unlike the ragged volley from the woods behind him, this had the sharp crack of well-trained infantry and the results were immediate: cries of pain and shock behind him, and that same frontiersman, screaming, 'Back! Back!'

The familiar voice spoke again. 'You! Come forward and be quick about it, see.'

It was the 'see' that placed it for him, as well as the slight burr on the 'r' of 'forward'.

'Well, Ted,' he said, as he stumbled into the red ranks. 'That's a fine way to greet a fellow Cornishman.'

Midshipman Edward Pellew stood just behind his company of Marines and gaped. 'Zooks! Jack! Jack Absolute! You're alive.'

'Only just, my lad. And I nearly fell at the last fence.' Ripping the shattered epaulette from the coat, he added, 'Thanks to you.'

Pellew had swiftly regained his sang-froid. 'Could only

improve your attire, Jack. You seem to have acquired a lamentable taste in clothing. Never took you for a macaroni.'

Jack grinned. 'I'm glad to see you.'

He thrust out his hand. Pellew gripped it and squeezed heartily. 'And I you. You've missed some brisk work this day, Jack. Welcome to Freeman's Farm.' Something dark came into the younger man's eyes as he glanced out across the field. Then the eyes cleared and focused again on him. 'But no doubt you've been about some hot action yourself.'

'Hot enough, Ted, aye. And now I must speak to General Burgoyne.'

'I'll take you to him forthwith.' Pellew unclasped Jack's hand, which he'd still been pumping vigorously. 'Wilson, you have the command.' As they moved off and the drill to reload began behind them, he contined, 'He'll be pleased to see you. And surprised. We all believed you was dead.'

Jack thought back. A few minutes ago he'd been lying in a log, musing on death, counting the number of times he'd faced it within just the last six months. He had exhausted his fingers in the tally. That run down the valley had moved him well onto his toes and he had a horrible suspicion that in what lay immediately ahead he would rapidly exhaust those too.

The camp was an appalling sight. Those who had limped or crawled or by some fortune been recovered from the field lay around before hastily erected tents in which the surgeons, their silhouettes monstrously distorted by the lamps within, operated continuously, while outside them amputated limbs grew into flesh volcanoes, with lava flows of congealing blood. In their shadows, men waited their turn, weeping, groaning, or just staring, mouthing silent prayers.

'And there's more left on the field, Jack, more than made it back. We try to get to them but the Rebels shoot if we stir. We must wait till full dark and then bring in those few who have survived.'

Jack heard the emotion in Pellew's voice and was careful not to look at his compatriot. He'd forgotten how young the lad was, barely eighteen. Out of the corner of his eye he saw a hand reach up, saw a tear flicked away.

'It was hard, the hardest day ever I saw in my life. I've been in the odd skirmish and scrap in this campaign but a battle . . .' Pellew paused and wrestled with his voice. 'We held the field, just, but each regiment in the brunt has barely seventy left, officers and men, and the gunners near wiped out. The Yankees kept coming and coming. Who thought they had that kind of courage? I think we was only saved by the Germans marching in from the left. And the rumour is that the General thinks to attack again in the morning. How can we do that, Jack, how—'

His voice was rising both in tone and volume, and Jack made to stumble, reaching out to steady himself on Pellew's forearm. Halting them both, he said, 'Burgoyne will only do what is right, Ted. For England. For honour. He will not sacrifice his men needlessly. He loves them too much for that.'

The words, calmly spoken, had their effect. The younger Cornishman breathed deeply and, at last, nodded. 'I know he will, Jack. I apologize.'

Jack squeezed and released his grip. 'No need,' he said. They resumed their walk over the rise and dip of the ground, and soon were passing down a wide central avenue made up of rows of tents, the campfires of the regiments before them. Men clustered around, content to squat and stare, while women moved among the cook pots. Even the swiftest glance told Jack that the rations were spare. No one seemed able to talk, a hush held the whole encampment. At the end of the rows, Jack could make out a structure through the gloom.

'Sword's House,' said Pellew. 'The General's HQ.'

He was perhaps fifty yards from the door when he heard a cry from a tent to his right. It would have been clear in a playhouse during the overture. In the stillness of the camp, it was piercing.

'Jack Absolute. My . . . oh my . . . *Jack*!'

He turned – in time only to open his arms to the blur that hurled itself into them.

'They told me . . . *he* told me . . . you were dead. Beyond all hope and prayer, dead!'

Though somewhat winded by the assault, Jack managed to breathe and speak. 'As you can see – and feel – Miss Reardon, I am not.'

Louisa gripped her hands up and down his arms as if to verify the solidity of flesh while her eyes searched and sought and still seemed unable to comprehend. Jack delighted in the touch, revelling again in those eyes. He had tried on many occasions, during many an uncomfortable night, to conjure their exact shade of green. He'd had it close; yet memory could never recall all their detail, their swirls and swoops. His grin spread – in London, aboard ship, she had always balanced coquettishness with an infuriating coolness. She was always in command. He suspected this would return once her surprise was past and she became aware of all the eyes upon her – not least those of the elderly man standing in the entrance of the tent from which she'd just burst.

He was sad though that awareness came just as he was bending to kiss her. The touch of those lips had been as tormenting a memory as her eyes and he was all for re-acquainting himself. He had been through enough, deserved a reward, and damn the audience! But Louisa had almost recovered. She stood back to look him up and down, and said, with a degree of tartness, 'Well, sir, and you have given your friends much aggravation, no mistake.'

Jack laughed and he was not the only one. 'I regret any upset caused, miss. It was entirely beyond my control, I assure you.'

'Well, you can make amends and shortly.' Jack marvelled. From full passion to coolness in moments. Only the reddish flush of her skin hinted of other emotions.

'Will you take a glass with us, sir, and tell us your tale?' She was gesturing to the tent entrance, where the elderly man still stood. 'I do not believe you have met my father?'

Jack inclined his head. 'Captain Jack Absolute, sir, at your service.'

The older man bowed stiffly. 'Colonel Thaddeus Reardon,

sir. At yours. I have heard much about you. And I have spent much time consoling my daughter at the loss of such a . . . friend.' The weight on the word was slight and not harshly meant. 'I am rejoiced to see that, like Lazarus, Christ has raised you up. Would you indeed join us for some Madeira? I believe it is my last bottle and I can't think of a better occasion.' He stepped wide and gestured into the tent.

'I thank you, sir, but I believe I must first make my report to General Burgoyne. May I return later?'

'You may.' The Colonel looked at his daughter, who was still staring at Jack, coolness and delight still raging in colours on her face. A smile came. 'Nay, I believe you must.'

'I vow it,' he said, making her a generous bow, then fell into step again with Pellew, the dignity of his exit somewhat compromised by the loss of the one boot and the hop that resulted. He didn't really care; for as he hopped, he grinned. He'd had doubts, during their separation, that her regard for him may only have been the product of five weeks' close company at sea. But her reception of him, her brief exposure, had reassured and delighted him. They made for the house ahead.

'If it is of any interest, Jack, she wept from the moment the German delivered the news till just now, I should think,' said Pellew.

Delight was displaced. 'Von Schlaben?'

'Aye. Said you'd been bit by a snake at Fort Stanwix and died horribly. Must say, it always sounded strange, a woodsman like yourself.'

The sentry already had the door swinging open. 'Is he still here, Ted?' Jack said. But any reply was cut off by a familiar voice from within the room.

'Captain Absolute. Well, well. I always believed reports of your demise were egregiously premature. Come in. Come in. You have arrived in the nick, as usual, sirrah. We have need of your specialist mind.'

Pellew squeezed his arm, whispered, 'There's a pillow for you with the Marines, Jack.'

Jack nodded and entered the room.

General Burgoyne stood facing the door, leaning on a table. He was dressed in his waistcoat, his jacket having been placed on a coat stand just behind him, its tails splayed so that the three bullet holes were clearly visible. Jack noted that someone had placed a lamp directly behind the coat, making the rents stand out like stars in a red evening sky. Burgoyne himself, undoubtedly, his sense of theatre never deserting him. The message was clear: They shoot at me in vain. I am invulnerable and so will triumph.

Burgoyne returned his attention to something on the table. Around him were gathered his war council, including many men Jack knew. Alexander 'Sandy' Lindsay, Earl of Balcarras, looking thinner and more frail than ever, started forward at the sight of Jack, then restrained his obvious joy and contented himself with a smile. General Fraser bobbed his head and winked. Baron von Riedesel and his interpreter gave curt Germanic nods and then continued their scrutiny over Burgoyne's shoulder. There were some there that Jack knew vaguely, such as the Artilleryman General Phillips; others, especially the Loyalist commanders, that he didn't. In the corner of the room, looking ill-at-ease, perhaps because he was the only one sitting, was a man in muddy civilian clothes. He was also the only one there who regarded Jack with something like interest. The rest took their cue from the General's insouciance and gave the prodigal but a cursory stare.

Lieutenant-Colonel Thomas Carleton, Burgoyne's adjutant, whose hair seemed to have turned near white from the time Jack last saw him, came and placed a glass of sherry in his hand, murmuring, 'Welcome,' then took him by the elbow and led him up to the table. Jack looked down. Spread out there was a handwritten letter, with various odd-shaped cardboard cards and bits of slashed cloth scattered around it. Another officer, Captain Money, was rather desperately pressing one after another of these cards and cloths over the childishly-scrawled words.

'Explain the problem to him, Captain Money,' Burgoyne said. His voice was strained and low when it was usually light and easy. 'In fact, Captain Absolute will be too quick for you, so why not explain it to us all. In simple terms.'

It was obvious that the unfortunate Money had committed some serious offence. Burgoyne was rarely anything other than polite with subordinates, even when aroused. That made his anger here all the more unnerving. It certainly unnerved the Captain, who stuttered slightly as he spoke, 'The p-p-problem is simple, Captain Absolute. Its solution, sadly, not so. We have lost the mask needed to decode this letter.'

'*You* have lost it, Money!'

'With . . . with . . . with respect, sir, it was hidden safe in your tent, and then it was—'

'Yes, yes. We've heard your excuses. On!'

Money chewed on his lower lip. He was explaining the obvious to people who mostly knew it. But Burgoyne was punishing him, making him recite his catechism. 'As you know, masks are an easy and effective means of encoding. The s-s-sender and the recipient have an identical piece of card or cloth, cut in a certain shape. It is placed over a piece of paper and the desired message is written to conform to the shape. It is then removed and the rest of the page filled in with innocent news. Trade, family illness, and the like. The message is delivered and the recipient places his card or cloth and—'

'Yes, all right, Money, that's enough,' Burgoyne snapped at the unfortunate officer then turned to Jack. 'D'ye see the problem? This letter arrived today from General Clinton in New York, borne by our gallant Sergeant Willis.' He nodded to the muddied man in the corner who tried to rise and was gestured down. 'He must return at dawn with an answer – but an answer to what?' The General angrily waved away Money's attempt to fit another of the silk shapes – something like a bolt of lightning – over the letter. 'Contained within this ill-spelled rubbish is the news we have been denied for eight weeks: Has General Howe finished his campaign in Pennsylvania and is at last advancing to our rendezvous at Albany? Or, at the very least, is Clinton about to attack the Highland forts on the Hudson and then march to our aid? Either will force our

American friends to divide the army here ranged against us. They outnumber me at least four to one. If that drops to two, by God, those are English odds and I'll take 'em on and thrash 'em, and obey my command to push through to Albany. The campaign, indeed America, will have been won, despite all our adversities.' He ground the heel of his hand into his forehead and massaged it. 'But as you have heard, the mask that would fit over this letter, that would render its meaning clear, that would tell us if help comes or no . . . is missing. Lost. *Lost!*'

Jack kept his dismay hidden. It was far more likely that the mask was not lost but stolen, no doubt by a spy at the heart of the British army. Von Schlaben? Could he have returned in time from Fort Stanwix to do it? Unlikely. And Burgoyne would never have left the Count alone in his tent. Could it be one of the Loyalist Commanders? One of the Germans? Surely not one of the red-coated offiers? That was, however, a concern for later. What mattered now was that the mask was missing, its disappearance near a disaster.

The General spoke again. 'So all we know is that "Mr Rhodes has had a delivery of fine cloth". Perhaps he can patch my coat, eh?' There was nervous laughter. He glanced up at Jack, who noticed, now he stood near, the closest he'd ever seen to desperation in those grey eyes. 'Can you cut this Gordian Knot, Captain?'

He didn't have much hope. But he had to try. So Jack read the letter. As Burgoyne had said, the spelling – and grammar – was poor, a further ward against unintended readers:

Dear Coz.
Have you lately seen that cur Will Piper? He owe me
5 pounds and so his vyle attempt to avoid me is contimtible.
I mean therefore to push ahead with your order, for because
I rieciev'd on Hudson's looms a delivary of fine cloth. Shall make cotes
then go fort'sell 'em. Give kind'st to my financee, Marge. I see her in
two or three weeks but it will seem no more nor less than three thousand.
  Yr. Affectionate Coz.
  T. Rhodes

Jack took a hefty swig of the sherry then set the glass down next to its decanter. He had never seen the mask the General referred to, and obviously no one could distinguish it from the several they carried for other correspondents. These – among them the lightning bolt, a Jewish star, a cross of Lorraine – had been laid out beside the page and Money had obviously tried them all. He had also made various random shapes from cards, the ones he'd been desperately trying when Jack came in, as well as some fair copies of the letter.

Jack lifted one now, slid it back and forth across the ink, looking for a pattern of words that would spring out, a sentence of military import among the detail of goods and gossip. He was aware of the men's attention upon him, the pressure of their expectation, their desperate hope. If Jack had had hardships on the campaign, so had they. The bodies lying in the stubble of Freeman's Farm were testimony to that, as eloquent as the holes in Burgoyne's coat.

He swallowed, his mouth suddenly dry, and placed another piece of card, stubbier, square. He'd been good at this sort of game, once. He moved it up and down, saw nothing. Licking his lips, without removing his scrutiny from the paper, he reached out to the glass at his side . . . and misjudged the distance completely, knocking the decanter, which tipped, splashing some liquid out, but did not fall.

'Absolute, have a care, that's the last of the Santa Vittoria,' Burgoyne exclaimed.

'Sorry, sir.' Jack reached out, his hand grasping the fine lead crystal vessel. A trickle of the golden liquid ran across the table, reminding him suddenly of that last supper on board the *Ariadne*, the river of port running between the glasses that signified this campaign, the blood-like flow of it, as Von Schlaben entered the room. His fingers ran over the decanter. It had a short, narrow neck, expanding, in an almost feminine way at the 'bosom', narrowing at waist, before spreading wide to the 'hips' of the flat base. Running his fingers down its curves stirred something in his mind.

The sherry was, of course, from the land where Burgoyne and he had first fought together in 1762. That Spanish campaign had made the General's reputation as strategist and commenced Jack's as lunatic when he was at the forefront in the storming of the citadel at Valencia de Alcantara. And he had seen his first masks in that country, for the Spanish were very attached to that method of encoding. When they'd captured the enemy staff in the surprise assault, several masks had been found on them. Burgoyne, already noting his young officer's intelligence as well as his courage, had ordered Jack to make a study of these devices. The first thing he realized was that most were derived from their Spanish enemies' greatest love – their native wines.

He traced the contours of the decanter again, then said, 'Has anyone here a reasonably clean handkerchief? And have you a pair of scissors, Captain Money?'

Several handkerchiefs were produced, in various degrees of cleanliness. Jack chose three of the least noxious and, with the scissors he was given, cut shapes from each to a different size but in the quite feminine lines of the crystal vessel before him. He then moved the smallest one up and down, read nothing. The second also produced no legible result. He was about to give up on the third when suddenly he saw something. It was in the sixth line, the misplaced apostrophe, the oddity of the words in the sixth line, 'fort'sell 'em'. Especially odd as they were beneath the word 'Hudson's'. He angled the mask to forty-five degrees . . . and smiled.

Burgoyne had never left studying him. A hand reached up to him, dropped back. 'You have it?'

'I . . . think so, sir. The mask is imperfect so you may not get it all but . . . perhaps enough.' Jack picked up a pencil and traced the shape of the mask around the isolated words. He then studied it again to make sure he'd got all he could.

Dear Coz.

Have you lately seen that cur **Will** Piper? He owe me
5 pounds and so his vile **attempt** to avoid me is contimtible.
I mean therefore **to push ahead** with your order, for because
I riecievd **on Hudson's** looms a delivery of fine cloth. Shall make coats
then go **fort's**ell 'em. Give kind'st to my financee, Marge. I see her
in two or three weeks but it will seem no more nor less than three
thousand.

    Yr. Affectionate Coz.

    T. Rhodes

'Colonel Carleton!' Burgoyne gestured down to the slashed
handkerchief and letter; his adjutant carefully reached over
and began to transcribe into a notebook. The General
squeezed Jack's arm. 'I lied, dear Jack. I do have one more
bottle of the Santa Vittoria. And it's yours.'

'May I suggest that we all drink it together, General?'

A cheer went up at that, the sherry was broached, decanted
into the revealing crystal, poured out. Carleton meanwhile
scratched with his pencil while men sipped and never took
their eyes from him. Fraser came and clapped Jack on the back
while Balcarras, ever the Old Harrovian, whispered, 'Not bad
for a Westminster boy. I thought all you learned there was
billiards and buggery.'

Jack picked up one of the fair copies of the letter. 'I'll take one,
Captain Money, if I may. There might be something further.'

A much-relieved young officer was happy to agree.

The men watched the adjutant. Carleton scratched at his
temples. 'Well?' barked the General.

Carleton showed the extract to Burgoyne, who closed his
eyes for a moment and smiled. He then nodded to Carleton
who read aloud, ' "Will attempt to push ahead on Hudson's
forts in two or three weeks." '

The company sighed out as one.

'So Clinton assaults the Highland forts of the Hudson
in two or three weeks. Could the man not have been more
specific?' Burgoyne raised his eyes to the roof. 'Still, since

the letter has taken six days to arrive, the attack, gentlemen, is imminent. A week or two at most.'

Burgoyne looked around at each of his officers to make sure they understood the import of those words.

'And it is inconceivable that even if General Howe continues his operations further south, he would not have left Clinton significant numbers in New York to both take the forts then march on to us here.' Burgoyne was once again leaning on the table. But whereas before his attitude had been one of exhaustion, now his stance betokened vigour. 'We can anticipate a force at least seven thousand strong. That Rebel facing us, General Gates, will have to split his forces here to deal with the threat . . . or retire entirely. Either way, gentlemen, retreat for us is no longer a consideration, for Gates could then turn his full might on Clinton. We must hold the Rebel here, pin him down. When Clinton breaks through, or Gates turns to face him, we will catch the Yankee between us and crush him.'

'Does that mean the attack for tomorrow is off?' General Fraser asked.

Burgoyne smiled. 'It does, Simon. The men may stand down and rest. Issue an extra tot of rum and give three cheers for the King. We will convene in the morning to discuss fortifying our position. Yet I fear our Sergeant Willis, who has proved himself so fine a deliverer of good news, must haste again to New York at dawn to inform General Clinton that we are most happy with his plans and to find out a more definite date for his arrival here. So get some rest now, man. You'll need it.'

The Sergeant took the news well, considering his obvious exhaustion. He saluted and left the room, the others taking this as a signal to disperse. Burgoyne's voice halted Jack at the door.

'Captain Absolute, a word if I may?'

Balcarras whispered, 'I've a fine Bordeaux saved. Join me later.' With a quick squeeze of Jack's arm he was gone. The General and he were alone.

On the very click of the door, Burgoyne sat down heavily, his head coming to rest on the palms of both hands. 'Not so young as I was, Jack.'

'We none of us are, sir.'

'And perhaps I was a little hard on that boy, Money.'

'It appears to have been a hard day for all.'

'Indeed it has.' Burgoyne knuckled his eyes, then raised them to regard Jack. 'A nasty discolouration of your neck, my boy.'

'You should have seen it three weeks ago, when the snake had just struck.'

'Ah, so the Count's story was true?'

'Only to a point, General. I'm sure it left out some essential points. Such as how it was Von Schlaben who introduced me to the snake. Or vice versa.'

'He did indeed fail to mention that.' Burgoyne smiled. 'Damn, Jack! I can always rely on you for an interesting tale. Would you care to tell it while we dine?'

'I would. But first I have to know – is the Count still here?'

'He is not, I'm afraid. You missed him by hours.'

Jack leaned back. He suddenly felt very tired, as if the thought of an imminent revenge had been the only thing that had kept him awake. Meanwhile, the General's servant, Braithwaite, had entered with a bowl, placing it on the table. Burgoyne bent over it with distaste.

'I'm rather afraid that when I was forced to cut the rations for the army I let it be known that I would only eat the same as the common soldier. Pure bravado.' He looked up, smiled. 'I did not, however, mention what I would be drinking. To celebrate . . . the Chateau Veracin, I think, Braithwaite. And a bowl – this purports to be stew, does it? – for the Captain.' As his servant went off to obey, Burgoyne turned back to Jack. 'Your report, sir, if you will.'

They ate and drank, the wine exceptional, though he would have expected no less from Burgoyne's cellar, while Jack recounted all that had happened in the months since they'd last seen one another. The General had received St Leger's self-excusing reports though not the letter Jack had entrusted to

Captain Ancrum; withheld, no doubt, by the drunken Colonel, fearful of Jack's truer version of the events at Fort Stanwix. Throughout the tale, Burgoyne swore and chewed, drank and whistled, as good an audience as he was a dramatist.

'You say the Indians deserted in droves?' he interjected. 'It is the same with my campaign. I have scarcely ninety of the brutes left and I awake every morning expecting to see those gone. Even that Brant fellow, who at least came back from Stanwix, has disappeared again.'

He topped up Jack's glass, then continued. 'Which reminds me, your friend Até was with Brant. I think he would have stayed but as soon as he was informed that you were not here, he took himself off again. Wish I could have kept him. Apart from his fighting skills, the fellow has the damndest ideas on Shakespeare I ever heard. I believe he considers Hamlet to be part Mohawk!'

Jack sipped and cursed. 'We were meant to rendezvous. Von Schlaben's assault and my capture meant I failed to appear. Até has gone to look for me as I would for him.' He swirled his wine, considering. 'And you say the German only just departed?' He received a nod. 'That is a great pity, for I believe – and I feel, sir, after what I have just told you of the debacle at Fort Stanwix that you must believe it too – that not only is the Count Von Schlaben Diomedes, he is also now one of the most dangerous opponents we have.'

Burgoyne too swirled the wine in his crystal, observing the play of red against the lamplight. 'I do agree, Jack. And I must apologize. I promised to keep him close. I did not know for a week that he was missing, for I was . . . somewhat distracted. And then Von Riedesel told me he'd gone – hunting, would you believe? I did not think that you were part of the quarry he sought. That sot St Leger never mentioned his arrival or influence. I probably should have had him seized the moment he returned here. But there was a battle to fight and I was set to rely on the skills of his cousin, the Baron von Riedesel.'

'Do you believe, sir, that the Baron knows of his cousin's activities?'

'Von Riedesel? Countenance treachery?' Burgoyne shook his head emphatically. 'Impossible. I sometimes believe the Baron seeks to win this war single-handed, so ardent is he in our cause. Indeed, if he had not marched his men in at double time and turned the Rebel flank . . . well, we might even have lost this day. Not the actions of a traitor.' He reached out a hand, laid it on Jack's shoulder. 'No, my lad, I alone am to blame for Von Schlaben's attempt on you. Apologies, again.'

'Forgiven, sir. I believe you had enough to think on.' He glanced to the world outside.

Burgoyne sighed. 'Hot work today, Jack, as hot as you and I saw at Valencia de Alcantara. These Rebels have learned to fight, curse 'em. We held the field but . . .' He passed a hand over his eyes. 'As to the damned Count, he only arrived here on the eve of the battle. When the business today was concluded, I immediately sent my first messenger for New York and Clinton. Von Schlaben, bearing personal dispatches from the Baron von Riedesel, set out shortly afterwards.'

'He followed your messenger?' A confirming nod. 'Then I doubt your dispatch will make it through.'

'He will kill my messenger?'

'He will try. You must send another.'

'Sergeant Willis goes at dawn. But I always send at least three because it's possible, nay, likely, that two will be caught. There are spies everywhere. I sometimes believe that Gates knows my movements before I've issued the orders.'

'Speaking of which, that mask you were so in want of? Lost, you said, but stolen perhaps?'

'Stolen, for certain. And it was discovered missing before Von Schlaben arrived back.'

Jack nodded. 'So we do have another spy amongst us. The Count may not be Diomedes after all. Perhaps he is, in fact, Cato, the other name in the coded message from Quebec.'

'He may well be.' Burgoyne drained his glass and regarded Jack for a long moment over the rim. 'You look tired, my lad. Positively gaunt. I am loathe to ask—'

'Yours to command, General, as always.'

Burgoyne nodded. 'Then . . . care to be my third messenger?'

'Do you not need me here?'

'I always delight in your company, dear Jack. But I do not need you to help me build redoubts and dig entrenchments. I need you to persuade Clinton that he must not dally at the forts on the Hudson but come on with all dispatch. For if he does not . . .' Burgoyne stared above the younger man's head. 'Then we are finished.' He leaned across the table. 'That, I'm sure you realize, is for your ears only. Yours and Clinton's. He must come or . . .' he looked up at Jack and the younger man again noted in the elder's eyes that hitherto unseen desperation, '. . . or he must order my retreat. He is still my senior officer. He is aware of what General Howe is about if I am not. If he ordered me to retire in good order to Canada, to conserve my army to fight again then I would do so. I would, by God!'

Burgoyne's eyelids, which had begun to flutter, closed. As if summoned to the stage Braithewaite appeared, carrying what looked like a bundle of polished wood in his arms. 'Shall I, sir?' the servant said.

Burgoyne nodded. 'I'm afraid I must sleep, Jack. I'll dictate the letters to Clinton for you and Willis and sign them on the morrow. Not so young as I was . . .'

He got up and moved across to where his servant had transformed the sticks into an ingenious folding bed. A mattress appeared from behind a screen – there was always a screen with Burgoyne though Jack was relieved, for the General's sake, to see that this one concealed no mistress. Burgoyne swayed above the bed, as his servant decanted blankets and pillows from a chest.

Jack crossed to stand beside him. 'Three final things, sir.'

'Hmm?'

I will report to Captain Money all I have learned of the Rebels during my stay with Benedict Arnold.'

'Yes,' Burgoyne yawned, 'do that, please.'

'Até.'

'If he returns, I shall hold him here for you.'

'Thank you. And finally – the Count von Schlaben.'

The exhaustion left the General's eyes. 'There is no further point in keeping "mine enemy close." He must not be allowed to cause any further harm to us, nor threaten you. Kill him.'

'It will be my especial pleasure to obey that order, sir.'

The General was snoring by the time the sentry had swung open the door. Jack felt nearly as exhausted himself. Survival had taken precedence over sleep in the previous weeks. He would take up Pellew's offer of a pillow. However, he had one call still to make.

He found her at the flap of her tent, watching. As he approached, Colonel Reardon rose from his cot behind her.

'Jack.' She raised a hand to him, then, aware of her father, let it fall back.

'Have you come for that Madeira, Captain?' Colonel Reardon said as he reached the entrance.

'I fear I should be asleep before the glass was poured, thanks kindly just the same. I merely came to bid you and your daughter a good night.'

'On the morrow, then?' Louisa smiled.

'Perhaps, if there is time. I am away again.'

'When? Where?'

'Noon. I leave for,' he hesitated 'a small mission of the General's devising. Nothing dangerous, I assure you.'

'Do you think me a child, sir to be pacified with little lies?' The instant transformation of her face was again remarkable, the spirit he'd noticed sometimes when they 'jousted' on board fully and immediately in evidence, flushing crimson to her cheeks. ' "Not dangerous?" You go to New York as one of the messengers, I am certain. There is not a more dangerous job in the army.'

Jack stepped closer. In low tone, he said, 'If that were true, Miss Reardon, you would do such a mission no good by declaring it so loudly.'

She had the decency to look a trifle abashed. Yet in a tone that matched his, she continued, 'I must go with you.'

Jack, not for the first time in her presence, was astounded. His reaction was, as hers had been, monosyllabic. 'How? Why?'

'I have been awaiting just such an opportunity, haven't I, Father?' She turned to rest a hand on the old gentleman's arm. 'We received a letter from New York. Sickness has broken out there and my mother has been taken by it. She is gravely ill, and almost unattended. I begged the General to let me go to her but he would not allow it. He could not spare sufficient troops to ward me and would not let me travel alone.'

'I should think not. And even if I was going there, you would not be much safer with me. The woods abound with desperate men, of both allegiances and neither. Alone, I have a chance of getting through but . . .'

The obstinacy never left her face. He turned to the Colonel. 'Sir, I appeal to you. I must travel at speed and will live in the roughest of conditions. It will not be the place for a—'

'A lady? Do you think I was spawned in silks raised in lace? Before my father made his fortune, before he ever commanded a regiment in the field, we were ten years on the frontiers. I was formed in the very forests you will travel through.'

'It is true, Captain, she was.'

'But the speed at which I must move—'

'And I was born astride a horse. I have my own, my beautiful Caspiana right here. It is you, sir, who will be chewing my trail mud.'

The older man said, warningly, 'Louisa—'

Jack felt he was drowning. 'Sir, I entreat you—'

But Colonel Reardon gave him no succour. 'Captain Absolute, I confess I fear to let my daughter go. But I fear even more to leave my wife friendless and alone in New York. She is, according to the letter my daughter received, very ill. Deathly, I might say.' His voice caught at the word. 'And the Lord, in whom we must place all trust . . .' He paused and looked at his daughter. 'Well, at times, even the Lord needs a little help.'

In the twin appeal of their eyes, in his fatigue, Jack faltered.

'Well, sir, I suppose if you can get the General's permission—'

'Done!' said Louisa, as if she had just concluded a purchase. 'Shall we go now, child?'

Louisa took a step forward then halted. 'No, Father. The General will be sleeping and will not be apt for our appeal if disturbed. Besides . . .' and here a smile displaced the obstinacy, 'I have been saving a dress for just such an occasion. Nancy! Nancy!' She took a step toward the next tent from which there came a distinct groan. Over her shoulder she called, 'Noon then, Captain. At the farrier's.'

The words he would speak were lost to her retreating back.

'Since she was three years old I have been able to deny her precisely . . . nothing.' Reardon turned to a still-speechless Jack. Hesitantly, in a lowered voice, he continued, 'One thing remains. A boon I must ask of you. My daughter is . . . fond of you, Captain Absolute. By her talk, fonder than she has ever been of any man. She was heartbroken when she thought you gone. You would not . . . not take advantage of her . . . regard, would you?' Off Jack's puzzled stare, he added. 'As her father, I ask for your word as a gentleman.'

It was a consideration he had not yet had the leisure to dwell upon. Louisa and he, alone in the woods. No cramped sea quarters, close neighbours and resonant wooden walls, just the trees and the stars and themselves. It was the stuff of more than a few of his most pleasant dreams.

Yet . . . here was another man asking if he was a gentleman. The Count von Schlaben had discovered that he was not, not entirely. Indeed, he felt that if he had ever deserved that title, it had not been for many years; not in India nor the Caribbean, nor when living as a Mohawk. But now he had again assumed the role, if not the uniform, of a Captain in the 16th Dragoons, he supposed he once more also assumed certain obligations. Gentlemanly ones.

Sighing, he said, 'You have my word, sir.'

The older man smiled. 'Thank you.' He paused, then added, 'You have, of course, my permission to pay your addresses to my daughter once the Rebel is beaten and we are safe again in

Boston. We shall look forward to receiving you, sir. Good-night.'

With that, he turned into his tent and the flap dropped behind him.

Jack stared stupidly at it for fully half a minute. 'Addresses,' he muttered, at last, turning away. 'The only thing I intend to address just now is Edward Pillow's Pellow.'

— TWELVE —
Cowboys and Skinners

Mist shrouded the farrier's camp, rendering horses and men insubstantial, solidifying only at three paces. The swirls had not lessened since before dawn; Jack knew, for he had been awake since an hour before it, despite the distracting comfort of Pellew's pillow. There had been too many things to do before departure, items to gather, a man to talk to.

That man, Sergeant Willis, had made the journey to New York and back already. His information would be vital. And when Jack had approached him in that darkest hour of the night, though at first he seemed the epitome of a taciturn Dorsetman, barely grunting in response to comments on the weather and questions as to his sleep, he became positively voluble on the subject of the road ahead.

'Trust to yourself, Cap'n, and no other.' He was pulling at a loose thread on the front of his dark green coat. Like Jack, in his freshly-issued clothes, the Sergeant was dressed as a civilian. 'The country abounds with gangs, and though the Cowboys are meant to be Loyalist and the Skinners side with the Rebel, there's nowt to tell the two apart. They'll turn coats on a whim, 'specially if they scent gold. So carry coin in different pockets, use it if ye must, and allus keep your pistols primed. Best stay clear altogether, lookee, carry or find your own food and make camp in the woods. Do you know the country at all, sir?'

Jack nodded. Though he and Até had usually trapped and

warred and hunted further north, there'd been times when they'd followed these trails.

'You'll want to ride the lower slopes of the Catskills. Closer you gets to the Hudson the more Rebels you'll meet. Circle high and skirt the villages of Altamont, down through Schoharie, Greenville, Cairo, Kingston . . .' He took a stick and scratched shapes in the mud. Then he rubbed his boot across them and continued. 'If General Clinton has begun his attack, ye might catch up with him near his targets, the Highland forts. If he hasn't . . . try to get across the Hudson to Tarrytown. There's a ferry on the west bank. Ride down the eastern shore. Then you'll have to steal a boat and row across to the city of New York.'

A farrier brought Willis's horse to him. As he checked the girth, Jack asked, 'Do you know how many men Clinton will attack with?'

For the first time Jack saw something stir within the man's guarded gaze. 'I know that's General Burgoyne's most important question. But I am just a sergeant. I am trusted with letters only and no information that might spill out of my head.' Satisfied with his horse, he turned and saluted, adding, 'Good luck to ye, sir.'

Jack reached out his hand. After a moment's hesitation, the man took it. 'And good luck to you, Sergeant Willis. Perhaps we'll meet again in New York.'

The man mounted before he spoke again. 'Ye never know. Though if two of us were to make it through, it'd be something akin to a miracle. Yah!' Spurring his horse, he parted the mists and was gone.

That had been six hours before. The time since Jack had spent gathering supplies. Scrounging objects tradable from his friends he'd gone to the Indian camp and bargained hard for cornmeal, maple sugar, and some rolls of birch bark. When he'd returned to the stables, the Earl of Balcarras was awaiting him there and had given him two fine pistols with Lazarino barrels and horse holsters to hold them. And then he'd presented Jack with the horse to mount them on.

'His name's Doughty and he never falters.' He'd patted the shoulder of the great bay gelding, full sixteen hands of him, who'd curled his neck around to nuzzle at the Earl's hands. 'He'll carry one across three counties to run down a fox. So he'll carry you with ease to the island of Manhattan.'

'And back again, Sandy. I'll return him to you. I cannot thank you enough.'

The Earl had smiled sadly, wished him godspeed, and left. Captain Money was the next visitor, bearing Burgoyne's dispatch, concealed in a secret chamber within a water canteen. He also noted down all that Jack could remember of Benedict Arnold and his men. Money had then, in his dual role of Assistant Quartermaster, issued Jack with a fusil – one of the light and precious .65 calibres; Burgoyne had obviously given orders that Jack was to be well armed – and a hunk of equally precious bacon, as well as oats, this latter making up the bulk of his possessions. He could always find food for himself in the forest, but not necessarily fodder for the animals. He finally handed over a variety of coins, gold and silver, for purchases and bribes as the occasion arose.

The horse was saddled and the fustian haversacks slung by a quarter of noon. He paced as he waited, Doughty seeming as anxious to depart as he, hoofing the earth before him.

'Straight up midday is what I said,' Jack muttered, trying to broach the mists in the direction of the main camp. Then he wondered if, perhaps, the General had somehow managed to resist Louisa's assault and refuse her. He wasn't sure if it was disappointment or hope he felt at the thought.

Yet her horse, a pretty, blue-black filly, was already accoutred with a lady's side-saddle; straps hung ready to receive what she would need to carry. Turning back to it, Jack suddenly noticed a figure now stood at its head, fingers running down the filly's white blaze.

'A fine morning for our purposes, Captain Absolute,' Louisa Reardon said.

He had not heard her approach, which surprised him since she was dressed in a dark riding dress, full purple skirts swathing her legs, which rustled now as she moved to him. Her thick red-gold hair had been tamed into a bun and in her right hand she clasped an ivory-handled riding crop.

'You look as though you are riding to hounds, madam.' Jack could not keep the irritation from his voice, made up of disquiet at seeing her and an attempt to hide his delight.

'Oh tush!' she said, striking his shoulder lightly with the crop.

'So it seems you obtained Burgoyne's permission.'

'Indeed! It was not hard. The General always yields to reasoned argument.'

Jack looked at her and wondered if the General had been persuaded by more than words. He had been away a while; and Louisa was damnably attractive.

To cover the flush these thoughts brought to his face, he reached for the bag at her side. 'Since you are under my command, madam, I must see what it is you consider so important that you will burden our horses with such baggage.'

Indeed, her bag was not huge. And she did not release it to him.

'You would not seek to look within a lady's purse, sir? It is not very gallant.'

Jack said nothing, just kept pulling on the haversack. Reluctant to the last, she let it go.

'I have, or will find food for us both, madam, so you will not need this.' He removed the bag of bread, though the warmth and scent of it made him hungry. Handing it to the grateful farrier who stood by, he delved deeper. There was only a few spare clothes, a canteen of water – again unnecessary but he let it pass – and . . .

'What's this?' He pulled out a book with a soft, green linen cover. 'We'll have no time to read by day and no light to do so at night.'

Louisa regarded the book, biting her lip. 'It is not for reading, sir, but for writing in. My diary. I have pen and ink too.'

She did. He heard them clink when he shook the bag. 'The

same goes for writing as reading. You must send this back to your maid.'

'Please, Jack. It is a small luxury, surely. I cannot go a day without writing. I would rather give up some clothes. Here . . .'

She reached towards the bag then, made to reach inside. Perhaps it was because the appeal was made so genuinely that Jack relented.

He released the bag to her, handed her the diary. 'Keep it, Louisa,' he said. 'Let the man tie this to your horse and we'll be gone.'

The farrier attached the bag. They mounted, Louisa swiftly arranging her skirts around the side-saddle, her knee crooked around the horn, her feet in the single stirrup. Doughty jerked his head up and down in impatience while she did this. Jack brought the reins up tight, exerting his will.

'Away!' he said, and the two horses cantered into the still-thick fog. They headed down a path to the right, to the west. They would have to swoop wide to by-pass the American position on Bemis Heights and the out-flung Rebel patrols.

At last, thought Jack, thrilled with the off, with the shrouding fog, with Doughty, so vastly different from the sorry roan Benedict Arnold had lent him. The thought of that American oddity suddenly made Jack chuckle; somewhere, not very far away, Arnold was no doubt raging to all who could bear to listen about the ungrateful oath-breaker, 'Lord John Absolute'. The chuckle became a laugh as he thought to the road ahead. A dangerous one, to be sure, but the woods were his world, especially when he was this well armed and prepared. He had a mission of import, this magnificent animal under him, and, despite some misgivings at her presence, a beautiful companion beside him. It was a joy to be alive.

That joy lasted three hundred yards, till Louisa suddenly reined in. Jack did the same, circled back.

'Your girth, madam?' he said, the impatience ill-concealed.

'Shh!' was her only reply. She was squinting into the swirls to her left. 'I'm sure this was the tree. Nancy! Nancy!' she hissed.

There was a sudden stirring there that had Jack reaching for a pistol, though he knew they were still well within the British lines. Then Louisa's maid appeared. In her hands was a sack.

'What's this?' Jack demanded. 'Really, Louisa, there will be no more baggage.'

She ignored him, dismounted, then looked up. 'Pray, hold my horse for a moment, will you?'

Jack took the proffered reins and Louisa immediately became busy with straps and cinches. In a few moments her side-saddle was on the ground and she was reaching into the sack Nancy held.

'Now,' said Louisa and, with a flourish worthy of a stage conjuror, produced another saddle. A gentleman's.

'What the . . .' Jack was stunned, could only watch as the woman before him attached the new saddle as expertly as she'd removed the old. But this surprise was as nothing to his next shock. For Louisa now grabbed at her waist and swiftly undid the strings that held her dress there. Stepping out of the folds of purple cloth, she stood before him – in breeches!

He was wordless, as she took back the reins and straddled her horse, wordless still, as Nancy wrapped the side saddle in the purple skirt and tied the whole to the last three dangling straps.

'Now, sir,' Louisa said, 'why do you dally? Shall we ride?'

He watched her spur ahead of him into the mist. Wordlessly, he followed.

They rode hard most of the day, their horses seemingly tireless, though Jack took good care to walk them frequently and rest them when necessary. They followed an insubstantial trail that soon widened to parallel a small river, the Schoharie. Dusk found them on the edge of the forest just above the settlement of the same name, a dozen log cabins set among well-tended fields of ripe corn. Lamps were just being placed in windows, farmers returning from their work, beckoned by their light.

'It looks cosy,' Louisa said from beside him. 'Shall we seek hospitality?'

'I think not,' replied Jack. 'They may be Cowboys or Skinners or neither, but strangers rarely receive welcome this close to a war.'

He turned back beneath the trees, leading his horse. He'd noticed the tiniest of paths down a little stream. A five-minute walk and they came to an uprooted beech. A fire could be lit in its lee and never be seen.

While Louisa hobbled and nose-bagged their mounts, Jack cut the smaller, springier boughs from the felled beech and soon had them lashed together with withies into a frame. The birch-bark rolls he'd bargained for with the Indians were threaded through them and then this half-moon shelter was pegged down.

'Even cosier than a cabin, I'd say.' Louisa watched, as Jack slashed some sprays from a pine. 'Where are you going to sleep?'

Jack snorted and threw the pine on to the floor of the shelter, then gestured to the forest. 'Can you gather some firewood?'

She was back soon, with a good mix of tinder and smaller logs. From one, he pulled off a small strip of bark, rolled it into a cone, then stuffed it with dry leaves. From his pocket he produced something he'd spotted when they'd walked their horses earlier.

'A mushroom?' Louisa was watching him closely. 'Is it supper?'

'The Amada's not for eating.' He pulled out the inner layer of the mushroom, shoved it into the cone. 'Hold this.'

While she did, he pulled out his strike-light. A few hits of a rifle flint against its metal and sparks fell into the centre of the cone. The mushroom skin began to smoulder.

'Now, blow,' he said. 'No, gently, gently, that's the way. Now a little harder.'

She looked up at him, her lips forming a half-smile. Then she pushed them out toward the glowing cone and blew with more force. Suddenly, the leaves ignited and he took the cone from her, shoving it into the tinder of the fire. Kneeling, he piled more dry leaves around, and as the flames grew, he pushed in first smaller sticks, then larger. Soon the fire was crackling nicely.

'If you will be so kind as to fill our canteens from the stream, Miss Reardon, then tend the fire, I will set about catching us our supper.'

He found the ideal place two hundred paces from their camp. The stream widened a little, while its bed flattened, a little pool that, once he'd stripped off his breeches and stockings, only reached to just above his knee, a few inches below his shirt tails. The water was deliciously cool, refreshing on a mid-September day that had turned hot again once they'd escaped the fog. If he had been alone in the forest he would certainly have stripped off completely and dived in. But he was there, anyway, for another purpose. Forearms resting lightly on his lower thighs, he let his fingers sink into the water.

He had positioned himself so that his shadow fell behind him. The ripples of his entry, the slight stirring of silt, all had settled again. The pool was almost as it was. His breathing slackened. Only his eyes moved, following the brown shapes that flitted from pebble to tumbled branch across the stream bed. A trout banged against his ankle. Too small. It moved away; one of its larger brothers came near. Nearer. He struck. Tossing the fish on to the bank, Jack grinned and crouched again.

Later, he heard her coming but he did not move to the sound. He had been stalking the biggest of the fish, or rather willing it close. He had gone for it once and the beast, belying its size, had squirted agily away from his questing fingers. Enough time had passed, its fish brain had forgotten him, it was coming closer, ever closer . . .

'Well, now. That is quite the sight.'

Jack shot his hands in, a tail fin brushed his hand with silk and was gone.

'Zounds! You made me miss it, woman!'

He straightened, stretched, easing his now-cramped back. Louisa laughed. 'Have you not caught enough?'

She pointed to the six trout that lay on a moss-covered rock, all longer than Jack's hand. They had fat backs, brown and speckled, creamy bellies.

'Aye,' replied Jack, 'but what are you going to eat?'

She laughed again, a sound as good to his ears as any in that twilit forest. He waded to her, climbed out. 'You are a fine fisherman, sir.'

'You are kind. Yet I am but a novice. Would you care to see the master?'

On her nod, he beckoned silence, took her hand and led her a few feet forward, parting the leaves of an overhanging willow. They peered through. 'Now there's a fisherman,' he said softly.

The heron was perhaps fifty yards further down the stream, stiller than Jack could ever have been, more perfectly hidden, blue and grey feathers blending it into its world. As they watched the pencil neck straightened, craning out over the water.

'Does it know we are here?' Louisa whispered.

'It knows. That circle vision takes in everything. But we've been fishing side by side for an hour now. It doesn't mind me.'

Suddenly, the bird's head shot down. Scalpel beak sliced the surface, a glitter was impaled, there was a flickering of sunlight on silver, a bulge in the thin neck. Then all was still again.

'Perfect.' Jack let the leaves fall back. 'Mind you, they are ungainly flyers. And their call is a harsh croak.'

'And they have spindly legs. Unlike yours.'

She glanced at them, wet to the thighs, damp shirt-tails hanging halfway down. He smiled and she smiled back and for a moment all was still in the forest. Then he turned away to his clothes, and said, 'Come, Louisa. Let's have our supper.'

Full night was upon them when they finally lay back in their birch-bark shelter, sated.

'Well,' Louisa sighed, 'among all your obvious talents, I never would have guessed you a master of cuisine.'

Jack leaned forward to shove another log on to the fire — and to conceal his pleasure at her words.

'Camp fare only. Simple stuff.'

'The best I've eaten in many a week. The campaign's been hard on the commissary.' She reached to grab a last few crumbs from the wooden cooking plank. 'What did you call these?'

'Johnny cakes. Just cornmeal, maple sugar . . . and I was lucky to find those sweet chestnuts.'

'Chestnuts. Yes! So,' she sat up and looked at him with that peculiarly secretive smile, 'Jack Absolute. Soldier. Mohawk. Duellist. Dramatist. Chef! One feels quite outshone. What other talents have you yet to reveal?' Her tone was teasing.

Jack cleared his throat. 'A talent for trouble, perhaps. Recently I reflected on the number of people who have tried to kill me lately, the variety of their methods.' He poked at the fire with a stick, watched little blazing empires collapse, others arise.

'Maybe that is because you are too free with your opinions. Many are provoked by beliefs firmly expressed.'

'I don't know what you mean.' Jack threw himself back on an elbow. 'I was coerced into this war, as you well know. I only sought to get on with my business. I am the mildest of men. I seek to provoke no one.'

Louisa hooted so loudly at this that Jack, after glowering for a moment, was forced to join in.

'You? I remember that conversation our last night aboard the *Ariadne*. You were passionate in your defence of the Rebel colonists.'

'Was I? I do not remember being passionate about anything but your eyes.'

'Fie, Jack. I am serious. Curious.' She had sat forward, intent now. 'Curious as to why an officer so close to, so fond of General Burgoyne, would hold such dangerous sentiments?'

'I am an officer, it is true, albeit a somewhat reluctant one. And indeed I care for the General, personally and professionally. But . . .' He hesitated then went on. 'I am also the son of a rebel.'

'Your father?'

'Sir James?' He chuckled. 'I think . . . not. No, my mother. She was Irish and fierce, especially in her avocation of that country's freedom. So there's a curse of blood, if you will.'

'Intriguing,' Louisa had risen to her knees, the better to look at him. 'A war within a war. So the rebel in you would see the Colonists free of their allegiance to the Crown?'

Jack thought for a moment. 'In the end, I would not. Like many so-called Rebels, I would see them gain their liberty yet stay loyal to the Crown. They are English too, after all.'

'And Irish, Scots, German, Dutch – these have no loyalty to England, surely?'

'It is England that has opened this land to them; England that has near ruined itself in war after war to protect them from French tyranny. Do they not owe a debt for that? I say let them have their representation, along with every Englishman's birthright of liberty . . . then tax them accordingly!'

'Ah, there's the passion I was hoping to see again!' Her eyes sparkled. 'I agree with you, Jack. Many do not. What of them?'

'Beat 'em. For such men – I do not speak of the majority, perhaps, but a minority with strength – would seize too much power and use it to tyrannize others. They have proved that already.'

Louisa leaned forward still further. 'You speak of slavery? I am at one with you there, as well. I, too, find it abhorrent.'

'I do not speak only of that. But, aye, it is a monstrous thing. There are no slaves in the British Isles now. And yet, near half the signatories of the Declaration of Independence are slave-owners and would retain that detested institution if they triumph. Maybe it's my mother talking, but if revolution must come, let it be against *all* tyranny and for *everyone's* freedom.'

'Bold words from a man whose England brought all those slaves to us, whose traders continue to make vast profit in doing so. You may have banned them from your own shores but you still drop them by their thousands on the shores of others.' There was now a passion in her voice to match his. 'Are you not concerned about that hypocrisy?'

He nodded. 'More than most, aye. Because . . .' He paused.

'Because?'

'Because,' he sighed, 'I am a slave-owner myself.'

Louisa shot up as if she had been stung. 'You?'

'Aye.' Jack nodded, picked up the stick again, poked at the fire. 'So you have another title for me. Recently acquired. Shameful.'

'Where?'

'Nevis, in the Antilles. I . . . gained, I suppose is the word, a plantation there in my last dealings in India. It was where I was bound from London when,' he waved the stick at the surrounding forest, 'all this interfered.' He threw the stick down, turned to her. 'You must believe me, Louisa, I was bound to Nevis from London to do my utmost to divest myself of the title slave-owner. It will be hard and there will be many who oppose me, on the island, elsewhere. But I intend to run my plantation with free men.'

She studied him, nodded at last. 'I do believe you. But you said there was something else that made you want the Rebels to fail?'

'Aye. Something a little more personal.' He turned again to stare into the flames. His voice, raised to convince her, dropped again. 'It is to do with my adopted people.'

'The Mohawk?'

'All the tribes, really, despite my enmity for some. But the Iroquois especially. I lived among them . . . loved among them. There is so much to admire in their world; yet the white man has changed them already, unutterably. I would protect what's left.'

'And you think the Rebels will not?'

'I know they will not.' Jack rose to his knees, too. He was in the flow, could have been back in a tavern in London in his youth, arguing his passions with Sheridan or any other ranter. 'The British North America Act in seventeen sixty-three gave the Indians rights – especially the right to their own land. Boundaries were negotiated, limits many Americans – and I include native-born English-Americans here – cannot tolerate. They see wealth in uncontrolled expansion. Or rather, expansion controlled by them. George Washington? Principal shareholder in the Vandalia Company. They seek to expropriate all the lands designated tribal. Not only such lands as my brothers still control but west beyond the Alleghenies, into Ohio, Michigan, Indiana, Wisconsin . . .' He shook his head. 'It is the untold story of this war and it is the story of every war ever fought. Greedy men seeing someone weaker with something they want.'

'I see.' Louisa was staring at him. 'I had not considered this.'

'Joseph Brant once called that act of sixty-three the Indian Magna Carta. And that is the very cornerstone of English liberty. That is worth fighting for.'

'Indeed. Indeed it is.' Louisa was now looking above his head, into the trees. After a moment, her gaze returned to him. 'Well, Jack Absolute! I am glad I have glimpsed, once more, your passion. I had wondered if it was only the result of Burgoyne's exceptional wines, the rich food, and five weeks of sea air. I am heartened to see it is not.'

She reached for him then; took the front of his shirt and pulled him toward her. He did not resist.

His arms went around her and their lips met. It was the kiss he had wanted since the moment of his return, the first since that one snatched as she departed the ship, the one of which he had long dreamed, that he hoped she had dreamed of too. A kiss to banish the memory of all others, so long did it continue. It had to end – an ending that could signal any number of beginnings.

'Oh my!' she said, half actress, half a woman starved of air. She was falling back, still holding his shirt. He had to resist falling on top of her and sacrificed a button to that cause.

'Louisa . . .'

'Jack?'

And then he told her of a conversation he'd had the night before.

'You promised my father . . . what?' Amazement was

swiftly displaced by a fury she struggled to contain. 'And he presumed to guess at my actions? That I would be . . . what? Unable to make up my own mind?'

'I'm sure, Louisa, he presumed no such thing. He was merely—'

'He did! As did you with your promise. Thought yourself so . . . irresistible that I would be left with no choice but to succumb!' She jerked her hand away from the one he reached out. 'And *I* presume you gave your word as a gentleman?'

He nodded, though it was more of a flinch.

'And *are* you one?'

'Sometimes,' he mumbled. 'On occasion.'

This passion, clearly, could no longer be dammed. She was up and moving fast into the forest, twigs snapping to mark her furious passage.

'Louisa,' he tried, knowing it was useless. He watched her out of sight. Then, cursing himself, her father, his own, the war, all gentlemen and anything else cussable that came to mind, he stamped about, making the camp and fire safe for the night. Its warmth was held in the half-moon shelter and when he wrapped the blankets around himself he was quite snug.

She returned, maybe half an hour later and a little more quietly than she'd left.

'I am sorry,' she said.

'No, I am.' He shrugged. 'You know it is not because I do not want—'

'I know.'

'And you also know this is a . . . conversation we will have again. When my word is not pledged. When we are out of this bloody forest.'

He threw open the blankets. After a moment's hesitation she lowered herself into the space before him, her back to him. He covered them both and lay back down. Their bodies touched at various points and suddenly, desperately, he tried to think of other things – Whigs, the cold seas of Cornwall, his mother, billiard cues . . . *no*! Racehorses, nails . . .

He felt her shuddering, thought that tears may have come.

Until she spoke, and he heard the laughter in her voice. 'So! We need to add three more titles to your name. Let me see. You are already a soldier, Mohawk, dramatist and duellist. We have also discovered you to be a chef. A . . . *gentleman*,' she coloured the word with incredulity, 'and . . .'

'And?'

'A fool. Yes, indeed, Jack Absolute, you are most certainly a fool.'

He squeezed her body a little tighter to him. 'This is one title I have long owned. You should hear Até on the subject.'

She laughed again, yawned, her breathing slowed. It seemed she was asleep almost on the instant.

The fool, however, was awake a good while longer.

Sometimes he could almost believe that the war did not exist; that he was only on another extended journey through the autumnal forests of New York, like so many he had taken in his life. Though instead of Até at his side, this time he had, in some distinct ways, a more agreeable companion, one who did not seek to draw him into endless arguments about Shakespeare, challenge him to run or shoot or skin faster – or complain about his cooking. Indeed, Louisa was all compliments in that area, even when the cornmeal and bacon ran out on the fifth day and he was forced to scavenge for burdock and cattail roots. These he roasted in the ashes beneath two squirrels he'd managed to kill with thrown knives; further south, he would not risk a shot.

Louisa seemed to share his joy in the life, and though she, like he, got grubbier as the days went by, it did not diminish her allure; rather the contrary. He'd watch her sometimes, brushing strands of hair away from her face as she broke up tinder, leaving trails of dirt or charcoal there, sticking out her tongue at him when she caught him staring. Their nights were no longer combative, both accepting the binding of Gentleman Jack's word. Laughter came as easily as sleep beneath the reddening leaves of maples, the yellowing of horse chestnuts and hornbeam.

But the war was still there, goading them as fast as they dared push their horses; his mission was still vital, her mother still ill. And the late afternoon of the seventh day found them risking what they'd so far avoided – contact.

'Do you see the ferry?'

'Aye. It's about halfway across. Time we were moving down.' Jack turned from peering through the leaves of a walnut. Louisa was behind him, just cinching the straps of the side-saddle on her filly, Caspiana. The man's saddle lay at her feet.

Jack looked at the purple dress she once again wore. 'So you are a lady after all,' he said.

'Did you ever doubt it, sir?' She swished the full pleats a little then bent to the saddle on the ground. 'This?'

'Leave it. Throw it under the tree there.' He raised a hand to stay her protest. 'I know, it is a waste. But if we are to carry out this deception, a gentleman's spare saddle, crafted for a lady, will not help it.'

She nodded, reluctantly heaved the saddle into the undergrowth, then came and stood beside him. 'Well, husband?'

'Well, wife. Shall we attempt to catch the Tarrytown ferry?'

They were both silent, in their own thoughts and fears, as they directed their horses down the steep hillside that overlooked the dock. Jack, though his view of the settlement was partial, had been able to watch both the ferry's approach and the small group of would-be passengers awaiting transport. He had not seen any uniforms among them. But most who called themselves either Loyalist Cowboys or Patriot Skinners wore none. This enabled them to decide which way they should turn their coats, depending on how much money they could make from either side. Yet whether friends, enemies, or neutrals awaited them below, this was the ferry Sergeant Willis had recommended across to the Hudson's eastern shore. If they were to progress any further and eventually reach the city of New York, they had no real choice but to cross on it.

They rode along a well-made fence, joined the road at the end of the line of houses. A group of children, the eldest no more than five, chased each other in and out of one barn. In another, a man had just finished milking one cow and was now moving his pail to another. A woman opened a door to throw some scraps out into a pen of chickens. As they squawked and pecked around her feet, she raised a hand to her eyes and watched them riding past, lifting it in lazy greeting before moving slowly back inside.

'Where's the war to these people?' Louisa murmured.

'Not far,' said Jack tightly. He had looked ahead, seen three men detach themselves from the group on the dock. The last of the evening sun glinted on the pistols in their belts.

When their hooves echoed on the wooden platform, the largest of the men, barrel-bellied and heavily bearded, stepped forward.

'Greetin's to you folk,' he said, smiling and catching at Caspiana's bridle. The horse jerked it away and he let it go, transferring his hand to pat at the filly's neck.

'And to you, friend.' Jack moved Doughty closer to Louisa, let one hand drop with the reins, leaving the other free. He had removed the holsters from the saddle. They were now strapped around his chest, concealed under his coat.

'N-n-n-nice horseflesh, Amos.' One of the other men, the younger of the two, had moved around to gaze up at Doughty. He had an air of Hans-Yost about him, a simplicity in his stare. He kept taking off a much-holed hat and putting it straight back on again. But it was the third man who concerned Jack the most. He stayed his distance, rested his hands on the weapons in his belt, and stared at Jack silently.

'Mighty nice,' the first man said. 'You must be gennelfolk, like. Cain't see none but gennelfolk ownin' horses like these.'

Jack nodded. He had already spoken in an accent he knew well, the one most common to Boston. Louisa spoke with a touch of it herself.

'Indeed we are. On our way home. Had to come the long way around to avoid the war up north. Terrible times.'

Hoping to draw out a declaration of allegiance here, he was disappointed. The silent man spat to the side, the younger one giggled, while their leader's face took on an earnest, almost pious look.

'The devil's abroad in the land, that's fer damn sure. Taken man's heart, makin' him lust,' he looked with ill-disguised interest at Louisa's skirt when he said this, 'cheat, kill. Steal.' He nodded. 'Yessiree. Gold's the root of all badness, that's fer damn sure.'

'Fer damn sh-sh-sure,' the youth echoed.

'But every man needs a little, do they not, sir?' Jack could see the way the conversation had gone. He was not averse to paying some of Burgoyne's coin to gain passage.

'A little, aye, fer grub an' suchlike.'

'Fer grub and li-li-liquor,' the younger man giggled.

The bearded one gave him a look that made him cringe, step back, and mumble to himself, the hat going on and off still more swiftly. 'Quiet, you,' he barked, then turned back. 'Honest men, sir. But we guard the crossing for gennelfolk like yourself. Don't get no thanks from government. Any government.'

There was still no clue – he could be of either the Higher or Lower party. Or neither. Jack looked beyond, to the water. The ferry was being plied hard across the river and stood about a hundred yards off. This exchange required good timing and judgement – enough payment to pacify till the boat docked, not enough to prod their greed.

'Then, sir, may a grateful citizen offer some recompense for your troubles.'

The eyes narrowed within the bearded face. 'If recompense is real pence, then, yessir, ye may.'

Jack reached slowly into his jacket. His fingers brushed one pistol butt, went past; he had a single silver dollar in his waistcoat pocket there. He hoped it would suffice.

He never got a chance to find out. 'Here, my man,' said Louisa, moving Caspiana toward the leader, 'take this and kindly leave our path.'

Jack turned, startled, at the hauteur in her voice, at the coin suddenly spinning through the air. Even in the fading sunlight, he saw its colour. It was gold – and it was too much.

The man saw it too, verified it when it landed in his palm. 'A John, begod,' he cried, raising it into the light. Jack couldn't help a groan. A guinea they might have got away with. But a Portuguese John was more than these men would see in a month of good extortion.

As he'd thought, it was the hitherto silent man who was the danger. Crying, 'Rich, and a damned King's man, I'll swear,' he declared both his allegiance and his intention. His hand was on his pistol's butt; Jack's, still inside his jacket, was an inch away from his own. They drew near simultaneously, cocked, and fired as one. The man's ball buzzed past Jack's ear, while his own struck home, the man spinning away with a yell.

The youth had belied his slow appearance by leaping smartly for Louisa's reins. She struck him a good blow with her riding crop and he yelped, but held on, dodging from side to side around the horse's neck. Jack's interrogator had taken time to stow the coin and now drew his own pistol from his belt.

'You'll step down smart or the lady dies,' he cried.

Whether it was the threat to her mistress or the way the youth jerked her bridle in avoiding Louisa's blows, was hard to tell, but Caspiana, the high-strung filly, reacted. She reared, forelegs lashing out, and caught the boy in the chest, reeling him backwards. The bearded man's pistol tried to follow the lady and Jack took his chance. In a moment, he had pulled Angus MacTavish's shillelagh from behind him, in another struck down with it. The heavy stick with its iron ferrule connected with the wrist, dashing the gun from the grasp. As it fell, it fired, the bullet skittering off the wood between Doughty's legs. The horse reared, too and, for a moment, Jack had to fight to control him. There were screams from the waiting passengers, calls from the fast-approaching ferry-boat . . . and a shout from behind them, at the nearest house of the settlement.

Jack turned. There, standing in the doorway, was a trooper in a blue coat and silver-laced hat. He was slowly lowering a tankard to his side, beer frothing over its lip. Behind him in a barn, ready saddled – and, Jack now realized, impossible to see from the hilltop – were a dozen cavalry horses.

Doughty pranced, jerking Jack's gaze away; but not before he'd seen the trooper turn back into what could only be a barracks and begin shouting.

'Ride, Louisa!'

'I'm sorry, Jack, I—'

'Ride!'

They turned in unison, hooves striking splinters from the wooden dock. Then they were on the mudded earth of the slope. As they reached the road, just before they began to gallop, Jack saw the Colonial cavalry troop running to their mounts.

Jack led them southerly, though it was distance not direction that was important. There was no worth, while in sight, of making into unfamiliar woods where paths could peter out and roots might snag at galloping fetlocks. He used the shillelagh across Doughty's rump to speed him still more. Beside him, Louisa plied her crop. The wind of their passage took away most sound and the shouts behind them on the straight road faded but did not die entirely away. Still, Jack thought, they were pulling ahead. They had to be, for he would trust Doughty and Caspiana against any cavalry nag in Washington's army. Soon he would begin to look for concealment.

They had just rounded a bend. She was a pace behind him so he heard first rather than saw. But he turned in an instant, in time to watch Louisa's side-saddle slip. Caspiana slowed as she pulled on the reins but not enough. The saddle twisted and Jack could only look on in dismay as Louisa toppled to the ground.

He had reined up in a moment, was off Doughty the next and at her side one after, pulling her up. Caspiana, ever jittery, skittered away.

'Louisa—'

'No.' She coughed, drew a juddering breath. 'I am well.'

'Then we have to go on.' There were shouts, voices drawing closer to the corner.

'You must.' Her words came in gasps. 'I cannot ride bareback in a dress. Go!'

'I will not leave you—'

'You must!' She pulled herself a little up, gripping his arms. 'I will say we thought them robbers – which they were. They will not harm an American lady. But you . . .' They both looked back to the corner, both now felt the drumming on the earth. 'And your mission . . . for Burgoyne, Jack! Go!'

She was right. Mission aside, he would not survive long in American hands. They were on constant lookout for spies. They would soon find the General's dispatch, hidden in a half-hollow canteen. And he had probably killed the man at the dock.

He vaulted on to his horse. As he grabbed the reins, he looked down. 'I promise I will find you again.'

'I believe you.' She smiled, though her eyes filled with tears. 'For as we both know, you are a gentleman who keeps his word.'

He raised his fingers to his lips, saluted her with a kiss. As he drove his heels into Doughty's flanks, the cavalry troop finally burst around the corner. They reined up slightly when they saw the fallen body, the riderless horse. Then, when Jack took off, Doughty almost instantly into a gallop, some continued their stride, while others circled the prone Louisa.

The shouts for a moment were close, closer and Jack's shoulders instinctively hunched; then gradually they began to fade behind him. Sandy Lindsay had been right and Doughty well named. The horse *would* bear him over three counties!

As the road curved, at each bend, the cries lessened. They were still there but he was losing the pursuit.

As he rode, he swore. What had made Louisa pre-empt him like that with her gold coin? The impetuosity he admired in her in other situations made him curse her now. And he knew it was fear for her, laying back there surrounded by soldiers, that was driving his anger. Leaving her had been one of the hardest things he'd ever had to do and he'd only done it on the instant realization that she'd been right. If she'd been caught with him, they'd both hang.

The road went through a series of curves, thickly forested on either side. He began to look for a suitable path, one that might carry him up into the hills where he could really lose the hunters. He would trust himself in a forest over any Continental trooper. Then the road suddenly straightened . . . and immediately before him was a wagon drawn across it, its driver manoeuvring his team to extract it from the mud, other men heaving and pushing from the side.

Doughty was a hunter, bred for the hedgerows of England. Jack let the reins go slack, gave the beast its head, and he took the challenge majestically, clearing the wooden sides by a good foot. But Jack's joy was cut short by the landing; by the screaming men he plunged into, who threw themselves from the flailing hooves. Doughty nearly halted and Jack was thrown forward on to the great bay neck, his own face low down and nearly level with the face of another man.

'Aghh!' the man screamed and fell back, and he was not the only one, others scurrying away on each side. Blue-coated men. Looking up, Jack realized he had landed in the middle of – or rather the end of – a column of Rebel troops.

There was no choice now. The forest still reached down to the roadside and he directed Doughty toward it, brushing through the thinner undergrowth and on, under the canopy. There could be no more concerns over roots. He pushed the horse to a canter, hearing the shouts behind him intensify, more screams of fear and pain, from both horses and men, as the pursuing Cavalry arrived.

They were behind him soon, running men as well as mounted. Some carried weapons; he discovered this as he reined in at a fallen tree and tried to see which way to go around it. The sun was almost out of the sky and, as he squinted, a musket ball embedded in the trunk.

'Yah!' he cried, turning the horse's head to the left. They cleared the fallen beech and he noticed the glimmer of a path ahead. Digging his heels in, he drove his mount along it. Another musket fired, the bullet going he knew not where.

The path widened, went downhill, then up. Doughty was

struggling now yet still game, that magnificent heart pushing him on. Jack suddenly had hope, felt he could break his pursuit on this slope, both men and horses, less well bred, fading away. A smile came as he gave the horse its head again, leaving the wielding of his stick, nudging him along with the lightest tap of his heels, with whispered commands.

He could sense the slope beginning to peak. Soon he would crest it, a new world would open up, and he would lose himself in it. Near the summit, he turned to glance back through the dusky gloom . . .

The birch had fallen across the slope, its uprooting halted by another on the other side of the path. The trunk connected with Jack's head and even if Doughty was no longer travelling at full gallop, he was still going spiritedly enough. Jack didn't feel pain, didn't remember falling, or landing. Just the world suddenly dark.

— THIRTEEN —
The Brewery

He had no sense of how much time had passed since his encounter with the tree. The dark that had taken him then, held him still; though now not in the oblivion of unconsciousness but in the deep blackness of a prison cell.

Once awake, the cold kept him so. They had removed his clothing, leaving him a thin blanket, which had little effect against the chill and smelled strongly of horse; it also appeared to move when placed against his skin and for that reason alone he was grateful to his temporary blindness. As to his injuries, though the tree had conjured a lump the size of a crab apple from his forehead and his back was sore due to his tumble from Doughty, he had sustained far worse, and often, on the playing fields of Westminster School.

Carefully, he began to feel around him, touch being his most functioning sense, though as he moved he perceived the faintest light coming from some gap high up on the wall, too high for him to reach. There was straw on the flagstone floor, and a large barrel to his left. His hand then encountered another to his right, both on their ends. Crawling, with an arm before him, he felt other such rounded shapes further along the cell, upright or prone. So he was in a cooperage or . . .

It was then his sense of smell returned. He inhaled and detected something sweet, heady.

'Beer,' he said out loud, and then laughed. He had been

often warned in his youth that he would end up dead in a beer cellar.

Further explorations confirmed his discovery. There were sacks of grain, a large trough, some heavy wooden paddles. The whole room was about thirty feet in length, a dozen wide. It had two doors; a great double one set high up in the wall, from whose edge the light was coming in, probably used to bring the barrels in and out, and a second, smaller door in the wall opposite. Locked and very stout.

Explorations over, Jack sat facing this door and, despite his distaste, pulled the blanket tightly around himself. A little warmth allowed his abused head to function. He was a prisoner. He did not know how long he'd been unconscious nor whether he was alone. Perhaps Louisa occupied another cellar nearby. He must have been taken to a township of reasonable size, for this brewery served a large-ish community. He'd had worse prison cells. And he preferred this cold to the heat he'd once suffered in one in Mysore.

His speculations were interrupted by the tread of feet on a stair, the throwing of bolts. Light came in with the opening door, enough to make him wince and shade his eyes. Then the entrance was blocked by two men. One carried a tray, the other a blunderbuss.

The younger man with the tray came in and set it down before Jack, then scurried back, regarding him with a not-unfriendly interest. The older one – they could be father and son – stayed glowering in the doorway and kept his weapon levelled.

Jack looked at the tray. There was something frothy in a jug and a hunk of bread beside it. He smiled. 'Thankee, sirs, for this kindness,' he said, remembering to maintain his Boston tones. He had no idea yet what they knew of him.

The young man nodded and smiled back. The elder grunted and moved out through the door.

'One other kindness, if you will, young sir. Can you tell me where I am?'

'Pearl River,' the fellow blurted. His elder raised a hand to him, and his son – Jack had decided they were indeed in that relation – cowered.

The man swung the wide barrel of the gun toward Jack. 'Yous only gets this,' he gestured to the tray, 'so you stays alive for a little. You answers questions, not us, when the officer gets 'ere. And then yous get a rope. Spy!'

He spat with the last word, withdrew. The younger man actually shrugged at Jack, then followed.

Spy. That must mean they had discovered the canteen with its false compartment and Burgoyne's message. Well, that was set in a newly devised cypher and would take them some days to decode. But . . . Pearl River? That meant he was still on the west side of the Hudson then and not far from where he'd been caught. Well, it was not much, but any knowledge was a beginning. He groped for the jug, took a sip of the beer and grimaced; it was poor and sour stuff. The bread seemed fresh enough and he ate all of it.

More footsteps came. The door was pushed in, once more the blunderbuss was levelled at him. There was no son this time but two soldiers, Militiamen in blue coats. A man was slumped between them, his arms over their shoulders. With a relieved curse, they threw the body down. The door slammed, the darkness returned.

Jack sat and listened to the raspy breathing for a moment. Then he reached forward and sought contact. Finding a shoulder, he shook it gently.

'Fellow? Are you awake? Do you live?'

A groan, then a fit of coughing, horridly fluid. It sounded for a moment that the man was choking, and then his throat cleared and a whisper came.

'I am, sir. No thanks to our hosts.'

There was something to the voice, an accent. English, not Colonial, for sure, though that, in itself, meant nothing in this land. While he searched for an answer, Jack said, 'Would you sit up?'

'I would, but I might need some help, like.'

Then it came to him. The accent was from the west,

though not as far west as Cornwall. Dorset! 'Willis? Sergeant Willis?'

Jack could hear the other man check his breath. 'Name's Johnson, mister. And I'm a farmer out near White Plains. Who's there?'

It was definitely him. 'It is Jack Absolute, Sergeant.'

A gasp then. An arm reached out to him, a hand almost exploring his face. Then it gripped his arm and Burgoyne's other messenger was pulled into a sitting position.

'Well, I'm sorry for you, Cap'n, and no mistake.'

'And I for you. Here, man, would you like some beer? It's sour but—'

'I think not, sir. They . . . they beat me when they finally caught me. Drink's the last thing on me mind. And it's not often you'll hear Emmanuel Willis say that.' There was the hint of a laugh. 'So you tried the Tarrytown ferry like I advised. I'm right sorry for that.'

'Not your fault, Willis. I think the whole Hudson is in the hands of the Rebel.'

'Perhaps not for long.' He paused. 'Are we alone in this cell?'

'We are.'

'Good. Then I can tell ye – General Clinton moves at last. He sets out for the Highland forts on the third of October. In four days.'

'You reached him then?'

'Aye, sir. I was on my way back.'

Jack whistled. 'I thought I travelled fast. You have the speed of Perseus and the luck of the devil, man.'

'Ran out on me, though, didn't he, Cap'n? Knew I be pushin' it, like.' Willis's hand reached forward. 'Perhaps I will take a sip of that beer. Who knows when I'll get that chance again? We're to be stabbed with the Bridport Dagger, Cap'n, and no question. I've a wife back in Lyme Regis who cursed me when I took the shilling, saying I was born to dangle. I've dreaded it ever since.'

Jack placed the jug in his hand. The Sergeant drank, spat.

'Fuck, that's foul. The Americans call this beer? Give me a strong Dorset ale any day.'

He drank on, nonetheless and while he did, Jack thought. 'If Clinton comes,' he said after a while, 'then General Burgoyne may be saved after all.'

Jack heard the jug being laid down. 'I'd like to say that, sir, but—'

'Come on, man.'

'He gave me a dispatch for General Burgoyne. Being a sergeant like, he gave me no verbal message, of course—'

'The fool.'

'Yet I was there when he dictated the letter. He attacks up the Hudson, sure . . .' Coughing took him. When it subsided, he croaked, 'But with scarce three thousand men.'

'*Three* . . . three thousand, you say? He'll never force his way to Albany with so few.'

'He don't intend it, Cap'n. A distraction he can do, is all.'

Jack shook his head angrily in the dark. 'And did he at least order Burgoyne to retreat?'

'He did not. I believe the phrase was – "He cannot presume" aye, "*presume* to send orders to General Burgoyne".'

'He's washed his hands. By God, he's washed his bloody hands.'

'I believe he has, sir, at that.'

Jack slumped back, remembering the desperation in Burgoyne's eyes. If he retreated without orders he risked a court martial and ignominy. Yet he could only stand a little longer unaided before that option was cut off. He must do so now, or fight or . . . no, surrender was impossible. No British army had surrendered to a Colonial one in the history of the world.

'Well, Sergeant Willis, this news must be delivered.'

That fluid cough came again. 'I'm afraid my deliverin' days are past, beggin' your favour. But I'll help you as I may. Is there escape from this room?'

'Only through the door.'

'And I am not well enough to overpower any. Are you?'

'I'll have to be,' Jack sighed.

'Have you a thought on it?'

Jack hadn't. Groping around, his hands felt for anything that might be of use. Straw? A wooden paddle against a blunderbuss? And the man never came fully into the room. He'd have to be lured in. Then Jack's hand rubbed against the upright barrel of beer. It was a large one, stood at least his own height, more; the brewery may have skimped on quality but it produced large quantities. From the malt smell coming off it, and the heat of the oak, it was in mid-fermentation.

'You know, Sergeant, I may just have thought of something.'

'Have you, Cap'n? Have you indeed?'

It was warm in the beer. He had some chemically-minded friends who could probably tell him why that was. Some brewers of his acquaintance, too. They would also be able to discourse about the froth on the surface. Something to do with yeast, he presumed. Anyway, he was grateful for the little warmth it generated. He doubted he'd have been able to hide naked, in that chill cellar, in a butt of wine.

The liquid was buoyant, forcing him up to the surface where he'd created a small gap by emptying some of the beer out with his jug. But there was little breathable up there due to the exhalations of the brew; and the hole he'd pried with an iron nail pulled from another barrel would quickly block with scum. He'd despaired, until Willis had suggested a straw. He found one hollow and thick enough, and thrust it through the air hole. Though he panicked the first time the lid was pressed down on him and struggled out again, he was calmer the second time and managed to steady his breath.

Now he waited, while spume clogged his vision; the beer made his bruised head ache and he could not help taking little sips of it whenever he shifted slightly. He could not remain in there long, he knew. The gases, the heady, noxious liquid, the confined space; he was getting drowsy. Yet he'd close his eyes and still see things. The longer he was in there, the more like a coffin it felt. Buried at sea!

Twice, Willis had rapped on the outside of the barrel to warn of approach, twice he signalled the false alarm. Each time, Jack had clutched the wooden paddle tightly to his chest, thinking ahead to the movements he had to make when he emerged, the only movements that would save him . . . and perhaps Burgoyne and the King's army too. But after the second thwarted hope, he did think he could survive much longer.

Another single tap came – a warning one: that meant footsteps on the stair. Then another three – the lock was being turned. Jack found he was suddenly starved of air, that the straw was no longer sufficing. He felt his bowels clench and gripped the paddle's handle harder, trying to stave off the panic. Then there came a single tap – someone had entered the room. He awaited the next signal, desperate, his air nearly gone – a tap for each man there and a flurry for him to move, if, as they hoped, the man with the blunderbuss would rush in at the sight of his absence and be in range.

Two taps. Two men.

A flurry.

Forcing himself as deep into the liquid as he could sink, Jack placed one hand in the centre of the barrel lid and grasping the paddle firmly in the other, he used his legs as a released spring and surged upwards.

Froth obscured half his sight. But a large shape was before him and he struck at it, sweeping the paddle down from on high. There was a cry, an explosion, the room stinking of gunpowder in an instant. Wiping his vision clear, Jack placed his hands on the barrel's side and propelled himself up and out.

The man who'd held the blunderbuss was crouched on the floor over his expended weapon, clutching at the collar bone that Jack had obviously snapped. The gun had discharged, scattering its shot. Some had caught Willis, thrown him back against the wall, a bloody rent where his throat had been. The other man in the room was emerging from his shock at the suddenness of the ambush and reaching for a sword at his side.

He had to be the interrogator, a stout officer in a green

greatcoat, the bulk of it making the removal of his sword awkward. He had spectacles on his nose and a black tricorn hat on his head and it was the centre of this that Jack aimed for, bringing the wooden stave down hard. It crushed the hat and the man collapsed with a cry.

There was no time to pause. Willis was dead, at least spared the Bridport Dagger he dreaded, no noose for him. But the other men stirred at his feet, and moans would soon be turning to screams, so Jack ran from the cellar and took the stairs before him two at a time.

A door gave on to a corridor. There were three others leading off it and, as Jack hesitated, one opened and a soldier walked out, pipe and pint mug in hand, trailing smoke and the noise of an inn in full conviviality. They regarded each other but a moment, until the man yelped, dropped his smoke and beer, and ran back inside, yelling. Jack sprinted the opposite way.

The door he burst through led to a large kitchen. A maid, bent over a range, stood up and screamed. He had a momentary glimpse of himself through her eyes – a naked man covered in yellow froth, spattered with another man's blood, clutching a paddle. As she shrieked again, as shouts filled the corridor, he ran past her to wrench open the back door.

Cool air wrapped around him, as he fell down two steps into a walled kitchen garden. A gate stood open at the back of it and he was through it in four strides, just as the room behind him filled with voices.

He was looking at a fenced paddock. To his left, three stalls were occupied by three horses. He took a step towards them, already uncertain if he could get one backed out and mounted in time, wondering if he should just run. Then, from his right, came a familiar snicker. He turned . . . and there was Doughty before him. The big bay wore a nosebag; he swished his tail and carried on eating.

The shouting came from the garden now. Any moment and they would be upon him. So he ran at the horse, who skittered slightly at his approach.

'Easy, lad,' Jack said, bending to jerk the loose hobble from the animal's fetlocks. As the first soldier came yelling through the door, Jack hurled the paddle at the man, then threw himself on to the animal's back. If Doughty was upset at the interruption of his meal he didn't show it. Instead, when Jack leaned down and shouted, 'Go!' he immediately began to move. A pistol cracked behind them, as Jack pressed his thighs into the horse's flanks and urged him toward the fence. Doughty cleared it easily, nosebag and all, though he nearly dislodged Jack on landing, his body still slick with half-fermented beer. Clinging desperately to the mane, Jack righted himself just as another pistol fired, this bullet passing between his chest and Doughty's head.

'Yah!' Jack yelled, digging in his heels. A field of barley lay beyond the paddock fence and, riding down one row, Jack gained the shelter of the forest that bordered it. The canopy swallowed them and trees soon smothered the sounds of screaming, the shouted commands. Only the raucous cry of a bugle pursued them under the dusk-lit leaves. And soon even that was gone.

– FOURTEEN –
Saratoga – 7 October 1777

Jack had at least that much to be grateful for – the morning mists, which had concealed his departure with Louisa over two weeks before, covered Jack again as he limped down the trail he could only pray led to the British camp. He reckoned it was near noon, though only instinct told him so, time having no relevance in that spectral world. Sounds were muffled as if he listened to them through sheepskin; shapes that seemed human at ten paces turned to saplings at three. He knew that others also wandered these woods; indeed, the last few miles had been full of half-heard voices, phantasms moving in the distance, challenges called out, ignored, passed by. He had no weapon to reach for if he met an enemy, no way of identifying a friend; he would pass his father in this fog and not know him. Yet some sense still led him along the path he could barely see, towards the faintest crackling sound he wasn't sure he heard.

And if I was seen, what would they make of me then? Some Native Shade, wandered from the Village of the Dead? A scarecrow hopped off his warding pole, tired of chasing crows, desirous of chasing men instead . . .

Jack shivered, stopped, stared into the greyness. He had definitely been alone in the woods too long. The forest was disorientating, even to one, like himself, who had spent so much time in it.

Especially at this season, with the mists rising from ground that smells of mould, of putrefaction, of a world turning in, consuming itself. The fire in every second tree, every maple, spreading flame to the ground, to die there and rot . . . what would Até say? 'And Hell itself breathes out Contagion to this world . . .'

He'd lost count of the times he'd heard Louisa laugh. Each time he heard the chitter of a squirrel scrambling away, or a bird taking flight, he'd turn, almost call. Then he'd battle down his disappointment, returning to his fear for her, for himself.

He was shoved in the back. Gasping, he turned. Then smiled. 'Quite right, Doughty, old thing. Pull myself together, eh?'

He scratched the horse between its eyes. He didn't need to peer through any mists to see how thin the animal was. The blanket he'd managed to steal hung over flanks where ribs thrust through. And his own? He scratched at them now through the tattered blouse a pitying old Tuscarora woman had given him, the third day of his escape, along with a long-dead husband's second-best breech cloth, donated for his modesty. That was also the last time he had eaten – five, six days before? – anything other than walnuts or burdock roots. His legs beneath the cloth were marked and torn by their passage along the trails that led back to Saratoga.

He bent to the earth, ignoring his feet – *when had they become that colour?* – and tried to rediscover the deer track he'd lost in his musings. When he did, he clicked his tongue at Doughty, and they started forward again; he'd long given up needing to lead him. They were moving again towards that strange crackling. And as they hit a slope and began to climb, suddenly he could see five paces ahead, then ten. There was breeze in his face, the mists fraying in it, dissolving. And the crackling that had been puzzling before was suddenly much louder and now came as clear as his vision.

'Muskets, and lots of them,' he said, gripping the thick mane, swinging himself up. 'Pray God we are not too late.'

'Zounds! Absolute? What the devil's become of you?'

Lieutenant-Colonel Carleton, Burgoyne's adjutant, stood in the centre of the commander's tent, aghast at the apparition before him. To his left, Burgoyne's full-length mirror showed Jack to himself. He had to own he was not looking his best. The old squaw's blouse was barely clinging to his tattooed chest, the holed breech cloth scarcely preserving his modesty. Given a beard that was now over two weeks old and untrained, and skin that had barely a square inch unscratched or unbitten . . . Jack could see why his superior officer might be somewhat appalled.

But he could not concern himself now with fashion. 'The General, sir. I must speak to him at once.'

Carleton came forward, carrying a camp chair. He set it down and Jack, after a moment's hesitation, slumped into it. 'You have returned from Clinton? What message does he send?'

'You'll pardon me, sir; for the General's ears only. Where is he?'

'Where do you think?' Carleton gestured to the west. 'There!'

Jack did not need to turn his head. The sound of musketry had grown to a distant but distinct roar, like surf pounding on a Cornish beach; cannon added a staccato bass note to the song. Bugles brayed. Very faintly now, Jack could even hear voices. Shouts and screams.

'An American attack?'

'Ours. Though it's only meant to be a reconnaissance in force to test the Rebel left. And a chance for us to reap some grain that's growing there. But by the sounds of it we have stirred up the viper in his den.'

Jack winced at the reference, then sighed. 'I must go to him.'

He tried to rise. Carleton's hand on his shoulder held him effortlessly down. 'Not looking like that, me lad. You'll get yourself shot, arrested or, at the very least, laughed at.

Can't have a staff officer looking so disgraceful. Where's your uniform?'

Jack passed a hand across his eyes. 'Um, I . . . I believe the General was holding it for me.'

'Really?' Carleton crossed to the armoire that stood beside the mirror, threw open its door. A dozen beautifully tailored coats hung there from a rail. 'What regiment are you?'

'Regiment?' He was, of course, a captain in the Queen's Light Dragoons. But since that regiment was not serving in this campaign, and it was entirely proper for an officer to hold dual commissions in horse and foot, Burgoyne had had him appointed to . . . to . . .

'The 24th Foot, sir?'

'Excellent! Simon Fraser's own and down there now in the thick of it.' Carleton delved among the clothes. 'Yes, here it is.'

He pulled the red coat from its hanger, laid it out on the table. A shirt came from a drawer, which also disgorged a bearskin hat, a stock, belt, pair of breeches, stockings, waist-coat, sash, steel gorget . . .

'Sir, I feel time is pressing—'

'Time can pause, sirrah!' Carleton glared at him. 'We may be beaten this day – but we will not be under-dressed!' He turned back to the armoire. 'I know you have a reputation of being something of an eccentric planet, Absolute but . . . ah!' He emerged from further rooting. 'These must be yours. Yes, J.A. God alone knows how you get the General to cart this stuff around for you.' He plonked two shining shoes on the table, with the black gaiters that would be buttoned to the knee. 'Braithewaite,' he yelled at the tent flap. Burgoyne's batman appeared before the cry had faded from the canvas walls. 'Fetch me some hot water, soap, and a razor. And some food.'

The servant barely glanced at the prone Absolute before nodding and retiring.

The Colonel reached into a knapsack, producing a dusty bottle. 'Been saving this. Armanac! The very thing.' He swiftly poured two glasses and thrust one across at Jack. 'For King and Country, eh?' As Jack tried to stand for the toast, he waved him back down, and drained his glass. 'Yes, that's the stuff. Now, man, do you have a horse?'

'My horse is outside, sir. But he's exhausted.'

Carleton threw back the tent flap, allowing Braithewaite to bustle in under his arm and march to the table, setting stew and biscuit there before Jack. Jack did not hold back, just tipped the bowl, swallowing straight down the thin soup and bits of what he presumed to be meat that floated in it. The biscuit disappeared in three bites.

Carleton was staring out. 'But that's . . . that's . . . Doughty! Best horse on the campaign. Lost fifty guineas to the Earl of Balcarras at Ticonderoga jumping against my Nimrod. He's down there too, of course, young Sandy.' He turned back. 'Looks fine to me. Carry you across three counties, what? See he's saddled, Braithewaite. I'll do that.'

He crossed to the table, took the brush from the servant, dipped it in the steaming water, stropped it vigorously across the cake of soap.

'Now, my good man,' he said, smiling down, 'all off or leave you your sideburns?'

It was remarkable what a shave, a clean uniform, a bowl of hot food and a tot or two of fine liquor could do for a fellow. Barely thirty minutes after Jack had entered the Commander's tent in the guise of a scarecrow, he re-emerged as a smart, if somewhat skinny, officer, though all they'd been able to do with his tangled, thick hair was bind it in a bow. Yet Braithwaite had found time not only to feed and saddle Doughty, he had given him a quick groom as well. The horse snickered as Jack approached and danced sideways across the grass.

Mounting, Jack cried, 'To the guns!' and Doughty snorted, reared, and cantered off. Jack had no real need to control him; the horse knew the sounds of battle as well as he. There was a soft path that led from the tent in the forest clearing and emerged soon into the open, joining a larger one there.

Immediately they were passing companies of both Redcoats and blue-clad Germans, all staring nervously down the valley towards the great bank of gunsmoke that was obscuring everything there, from which only the driven waves of regimental volleys, the sharp explosions of individual rifles, the heavy bark of cannon, the shriek of bugles, and, more faintly, of men could be observed. Carleton had told him that, to make up a fully fit force, detachments had been taken from each of the regiments and formed into impromptu units. So it was these men's comrades that were struggling in that smoky hell, their colours that flew over that field.

Jack galloped past Freeman's Farm, which he had run through two weeks before to gain the British lines. Just beyond it, on a slight rise, stood a new, well-fortified structure made up of earth and thick tree trunks – Balcarras's Redoubt, Carleton had named it. And beside it, as the Colonel had predicted, telescope pointing down a path that cut through the wood ahead, was General Burgoyne.

Jack reined in just behind him, dismounted, and handed his reins to a groom who already held those of the staff horses. Captain Money shook his hand quickly then turned to his commanding officer.

'General?'

'Can't see a damn thing. Smoke and trees as ever. Does Fraser hold the Barber Wheatfield or no?' Burgoyne lowered his scope, but still squinted ahead. 'Yes, Money?' he called over his shoulder.

'New arrival, sir.'

Burgoyne looked back and instantly smiled. 'Why, Jack Absolute! A little late, eh? Nearly missed your entrance.'

'A few problems, sir. Unavoidable, I am afraid.'

'Oh, I am sure.'

A burst of shouting caused all to turn to see a man dashing toward them from the forest to their left, along the front of the redoubt. He tripped and fell, then stood immediately to attention before them. He wore the markings of a grenadier, the button of the 62nd, the crimson sash of a sergeant. That he was away from his company indicated that something was very wrong.

'Beggin' your leave, sir,' he said, his Welsh accent thick, 'but Major Ackland fears he cannot hold the wood. We are pressed hard, sir.'

'Major Ackland would not send such a message if it were not true,' Burgoyne said, 'and if his Grenadiers fail, our right flank will fold. Go back, man, and tell him he has my permission to withdraw to the redoubt.'

The sergeant saluted, turned and ran. 'Francis?' Burgoyne called, and an exquisitely tailored young officer stepped forward. 'Be so good as to convey to Generals Fraser and Riedesel that they should retire on us in good order, at their earliest convenience.'

'Sir!' A salute was snapped up, returned, and the man mounted and was away.

'Now, Captain Absolute,' Burgoyne turned back to him, 'what news do you bring me? Does General Clinton march to us or no?'

Jack glanced at the staff officers, who stared back at him, their expressions intent. 'Perhaps, sir, I should convey the news in private.'

He saw Burgoyne's urbanity waver a little at that – for he had to realize that private news would be bad. But his voice was still light when he said, 'They must all know soon enough and base their actions on your report. For if you and I were killed . . .' He waved his hand. 'So – does Clinton come?'

Jack knew that the news, bad as it was, must be conveyed without honeying. 'He moves, sir, upon the Highland forts,' he continued over the gasps of relief, 'but with just three thousand men.'

Even Burgoyne's composure cracked at that. '*Three*? Three thousand, you say? By God, that may be enough to take the forts but not to hold them and march to us here.' He looked around at the exhausted, grim faces before him; all eyes avoided his now. So he looked up for a moment into the clouds as if to seek there for a better omen, then sighed, looked back. 'Well, gentlemen, it appears we have been left to our own resources.' Snapping his telescope up, he turned back to the field. The noise, that had seemed to slacken for the duration of Jack's report, returned now five-fold. ' "I have set my life upon a cast and I will stand the hazard of the die," ' Burgoyne declaimed above it. 'What's that? *Henry the Fifth*? Agincourt?'

Captain Money coughed, spoke. '*Richard the Third*, I think, sir. Bosworth.'

'Surely not? Damn, I would hate to be quoting the vanquished. A bottle of Bucellas on it, shall we say? Your savage, Jack, would be able to tell us. He's around, by the way, somewhere. I kept him, as you requested.' Burgoyne waved his hand toward the British right, as Jack's heart gave a little jump. Then the General turned the scope again to the path ahead. 'Good God. Is that Francis?'

All looked. Indeed, the body of the messenger, Sir Francis Clarke, was being carried by four men back toward them, among the scores of wounded, desperate soldiers coming down the path and from the woods.

Silence held them for a moment as they studied the body for any sign of life. But when he was laid out nearby, all could see the ragged chest, ripped open by at least three rifle balls.

'Poor lad,' Burgoyne murmured. 'The Countess will never forgive me.' He turned to his officers. 'We do not know if he delivered his message. And we need to. Does Fraser rally? I would not order another and yet . . . would anyone go?'

Those designated messengers must already have been sent. The staff officers who remained all lowered their eyes, avoiding Burgoyne's. Until they reached Jack, who held his gaze and nodded. 'Since I have missed most of the fighting, sir . . . and Fraser's 24th is, technically, my regiment . . . I should be the one to go to them.'

There was a long pause. Burgoyne looked as though he would not have it so, then turned to gaze out once more over the field before speaking. 'I should not doubt but Simon is somewhat short of officers by now. Help him to rally them,

213

Captain, and to bring him and his men back here. Perhaps we can break the Rebel on this redoubt and yet win this hazard.'

'General.' With a swift salute, Jack once more mounted Doughty. There was another route than the one Clarke had taken to his death, a path that led around rather than through the wood. Less clogged with retreating soldiers, it would bring him quicker to the fray. Pausing only to check the two pistols in their saddle holsters – Carleton had lent him a matched pair from the French foundry of St Etienne, one of the finest in the world – and that his sabre was unhindered in its scabbard, Jack mounted.

Doughty, as usual, responded to the merest touch of heels. They cantered along the edge of the wood. The trees and a slight dip seemed to absorb most of the noise, if not the smell, of battle. To his right, he could see a second redoubt, Breymann's, garrisoned by that German officer and detachments of his men. Between the redoubts were two fortified cabins and, even in a swift glance, Jack could see that the men who held them wore a variety of uniforms or none at all. Canadians and Mohawks. He suddenly knew that Até would be there among them. He would see him soon, he hoped. If he survived what lay ahead.

Then he rounded the wood and all thought of reunion was swept away in sound and smoke.

'Fire!' yelled an officer immediately in front of him, and the company of Redcoats, two ranks of twenty, discharged as one man. Their targets stood less than fifty yards away, some blue-coated, some in the fur and buck-skin of Daniel Morgan's riflemen, yet others in varying shades of grey or brown or green. There was a huge mob of them and while some fell to the volley, others leaped up from the ground where they'd thrown themselves and immediately returned fire. It was not a volley but it was perhaps more accurate. The officer sank down clutching a shoulder, three men fell. But their bodies were swiftly dragged to the rear, the ranks redressed at the bellows of an NCO. At his command, muskets were reloaded, presented. Another volley crashed out. It may have been somewhat more ragged this time but it checked the gathering to their front. The Rebels seemed to split into two groups and seek to run either side of the tight body of men.

Jack peered to his left, sulphurous smoke making vision hard. But he could just distinguish another horse there, a splendid grey, in the centre of the corkscrewed British line. He tapped Doughty and his horse spurred forward towards the other. At twenty paces, Jack had his guess confirmed. Simon Fraser sat on his huge gelding, calmly calling orders to the bugler and drummer at his side, who responded in note and beat. Soldiers were receiving the messages and rallying to the colours that waved above the General, both the King's Union Standard and the blue of the 24th.

'General!'

'Captain Absolute.' Simon Fraser gazed down – his horse was two hands bigger than Doughty at the least. 'Auch, it's good to see ye, lad. The Commander will be unco pleased. Though you seem to have lost some weight. Either that or you'll be needin' a new tailor.'

As he spoke, ball was whispering past their heads. 'His compliments, sir. And he urges you to withdraw and rally at the redoubt.'

'Exactly what I'm trying to do. But I want to bring my men along with me, ye ken.'

A ball passed through the General's sleeve, just at his wrist. He seemed not to notice. 'Lad, I'm bereft of officers. Could you help me straighten this line?'

He gestured to his left where a body of men were milling like sheep harried by a collie.

Without another word, Jack leaped from Doughty's back, thrusting the reins into the hands of a dazed young officer, scarcely more than a boy, who took them, mumbling the while. The lad's spontoon, the spear such officers were meant to carry and often didn't, was discarded at his feet. Though it was considered old-fashioned, Jack had always quite liked the half-pike weapon. Keeping your enemy three arm-lengths away had obvious advantages over a sword; and it was perfect for the job before him.

He grasped the wooden pole and ran to the distressed men. 'To me,' he bellowed, waving the spontoon above his head. He saw a corporal. 'Seize the end,' he ordered, and when the man had taken the butt, Jack pushed the tip out flat before him. It became a line and six men were suddenly against it. Setting their feet, somehow the two of them held on, as six more pressed.

'Handle your cartridge,' Jack shouted, and half of them did just that. Some of the others, seeing the rally, joined it.

'Prime!' Jack marched to the side of the swelling ranks, stood there, chest square to the enemy, despite the close passage of lead ball, his spontoon now at half-port, butt to the ground. If he was steady, then perhaps they would be. He only hoped he would remember the drill. He hadn't trained as an infantry officer in many a year.

'Shut your pans!' he bellowed. 'Steady there! Charge your cartridge! Draw your rammers! Ram down your cartridge! Return your rammers! Poise your firelocks! Cock your fire-locks! Present your firelocks! Hold now, men. Hold!'

Jack held them there for that moment, the one that would bring them together as soldiers and comrades, not targets. Then he shouted, 'Fire!' It was not the most effective volley the British Army had ever discharged. But the men had held, and soon dozens more had joined them, rallying NCOs forcing them into the ranks. The milling stopped.

'Good men. You, Corporal, there! Once more, if you please.'

'Sir!'

As the man shouted the commands, Jack leaned forward into the smoke, trying to see. Suddenly, a gust of wind swept the warcloud away and his vision cleared. The first thing he noticed, strangely, was a heron, on the wing, its long neck scrunched, as ungainly in flight as ever. The bird seemed not disgruntled in the least by the noise below it, giving out its harsh croak, off to fish in a different stream with that deadly elegance Jack and Louisa had observed. Smoke and rifles and man's petty quarrels would not bend it from that purpose.

Looking down, the second thing Jack saw was Benedict Arnold. The man was maybe seventy yards away, a sword in one hand, a pistol in the other. Beside him stood a buck-skinned rifleman.

Perhaps it was the sight of the bird, the calmness of its passing, but Jack had a moment of sudden clarity. Above the tumult, he could not hear what Arnold was saying. But he understood as if he were next to him when the General tapped the buck-skinned shoulder with his pistol barrel then pointed with his sword towards Simon Fraser.

Lethargy held his legs. He found it hard to turn, his voice coming as if from some far away place, too long in arriving. He saw the rifleman raise his weapon, sight . . .

'General!' screamed Jack, but the noise was too much, the distance between them too great. Yet he was near enough for all that; when the bullet struck home and Fraser jerked and began to fall from his saddle, Jack was at his side, catching him, lowering him to the ground. The great grey reared and plunged away toward the Rebel line. As Jack supported General Fraser's head, the eyes rolled open.

'Am I hit, Jack?'

'I'm afraid you are, sir.'

'It is nothing, I am sure.' Fraser said, tried to rise, then fainted. Jack lowered him to the ground, appalled at the source of the blood spreading down the white waistcoat, staining the breeches. Gut shot, the worst of wounds.

'You! Ensign!' Jack yelled at the young man who yet retained Doughty's reins. He started forward as if he were the one hit. 'You must help me get the General on to the horse. You must ride him back to the surgeons. Now!'

Somehow – for Fraser was a big man – they hoisted the mercifully unconscious General across the saddle. The ensign, at Jack's urging, mounted behind. Once up, Jack removed his two pistols from their holsters, then slapped the horse on its withers; Doughty, responding instantly, as always, to the command, galloped away.

The sight of Fraser's fall had broken the spirit of even those who would rally. Men everywhere began to run and Jack could see he had no hope of stopping them. They would probably kill him if he tried. For just one moment he was tempted to run at the enemy ranks, to seek out Arnold and slaughter him as he had slaughtered Fraser – for what he had ordered, the murder of an opposing general, was against all the rules of war. He even took one step forward, the only Redcoat doing so . . . then through the smoke, two blue-coated figures were running at him, bayonets fixed, yelling in their triumph. Jack's first bullet took the leading man in his shoulder, spinning him away. The other paused for just a moment, to look down at his fallen friend, then screamed and levelled at Jack. But the pause did for him. Jack, sighting briefly, put a ball between his eyes. Then, like all around him, Jack turned on his heel and ran.

This time he took to the woods directly behind the fracturing British line, for the trees would give some cover from the American riflemen. More Redcoats were streaming down from his right, from the higher ground there, buck-skinned pursuers clubbing at their backs. He kept away from the path where men were bunching into a mass target and dying, and instead ran through the undergrowth between the maples and the birches, vaulting many bodies, both red-coated and dark blue. Men screamed at him from the ground, cursing, pleading, but he did not pause. He could do nothing for any of them, would only join them, shot dead on the ground, if he were lucky, bayoneted and left to bleed to death if he was not – for the Americans had the killing fever and would not yet think of quarter. The rout held even him in its terrorizing grip. His one hope lay ahead.

The trees thinned, the wood ended. Then there was a meadow and, a couple of hundred yards across it, Balcarras's Redoubt. Before that, a smaller earthwork occupied a slight rise in the ground. By-passing this at a smart sprint – Rebels already had it under fire from the forest's edge – Jack ran straight to the wooden palisades beyond. The gates had to be on the far side, away from the enemy, but Jack knew they would be blocked by scores of desperate men. So he followed the example of an equally tall sergeant of grenadiers before him and hurled himself straight at the wooden wall. Grasping the top of the stake, which was cut into a sharp point, he heaved himself up and over the parapet. Men were crowded thick on the walkway and he nearly took two with him as he fell to the ground the other side.

The order within was the reverse of the chaos without. Light infantrymen and others from the Advance Corps stood to at the walls, muskets held across their chests. Beneath each one stood another, weapons loaded, ready to be passed up. The central ground of the fort was filled with companies standing to, ready to be sent wherever they were needed. And, descending a stair from the parapet and walking up their ranks toward him, a smile on the ever pallid face, was Alexander Lindsay, Earl of Balcarras.

'Why, Jack! Never took you for a sprinter.' Suddenly the smile disappeared. 'But if you're running, then where's my blasted horse?'

'Bearing General Fraser to the surgeons, Sandy. And with the same devotion he always showed to me, I trust.'

The Earl laid a hand on Jack's arm. 'Not bad, is it, the General's wound?'

'The very worst, I fear.' Swiftly, Jack related the story and Arnold's part in it. It was one of the few times he'd seen colour come to the younger man's cheeks.

'By God, let me but meet him on this field,' he said. 'I'll pay him for Simon Fraser.'

'I think you'll get your chance soon enough.' Jack had been loading his pistols as he spoke. Slamming down the second pan, he added, 'For if I am not mistaken, that's him coming.'

Jack had cocked an ear to the parapets. Indeed the noise from beyond them had swelled even in their short conversation. Both men ran up the stairs, looked over the parapet. The defended knoll that lay in front of their position was smothered in musket smoke, surrounded by screaming Yankees. Even as they first looked, a group of Redcoats broke from it, through the blue ranks, fleeing back towards them.

'Arnold will be there, leading them,' Jack said. 'As well as being no gentleman he's mad as a Bedlamite. He'll be on you in a moment and he has men to spare.'

Balcarras glanced around. 'Unless he brings up cannon – and it looks like he's in too much of a hurry – I'll wager a guinea to a grouse that we'll break him here. That will give General Burgoyne time to set up the secondary defence. He's ridden back to do so.' Balcarras sighed. 'So long as Breymann holds his redoubt, there, to the right.' He pointed and Jack looked. 'It is our weak point to be sure, I warned them before. Those cabins beside him, they can be too easily taken and his flank turned.'

The firing had doubled in volume even as he spoke. Lines of men in every shade of coat had begun to move across the meadow. Ball, in ever increasing numbers, was thrumming by or smashing into the logs before them.

It made concentration difficult. 'Cabins,' echoed Jack. He had noted something about cabins in the eternity that was the last hour, had ridden past them. They were held by . . . held by . . . Canadians. And Indians.

Até.

He grasped Balcarras's forearm. 'I'm for those cabins, Sandy.'

'Take your pick, Jack. It will be hot wherever you go. But perhaps there will be the hottest.'

'Have you a spare musket and bayonet?'

'Take mine.' He passed over both weapons. Jack checked the charge under the pan and thrust the blade into his belt beside his charged pistols. 'Now,' the Earl continued, 'that's a horse you owe me, a musket, and a bayonet . . . don't get yourself killed, dear fellow, you are too much in my debt.' He turned, yelled down the ranks of waiting men, 'Cock your firelocks! Present! Hold on my command!' Sergeants echoed the cry along the ramparts.

The cry of 'Fire!' came moments later, as Jack grasped the rear log wall of the stockade, the guns roaring almost as one. The vibration transferred through the wood to his hands, stinging them as he vaulted over. He landed somewhat awkwardly on the earth that had been thrown up against the redoubt, fell, his bearskin hat rolling far into the scrapings below. He left it, crouched and began to walk swiftly forward. It was when he cleared the cover of the walls that he realized how exposed he was. To his left, the lines of American troops had already crashed against Balcarras's Redoubt and, like a wave around a beach boulder, had spilled around it. Some were now paralleling his walk down toward the Breymann Redoubt a few hundred yards ahead while, behind them, more solid bodies were marching there beneath banners. To his right, two companies of Redcoats had formed a double rank. He saw their colour, noted that they were the regiment he'd been rather casually assigned to by Burgoyne, the 24th. They stood, muskets levelled at the Americans. He was directly between the rivals and equidistant from each, which was probably all that was saving him – from blue ranks to red, it was a long shot for both. Still, after those initial glances, Jack decided to work on the – he had to admit – somewhat childish principle that if he was not seeing them, they were not seeing him. He ground his teeth and kept his eyes fixed forward on his destination. It took only a minute, yet his shirt was soaked in sweat when he arrived. Just before the redoubt, a large shrub offered a little cover and he took it.

Though he was no engineer, even he could see what Sandy had meant. The German redoubt, while not as large or impressive as the British one, looked sturdy enough; but it was the cabins on the flanks that were its true weak points. Capture them and you turned the whole position, exposed the main fortification to fire from all sides. And unlike the palisades that were lined with men who would die for their dukes and their prickly honour, the cabins had apparently been garrisoned by the half-trained Canadian volunteers and the men who least liked such a static form of fighting – the very last of Burgoyne's Native allies.

Someone on the American side had obviously noted the same weaknesses. Mass and rapid firing was being directed at the musket slits of the larger of the two cabins, making it hard for the defenders to fire back. This was enabling parties of Rebels to draw ever closer, bearing firebrands and brushwood, and hurl these against the back wall. Another party carried a cedar trunk, its end roughly hewn into a point, to batter in the cabin door. With that, it would not be long before the door crumpled and they were inside, massacring the defenders.

As the Rebels began their charge, Jack stripped off his red coat, and threw it under a bush. Then, slinging his musket over his shoulder, he ran forwards, screaming the cry he'd most heard on the battlefield that day . . .

'Kill the bastards!'

A man fell away from the rear of the log, clutching at his neck. Jack shoved two men aside to take his place, just as the door's planks began to sunder. Three more thuds and it gave and the men at the front of the log died when it did, felled by a volley from within. The rest began to thrust through the gap, some dying, many making it in.

He was maybe the twentieth man inside and it was as if he'd been whipped fast to hell. Fire was already encasing the rear wall in crimson flowers of flame, smoke spiralling up in columns. Screaming men were everywhere engaged, bayonets plunging, guns exploding, tomahawks scything down, jerked from bodies to strike again. The floor was already slick with blood-soaked straw and men would fall and rise only to fall again.

It was hard to discern anything in that human abattoir. Jack, using his musket like a quarterstaff, parried blows from men who believed him to be an enemy while he sought for a friend. And there, in the darkest corner, where the most bodies lay, he found him.

It took five strides of slip and slide, strike and block, to get to him. By that time Até had felled the largest man before him and was engaged with four more, a tomahawk in one hand, Ironwood club in the other. But the dead before him testified how long he had been fighting. His arms were clearly growing weaker; a bayonet grazed his hip, two men with sabres were cutting down . . .

Jack stepped in, chucked his musket, taking one opponent full in the chest. Crossing his arms, he pulled the bayonet from his belt with his left hand, his sword from its sheath with his right, needing both weapons to counter the two that came, one for him, one for his brother. Parrying the sabre of a Militia officer, who had overstretched on his lunge, Jack pulled his own sabre back and hit the man, fist to face. He went down but Jack barely noted it, for he felt the bayonet in his left hand twitch as the sword he'd blocked with it withdrew to strike again. The man he'd punched falling away freed his sabre and he span out, ripping it straight across the white-clad chest, this man screaming, staggering backwards. The last one before Até, seeing the odds, turned, ran. The smoke was thickening around them and, for just a moment, Jack and Até were quite alone within it.

'Daganoweda!' Até's dark face split in a huge smile. 'I thought you were dead!'

'Very nearly. Very often. And that,' he said gesturing with his bayonet to the bodies before them, 'pays you for Oriskany.'

Até's smile disappeared. 'What . . . *these*? Only four of them? I could . . .' But the rest of his protestation went unheard, lost in two distinct sounds – the screaming of the remaining defenders, offering, almost as one, their surrender; and the burning rear wall of the cabin suddenly dissolving in a cascade of flame a foot from Jack and Até's backs.

All there, on either side, bent away from the sudden gust of heat, the surge of spark. Then Jack saw clear sky beyond the fire.

He yelled at Até over the roar. 'Surrender or . . .?' He gestured.

'Or!' Até shouted back and, on the word, dropped his powder horn and ran into the inferno. Jack dropped his, sheathed his sword and, a pace behind, leaped too, felt the fire snatch at him, sear his skin, crisp and dissolve some hair. Then the two of them were slipping down a slope to the rear of the cabin, rolling to dampen the flames, slapping themselves, each other.

'Up there!' Jack pointed, and the two of them ran towards Breymann's Redoubt. Bullets came, from behind and before – the Germans were trying to shoot them as well. But when Jack yelled, 'Officer of the Crown!' someone up there held the muskets back long enough for them to scramble through a door hastily opened, hastily closed.

At first, they were most concerned with extinguishing the flames that seared and burned them still. No sooner was one damped out than another made itself known in sudden pain. Até's brown skin had gained a feverish hue and he seemed to have mislaid one of his eyebrows. From the rawness he himself was feeling, Jack thought he must have fared no better. And Até, when he pointed at Jack's clothes, confirmed this.

'A king of shreds and patches,' he roared.

Jack looked around. If he thought they'd escaped from hell he was wrong; they had merely descended to an-other level. The green-jacketed Jaeger, the huge, blue-coated German Grenadiers, each were engaged in a fierce and increasingly unequal contest. The walls reached only just above the men's conical, metal-plated hats, and the Americans were hurling themselves over at many points. If one was shot, three more would take his place. The earth floor of the redoubt was breaking up into a series of savage individual contests.

'Look there!' Jack pointed. The main gates were being subjected to the same battering technique that had stoved in the cabin's doors. A tall and extravagantly moustached officer – it had to be Breymann himself – was mustering two ranks of men before it. Até snatched up a discarded musket; Jack pulled out his pistols, which miraculously had neither exploded in the flames nor been lost in the tumbling. Together they ran toward the rallying men.

They did not make it. With a noise like a drawn out-scream,

the gates crumpled in. The German volley was ragged, ineffectual; Rebels poured through the breach and in their midst was a man on a horse, screaming like a goblin, sword swirling above his head, urging his men on. Jack recognized him instantly.

'Arnold!' he cried, raising both pistols to fire. But a Grenadier beat him to it, shot the horse, which staggered, reared, both Jack's bullets passing through the point where the American General's head had just been. Then the stallion fell and Jack was close enough to hear the snap, the shriek of pain, as the full weight landed on Arnold's leg.

Up to now, Jack had been more concerned with preserving his own life and that of his friend. Now, with the man who'd ordered Simon Fraser shot lying before him, the blood rage descended. Throwing his pistols aside, snatching out his sword, he advanced on his enemy, seeing only him and this chance for vengeance. As he came, he shouted, 'Benedict Arnold! Murderer!'

The General, despite his agony, despite the cacophony of chaos that surrounded him, somehow heard Jack's shout and looked up.

'Lord John!' He cried, surprise paramount. Then his pain-wracked visage twisted into fury. 'Oath-breaker,' he screamed.

Arnold groped to his saddle, drawing forth a pistol. Jack advanced, senses centred on the man ahead. Até was two paces behind him; one pace too far to prevent one of Arnold's officers raising his rifle, firing. Something struck Jack, gouging fire across his temple. White light took him and he was down.

Yet this time there was no relieving dark to receive him. He watched the men before him – fighting, falling, dying – yet they were doing it quite slowly and in a world without sound. He watched Arnold's mouth, edged in white foam, forming curses directed straight at him, until he was pulled from under his horse and his head rolled back in a faint. He felt arms slide under his own shoulders, hands gripped across his chest, noted that the hands were streaked with soot, reddened with burns. He was being dragged backwards then, his sword slipping free though his fingers stretched for it, his heels carving twin trails in the earth. Once, the hands left him and he was aware of swift movements behind, and a soldier, a Rebel, falling to his side, lifeless eyes staring wide at him. Then he was gripped again, dragged again until his back rested against wood. Still in that slow silence, he watched more Americans come screaming into the stockade, watched the Germans finally break, watched Breymann cut down several deserters with his sabre, until one of his own men shot him then used his body to climb the wall.

The grip was on him again, he was being lifted, balanced on the rough planks tops, tipped over. He reached out and felt something snap in the wrist that would stop his fall, though, strangely, this came with no pain. Then the hands were under him and manoeuvring him over a shoulder.

He had only two more distinct thoughts as he was run across the stubble of Freeman's Farm. The first was that Até had once more stolen the lead in the saving of lives. The other arose from a sight, made more beautiful by the silence of that world. Clinging to a grass stalk was a butterfly, a monarch, its huge wings, red and black-veined, tipped in ovals of white, spread wide. Like Jack, it too hung upside down and as they passed, he saw it thrust its furred head into a tiny mauve flower.

— FIFTEEN —
The City of Brotherly Love

At the beginning, there was little to differentiate between day and night, the two made one by the rain that fell ceaselessly, not in drops, but in slabs of water from a sky that simply changed from dark to slightly darker. His fever provided another unity to time's passing, holding him in a deeper darkness, tides of consciousness that paid no attention to the hour of the clock, or what was being done to his body. He woke to find his hand and wrist set in splints and bandage, and having no memory of it being done. Woke again staring at a horse's mane, someone's arms around him while that person argued with men who wanted him removed from his mount and laid in the thick mud beside the road where other wounded moaned. That had not happened, for when he next awoke it was to Até forcing some sort of broth down his throat. When conscious, he had no connection with what was going on around him, except the sight of it; yet that was clear, and every object he regarded was haloed in light. When he slept, which was nearly all the time, the darkness was total, admitting no sound, no image of dream, only a simultaneous sensation of heat and terrible cold.

Finally, the movement ended, the army settling into a rough camp. Words penetrated, voices passing the tent he'd ended up in, telling that they were near Saratoga itself; for the battles, as was the custom, had been named for the nearest larger town, though fought ten miles to its south. People came, tarried, left, and it was these visits that gradually pulled his mind back to the world, helped him fix his place in it again. Até was nearly always there and when he wasn't he would soon return with food, sometimes with a grimace and thin gruel, other times with a grin and fresh-roasted squirrel or even venison. The Earl of Balcarras came one morning and sat for an hour while Jack listened to his tale, following the slow progress of the single tear trickling down that pale face as he described the burial of Simon Fraser on the battlefield the night of his death, just before the retreat began. He told of the roar of Rebel cannon that first were aimed at them, earth flying up into the faces of the mourning officers and men. And how, when the Americans realized it was not a gathering to assault but to bury, they switched to a Minute Gun, its salute punctuating the sad, proud eulogy delivered by the chaplain.

Two days later, with the balance now swinging to wakefulness in Jack's hours, it was Midshipman Edward Pellew who came and made Jack laugh for the first time in an age with his fury at what was being planned for him.

' 'Tis not the fact of surrender, Jack,' the young man declared, his Cornish accent growing ever stronger with his passion, 'but 'tis my part in it, see. I command the Marines, so am the senior naval officer present. I told them all in Council – "Fair do's," I says, "I can see the Army has no choice. But the Royal Navy never surrenders." I mean, Jack, if they're lettin' the Loyalists slip away, and your savage is the only Native who hasn't absconded, why not let me take my twenty lads and break out? But the General wouldn't hear of it, for some reason.'

Balcarras had been the first to mention the negotiations. Até had confirmed it with a few disapproving grunts. It seemed inconceivable, a British Army yielding to a Colonial one. It had never happened before. Yet it was Jack's third visitor who confirmed the inevitability.

He was up from his cot for the first time, attempting a few foal-like steps across the tent, when a voice halted his progress.

'And that's the first gladdening sight to meet these eyes in many a day. Are you then recovered, Captain Absolute?'

Jack turned, nearly lost his balance, held himself on his stick.

'General . . . I am better, yes. The ball skinned, but did not enter, my much abused head.'

Burgoyne stood clutching an edge of canvas. Jack was shocked – for the normally ruddy face was almost white, its only shade deriving from the great patches of darkness under each bloodshot eye. His thick, snowy hair did not have its usual abundance but looked thin, plastered down. It was only in the exquisite cut of the uniform that Burgoyne was himself. It had to have been altered to suit a loss of weight and the thought made Jack smile. 'Gentleman Johnny' would sooner go on campaign without a company of Grenadiers than his tailor.

'Sir, come in, please. Would you care to sit?'

Burgoyne entered but shook his head. 'I fear, dear Jack, that if I do I shall not rise again. But you must, please.'

He gestured and Jack sank gratefully down. 'I have little to offer you, sir.' His gaze moved around the canvas. 'Unless . . .' He reached forward and pulled down a bundle of fibrous strands from the tent pole. 'Dried meat?'

Burgoyne took one of the strips and chewed. 'Venison, eh? By God, Absolute, you eat better than any in the army. That will be your Até, I suppose?' Jack nodded. 'Where is he? I would like to talk with the fellow.' He sighed. 'My last loyal savage.'

'Out procuring more of this, I should think.' Jack took a strip, gnawed at the gamey meat. 'So I'll give him your good wishes. And I'm sure he'd wish you to take this. A guest's gift.' At the man's hesitation, he continued, 'There'll be plenty more for us, General, never fear. And you know the hospitality of an Iroquois.'

'Well, one would not wish to be rude.' Burgoyne took the proffered bundle of jerky and tucked it rather swiftly into a capacious pocket at the back of his coat. 'Now, sir, I have something of import to discuss with you. Perhaps I will share that seat, if I may?'

Jack shifted and Burgoyne sat heavily down. There was a time when their combined weights would have tested the camp bed's construction. *No more*, thought Jack, somewhat ruefully.

'So,' began Burgoyne briskly, 'you know about the result of the negotiations, do you?'

'I have heard . . . something. Is it capitulation, then?'

'It is not!' Burgoyne tapped Jack's knee with one finger. 'I may have lost the campaign but I have undoubtedly won the peace. It is a "convention". We are to be known as the "Convention Army", and will march by way of Boston to a British fleet and thence home. We will not be allowed to fight in this war again, none of us, but . . . it will at least free His Majesty to send replacement forces here.'

'It seems . . . generous of the Rebel, to say the least.'

'I bamboozled him, Jack,' Burgoyne declared proudly. 'Told Gates that we'd hurl ourselves upon him with bayonets fixed and die rather than submit to humiliation. And he still fears that Clinton will come, even if I am now certain that he will not. So he signed the Convention with alacrity. We march out on the morrow with full honours of war.'

For all the bravado in the speech, Burgoyne would not look at him. Jack struggled to choke down both his anger and the thoughts he would express. Whatever sweetening euphemisms were used, it was still surrender. Whatever the terms, the Yankee had triumphed. He thought of Simon Fraser then, his sacrifice, and of all the hundreds, thousands, who had marched down from Canada, never to march back. And he felt something he'd never experienced before as a Redcoat – shame.

His throat was full yet he managed to speak. 'So we are prisoners, sir, at least for a while?'

'We are in their hands, yes. All of us.' The older man paused, at last looked up. 'All, that is, save three.' He let the words sink in, continued. 'That is what I would talk to you about. One of my conditions was that I was allowed to inform my superiors of the . . . debacle that has been so much their fault. So three dispatch bearers are guaranteed safe passage. One to Boston and thence by swiftest frigate to Lord Germain in London. One to General Clinton in New York. And one to Sir William Howe, our Commander in North America, who has had some successes against Washington and taken Philadelphia.' Burgoyne's voice could not help but edge with bitterness as he spoke those words. 'I want you to be that messenger and ride to Philadelphia.'

Jack's heartbeat quickened. *To not be part of this surrender, to be free to carry on the fight!* Yet a soldier's honesty made him caution.

'I thank you for the honour and the trust, General. But,' he gestured to himself, 'I am not in the rudest of health. My progress may be slower than you would like. Does General Howe not need this news urgently?'

Burgoyne said, softly, 'I am sure he will know it within a week if not in days. The Rebel will trumpet his triumph swiftly, both here and in the courts of Europe. Especially in Paris. The French have been aiding the rebellion since its beginning and not very secretly. Who knows what those curs will do now.' He sighed. 'No, it is not truly as a news bearer that you are needed there, Jack. It is for . . . something else.'

The vigour with which he'd proclaimed his skills in negotiation had left him. He leaned forward now to rest arms on knees, rubbing his hands first against each other then reaching one up to his brow. His eyes seemed to darken still more as they stared forward.

'There are several reasons I could give why I lost this campaign. Some, no doubt, my fault; others, certainly the greater number, clearly not. But one remains prominent in my mind: I have been consistently undermined from within. Somewhere out there, in that rabble of Germans and Loyalists, there is still, as we have discussed, a traitor, a spy. He has stolen my decoding mask, spread dissension between my allies, consistently betrayed my secrets to my foes. I do not speak of von Schlaben – as we said, he was not in the camp when our mask went missing – though I am sure he was involved. The Count may well be this other, this Cato. But the one he controls, this . . .'

'Diomedes?'

'Just so. Diomedes. Whoever he is, he will move on to plague General Howe, attempting to ruin him as he has helped to ruin me.'

He turned back to Jack, reached out to grip his arm. 'You must find him. Root him out and kill him before he does to Howe's campaign what he did to mine. It may be the last action I can take to help win this war. Set a spy to trap a spy.'

Jack looked at his leader, noted the sadness, the desperation in him. And he realized that the terrible feeling he'd had when he thought of surrender and the wasted death of Simon Fraser was dispersing like a weight pulled off his chest.

'I will go to Philadelphia, sir. And I swear this to you – I will see this Diomedes dead.'

Burgoyne held his gaze for a moment. 'Good,' he said on a sigh. 'And I am going to promote you, lad. To Brevet-Major. A field promotion only, alas, that those fools in London will no doubt rescind at war's end to save themselves a farthing. Captain Money will be by later with the commission, the dispatch, and a generous supply of gold. Enough even for a spendthrift such as yourself.' A brief smile came as he rose from the bed, Jack rising behind him. 'You'll take your savage?'

'If my savage will come, aye. He has concerns of his own in this land. And he has no obligations to me. Quite the reverse, damn the fellow!'

Burgoyne nodded, his mind already moving beyond the tent. He was at the flap when he stopped, turned back. 'All the luck in the world, *Major* Absolute. I know we shall meet again. Perhaps at Drury Lane, eh? Where the prologue of our own little play began. That was quite a night for you, wasn't it? Long as I live, I'll never forget your entrance, Stage Right. Barely had your breeches done up.' He chuckled. 'But try not to get into any duels this time, eh?'

The tent flap had barely settled before it twitched up again and Até was there.

'You just missed the General. He wanted to see you.'

Até came in, two squirrels dangling from his belt. 'I did not want to see him. He smells of defeat. It's not a smell I like.'

Momentarily annoyed, Jack grunted – nothing could persuade an Iroquois that Burgoyne had no choice. Then he told Até of his new mission. 'Will you come?'

'I do not think you could reach this city without me. But I will not stay. There are things afoot in the land of the Mohawk, bad things. I must return.'

'Fair enough,' Jack said. He looked down at his bandaged arm. His sword arm, of course. He did not need Burgoyne's warning about duels, he would not be fighting with a sword any time soon. But a pistol he could fire with his left hand. As he hoped Diomedes would soon find out.

'So what, exactly, are you doing in Philadelphia, uh . . . Major Absolute?'

Major Puxley sat behind his desk, staring up at his visitor, unease plain on his large, farmer's face. Jack understood his discomfort, indeed shared a little of it. When he'd last seen Puxley, the Welshman had been the Senior Sergeant in Jack's company of Dragoons. That had been in 1767, the year Jack had resigned his commission in the 16th and first gone to India. He was pleased to see that the man had risen from the ranks; he was more than capable of the responsibility. But the reversal of their positions – Puxley was a full Major, not a Brevet like Jack – was awkward.

While he considered his answer, Jack glanced out into the stable yard. A platoon of troopers was saddling up, a corporal stalking among them checking equipment. Though Philadelphia was firmly in the British grasp, the surrounding country was still hard contested. The patrol would need to be well accoutred and prepared.

Puxley had followed Jack's gaze, misinterpreted it. 'I mean, if you should wish to resume your regimental duties . . . it might be a little difficult. Your commission makes you superior to Kelly and Craddock, whom you might remember. Captains now, but they've been serving for years and, to be truthful, the regiment is functioning so well . . .'

He petered out. Jack regarded the man. He had always got on well with him, ever since they had fought together under Burgoyne in Spain and Portugal. He had no desire to discountenance him now – and even less to take up the normal duties of a Dragoon officer. He was there for different reasons, which need not concern this honest soldier.

'Sir, may I?' He tapped the chair before the desk with his cane.

'My dear fellow, of course. Please.'

Jack sat, leaned forward, his voice lowering. 'I wouldn't conceive of disrupting the running of the regiment. I took my commission again on General Burgoyne's insistence. But he wanted me at his side, to aid him in . . . certain areas where he felt I could be of most use.'

The other man shifted, looking uncomfortable. 'Areas of . . . intelligence?'

'Yes, sir. You understand I cannot be more . . .' Jack waved a hand.

'Quite so! Quite so!' Puxley too had leaned across the desk, his tone and volume matching Jack's. 'Rather you than me, to be honest. But what is it then, that you require of the regiment?'

It was all quickly arranged. Jack would once more assume the privileges of an officer of the 16th but without any of the duties. His bandaged arm, his fever pallor, these would be enough to excuse him while his new rank of Major, even if it was only a field promotion, would give him access to the more elevated echelons of society, free to roam the city engaged on . . . whatever his mission was.

'No need to go into any of that, eh?' Puxley rose, so Jack did too. 'You are, of course, welcome at the Mess any time. In fact we would be thrilled if you'd come tonight. We are all so keen to learn first-hand of the travails of poor General Burgoyne.

Hear it was the Germans let us down again, what? Anyway, you have a billet, yes? Good, good.'

He was ushering Jack out, obviously greatly relieved that this new problem had solved itself. Jack halted in the doorway. 'One other thing, Major?' He indicated the very tattered and mismatched remnants of his infantry uniform, under his borrowed greatcoat. 'Is there a tailor in the city who could make me a Dragoon uniform?'

Puxley nodded. 'Indeed there is. Alphonse of Locust Street. A splendid worker, though he can't help being French. Problem is he is very busy as he also makes dresses and many of the ladies of the town go to him. Every evening is spent in balls and recitals and all sorts of damned fripperies.' He gave a very soldierly shrug. 'Gold speeds things along, of course.'

'Well, I have that.' Jack stepped outside, into chilly November sunshine. 'Thank you so much, sir.'

He saluted, Puxley returned it then reached out his hand, his voice suddenly full of the Welsh tones he'd restrained. 'Glad to see you again, Jack. Come to the Mess, will you? We're pretty informal there, see. We can talk of old times. Spain, eh?' He shivered. 'Damn sight warmer than here. And the women . . .'

He smiled, tipped a finger to his brow, and closed the door. Jack watched the now mounted patrol ride smartly through the yard gate and followed them out into the street.

As he walked away from the barracks, Jack reflected that at least the second of his official meetings had gone better than the first. That had taken place the day before when, on his arrival, he had presented Burgoyne's dispatches at the mansion commandeered by the British Army for its headquarters. Once his credentials were established, he had been brought quickly enough into the presence of the Commander-in-Chief, Sir William Howe, but then sent on his way as swiftly as bare civility allowed.

He and the General had some history. Howe had also been in the vanguard of that assault up the cliffs at Quebec in 1759. He'd been a Colonel then, so had paid little attention to the young Lieutenant fresh from England, despite Jack's brave actions that day. Or perhaps because of them – Howe was notoriously chary of sharing glory. They had seen each other at times over that campaign and intermittently over the years since. Each time, Howe had contrived to forget Jack's name and confuse his rank. At this meeting in Philadelphia, he not only did both those things, he also gave the impression, in the way he barely looked at the messenger and addressed remarks to him through a third party, that Jack was Burgoyne's man, associated with something distasteful – failure, defeat, an unthinkable surrender. Jack would have put some of this down to guilt, since, in not marching to rendezvous with Burgoyne in Albany, Howe had contributed so much to that failure. But this was crediting the Commander-in-Chief with a capacity for concern he undoubtedly did not possess. Indeed, if the rumours Jack had already heard in the city were true, Howe's only real concern was to return as soon as possible to the soft attentions of his mistress, Betsey Loring, just brought down from New York. Whatever the reason, Jack was in the Commander's presence no longer than five minutes. Howe wanted nothing from him. He'd already had innumerable reports from spies, deserters, and Rebels as to the battles at Saratoga and the Convention that had been signed two weeks previously. He probably regarded the dispatches Jack brought as mere exculpation on Burgoyne's part. He'd asked that they be handed over to his intelligence officer – some fellow named Major John André, not present at the meeting – to analyse, précis, and report. Jack was barely acknowledged and quickly dismissed.

Which suits me perfectly, Jack thought. He had not revealed himself to anyone on General's Howe's staff as anything other than a messenger and convalescing officer. He did not know how infiltrated that staff might be. Working alone gave him his best chance of discovering the identity of Díomedes. And alone, he had a better chance of exacting Burgoyne's – and his own – revenge.

Philadelphia was a well-made place – broad, tree-lined

avenues behind which sat handsome, two-storey houses. No doubt, several belonged to the signatories of the famous Declaration with which they had proclaimed Colonial independence from this very city the previous year. Men now driven away to shiver with Washington in the field, while British officers enjoyed their well-appointed residences, their servants, and, Jack was sure, many of their daughters and wives as well – for the city appeared full of women, all claiming to be Loyalists, strolling down the streets despite the chill wind, smiling at British officers, giggling and gossiping in groups on every corner. Jack had secured fine quarters on Chestnut Street, sharing with just two other officers of General Howe's staff. It was costly but after what he'd been through, he saw no reason to scrimp and, with Burgoyne's generosity, no need to. Até had paid a swift visit, grunted his disapproval of such luxury, and departed the next day, pausing only to stock up on second-hand books. After toting the hefty *Clarissa* throughout the campaign, he had developed what Jack found to be quite a disturbing taste in novels, the more sentimental the better. Jack couldn't abide novels himself. Give him a good play any day! Yet it was sad to see his comrade go, back to the dangers of the Mohawk valley, to the civil war of the Iroquois. They made arrangements to keep in contact, hard though it would be in that fractured world. At the least, the plan was to rendezvous in the Cherry Valley when the blossoms came.

Locust Street was more of an alley, lined with stores of varying size. Above the door of one 'Alphonse' was lettered in gold leaf. A half-crown to the elegantly attired and be-wigged doorman gained him entrance and a private room. The sight of silver also brought *le patron* quite swiftly. Jack's French was praised as much as his physique – mere flattery given his privations – but the greatest approbation was reserved for his coin. A price that would have shocked the denizens of Jermyn Street was eventually agreed. Jack felt that, if he was to honour the command of his General, he would have to operate in the same circles, the same balls and events Diomedes would to glean his information – the very highest. Besides, Burgoyne would not begrudge him. The two men had always shared a love of good tailoring. And Jack had been grubby in this campaign quite long enough.

The only difficulty, as Puxley had foretold, came over timing. Jack wanted it yesterday and at that the diminutive Frenchman baulked.

'Impossible, monsieur. It is the Governor's Ball next week and all the ladies of the city will only come *à la maison Alphonse.*' He sighed and looked as if this was the greatest source of regret instead of the reason his own coat was so threaded through with gold.

'And I am to attend the same event. Do you wish me to go like this?'

Alphonse looked with ill-concealed distaste at Jack's apparel. 'Perhaps we could adapt something already made—'

'Already *made*?' Jack's voice deepened. 'I will not be seen in cast-offs, sir. I don't think you quite realize who I am. I am to be fêted at this same Governor's Ball. For I, sir, am Lord John Absolute – hero of Saratoga.'

The name meant nothing, the title only a little – Jack knew you could throw a stick on any street corner in Philadelphia and strike three lords – but the idea that a man dressed in one of his creations would be the focus of the festivities obviously appealed. As did the producing of a two-guinea gold piece as down payment. Alphonse pocketed it with the sigh of a martyr while agreeing to all. Then the footman informed him that a large party had arrived for final fittings and he rushed away, promising to send his subordinates to take measurements.

Soon Jack was stripped down to shirt and breeches, while Alphonse's assistants – who somehow achieved the near-impossible by being more haughty than their master – moved around him taking down his every detail. A middling white port was served, which Jack happily sipped. Indeed he was beginning to feel more relaxed than he had in many a day. He had a mission, and a deadly one at that. He'd always found it intriguing when pitted against a worthy opponent, which this Diomedes certainly was. But the mission's pursuance required a role of him, the elegant officer. One for which he was – or soon would be – well suited.

Laughter came from the next room, only a little muffled by the thin walls. Both men and women were there and Jack enjoyed listening to the cadence of the bantering, if not being able to distinguish many words. When was the last time he had heard people really laugh? At Drury Lane? In another life, certainly. He half-listened, as the assistants wielded tapes and sticks around him.

Then he heard something else, a fall of pure merriment in a woman's voice. There was something especially musical to it and he had heard something like it before. When he realized where, he was through the door in a moment, protesting tailors scattering from his path.

The next door was ajar. A male voice had joined in the laugh, so Jack felt no need to pause and politely knock before intruding on ladies. Besides, his accelerating heart would allow no such niceties. Shoving hard, he swept in.

They were obviously used to people coming in and out, for no one looked up. Two young ladies sat on a divan, each tugging at an exquisitely dressed young gentleman between them, who was clutching a paper pad in one hand while endeavouring, despite the wrestling, to sketch a third young lady with a soft crayon. She was standing across from the divan, surrounded by kneeling tailoresses with pins in their mouths and it was her, fighting for balance, trying to hold a pose, who was still laughing the laugh that had drawn Jack there.

The third young lady was Louisa Reardon.

She saw him last. One of the young ladies looked at him with interest, the other with distaste, as her eyes climbed from his stockinged feet to his stock-less neck. The gentleman rose, laying the pad down. Jack took them in as if he was in some sort of dream, or at that moment in battle when time moved slowly. When his regard returned to the model, her eyes rose for the first time and met his.

They widened. She gasped, tottered. There was a cry of

dismay from the women at her feet as pins popped and something ripped. Louisa struggled for balance then, heeding the shrill warnings, settled. He could, however, move and did and was across the room in three strides.

Only the assistants at her feet prevented him from seizing her.

'Jack! How . . . When?' Colours chased each other across her face.

'Louisa!' He saw a gap, moved to go through it – till her hand, thrust out, halted him.

'Jack, have a care, or you'll ruin this dress.'

'I *don't* care, I . . .'

'Jack!' The hand now gestured, to the man and the two ladies rising from the divan. He did halt then, even turned partly to them.

'Another admirer, Louisa?' The man's voice was pleasant, full of laughter.

'An old friend.' Her voice shook. 'Jack, this is Major John—'

It was not the time for tedious, polite introductions. 'How are you here? How did you escape? How, by all that's holy—?'

'It's a long story. Jack, these are my good friends—'

'I thought you . . . a prisoner at the least, if not—'

'Dead?' The word at last halted her attempted introduction. 'I heard you were taken but only later, for they had already let me go and I did not linger for them to change their minds. They'd believed my story of fleeing those who would rob us. But I learned, once I reached New York, that you'd been proclaimed a spy. They were going to examine then . . . then hang you.' She shook her head slowly. 'Oh, Jack. I believed *you* were the one dead. I mourned for you – once more.'

Confusion stirred something in him, compounded by the presence of this handsome young man, the laughter he'd over-heard, that had drawn him here.

'Yes, I can see how well black suits you,' he said, looking at the vibrant pink of the skirt, the canary yellow of the bodice.

The blow struck home and she blushed, nearly the colour of

the dress. Before she could speak, the young man had come forward, arm extended. He took Jack's unbandaged left hand.

'Major John André. And these ladies are my two adorable Pegs – Miss Peggy Shippen and Miss Peggy Chew.' Both misses curtseyed, giggled, then turned to whisper to each other, their gaze still upon him. 'And you must be the officer who accompanied Miss Reardon on that hazardous ride. We all rejoice to see you alive, sir. We have heard so many tales of your forest skills, your gallantry, "Jack, this" and "Jack, that." The only thing she failed to supply us with was your surname.'

André was in his mid-twenties, Jack guessed – closer in age to Louisa than himself. He was small, in height and physique, almost delicate, with a face that would have been called pretty on a woman. Each of the Peggys would have fought the other for his eyelashes. He reminded Jack of Banastre Tarleton. Yet in Tarleton's face the man's cruelty revealed itself in a thrust of jaw, the mad-dog gleam of his self-regard, the fanaticism in his eyes. André's displayed nothing so much as a profound amiability. Intelligence was there too, keenly so. But he was obviously a lover of life – and life returned the compliment. Indeed, if the ladies' marked attention to him was anything to go by, life returned the compliment in trumps.

'Major Jack Absolute of the 16th Light Dragoons.'

'Burgoyne's own,' André murmured. 'You weren't with that noble man at Saratoga by any chance?'

'I was. I brought his dispatches here to General Howe.'

'Oh, that was you? I am on the General's staff but was absent when they arrived.'

Of course. He knew he'd heard the name before. Major John André was the officer responsible for précising the reports Jack had brought. He was Howe's Intelligence as Jack had been Burgoyne's. It suddenly put the amiability of the man's face into a different perspective, as a mask always will.

André still held Jack's hand quite in the manner of an old friend. Suddenly, the pressure of his grip increased. 'Wait! Jack Absolute? You're not *the* Jack Absolute, are you? From Sheridan's *Rivals*?'

Jack flushed. His infamy had leaped the ocean then. 'I rather think it is the other way around, sir. That . . . Irishman misappropriated my name and certain . . . aspects of my past, for his drama.'

André's hand was now pumping Jack's. 'By all that's marvellous! I have just formed a little theatre company. Think of me as Philostrate – "For how shall we beguile this lazy time if not with some delight."' He laughed, as musically as Louisa. 'We call ourselves The Thespians and there is a small but quite acceptable playhouse here, the Southwark. And, sir, sir, this is the most wonderful thing! We open next week . . . with *The Rivals*.'

Jesus! Would that play never cease to haunt him?

Holding on still, André continued, 'You don't, by any chance, perform, do you, Major?'

Summoning his disdain took a little time. Louisa jumped into the gap. 'He does indeed. I acted with him on the voyage over. Jack has a wonderful presence upon the stage.'

'And one of our Thespians has just dropped out,' André continued. 'He was inconsiderate enough to get himself shot in the leg while on patrol. He'll walk again but not act any time soon. Left me in a predicament, I have to say. Thought I was going to have to go on for him as well as stage the piece. Too important a role for a divided attention – for he was to play your namesake, sir.' André added his second hand to Jack's single one. Those heavily-lashed eyes were at their most imploring. 'Why don't you take it on?'

It was such an outrageous idea that it actually stopped Jack's breath. While he sought for it, Louisa gave a delighted laugh.

He looked from her back to the Major and, detaching his hand from André's fervent grip, he said stiffly, 'Since that jackanapes Sheridan abused me so, I have been pestered by every chairman, porter and ladies' maid crying, "Are you *that* Jack Absolute?" And you would have me, in a land so far blessedly free of this calumny, personify *myself*?' The words could not have been laden with any more contempt.

Yet they seemed to do little to put off the Major. He

countered, 'But who better to defend the reputation, to give us the truth of the man than the man himself? Also . . .' and here he glanced briefly at Louisa, 'I can assure you the rest of the casting is equally strong. For example, could you wish for a better stage partner than our lovely Miss Reardon?'

Of course. Louisa would be playing Lydia, Jack Absolute's stage lover, based on the bloody girl Jack had made such a fool of himself over in Bath all those years ago, the story Sheridan had stolen for his bloody plot. And they wanted him to play himself, to make stage love to the incarnation of his youthful folly, played by a woman he so desired. To parade his history and his feelings before an audience that would include the General staff of the British Army, the cream of Loyalist society, as well, no doubt, as every spy in Philadelphia, including the man he'd been sent there to kill?

'Never,' he roared. 'If I was to be boiled alive, pulled apart between stallions, offered the key to the Seraglio of the Sultan and a thousand nights to enjoy it. Never! Never. Never. *Never!*'

— SIXTEEN —
The Rehearsal

'If she holds out now, the devil is in it.'

Jack looked out into the emptiness, waited. Nothing. At the first rehearsal, that line had conjured a huge laugh from the cast. In the week of rehearsals since, it had received not even a chuckle.

Perhaps he had delivered the line badly? It was the cursed thing about this playing. Did one let the line speak for itself? Or did one need to emphasize it for the audience, lead them to the laugh? 'Speak the speech, trippingly upon the tongue,' Hamlet had cautioned.

But Hamlet never played Philadelphia on a freezing November night! Jack breathed out, saw his breath stream away above the candles on the forestage. He shivered, not just from the cold November air, then turned his attention back to the one warm thing there. Before delivering the line, he had kissed his Lydia. And Louisa was still in his arms.

Was it the kiss that had affected his delivery of the line? Three times they had played this scene, three times they had kissed; and each time the kiss was different. The first, on the day after their reunion at Alphonse's, had been passionate – at least on his behalf. She had broken it off quickly, embarrassed before the other actors it seemed. With the second kiss, two days later, she was the one with the passion, he who felt strained.

And this third? He looked at Louisa now as she rose up in his arms, drawing breath for her next line. Yes, it was indeed why he had said the line so poorly.

For this third kiss was cold. Functional. For the stage alone.

'Now could I fly with him to the Antipodes! But my persecution is not yet come to a crisis!' Louisa declaimed, a hand to her brow in the approved style. The other actors, playing his father and her aunt – a colonel of engineers and his wife, both much given to over-egging the comic aspects of their roles – came on. The scene concluded and Jack was soon in the wings, Louisa beside him though rapidly moving away to change her dress for the next scene, leaving Jack to reflect on the quality of kisses.

Those three dissatisfying moments were the most intimate exchanges of his whole time in Philadelphia. Louisa's coolness, which he'd sensed almost from the moment of their reunion, had, to his confusion, persisted, grown, like the ever-heavier snowfalls that covered the city each night. And the rehearsals were indeed the only time they seemed able to be together. Though these only occupied a portion of each day, the rest of her hours were divided between caring for her ill mother – who she'd brought down from New York and who was still sickly and house-bound – and the social swirl that was the city's society. Balls, dinners, recitals – Jack, resplendent in his new uniform, attended them too, knowing that somewhere among the elite crowd might also be his quarry, Diomedes, or another who would lead Jack to him, and perhaps also to Cato, Diomedes's superior. He circled, talked, questioned, his passion for vengeance undiminished since parting from his betrayed General. He had so far discovered nothing but rumour. Yet, in the deepest part of his heart, he knew his motives were not pure, that there was another reason he attended these functions – to see Louisa. This was not HMS *Ariadne*, with people always a thin plank away. This was a city; and the mansions, where the balls were held, had many rooms. Surely, he'd reasoned, it would be possible to steal Louisa away to one of them, to be alone, to talk, at the very least? In the forest they had seemed to share every thought in the long evenings lit by the campfire's light. He missed that intimacy, especially in its contrast to their conversations in Philadelphia, limited, as they were, to Sheridan's on-stage exchanges and snatched whispers in the wings. At the balls and gatherings, he'd watch her, wait for an opportunity. But she was never alone, being either with the two Peggys, or at the centre of a circle of admiring young officers; conspicuous among whom, for both his looks and his captivating ways, was John André.

Each night Jack would return to his lodgings alone and brood on the changes in her. Was it possible that the feelings she'd had for him, so strong in the forest, had dissipated during their brief separation? And had those affections transferred so swiftly to another?

Jack peered now around the proscenium arch into the darkened auditorium. Their director was out there, and with a little time before his next entrance, he decided to visit him. André was the other reason he'd agreed to play himself in *The Rivals*. Who better to glean information from, as to spy rings and double agents in Philadelphia, than Howe's Intelligence?

He'd even thought he might confide in André. Caution had held him back; for it was possible that Diomedes lurked undetected at the heart of Howe's command as he had at the heart of Burgoyne's and Jack did not want another officer scaring him off. Also, conversations with the younger man did nothing to make Jack want to take him into his confidence.

In a week of hints and gentle probing, Jack had confirmed little other than, yes, there were undoubtedly spies in Philadelphia and, yes, once the play was up, the Major would devote himself completely to hunting them down. Indeed, André, in his casualness, was quite unlike any other intelligence officer Jack had met. With almost daily Rebel raids on the city, with English patrols being ambushed as if news of their coming had been sent ahead, there should have been plenty to concern and occupy André. But he seemed to wish only to talk of London theatre, his obsession, and Jack's friendship with the admired Sheridan. The war, their similar roles in it, seemed to interest the younger man hardly at all. The only other times the languid young man would animate was when he was addressing Louisa. Could Jack be the only one who noticed how André's eyes glinted when he regarded her, how his attention pulled his whole body towards her when they talked?

Jack made his way into the auditorium. His rival was near the back, his sketching pad as ever beside him, though now it was filling with notes to himself and the players. Jack, with a nervous glance at the scribbles – he had no doubt that some of the criticisms would be aimed at him – sat beside him and watched the next scene. Quite soon, it reached the point where the stage Irishman, Sir Lucius O'Trigger, was due to make his entrance. As usual, he didn't

'Henry,' André called to the Colonel, 'read in for him, will you, so the others can say their lines?' As an appallingly faked Irish accent came down from the stage, André turned to Jack, saw his expression. 'I know, dear fellow. But he will be here.'

'When?' The actor personifying Sir Lucius had suddenly decided, after only one rehearsal, that he did not want to be a player. But instead of recasting, André had learned that an officer who had only just played the part in New York ('Alas, Jack,' André had said, 'it appears that ours is not to be the premiere performance in this land') was bound for Philadelphia. Each day he was promised, each day he failed to arrive.

'Tomorrow.'

'On the night we open?'

'Jack, rest easy. He knows the lines. I can take him through the blocking in an hour.'

'And the duel?' The characters, Jack and Sir Lucius, were meant to cross swords over Lydia. Despite his dislike of most aspects of playing, Jack had been almost looking forward to a spirited stage duel – even if, with his injury, he would have to fight left-handed. Most theatrical fights were dreadful – if he had to sit through one more Mercutio and Tybalt limp-wristedly flailing at each other! So he'd carefully worked out a few ideas.

'Sorry, Jack. I know your hopes but we'll just have to do it as play-scripted. You cross blades only and then the rest will rush on and separate you.'

Disappointed, Jack rose and walked back to the stage. His next entrance was coming up. *Why did I let myself be talked into this?* he thought, mentally giving himself a good kick in the rear. *Why?* And then he saw the ultimate 'why', standing in the wings, leaning on a pedestal, wearing her change of dress. This one was cut especially low and, even though it was just the rehearsal, she had used some powders there, highlighted and shaded, though her charms had no need of enchancement. Whose benefit was that for, he wondered. She was leaning forward slightly, those eyes alive with mockery at some compliment the very young Ensign, Anton Hervey, who played Acres, was obviously paying her.

The Ensign left her for his scene. Jack moved behind Louisa. Her face was to the stage and she did not hear him come.

'Can we meet tonight?' he whispered.

'Oh, Jack!' She turned, startled. 'What did you say?'

He kept his voice low. 'Tonight, Louisa. Come to my house. The other officers are on patrol. We . . .'

He hesitated. She flushed. 'Oh, Jack. You know how I would love to. But John has called an extra rehearsal at his lodgings, for myself and Julia.' She pointed at Peggy Chew, mouthing lines in the wings opposite. 'And then he will give us a late supper.' She looked away, then back to add, 'You could join us?'

She had splayed her fan, fluttered it now before her face. Was it that prop that gave something of the stage to the invitation? Was there not something more than half-hearted about it? He felt heat now, at last, rising in his face. 'I would not wish to intrude, madam,' he said, bowing slightly, though to her back, as she was already making her next entrance.

He had attended one such supper before. But the two Pegs, André, some of his brother officers . . . they were all so damnably young! The men had barely seen combat, the girls – they were little more than that – had been raised in a restricted, harmless society. He enjoyed company, was considered a spirited companion; he could carouse with the best. But with his splinted hand and his fever pallor, his recent experiences still haunting his face . . . he felt like a gnarled old wolfhound allowed to lie before the fire with tumbling puppies. He'd said little, drank too much . . . especially when he'd again noted the exchanges between Louisa and John André. Of course she flirted, it was society's way and indiscriminate; yet for the handsome Major she seemed to reserve a special attention, a lingering of eyes.

He watched her from the wings, his heart quickening, driving heat again into his face. Again, he thought back to the forest, their time there, curling around her each night, bound by the word he'd given to her father. And another word came to him, the one she'd called him then.

'Fool,' he muttered. 'Bloody fool!'

Rehearsal over, comments on their performances given, the cast dispersed.

He had no further conversation with Louisa, no desire to. He watched her helped into a cloak, spread over the last dress she'd worn on stage, the low-cut one. Obviously what enticed in the theatre would do so equally over supper.

Jack left, saying goodbye to no one. Once outside, he was somewhat at a loss so he tucked himself into a doorway opposite the playhouse to consider his options. Snow was falling again, adding to the prodigious quantities that had already transformed the city into a slippery, muffled cocoon. A bitter wind came with it, so that the snow fell slantways, driving into the very few people who struggled through the streets. Shrugging deeper into his greatcoat, pulling down his tricorn hat, Jack wondered where to seek shelter. There was always the mess of the 16th. Jack had already passed several pleasant nights there, taking comfort in the simple conversation of fellow soldiers, men he'd known in that other life, those other wars. There was good food, plenty of grog . . . and not a mention of which greasepaint provided the greatest effect, or the absurd inflexions of a fellow performer. Suddenly it seemed a very good place to be and Jack was just about to forsake his paltry shelter when the playhouse door opposite swung open and Anton Hervey, Peggy Chew, John André, and Louisa Reardon stepped out. Without even considering it, Jack let them get fifty yards ahead then began to follow.

He had stalked many people down numerous city streets and he knew how to remain unnoticed, but in this case there was little need for caution, his quarry quite absorbed in their own, high-spirited company. He followed them down the main thoroughfare, then through some winding back streets. They were undoubtedly heading toward the Major's lodgings. It was in a less favoured area than Jack's, for André, though of good enough society, did not possess Jack's sudden wealth. He shared a sprawl of rooms above a baker's with six other officers from his regiment; the heat from the ovens below kept them snug, he said.

They were soon there and the party went up immediately. Opposite the house, noise and smoke leaked from the half-open door of a tavern. There was a grimy, lead-framed bow window that gave on to the street. Considering that he may as well be warm and liquored while he waited and watched, he entered.

It was a soldier's place, not an officer's, but the inhabitants were too far into the evening to give his well-cut clothes much notice. Their attention was largely focused on a civilian fiddle player in the corner, who sawed and bowed with vigour and some skill, his efforts luring several couples to the jig. Fetching himself a large mug of heated rum, Jack pushed to the window. The corner seat was taken by a corporal from a Highland regiment, who balanced a tough-looking, pock-marked, 'lady of the town' upon his bare knee. When Jack opened his coat enough to reveal the officer's gorget at his neck, she looked as if she would argue, but the Scotsman dragged her off by the hand, saying, 'Dinna fash, limmer. Awa to dance!' A little smile came as Jack thought on Angus MacTavish and his unintelligible ways. Then he rubbed a patch of the window clean, loosened his coat, and settled to his vigil.

An hour passed, people came into the house opposite but none left. Jack finished the rum and, despite a sudden desire to get drunk, now ordered a pint of beer from a serving girl. She appeared to want more than the four pence he slipped her and she was comely enough beneath her grubby face and patched clothes. But Jack had thoughts for only one woman that night. He would wait and watch for her.

And then? He had not thought it through. When he saw her, perhaps he'd know.

He was halfway down his second, somewhat sour pint – *Did no one in this damned land know how to brew a decent ale?* – when she appeared, just as the bell in the nearby church tolled midnight. Anton Hervey was with her, cloaked against the weather. André was merely in his shirt and waistcoat, shivering while he made his farewells from the doorway.

She leaves him, Jack thought, *and the young gentleman escorts her home. And I will see her there! I will have an answer to her behaviour this night.* As Jack was pulling on his greatcoat, he saw André close the door, Louisa take her companion's arm, and the two begin to walk up the street. Yet as Jack finished his last button and reached for his hat, he saw them halt no more than fifty yards away, just past an alley entrance, under the wooden shutter of an ironmongery. He watched Hervey kiss her gloved hand, then retrace his steps, walk past the house, around a corner. Then, at the same moment the Ensign disappeared, someone else emerged from the dark mouth of the alley – a man in a black cloak and hood, this pulled down so far that only his jaw was exposed. He took Louisa's arm, and the two began to hurry away down the street.

Of course. As Jack hurried from the the tavern, he cursed himself for every kind of an idiot. Miss Reardon would be preserving her reputation! She could not stay with André – for that was whom the man in the black cloak undoubtedly was – not in a houseful of officers. They were not going to her lodgings, not with her mother there. They were going to a third place where they were unknown, where their secret, and her honour, would be safe.

Now he was in this deep, he had to know the limit of it. He would follow them wherever they went . . . *And then what? A duel? Playing the role he'd despised Tarleton for on another snowy ground? Or kill them both, then fall upon his own sword? 'Put out the light, and then put out the light.'*

He did not know what to do. So he followed the couple ever deeper into the tangle of ill-lit, filthy streets that made up this poorer quarter of Philadelphia. Still did not know when he stood opposite the house they'd entered, the one with the notice on the door that said, 'Clean Rooms – One Shilling and Sixpence.' It was only when a lamp was lit in one of those 'clean rooms', when a grubby drape was pulled over its window, when he did finally know, that he remembered something; and remembering, he turned instantly, putting his back to the lowered curtain and the shadows moving behind it, went down the street, almost the way he had come. Not quite. Her lodgings did not quite lie the way he had come.

He had to know how much of a fool he was. And what he'd remembered was that Louisa kept a diary.

She had taken over a fled Rebel's small but well-appointed house, almost a cottage, in a quiet street filled with many similar ones, not far from the theatre. Jack had been of a party that had escorted her home one night but as far as he knew, no one had ever been admitted inside – her mother's illness, somewhat hysterical in nature, did not allow for visitors. She had said that Nancy, her maid, had been allowed to join her from Saratoga and also lived there. She had hired two other servants locally but these had their own dwellings and left at day's end.

An invalid and a servant. With luck, both would be asleep by now and in their own rooms.

The new-fallen snow made a soft surface for his boots; no gravel to betray him, just an almost inaudible squeak. He circled the house twice. A lamp above the front door set for the mistress's return was the only light, but the moon, near full, darted among the snow clouds and Jack could see his way tolerably well, indeed could wish it a little darker for his purpose. But the rear of the house had an overhanging ledge that put the door and windows on the lower floor in sufficient shadow. Like many rear entrances the owners had not thought it necessary to furnish that door with expensive glass. It was quartered in wood panels and one had been recently replaced, though not yet treated for the weather. Taking out his penknife Jack used the blade to scrape away the softer wood around each steel tack. It took some minutes before the panel came out. Reaching in, he blessed both the negligence of a maid who had left a key in a lock and his longer than average arms that could reach the bolts above and below.

It was even darker inside and he had no wish to stumble around. So he slipped out again, went to the front of the house, and removed the oil lamp glowing there. Back in the kitchen – for that was what the lamp revealed it to be – he took off his hat and gloves, thrusting both into the coat's ample pockets. Then he slowly opened the kitchen door.

There was little to disturb the silence, aside from the creaking of the house in the wind, the ticking of a clock down a corridor. He followed it, noted the hour. Not even half past midnight. Louisa and André would be . . . about their business for some time yet. *She is worth the hours*, he thought bitterly.

He became angrier, bolder. A dedicated listening at the few doors gave no sound of sleepers within, so he tried them all. The rooms beyond consisted of a water closet, a handsome dining-room and parlour, and a room with a chaise longue, with chairs laid out as if for a party. There was a desk, but the drawers were all unlocked and empty, save for some playing cards and two old newspapers. He had no choice but to mount the stairs to the first floor where the occupants of the house had to be sleeping.

There were three doors up there. Again, he listened at the

first, again heard nothing, so he carefully turned the handle and discovered a cupboard only, filled with blankets and basins. The second door opened on a small bedroom with just a bed and an armoire, in the drawers of which were some clothes, maid's pinafores, and headscarves. It was Nancy's room but without a Nancy in it. Blessing whichever soldier was occupying the maid's time, Jack moved to the third room, the one, he now presumed, that Louisa must share with her mother. He had no wish to startle an old and infirm lady, but he hoped that what Louisa had told him of her was still true – she took a thousand drops of laudanum a night and could not be woken from their effect till long after dawn. All he had to do was slip in, find the diary, slip out . . .

The door creaked, making him wince. Nevertheless he pushed it full open, held the lamp into the room . . .

No one. There was no one there. The bed's coverlet was pulled down, as if it expected its occupant. Nancy had done her work before taking her pleasure; a small fire glowed behind an iron guard. But of the invalid mother there was not a sign.

He had no time to worry about that. Pushing the door to, he began searching; such an intimate treasure had to be well hidden. So it took him near two minutes before he found it, just where a diary should be – on the blotter on the desk, a pot of ink to its right, a metal-tipped dipping pen in a stand to its left.

He held the book up. It was the same Louisa had taken on their journey, a thick tome, wider than his spread fingers and longer. It was unusual, for it had soft covers, bulging as if filled with down that was trapped between the green linen covering and the card of the book proper. A golden clasp locked its middle, no key in its tiny hole. He turned the journal this way and that, not opening it yet. In fact, now he had it in his hands, he found the urge that had brought him to it had almost vanished. What could be written inside to make him feel better? That she had loved him once perhaps and her feelings for him had died, that he had been replaced in her affections by another? Or that she never had, that it was just one of many such amours she used to while away her time?

He had his anger back. The lock provided no resistance to it.

The hand was bold, the blue letters slanting to the right across the thick, cream paper, great loops on the L's and S's, curlicues on the tip of each Y. She was profligate with her words, for the paper was of the very finest, as expensive as could be purchased, yet she left great gaps between each line, almost a line's depth for each.

He turned from the labour to its content. The dates were scrupulously marked, even if she did not write every day. This diary commenced after their arrival in Quebec and their first parting, had been begun sometime when he was away with St Leger and she was on the march with Burgoyne.

An entry drew his eye. It followed a long description of the country through which they were passing, from Ticonderoga down. It was written just south of that fortress.

How that fellow still runs so strangely in my head, though I know he should not. How did he ingratiate himself into my heart so quickly? He is far away, risking all sorts of dangers. Let heaven bring him safely away from them and once more to my side.

How long had she known André? She had said he was an old friend. It was entirely possible that they had met in New York before she came to England. Likely, in fact, for he had been on General Howe's staff at least that amount of time. But surely, Louisa's behaviour towards himself, on board the ship, afterwards, could not have been so . . . so encouraging if she was still longing for an older love in André?

He flicked on, came to a page where the writing was not so measured, nor the tone.

I can hardly see the page for tears. News has come. He's dead, dead, de—

The last word was cut off, just so, the next entry a turgid

description of a dinner hosted by Burgoyne, each course described in full. But '*dead, dead, de . . .*' Did she hear that André had died and was mistaken in the report? Or was there another lover, whose name he was yet to discover?

Then something made him pause. His passion was making him see things only one way when he had trained himself to consider every option. And a tiny hope still smouldered, the flame of which he'd not, despite his misgivings, quite extinguished. Had his jealousy so misled him that he could not now see the truth?

He turned the pages more swiftly, seeking a date.

They had raised the siege at Stanwix on 23 August. He was bitten the same day, saved by MacTavish, was taken by Arnold three days later, escaped from him two weeks after that, more, returned to Burgoyne on the evening of the battle, 19 September . . .

19th September, 1777. He has returned. He is not dead. Jack. My Jack.

He stared at the word, the name, could not quite take it in. Wanting to more than anything, not wanting to . . . for what was he doing in the room of a woman who did indeed love him, or had, at the very least, and thus could again, desecrating the very basis of love – her trust – by reading her most intimate thoughts? How could he atone for that?

And yet the vision came, of a curtain dropping in a grubby lodging house . . .

He could not help flicking on. There was only one entry from the forest, cryptic, short:

Here, beneath the trees, I could, if he would but . . . I called him a fool but he is not. I am.

The entries from Philadelphia came near the end of the book. She would have to buy another soon. Perhaps that could begin his atonement, to plead the recklessness of his passion then scour the shops of the city for a journal even more lush than this? But one entry, as he read it, pleased him less.

He is returned, again. I had given up all hope, had reconciled myself to duty alone. And yet, here he is. What can I do now?

There was a mark on the page there, the ink blotched.

Ay, let my tears fall. I weep for an answer.

An answer to what? Had she presumed him dead? If so, had she mourned as she had said then transferred her affections to someone else? Jealousy returned instantly . . . yet could he blame her? She was young; men died in war. What this truly meant was that her love for him had only ended when she was sure he was dead. She had grieved twice; perhaps it was too much. But, if it yet smouldered, could it be revived, like a fire log at daybreak, with his breath? Despite . . . whatever was occurring with André that night!

He turned the page more to the light to gaze upon the teardrop. And it was in the glimmer of the lamp that he saw something, sitting within the stain. He turned the book one way and it disappeared; another and . . . yes, there it was again. A number – 2 – sat in the middle of the smudge. It was a phantom, barely there, and nothing else showed on that page or any nearby. But he could not make it go away once he'd seen it.

The number was written in invisible ink.

He could not allow his mind to focus on what this might mean. It could be a game with which Louisa amused herself. Perfectly normal people wanted their secrets hidden. Was not a diary a place for that?

There were different methods of reading such ink markings and he set about trying the easiest. But held close to the fire grate, the book produced no more glyphs, so heat would not bring it forth. It was not lime juice then, nor milk. The fact that a tear had displayed it, however faintly, meant that something in the tear – the salt perhaps – had done so. But remembering his own use of such inks, he thought that unlikely to be the full answer. This was more sophisticated, a chemical. He would need an acid of some kind; but where was he to get one in the night, with the clock downstairs just striking one and Louisa perhaps on her way home even now?

He looked around. The bedroom had the usual furnishings. An empty basin stood on a table at the side, a jug full of water beside it. Beneath the bed, the edge of a chamber pot held up the coverlet's uninterrupted fall to the floor. He looked on the bed, thought of going to the kitchen, rooting for lye there or . . .

His stare returned to the chamber pot. At the same time, by association, his mind went to his bladder, to the pints and the rum he'd had that night. On the thought came action. He unbuttoned his breeches, stooped, filled the vessel near to halfway. Then he carried it to the desk, set it down beside the diary. Cursing himself, unable to stop, he ripped away a corner of a page. The quality of the stationery, before a sign of indulgence, of luxury, now meant something else; for invisible ink only took well on the finest vellum.

He worked carefully, mixing the contents of the chamber pot with water in different strengths in the basin, trying a little on an eye brush he'd found on the dressing table, spreading it beneath one letter on his scrap at a time, pouring out the basin when no effect was achieved, starting again. After five attempts, numbers and letters began to appear in the gaps between the written lines. Certain of his proportions now, he made as much of his 'revealer' as he thought he'd need, sat down at the desk, and began.

Invisible ink appeared only on certain pages, swiftly as-certained by a stroke of the brush down their length. The ones that did had a lot of writing, as cramped as that in blue was luxuriant. It was in code but it was a code that Jack had already broken once on board the *Ariadne*. He did not trouble to transcribe it all, one page was enough to show that the writer had noted the strength of certain regiments in the city, the level of their morale, which Loyalist Commanders were wavering, could be bought, blackmailed, seduced. From that one page alone, he was sure the book would yield up a pretty exact rendering of General Howe's entire command.

He sat back, rubbed his eyes. He still did not want to believe it. Closing the book, he pressed his finger into the sponginess of its cover. On a whim, snatching up his penknife, he slashed the point down and across. The linen parted and his fingers did indeed encounter goose down, but underneath it lay something else. Jack's fingers closed on an edge of material. Slowly, he extracted it, laid it on the desk, spread it out.

It was the decanter-shaped mask, the one 'lost' on the road to Saratoga, and as soon as Jack saw it, he groaned. The replica mask he'd created from a handkerchief did have a similar shape to this original. But it was different in one important detail. His copy had not had the small flap, almost a curling tail, that came off the bottom and to the right. There was a cut in that tail that would isolate further words, another key part of the message.

Jack had kept one of the fair, exact copies Captain Money had made. It was in his coat pocket along with certain other papers. Fetching it now, he unfolded it, lay it down beside the diary, laid the silk mask atop it. He was pleased to see he had at least gotten the main part of the letter. But it was the tail that came, of course, with the sting:

Dear Coz.
Have you lately seen that cur **Will** Piper? He owe me
5 pounds and so his vile **attempt** to avoid me is contimtible.
I mean therefore **to push ahead** with your order, for because
I riecievd **on Hudson's** looms a delivery of fine cloth. Shall make coats
then go **fort's**ell 'em. Give kind'st to my financee, Marge. I see her in **two
or three weeks but** it will seem no more nor **less than three thousand**.
   Yr. Affectionate Coz.
   T. Rhodes

He stared at the new words isolated: 'but less than three thousand'. Clinton had stated that he was coming with too few men to make a difference. He was advising Burgoyne to retreat, without taking the responsibility of ordering him to do so.

Jack picked up the paper, scrunched it into a ball, hurled it into the corner of the room. This betrayal had cost Burgoyne his army. It might yet cost England the war. All caused by the theft of such a little thing, this small piece of silk, by one agent known as Diomedes.

Jack picked it up, ran it over his fingers, then crumpled it again, stowing it in the pocket of his waistcoat. He would save it for the General. When his conduct of the campaign was questioned at the court martial – the surrender of an army would certainly require one – the stolen mask would be proof of just how treacherously he had been undermined.

The bedroom door creaked behind him. He had not heard the tread on the stair but he heard it now as someone quietly entered the room behind him.

He did not turn. 'Diomedes,' he whispered. The spy who'd helped lead Burgoyne to disaster, who now sought to do the same to Howe. The spy he'd vowed to see dead.

'Hello, Jack.'

He turned then, to the voice, to the woman standing in the doorway. One gloved hand lay on the edge of the frame. In her other, she held a pistol.

— SEVENTEEN —
Entr'acte

He rose, very slowly, sliding the chair back. Turning, he placed it between them.

'Hello, Louisa,' he said.

If it were possible, she looked more beautiful than he had ever seen her. She must have walked quickly for there was a flush to her cheeks, her brow, snowflakes melting there, trails of water like wayward teardrops running down her face. Some little crystals still lingered on her eyelashes enhancing those which needed no help, her eyes. Yet within them was a look he had not seen there before, a coldness to go with the ice.

He looked down at the gun in her hand. It was a Dragoon pistol, heavy, expensive, he could see the distinctive Lazarino stamp on its barrel. It was by no means a ladies' pocket weapon. And it was not wavering a jot.

'Will you mourn for me *again*, Louisa?'

She did not speak, carried on regarding him in a way he could not read. Silence, he realized, could lead to action. In dialogue there was delay. 'John André has already lost one Jack Absolute to a bullet. I doubt he'll care to lose another. And neither, may I say, would I.'

At last, she spoke, her voice as firm as her regard. 'I think that production is cursed. Whatever happens to its Jack, its Lydia will not be in the city to play.'

'Going somewhere?'

'I think I must . . . now.' The pistol point moved a fraction away on the word but only to gesture to the diary on the desk, goose-down exploded from its cover like guts from a freshly slaughtered bird.

'Ah, yes.' Jack glanced back to it. 'I don't suppose Lydia can be portrayed by a traitor.'

No hesitation now to her words, which came quickly, angrily. 'I am a patriot, sir, and more loyal to my cause than you are to yours.'

He spoke softly to calm her anger, the possible consequences of it. 'And how do you calculate that?'

'You have doubts as to the merits of your loyalty. I have none. Your eloquent defence of American rights? I am sure that were you born on this side of the Atlantic you would be wearing a blue coat now rather than that red one.'

'You may well be right,' he murmured, sinking back till his red coat-tails rested on the desk's edge. His good hand too went slowly backwards, hidden from her, eventually finding what it sought – the hard edge of a crystal ink well. He continued, 'Nevertheless, I have other loyalties. To honour. To a man.'

'Burgoyne? I am sorry for that, in a way. I like the General. I hope that after our freedom is gained he will recognize that I did for my country what he strove to do for his – merely my duty.'

'Duty? It can be a burden sometimes.' His hand had tightened on the crystal and he was alarmed to feel it shaking, ink spilling down his fingers. By contrast, Louisa's hand was firm; but, then again, she was holding a pistol.

Jack looked at it and suddenly couldn't help the soft chuckle that came.

'You laugh?'

'I was thinking back to another gun, the one I used on the man at the Tarrytown ferry. I thought I was rescuing you from your recklessness, the consequences of the gold coin you tossed him. But I was actually shooting your comrade, wasn't I?' She looked to speak but he went on. 'I should have known

262

when your saddle slipped. You, the consummate groom, mis-tie a cinch? Impossible! Yet there you were upon the ground with Washington's cavalry galloping to your aid. You'd let them know, somehow, hadn't you? The rendezvous was long arranged?'

'Not long,' she murmured.

'Of course. For you needed someone to bring you to it.'

He raised himself from the desk, stood, still holding the inkwell. He did not step near, but she took a step back anyway. His voice became softer. 'And would you have watched me hang, Louisa?'

There! The pistol point wavered, just a little. His ink-slick fingers tightened on the crystal. But her voice, unlike his, did not soften. 'I would not have seen that. I did not loosen Doughty's cinches. I presumed, with luck, that he should carry you free.'

'You presumed much.'

'I did. One must take chances, make . . . sacrifices . . . in our secret world. There are things that I have done—'

He raised a hand, the splinted, unstained one. 'A word of advice, Louisa. From one spy to another. Don't tell me too much. Even if you intend to kill me. You might, after all, miss.'

'I will not.' Her jaw tightened. 'I might regret it. But I will not miss.'

The hand that had held the door now came to support her wrist. Lazarino barrels were heavy. But in case the movement meant something else, a gathering of will, he spoke quickly. 'There is one secret I would know, before we put your ac-curacy to the test – come, Louisa, we both know the business of this Scene even if we are not completely sure how the Act will end.'

Her gaze was still steady. 'What secret?'

'Your diary. Is it all encrypted?'

'You decoded it, didn't you?'

'Not all of it. Enough. I do not refer to the invisible ink, however, but the blue.'

'The blue? I do not understand.'

'Did you mean what you wrote?'

He saw it come then, her understanding; saw, for the first time since she'd entered the room, some doubt, even confusion. She wavered, if her pistol point still did not, and her voice, when it came was, at last, gentler. 'The space between the lines belongs to Diomedes. The blue-inked words . . . are mine.'

'And the tears? What of them? They fell between the lines.' She stayed silent, looking at him. 'Did you mean them, Louisa? Did you mourn when you thought me dead, rejoice at my resurrection? Did you truly regret the word I'd given to your father before we went into the forest?'

'Yes, yes, and yes, I did, damn you . . . and stop! Stop where you are!'

He had pushed himself off the desk, abandoned the ink well, moved past the chair. He raised his hands to his side, never stopped moving slowly towards her, never stopped looking into her eyes, into the indecision there, waiting for the moment she decided, not certain what he'd do when she did. When he reached her and there was still no change, he stepped in close and pressed his chest against the barrel.

They stood like that for a long moment. He had not really stared into her eyes since he'd arrived in Philadelphia, had almost forgotten their extraordinary green. Almost. He stared now and finally, whispered, 'You honoured me with a title once, there in our forest camp. You called me a fool. So prove to me how I deserve it. Prove to me now how great a fool I am.'

Her eyes moved back and forth, focusing now on one of his, now on the other. In the movement, he saw the doubt. He could have grabbed for the gun. He might have wrestled it away.

But then he would never know.

At last he said, 'You've broken my heart already, Louisa. You may as well put a ball through it.'

Her voice now came in a whisper. 'You know of my love now, Jack Absolute. You have read of it. But what do I truly know of yours? How can I believe it is strong enough to . . . do what must be done?'

'Pull the trigger and you'll never find out.'

He felt the gun begin to shake and he closed his eyes. Then he felt it withdrawn from his chest, moved away from him, and he opened his eyes again to hers. The challenge in them was gone. 'Oh Jack,' she said, simply, wearily. 'Oh . . . Jack.'

He reached down, took the pistol from her, uncocked it, went to set it on the chair. She kept her eyes downcast, staring at the floor. Only when he moved back did she look up, speak. 'So . . . what shall we do now?'

He raised his hand, reaching to the side of her head, touching her there, a light pressure, letting his fingers slide further up and into her red-gold hair, still pinned high for her role. He found the pins there, tugged gently at each one till it came away, one by one, dropping them to the rug, till the whole thick mass tumbled down. He brought the other hand up, used his fingers like the teeth of a comb and her head leaned into them as they worked at every knot, resting her weight against his palm as every tangle came free. His healing wrist hurt a little as she did and he didn't care. It was only when it all lay spread over her shoulders that he replied.

'This is what we shall do,' he said, taking her hand, pulling her towards the bed.

She resisted, just slightly, a little smile coming. 'Whatever impression I may have given you to the contrary, Captain, I . . . I . . .' She gestured to him, to the bed. 'I am not . . . not greatly . . .'

'Experienced?'

There was the slightest of nods though her smile grew and held little nervousness. Nonetheless, Jack moved to the table, turned down the lamp, which guttered, died, the only light in the room now coming from the snow-reflected moon and the fire behind its guard.

The kiss was long, began slowly, lips finding lips, tongue-tips tongues. Then it sped up, while hands went to their work.

Yet if his clothes were hard enough to remove while their mouths met, hers were impossible.

'Hold, sir!' she gasped, staggered away from him, laughing. There were only a few of her ties that she could reach. Turning her back to him, she looked over her shoulder and gestured down with her eyes.

He was not a novice in the matter of ladies' dresses. Each had their variation, a code to be deciphered. Her saque dress was exquisitely cut, one of Alphonse's finest, and the concealed silk tapes that held the bodice's covering pleats separated smoothly. But beneath, the bodice itself was intricately laced, the knots proving hard for his soldier's fingers, his one splinted hand. He had to pull her close, brush the tresses of her long hair out of his way over her shoulder and his breath, coming faster as he struggled, fell on to her exposed neck. She tipped her head forward, closed her eyes.

He looked to the desk, to the penknife there. In a moment he had it, had slashed the fine steel the length of the bodice, the laces parting like wheatsheafs, scythed. And at their parting she groaned, shrugged from the bodice, stepped from the skirt still attached to it.

There was another layer of laces beneath. These joined her stays, that were, unusually, of leather and released now the heady scents of that material and her own warming body. These bindings were simply secured with a bow and when he'd undone it, he took hold of one end and slid the lace slowly past each of its restraints. As the string slipped from the last hole, he pulled the stays away, throwing the supple leather garment to the side. Louisa now only wore a knee-length chemise that fell from her bare shoulders to her scarlet stockings. She stood directly before the fire and her legs were silhouetted through the cotton.

He shed the remainder of his clothes as she watched. Soon he was clad only in a shirt that reached to just above his knees.

'I discovered you fishing once dressed in just such a way,' she said, softly.

He went slowly to her, stepping between her opening arms,

bending to lift her, arms behind her knees at her back. Their lips met again as he carried her to the bed.

In midnight and noontime dreams, he had done this a thousand times. Yet the reality of her skin, her strong, long legs, her small, full breasts, that cascade of golden hair half-concealing them like a veil, all this, and secrets unimagined, proved dreams to be the poor imitation they were. He took his time, kissing everywhere he had always wanted to kiss, leaving little untouched by lips or tongue or fingers. She responded, tentatively at first, increasingly bold, going where his moans led her, as hers led him, until the heat grew too hot for them both, could only be taken off in one last way. Remnants of clothes fell away and they were joined.

The snow, newly falling, had built a deep lining in the leaded frames of the window before they parted.

It was not unusual for Jack to experience some sadness after lovemaking. He understood, from friends, fellow officers, that he was not alone in this – though Até mocked him relentlessly when he'd been unwise enough to confess it. It was usual, though, for the sadness to be general, to have no specific cause. Something to do with endings perhaps, of a wish fulfilled that could be wished no more.

This time the reason was plain, lay in his arms within the tangle of blankets, sheets and pillows that he had fashioned into a nest on the floor near the fire. His back rested against the bedstead, one bare foot exposed to the little flame that remained in the grate. Her fingers lightly traced the patterns of the Mohawk tattoos on his chest and shoulders, ran down the leaf wreathes, followed the jaws of a wolf.

It was her voice that put a question to his thoughts. 'What now, Jack?'

'What now, indeed.'

She pulled away, looked up at him, without words, the blanket over her back making a cave within which he stared at her hair, her face, her glowing body.

'I presume we are not to be disturbed by your mother.'

'I think it unlikely as she is in Massachusetts.'

'Not sick then?'

'In fierce health when last I heard.'

He smiled. 'I invented an invalid aunt once, in Bath. Had to spend all sorts of time tending her. Or rather, going to her rooms and slipping down a secret stair that no one knew of. I grew fond of her. Was ever so sad when she recovered and moved back to Truro.'

She laughed and he joined her, both enjoying the moment. Until a new question came to him. 'Wait. Does that mean your father—'

'No. He truly is loyal to the Crown. I cozened him as I cozened you in that. It has given me much grief.'

Once questions came they came not in single spies but in battalions, no matter how awkward. 'And André? Is he also your lover?'

She pulled the blanket tighter around herself, shook her head.

'But you encourage him?'

She sighed. 'Jack, he is Howe's Intelligence as you were Burgoyne's.'

'So that's why you made love to me?' The tone of the question was half jest, half not.

'No. Your usefulness in that regard ended with Burgoyne's surrender.'

The cold way she said it – an item of commerce. It made him laugh again.

'Well, I am sorry if I am no longer useful to you, madam.'

'Nay, sir,' she said, rising above him, throwing back the blanket, 'now did I say that?'

Afterwards, he could sit no more. He dressed and she watched him, from the bed now. The sadness had returned to blend with his confusion.

'You have not answered my question, Jack.'

He pulled on one boot. 'Which was?'

'What now?'

He pulled on the other boot, sat to tie his stock. 'What would you have?'

She considered him. 'We have discovered that I am a patriot. We have noted that you have your doubts as to the rightness of your cause. Is there not . . . some room there?'

He finished tying, put his hands on his thighs. 'You would have me be a traitor.' It was not a question.

'I would have you follow your heart.' She clutched the blanket tight to her neck, came towards him down the bed. 'You are America's friend, not its enemy. Yes, you have doubts about our cause, the hypocrisy of slavery, fears for your Native brothers. I share many of them. But do you not see that we will deal with those once we have our freedom? We will disagree and bicker and resolve as families must. It matters not that all Colonists agree on everything now – for what we do agree on is a principle. Such a principle! It is enshrined in our Declaration of Independence – the right to the pursuit of happiness.' She stared above him for a moment, then laughed. 'Happiness! When, in the history of the world, has that ever been a universal aspiration? When has it not been reserved only for the wealthy, backed by tyrannous power? We will make it something that every person can seek, no matter how lowly born.'

Jack sighed. 'My fear, Louisa, is that, in seeking happiness for yourselves, you would coerce others into providing it for you.'

She reached a hand out to him. 'No, Jack. This is a new world we strive to make now, based on new principles. I have heard you speak with passion on just such freedoms. You talked of your own mother's quest for them. Why deny your truths, your blood?'

'You do not know what you ask of me.' He rose, lifted his red coat, held it towards her. 'You would have me deny other truths, different blood. Bring dishonour to this uniform. To the name of Absolute. Give up that name, abandon my estates, my father. You would have me break faith with General Burgoyne.' He was squeezing the material hard between his fingers. 'I swore him an oath to see you dead, "Diomedes".' He shrugged into the jacket. 'You are asking me to give up my life.'

'One life! You have another. I saw you in the forest, saw how you love this land. And you have another name – for are you not Daganoweda of the Mohawk? There are estates here, greater than the whole of Cornwall, waiting for a man such as you to claim them. And as for family, you could start a new one . . . here.' She pressed her fist into her chest.

He stared at her, her words resounding inside him. He had to get away, to consider answers for all this. They would be hard to find, while too many questions kept coming.

'I followed you and André to that lodging house.'

She clutched the sheet tighter to her. 'When? Tonight?'

He nodded. 'He wore a black cloak.'

'That . . . that was not André. It was another agent.'

'Cato?'

Her eyes narrowed for a tiny moment, and Jack only saw it because he was studying her so closely. Then she looked puzzled and said, 'Who?'

'Come, Louisa! That first message I decoded in Quebec. It was meant for Diomedes. You! And no doubt you did receive one of the other two messages for your number – 642 is clear in your diary. But the message also talked of your superior, whose orders you would obey. Is the man in the black cloak Cato?'

She studied him for a moment, then shrugged. 'Does it matter? You know I cannot tell you his real name. Will not . . . until you have decided what you are going to do.'

He considered her, then nodded, reached for his sword belt, buckled it, put on his greatcoat. With his hat in his hand, he turned to her, to the question on her face.

'I need time to think on all this. And tomorrow night – no, tonight, we perform a play.'

He startled her with that. 'You would still do that. Now? After—'

'It is one more day, Louisa. One more night. The world will keep turning without our guidance. Nations will not be formed or enslaved by our lack of action. If we were to disappear now . . . suspicion would be upon us.' He smiled. 'And maybe I am enough of an actor after all to want the play to go on. Even this one. So let us lose ourselves in the drama and let us decide our future afterwards.' She made to speak but he overrode her. 'I will do nothing, report nothing until we have decided . . . together. I give you my word. And you know that, whatever my other failings, I always keep my word.'

She studied him, then nodded. 'I do. Till tonight then and the end of the play.'

'Till tonight.' He did not go near her again; he knew if he did he would not be able to leave. He went through the door, down the stairs, out the front door. Enough snow had fallen to hide his prints from the night before. With a sigh, he began to make new ones – back to his lodgings, on to his future.

— EIGHTEEN —
The Rivals

'Am not *I* a lover; aye, and a romantic one too?'

A roar rose at the words. It was extraordinary what people found to laugh at. Yet André had warned them before the performance that the audience would have dined and drank heartily before crowding into the small auditorium to be entertained. And since *The Rivals* was a cunning and proven piece of craft, they had come prepared to be amused by it, to leave outside the cruel winds and the threat of Rebel raids – they had been growing ever bolder in their assaults – and lose themselves in the comedy. Each entrance was cheered, every exit applauded, demands made for especially good lines or bits of business to be repeated. It was intoxicating, Jack had to admit. He had only experienced it before t'other side of the footlights and had found it pleasing enough there. Now he was learning what various player friends had tried to tell him – to be the focus of all that attention, the centre of that vortex of power, to shape and direct it . . . well, it was akin to drunkenness on the finest champagne. Or very much like being in the first passion of love, making it easy to forget anything else.

Which reminded him . . . *What a stew this is*, Jack thought, staring out, his mind in three worlds at once. There was himself, Jack Absolute, playing the character Jack Absolute, re-enacting a very partial view of an episode from his own past.

There was the actor mouthing the lines, waiting for the reaction. And somewhere shoved away behind these two, there was the spy who had compromised himself with an enemy agent, worse, fallen in love with that agent – who was also his on-stage lover! And before the midnight bell tolled, a decision must be made about that agent. One that would change many lives, his own not least, and could even affect the outcome of a war.

A stew, indeed. While the audience still enjoyed his line, Jack looked out, let his gaze sweep over the entire house. It may have been considerably smaller than Drury Lane, a mere five hundred crammed in, but it was its match in miniature, with the open space of the pit crowded with benches, a gallery above, a box just encroaching upon the stage on each side. He looked at the one Stage Left now, then looked swiftly away. General Howe, with his mistress, Mrs Loring, and several of his most senior officers, occupied it. Suddenly it felt most peculiar to be observed in this role by his commanding officer when he, and indeed the entire audience, believed that Jack was playing 'himself', and revelled in the fact. Unnerved, he turned to the box Stage Right. André sat there, leaning forward, apparently more nervous than any of his players.

Jack spoke his next words straight to him. André had encouraged them to make direct contact with members of the audience. Line delivered, he glanced to André's right. There was another man there, leaning back, talking to someone behind him. His face was in shadow but his hand was before him, thin, pale fingers moving ceaselessly across a cloak draped over the box's front. Heavy, blue-black, its hood was pointed and Jack recognized it instantly from the night before. Its wearer had escorted Louisa to a lodging house where rooms could be rented for a shilling and a half.

His mind, so split before, now focused on one need – to learn the identity of the agent that Louisa had concealed from him, Cato – and find out why that man was now sat next to John André. That identity could be a vital part of the decision he was to make at play's end.

Returning his mind reluctantly to the stage, he realized the other actor was staring at him peculiarly. He glanced into the auditorium. The audience looked back expectantly and sudden heat surged through him, bringing sweat instantly to his forehead. It was his line and he had not an idea what it was! He stared again at the man playing his servant, Fag, and shook his head slightly. The fusilier lieutenant swallowed and spoke, repeating Jack's cue.

'Were I in your place, I should certainly drop his acquaintance.'

Yes, Jack thought, *that's your line. But what the devil's mine?*

And then he just said it and eternity ended, for somehow it was correct. Pushing the man aside, as per his stage directions, he exited. He didn't have long. A scenery change and then the first entrance of Sir Lucius O'Trigger. The actor playing him had cut it very fine indeed and had only arrived at the theatre after the play began. Jack had not even met him yet; the man would just have to stand still and say his lines. And of course, the climactic duel, that Jack had desired, could not now take place.

But, as he left the stage and proceeded to the corridor that led to the Stage Right box, it was not actorly considerations that preoccupied him. He was an agent again and an enemy spy, who wore a black cloak, who had been alone with Louisa in a cheap lodging room, was ahead of him.

'What are you doing here?' hissed André, as Jack pushed open the door.

'I need to be introduced to your friend,' he said, stepping in. André was between him and the seated figure whose face was still in shadow. But the man rose and spoke as he did.

'Surely we need no introduction, Captain Absolute. For are we not old friends?' said the Count von Schlaben.

If it was hard for Jack to find words on stage, it was worse now. Similar feelings came, a difficulty in breathing, a flush to skin, a prickling of brow. He reached to grasp the back of André's chair.

His director had risen between them. 'You know each other?'

'But yes. Did I not mention that fact?'

André frowned slightly. 'Not a word of it, no.'

Von Schlaben's voice was as soft, as insinuating as ever. 'Really? Oh, I have long been a great admirer of Captain Absolute's remarkable and varied talents. Not least his one for survival.'

'You—'

Jack had left his grip on the chair, taken one step toward the man. But André was in the way and, as Jack moved to go around him, two shapes cleared the shadows in the box. An Abenaki rose from his squat beside Von Schlaben's seat; and the huge German Sergeant, his face now half-obscured by a full moustache and sideburns, stepped away from the wall.

Jack halted, a measure of calm returning with a deeper breath. He turned to André, who was still looking quizzical, and said, 'The Count and I are indeed old acquaintances. Or perhaps I should say, *rivals*. How appropriate that we meet here.' He took in each of the bodyguards, letting his gaze meet and hold theirs, before returning it to Von Schlaben. 'I so look forward, Count, to the end of the play and the renewal of that rivalry.'

'As do I, Captain. As do I.'

Music had underscored their last words. Now someone hissed at them from the pit just below the box. 'Shh, sirs. The play continues!'

Von Schlaben's voice lowered to a whisper. 'I hope you will not be offended but, despite your talents, it was really this next player that I was most looking forward to seeing. It was I who recommended him to Major André, you see. I do hope he justifies my confidence.' He gestured behind Jack to the stage.

'Here he is, Jack.' André had taken him by the elbow, was swinging him around. 'Talk about a late entrance! Here's your other rival, Sir Lucius O'Trigger.'

Though he was meant to be playing an impoverished Irish

baronet, the figure who entered was dressed in the smartest of uniforms, a beautifully tailored green jacket with three columns of silver buttons up the front, braid at sleeve and neck, buff trousers, gleaming black riding boots. He had a cavalry sabre at his waist, his hand, resting on the pommel, tipping it up to a jaunty angle. And it was the weapon that brought the man's name to Jack, rather than the voice, which was anyway speaking in a rather well-done Irish accent, or the face, even more eerily beautiful in the underlit glow of the footlights. It was the weapon; because when he'd last seen this man it had been on Hounslow Heath in London and the sabre in his hand was descending from a winter sky to snuff out Jack's life.

'Banastre Tarleton,' Jack breathed.

'It is he, indeed. And how delighted my young friend will be to see you again.'

He had no time to pause, to consider. 'Jack,' whispered André, taking him by the arm, 'you're on.'

Somehow he walked to the wings, waited while the actors talked before him, watched Tarleton exit on the opposite side, leaving the servants to their gossip. He saw the action, heard the words spoken, but it was as if everything before him now was a stagecloth against which his whirling thoughts played.

Von Schlaben, he wanted to scream to General Howe, to the audience. *He is the head of a secret society and a Rebel spy, plotting against the Crown!* But what was this dangerous man doing with John André, Howe's intelligence officer? Was André aware, and drawing the German into a trap? If Jack cried out against him, would he tear apart an intricate web André had woven? And if he exposed the Count, would he not also expose Louisa? All he knew for certain was that Louisa had been consorting with this enemy. He had probably controlled her as an agent from the moment they docked in Quebec. He remembered Von Schlaben's grip upon her elbow. Louisa had said he was a spurned suitor from London. She had lied to protect him. For if, in that first secret message he had decoded, Louisa was 'Diomedes' then Von Schlaben was, undoubtedly, 'Cato.'

The play was accelerating toward his entrance. He could see his 'father' in the wings opposite. But he was trapped there by a thought: what if Louisa truly was a sublime actress? What if she had seduced him to turn him to their cause?

He shook his head, though the thoughts refused to vacate. He could only do one thing now – finish the play and get Louisa out of the city, there to uncover her true nature. Only when he knew everything could he return, expose – and kill – Von Schlaben.

There was applause. Actors left the stage, scenery changed and his 'father' was on. He walked to meet him.

The play, somehow, continued. If the audience noticed a change in him they did not show it. They 'ooh'd' and 'aah'd' where appropriate, laughed on worthy and unworthy lines, especially when he said the words that had exercised him the previous day in rehearsal. But as these followed his kiss with Louisa, he barely noted it. The kiss was strange – chill and at the same time desperate. He had seen her glance into André's box; she had paled and been less animated since.

Yet it was Tarleton who brought the blur into focus for Jack. They came to the scene in which Sir Lucius challenged Jack Absolute to a duel. Tarleton looked at him as a fox would regard the occupants of a chicken shed. And he changed a line. When he chose weapons, he did not say, as scripted, 'Sir, there will very pretty small-sword light,' but instead 'There will be very pretty light – for sabres.' As on Hounslow Heath, Tarleton wanted to fight with the weapon that would inflict the most hideous wounds. Jack now recalled André's words, which had annoyed him before, with relief: 'You only cross blades, then the rest will rush on and separate you.'

The play marched to its climax – the duel at Kingsmead Fields, Bath. As all the actors gathered in the Stage Right wings for this finale, Jack managed to pull Louisa aside.

'Be ready! As soon as the epilogue is spoken we must leave the city.'

'Leave?' She turned even paler. 'Have you then decided?'

'I have decided nothing. All I know is the man who wants

me dead more than anyone on this earth is your man in the black cloak. I believe the Count von Schlaben will try to kill me after the play tonight and with four of them and this cursed arm . . .' he raised his right hand, just that night out of the splints and bandage that had held it for four weeks. 'I doubt I have the strength to stop him.'

'Jack . . .' she said, trouble in her eyes. But then his cue was called and he was walking on to the stage. Towards Banastre Tarleton.

'Well then, Captain,' he said, the Irish accent still perfect, ''tis we must begin – so come out, my little counsellor,' he drew his sabre with a flourish, 'and ask the gentleman whether he will resign the lady?'

Jack drew his sabre, buckled on his right so he could draw it with his healthy left hand. 'Come on then, sir,' he said. 'Here's my reply.'

The blades crossed, they both settled into their stance. Jack looked to André's box. The Major was still there. The black cloak had gone.

His eyes came back to look into Tarleton's. That hunger was clear, stronger than ever. And it seemed that meeting Jack's gaze was all that he required now. Disengaging his blade, he swung it, not with a full force but hard enough. Jack watched it come, disbelieving. Even when the blade bit into his right upper arm, when he heard the cloth of his jacket shred, when he felt that familiar, peculiar coldness of steel cutting into flesh, he still could not believe it. It was only when he looked into the wings and saw the black cloak spread out to block the entrance of the other actors, saw the Abenaki and the giant Sergeant with their own weapons unsheathed that he knew. The Illuminati, through their representative, the Count von Schlaben, would pay him for his opposition. He did not need Tarleton's words to confirm this.

'First Blood, sir,' the younger man whispered, gesturing to Jack's arm, where a darker red was beginning to stain the coat, 'just a marker, to begin. But this time first blood shall not be the last.'

With a cry, he whirled his sabre above his head and the other on-stage actors stumbled away from the curving blade. Then he charged, the sword going back, then coming down straight from overhead. Aware now, Jack managed to get his own weapon up just in time, holding his grip in two hands. The shock of collision shot pulses of intense pain through his barely-healed wrist. He gasped, staggered back, let Tarleton's blade slide down his own. Still two-handed, he thrust the tip out before him, as Tarleton took his own sword out to the side, parallel to the floor, then attacked again to Jack's right. Jack tipped his own point toward the stage, at the same time stepping through with his front foot. Though he stopped the blade, his own was knocked backwards, bouncing into the very place where Tarleton had already cut him.

'Fine swordplay, what?' came a gruff voice from the audience.

'Brutish,' a woman lamented.

'Bravo,' shouted three more, while from the wings he heard Louisa cry, 'No. No!'

Tarleton's edge rested on his own, his tip still down. Flicking his wrists, Jack sent both blades flying up, stepped back again, again stood square with his sword held two-handed before him, point to face.

'Oh, good.' Tarleton was smiling. 'It's so much better when they struggle.'

He came at Jack, smashing his blade aside, thrusting up at his groin, Jack staggered backwards, just bringing his weapon across to deflect the thrust in time but off balance, which his opponent saw and scythed down again at his head. Jack stopped the blow, just, but the shock that went through his arm made him think he had broken his wrist again.

Tarleton noted it, savoured the pain. As someone in the audience called out, 'Is this not a little much?' Tarleton smiled once more.

'Oh well,' he said, 'all good things must end. I'll just make it look like an accident.'

The attacks came now in a flurry that was almost impossible

to predict. Somehow, Jack managed, getting his weapon across just in time, though with each blow he felt his wrist shudder, his strength failing. Finally, he slipped, went to one knee, and Tarleton stepped in and swept his sword up, knocking Jack's out of his left hand. He barely held on to it with his weakened right. The blade hovered out there, with all of Jack open, exposed, his sword tip resting on the floor and the whole weapon as heavy and cumbersome as a tree trunk. He could not lift it if he tried.

'Quel dommage!' tsked Tarleton, stepping back to deliver what would be his last blow. Yet just as he did, something strange happened. There was a noise from outside the theatre, a rumble that became a roar in an eye blink. Tarleton's blade had not yet reached the backward point from which he could deliver his death blow, when, directly above him, it looked as if some malevolent god had reached down and ripped the roof off the theatre.

There was a brief sight of stars and snow, then the flies and their rails were tumbling down. Jack rolled to one side just before a sheared pole impaled him. Tarleton vanished in the swirl of a backcloth as if he'd fallen down the well that was painted on it. Before people had time to rise from their seats, a second blow struck the theatre and a cannon ball came through the riverside wall, passed a foot above the audience's heads, and exited the city side wall without touching anything else in its flight.

'The Rebels attack,' came the cry from more than one voice, and in an instant the theatre was transformed into the hall at Bedlam, men and women screaming, gender ignored, as they struggled over each other to get out. Jack saw that Von Schlaben and his bodyguards had disappeared; while at his feet, entwining himself further into the backcloth's folds with every roll, Tarleton ranted and cursed. Without a qualm, Jack suddenly found the strength in his sword arm to plunge the point into the mouth of the wishing well. Annoyingly, he felt it lodge in wood. At least Jack was gladdened by the yelp of rage and fear from the writhing body before the stage swirled with people and he was jostled away. Striking out against the panic, Jack managed to force his way through to Louisa, who was striving as desperately towards him.

'Jack! I thought he was going to kill you.'

'So did he.' As further Rebel shot flew over the roof, he was crushed against her by the press, and found her lips with his. Then he said, 'Do you trust me?'

'Yes.'

'Then go to your lodgings, make sure you are not followed, gather what you can fit on a horse and I will bring two there in an hour.' He saw her baulk. 'Louisa, either you or I or both will die this night if we do not flee. You will be exposed . . . for your Cato consorts with André. Let us use this attack as cover.' She still hesitated. 'We can talk on causes, on what is right, when we are safe.'

She nodded at last, kissed him, and was gone, pushing through those who yet circled in fear. He turned the other way.

One hour, he thought. *Pray God one hour is enough.*

It took him two, for the streets were swollen both with soldiers marching to counter the Rebel raid and civilians fleeing it. The 16th had been mustered and ridden out, so there was only a groom in the stables who did not question an officer taking his own horse, Doughty, and requesting one of the regiment's reserves plus two weeks supply of oats. The rest of his needs were provided by the Officers' Mess and Jack was glad he'd stored most of his few goods there and not at his lodgings. He could not return to them. Von Schlaben, Tarleton, and others of the hellish Illuminati would no doubt await him to finish what they had so far failed to do. But the regiment provided all he needed to survive a time in the forest. He could live through a winter there, if necessary. He had done it before.

The bell was sounding from the church on her corner when he led the horses down the alley at the back of Louisa's house and tied them up. Midnight, the temperature exceedingly low, a cutting wind. The sounds of battle had diminished as he rode over, the Rebel driven back or withdrawing. It had been a raid in force, the biggest yet. Washington would not allow the enemy to hold his capital untroubled.

There had been no welcoming lamp at the front and the back was as dark as ever, even if the door was unbolted. Louisa was being suitably cautious. There was no sign that the house was occupied and Jack struck no spark, groping along the passage, mole-blind, feeling his way along the balustrade up the stairs. He went silently and only on reaching the landing did he whisper, 'Louisa?'

The silence held for a moment longer until a whisper came back, her voice. 'Here,' she said from her bedroom, and there was something in the monosyllable, some quality, that had Jack reaching for one of the two pistols in his belt. The cocking made a huge sound in the still house, echoed around the corridor, down the stairs; now there could be no delay. Placing the barrel against the door, he pushed and it swung in with that familiar creak.

The blackness was almost complete, some lighter shade of it alone at the window, which let in the night. Then it was pierced by flame, startling in its suddenness. At the desk, a lamp that had been muffled by a hat was uncovered. In that darkness, it was like the sun at midday, and Jack squinted against it to seek for target or threat. But when he'd seen that there were at least five figures in the room, he let the gun barrel slowly sink toward the floor.

'Jack, come in, dear fellow, do come in.' John André was sat at the desk and had twisted around to look at him. 'And put that gun down, eh? There's really no need.'

He stayed in the doorway till his eyes had adjusted and he could see everyone. One soldier stood behind André at the window, another rested a blunderbuss on the armoire. Anton Hervey, 'Bob Acres' of the play, was by the bed. He had a pistol in one hand while his other rested on Louisa's shoulder where she sat, her back against the bedstead.

'Jack, I—' She tried to rise, but the Ensign pressed her down.

'Oh, he knows it is not your fault, my dear.' André nodded solicitously toward her then faced Jack again. 'Fact is, we've had her under scrutiny for some time. Useful she was such a damn fine actress. Nothing like the theatre for bringing people together, eh?'

'And what need would you have to scrutinize Miss Reardon?' Jack was quite pleased with how steady his voice sounded. 'Apart from the most obvious.'

'Oh, Jack!' André's laugh was pleasant. He turned back to the desk. 'Do come over here. I'd like your opinion on something. Sergeant, unencumber Captain Absolute ... sorry, Major Absolute, of all that heavy weaponry, will you?'

Jack uncocked the gun in his hand and passed it over, the one at his belt following. Then he went and stood behind André. Before him, spread open on the desk, was Louisa's diary.

'You know, she was trying to burn it when we came in. But the wood was wet. Only damaged it a little.' He flicked a page over to one where both blue and invisible ink was revealed. 'What I am thinking, Jack, is that she has been ... how shall I put it? Playing you? And that you have only just discovered it. You did this?' He gestured to the decoding.

Jack shrugged. There seemed little point in denial.

'How long did it take you to break the code?'

'Half a night.'

'Ah.' André seemed pleased. 'I did it in an hour.'

'Well,' grunted Jack, 'You are younger than me.'

André smiled. 'And the secret ink? I have a sympathetic developer.' He picked up a small glass bottle. 'But it has only just been discovered, since we captured an agent with letters written in this ink. And it usually stains it green, while yours is,' he peered, 'yellow. So how did you manage? Professional curiosity, is all.'

Jack looked at Louisa. 'I'd rather not say. Perhaps another time?'

André frowned. 'Yes, well, I do hope we get that chance.' He looked again at the text before him. 'Diomedes is obviously Miss Reardon, as she is also 642. But this person,' he pointed,

'597. He crops up so often. Must be her director, what? Hiding on our side rather than on theirs. So, a traitor. Who is he, if it is indeed a he?' He looked up. 'Any ideas?'

'Perhaps.' Jack did not know the way this game was going. And if André wanted to take him for Louisa's dupe, only recently enlightened, that was fine. He could bear the title of fool a while longer. And until he knew more, he would keep his trump card – Von Schlaben and all he knew of him – in his hand. It was the old rule of interrogation, that he and André, both trained in His Majesty's Army, understood. You gave a little, only when forced to – by whatever means – and always in return for something.

'No perhaps about it.' The Major's voice had dropped to near a whisper. 'You certainly know. Rather better than anyone, I should say.' André's boyish face suddenly lost all its youth. Leaping up, he thrust his face into Jack's and shouted, '*You* are the traitor, sir. *You* are 597.'

As Jack stepped back, outrage rose like a physical presence in his throat, preventing him from speaking. And anyway, Louisa was as quick as he would ever have been.

'It's not true,' she said, shrugging off Hervey's restraining hand and rising from the bed. 'Jack knows little of all that. And he found out that little only when we became lovers.'

'Lovers? I presume the desperation of your situation makes you careless of reputation.' André's face had lost none of its sourness. 'Jack Absolute, on stage and off, the Lover Personified' He snorted. 'Then, madam, for Love's Sake, perhaps *you* would care to reveal the identity of 597?'

Louisa looked as if she would speak. Then she merely lowered her head.

'Thought not,' André snarled. 'Ensign Hervey, escort Miss Reardon to the gaol. And if she tries to speak again, gag her. I will be along to examine her presently.'

The Ensign did not take her arm as gently as he had the night before, when leaving André's. The soldier by the window took the other and they almost ran a grim and silent Louisa out of the door.

'Now, Jack.' André's voice had again become soft and moderate. 'Would you like to hear why we know you are not just Fortune's Fool but the traitor 597?'

'I would be thrilled – since I am not.'

'Sit then, and I will expound it to you. No, Jack, really. I would prefer it if you sat. You are such a dangerous man even a blunderbuss might not deter you.' He gestured to the soldier by the armoire whose hand tightened on the gun stock. André began to pace, just as he did when commenting on the actors' performances after rehearsals. 'We know Louisa is a spy. Quite a successful one too, as—'

Jack interrupted. 'She is an idealist, naïve and young. And she has been coerced into this role.'

'Oh, I am sure. By 597, yourself, in fact. But you *would* try to protect her, now you are her lover and, when that story emerges, the envy of every man in Philadelphia!' He beamed. 'I am very fond of her myself. But our regard will not save her from the noose.'

Jack swallowed. 'You would not—'

'I would have to *pour encourager les autres*. They will hang our lady spies as we will hang theirs. We will wrap her lovely neck in a silken noose, push her off the scaffold, watch her kick and wriggle, and unless,' here the smile that had never left his face widened, 'you reveal the full extent of your treachery, give us other names, other circles of spies. It could then be made out that you were the cold manipulator who led this young girl astray. Wouldn't save you, of course. But she might then find some sympathy in the court.'

It was almost tempting. To take the blame upon himself, to save her. But he did not think he could make up enough lies to credibly satisfy such a mind as André's.

'This is absurd. Everyone knows my loyalty, to Burgoyne, to the army. I have worn the Redcoat for almost twenty years.'

'I'll tell you what everyone knows about Jack Absolute.' André was walking behind Jack now, hands clasped behind his back, always turning just when he edged Jack's vision. His

285

voice was soft. 'Your mother was an actress – not an amateur one but a professional with all that implies—'

'You may insult me by whatever title you choose but you are no gentleman if you attack a woman long dead.'

'True.' André smiled thinly. 'It is unworthy of me. So let us assume that Jane Fitzsimmons was as pure as many of that profession are corrupt. You would not deny that she was Irish, hmm? And that she held Rebel sympathies?'

'People speculated so. As you do with me.'

'There is a taint of blood though, is there not? Speculation perhaps, I acknowledge. But it serves as a neat prologue to the facts. So to deal in them.' He halted, looked out the window into the darkness, into the snow falling there again. 'You resigned your commission ten years ago to pursue personal wealth in India—'

'I was also commissioned into the East India Company. I still wore the Redcoat and was serving the Crown when you had barely been breeched.'

'You served yourself, sir. *Yourself.* All know how desperate you were for money to save your family estates, bankrupted by your mad father – another taint in the blood there, eh, for do not lunatics tend to beget the same?' He began to pace again. 'And all know you were coerced into this war, one for which you had little sympathy. I heard of an extraordinary speech you made at General Burgoyne's table the night you arrived in Quebec. Full of praise for the American and compassion for his cause.'

'I have compassion, yes. As do nearly half the Members sitting at Westminster.'

'But none of them are called Daganoweda, are they? They have not established homes in this land, fucked the squaws, sired bastards—'

Jack came out of the chair. 'Again, you insult when you know nothing about me or my life—'

'I. Know. Everything.' André motioned away the soldier who had stepped forward, gun levelled, when Jack rose. His handsome face a few inches away now, he continued, 'You think we only find out about enemy agents? We also discover everything we can about our own. I have a drawerful of reports on you. What a colourful life you have led! They should put you in a novel, not just a play. You would rival Tom Jones in ribaldry, out-peregrinate Peregrine Pickle! But as a spy, sir, you are an amateur, a dabbler. That world has changed since you first donned war paint and feathers and impersonated a savage to peek at the French.'

Jack deflected his growing anger with the sudden realization that André sought to provoke him, with insult and insinuation, into an outburst, into carelessness. So, breathing deep, sitting again, Jack gave his most charming smile and said, 'That may well be. I seem to acquire new titles by the month so . . . dabbler? Why not? I also acknowledge that I am a man in love and I readily own the title of fool. But you, young sir, have not yet produced any proof of anything beyond that.'

'No?' André sat on the edge of the desk, lifted a piece of goose down, blew it into the air. 'Oh, I think the contents of this diary, the references to you by name in the blue ink and to 597 in the invisible, together with your reputation, your documented outbursts, your family's legacy, your Indian dalliances, and, above all, your romantic liaison with a proven spy, would be more than enough to condemn. You are a lone wolf, sir, and their Lordships, who would sit upon your Court Martial, don't trust those who run separate from the pack.' André leaned down. 'But you want harder proof, you say? I think we can find that as well.' He looked past Jack to the door, whispered, 'Where is it, Jack? In your saddle pack? On your person?'

'Where is what?'

'Jack! Burgoyne's stolen mask, of course. The one thing that, by some interpretations, including his own speculation in his dispatches to General Howe, cost him the campaign.'

Jack felt chill creep into his scalp. He blustered, 'Burgoyne . . . lost it. I arrived in time to fashion another one.'

André laughed. 'Oh yes, I heard that story too. Jack

Absolute – saviour! A marvellous piece of cover. Perhaps you are not such a sorry dog after all. But I suspect you didn't fashion the perfect replacement, what? Perhaps some details still remained hidden?' André's eyes gleamed. 'I also heard you still have it.'

Jack was motionless. 'And who told you that?'

'A friend. Who heard it from a friend. Come, Jack, shall I get my man here to fetch up your bags? No, wait, it is too important to be left on the back of a horse. You'll have it on your person.' As Jack said nothing, André continued, 'Corporal, give me the gun and search the Brevet-Major, will you?'

'Sir.' The big soldier moved over, handing the weapon across to André, who moved so he could rest its barrel on the edge of the desk, its wide mouth level with Jack's chest.

As the man took a step toward him, Jack raised a hand. 'Here.' He reached into his waistcoat pocket and pulled the piece of cut silk out. 'I suppose it will do me no good to tell you that I was keeping it for the General, to help him clear his name.'

'None whatsoever.' André had taken the cloth and was holding it to the light. 'Such a little thing,' he murmured, running it through his fingers, 'to cause such harm.' He let the mask slip, its lightness causing it to float, then snatched it from the air, stuffed it into a pocket. 'But it's always the little things that trip us, eh, Jack?' He turned to the Corporal. 'Bind his hands. We'll take him to the gaol.'

As he was jerked to his feet, his wrists roughly grabbed, pulled back, pain sharding through the barely healed one, Jack leaned into André. He only had that single trump to play now and strangely, the only one left was the truth. 'Listen to me. I am not 597 nor guilty of anything of which you have accused me – apart, yes, from being a fool and falling in love. But I know the identity of the man you seek. He has tried to kill me three times. He successfully interfered at Oriskany and helped in our defeat there. This man controls a spy network here and in Europe. He is the most dangerous man on the continent, because he works not for us or even, ultimately, for the

Americans but for a tiny, powerful secret society. And they desire to control us all.'

André's face had changed. 'Who? What secret society?'

'It is called the Illuminati. And their leader in the Colonies was your guest tonight – the Count von Schlaben. *He's* your 597, and his code name is Cato.'

André stared at Jack and Jack stared back, desperate to be believed. It was suddenly beyond himself and Louisa, beyond even this war. Von Schlaben and the Illuminati, bastard offspring of German Masons, they had to be stopped. André, General Howe's Intelligence in Philadelphia, had to stop them.

The Corporal made the final adjustments to the ropes. 'Done, sir.'

'Thank you,' André said, handing over the gun. 'Take this and wait outside.'

As the soldier retired and André stepped towards him, Jack whispered, 'You must believe me, John. You must!'

They were so close now their faces were almost touching. 'I would so like to, Jack. But unfortunately, I cannot.'

'Why not? For God's sake, man, why not?'

André smiled. 'The Count von Schlaben is not the leader of the Illuminati in America, Jack. I know this for certain. Because, you see . . . *I* am.'

— NINETEEN —
The Traitor

Jack had spent much of the morning thinking on his child-hood. He presumed it was because his life was to end with the midday bell that his mind kept returning to its beginning; to the country about Land's End, its granite cliffs, rock-strewn fields, sandy beaches. Disturbingly – for he had not cared for the fellow at all – he seemed to dwell most on his uncle, Duncan Absolute, his guardian for the first nine years of life. 'Druncan', as he was inevitably referred to by all who knew him, was perpetually incapacitated with brandy, and thus easy to elude. It was a rare day that Jack would be apprehended and thrashed for some misdemeanour, which he had undoubtedly committed. Far more often he would hear his uncle yelling after him down the lanes, 'You'll hang one day, Jack Absolute. You will hang!'

So the sot was right after all. It was most annoying.

As death cells went, this was one of the more comfortable Jack had occupied. It was within the town gaol, a recently built brick building that formed one side of a square. A ventilation hole set high up in the wall – too high for him to reach, too small to squeeze through anyway – gave on to that square, allowing in the sounds that had stimulated many of Jack's thoughts. In the two days that he had been there since his trial, there had been much hammering and sawing of wood, many shouted commands and curses, much heaving and grunting as the scaffold and gallows were erected. They had only finished last midnight and Jack had barely got to sleep when the first spectators arrived to claim their sites, waking him with squabbles and loud speculations. Long before the dawn the hawkers and stall holders had set up and there was much trading when the sky was yet dark. Bakers were there and the scent of warm bread reached him, soon joined by brewers proclaiming the merits of their stock. Such was the enthusiasm of one bass voice that Jack had determined to bribe a guard to fetch him up some of the fellow's product. He still felt, on considerable evidence, that Americans did not know how to brew a decent ale, but perhaps his last quart in the Colonies – on earth – would persuade him.

So far that morning he had managed to keep his mind fixed on such trivialities; to let it wander would be to succumb to despair and he was determined, whatever else, not to cut a sorry figure at his noon appointment. Also, he still had one little hope. Not for himself – on the evidence presented in the court martial the day before he would have donned the black cloth with the judge and condemned himself to hang – but Louisa! An appeal had been made, based on her youth, her father's loyalty, the influence upon her of evil traitors such as Jack Absolute. General Howe did have the power to commute. Jack was not and never had been a praying man. He would never think of beseeching anyone for himself. But he prayed that morning for Louisa. He wondered if, somewhere in the building, she was doing the same for him.

The clock in the square was striking half past eleven, its toll barely audible above the people now thronging out there, when bolts were thrown, the door pushed in. Jack rose to meet his visitor.

'Good news, Jack. The first of two gifts I bring you.' John André said, striding into the room. He was dressed, as befitted the day, in the most elegantly cut of uniforms and his hair had been some time in the styling, falling in ordered waves on to his neck, held there in a black silk bag and solitaire. With a smile that seemed to bring sunlight into the cell, he was once again the friendly young buck and theatre enthusiast, no longer the cool interrogator who had examined Jack again and again during his week's confinement.

'Louisa?' Jack could not hold back the desperation in his voice.

André stopped, the smile vanishing. 'Alas, Jack. I did not mean to toy so with your hopes. No, indeed, the sentence of the court will be observed. While recognizing the necessity, I am most truly sorry for it.'

Jack had sunk down again on to the cot. 'And the good news?' he muttered.

André swung the one chair around, sat, leaned on its back toward him. 'They have commuted your sentence.'

Jack looked at him dully. After his disappointment for Louisa, what joy could there be in this? 'They kill her and let me live?'

'No, Jack, be serious.' André had pulled a pouch from his pocket and made busy cramming tobacco from it into a pipe. 'The good news is that my representations were accepted. You will not hang.' He placed a taper over Jack's lamp and, when it caught, held it to the bowl, sucked, then exhaled a deep plume above Jack's head. 'You will be shot.'

Jack chuckled. He could not help himself, it was so absurd – and his uncle had been wrong, after all! 'Oh, thank you,' he said.

André looked offended at the sarcasm. 'It is a tribute to you as a soldier, your loyal service before you . . . strayed.' He sighed, sending smoke up towards the corner of the cell though he seemed to be looking beyond it. 'I just hope that, were I ever in your situation, someone would be as kind to me.' He looked back. 'So Jack, in view of this benevolence, and the lateness of the hour, have you finally anything to say to me?'

It was spoken without any real hope. André had sought information every day in the five before the trial and every day Jack had told him the same – nothing. There was nothing he could tell him, for André had no interest in the truth. He already had his own version – that Jack was Washington's spy and, for a reason he had yet to divulge, a hater of all things to do with the Illuminati.

'I will merely say at the last what I have said all along – watch the German. You say you are his superior in the Order. I know you are not, that the tail wags the dog.'

'Jack! Jack!' Andre coughed some smoke out. 'I still do not understand this unreasoning fear of yours. I wish you could be persuaded, even at this late hour. For it is English Illumination that will shape the society to come. When we win this war for England, enlightened men from both sides will come to a just peace. The arrangements will set an example of what a society can be like. That model will then be transferred to Britain, to Europe, to the World, for the deliverance of all humanity from the dark. That is what we have sworn.'

'Do you not find that oath a contradiction to the one you swore to your King and Country?'

André shrugged. 'To my King? Perhaps. But are kings what we truly need in this world, Jack? George the Hanoverian? The Tyrants of France and Spain? The deranged monarchs of Germany? And as for England . . . what greater loyalty can I show than to seek to deliver my land out of that darkness? To join it to other lands in a Commonwealth of Illumination?'

'With you in charge.'

'With me and people like me, yes. But for the benefit of all mankind.'

Jack looked into the man's eyes, lit now by his fanaticism. There was nothing more he could say to persuade him had he all the time in the world, which he had not – the building hum of the crowd outside was testament to that. There was something he would know though, which had troubled his sleep.

'Burgoyne?'

It had been his hope, unreasoning though he knew it to be, that somehow John Burgoyne would sweep from his imprisonment and deliver Jack and Louisa from theirs. Or, at the least, send a message of such outrage that the proceedings could be delayed. Even at this hour it was a hope.

But André shook his head. 'Alas, Jack. The messengers sent have not returned. The rumour is the imprisoned army is scattered. Given the speed with which justice has moved in your case, and this snow . . .' He gestured outside. 'And what could Burgoyne send, if he was reached in time and the message got back? That he trusts you? The judges that condemned you would say he was merely the most cozened of all your dupes. So, I am sorry.'

It was what Jack expected, disappointing nonetheless. But one last thing rankled with him.

'I cannot believe the General, preoccupied as he was after the surrender, said nothing of the dangers presented by the Count von Schlaben in the dispatches I brought for General Howe.'

'Ah.' The pipe had gone cold. Rising, André tapped the remains of tobacco out on the back of a perfectly shined boot. 'He did. And I'm rather afraid that I chose not to highlight that warning when I précised the contents of the dispatches for General Howe. It is one of the advantages of having a Commander whose interest in detail is confined to the softer parts of Mrs Loring's anatomy.'

There! It was the last part of the puzzle, the last rope tied around him, binding him to the stake. And yet, instead of anger, he felt almost nothing. In the half hour that remained of his life, less, what was the purpose in railing now against those bonds.

He came off the cot, held out his hand. 'Goodbye, John.'

André shook it. 'Goodbye, Jack. It's been a delight. Apart from . . . well. You missed your vocation, you know. You are an excellent actor. Would that I had you now! The artilleryman playing Marlow in *She Stoops To Conquer* is more wooden than the furniture.' He half-turned, turned back. 'Oh, there is one last and, I'm afraid, disagreeable thing to tell you.' He bit his lip. 'Tarleton commands the firing squad.'

The ironies kept gathering. Jack could only smile. 'Of course he does.'

André shook his head sadly, moved to the door. He was just

about to rap upon it to summon the guard when his hand froze. 'Faith!' he said. 'Nearly forgot.' He went to the wall opposite the cot, searched along it for a while, bent to waist height, his head moving back and forth.

'What are you about, sir?' Now he was near the end, Jack only wanted to be alone.

'Well,' said André, 'a fellow spent some time in this cell once. Occupied that time with thoughts of escape. Ah!' His head stopped moving. He reached out, fingernails digging into a line between two bricks. To Jack's amazement, one of them came loose, then was out and in André's hand. 'The second gift I promised, Jack. Goodbye.'

Laying the brick on the floor, André left the room. Jack waited until the three bolts had been shot before rising and crossing to the gap. It was not the dim light in his cell that failed to enlighten him. There was nothing to be seen, a brick-lined hole was all there was, another brick to the back of it. Then, as he watched, that other brick shifted, waggled, was removed. There was air, a little light from the far side. Then a voice came. 'Thank you, John.' The voice of Louisa Reardon.

A door slammed, bolts thrown in the other cell. 'Louisa?' Jack called softly and in a moment she was there. He could see little of her face. Her brow, fringed in red and gold. Those eyes. Enough.

'Jack?'

'Yes.'

He stared, scarce believing. The noise outside, the increasing frenzy of the hawker's competing shouts, the fiddle and fife that had struck up a series of tunes, the swelling voice of a crowd merging into one eager entity . . . all these faded away, to a world beyond them, the two of them.

'Have you a chair there, Louisa?'

'I have. I'll fetch it.'

She did and he did the same, then they sat opposite each other, discovering that they could not get too close or they blocked out all light and could not see. And he needed to see her, more than anything. To hold her in his sight where she was safe.

They sat in silence, simply looking. Then they both spoke at once.

'You have—'

'I wanted—'

They stopped, started again.

'I must—'

'Will you—'

They laughed. When had he last laughed? Lying beside her at the foot of her bed, wrapped in blankets and the scents of their love-making? As long ago as that?

'Jack. I wanted to . . . there is so little time . . .'

'To?'

'To tell you I am so sorry.'

'For what?'

'For what?' She looked up, away, back. 'You are about to die because of my actions.'

'Because of mine too. And my lack of them.'

She hesitated, her eyes moving back and forth, searching each of his.

'John André told me you kept silent at your trial. You did not defend yourself. Why?'

Jack sighed. 'Any justification I uttered would have condemned you further. I could not do that. And when they discovered the mask, I was lost. The reason I gave them only sounded like an excuse.'

She shook her head. 'Oh Jack! I told Von Schlaben that you took the mask. He would have told André.'

'I thought so.' There was something else that had been nagging at Jack in his cell. 'He was your controller here from the start, wasn't he? Even before Quebec?'

'No. He revealed himself to me as Cato that last night on the *Ariadne*. After the General's dinner, when you saw his hand upon my arm.'

'I remember. You were flustered but covered it up with a tale of his amorous pursuit of you in London and taxing me with my former loves.'

'I did.'

He hesitated but he needed to know. 'And did you tell him much of us?'

Even within the darkness of the brick hole, he could see the light pour into her eyes.

'No, Jack. I told him nothing of that. I thought,' she sighed, 'I thought I could keep it separate. We had not much contact after we arrived, for he went off to St Leger's expedition and then on to here. But a week ago, that night,' she bit her lower lip, looked away for a moment, 'that night when you and I . . . later, I told him everything. I'm so sorry. But I did not know what you would choose to do, whether you would betray me or no.'

'You did not know? How could you not know?'

'I was confused – by everything. The feelings I'd had, our . . . coming together.' Her eyes suddenly lost their sadness. 'You must remember that unlike you, sir, I had had little experience of such matters. While you . . . Gemini! They wrote a play about *your* amours!'

He smiled. The innocent country maid was so well done. 'And you mistook the Jack Absolute of the stage for myself. Understandable, madam. And forgiven.' He peered in, made sure she could see his eyes. 'I mean it, Louisa. Von Schlaben. Everything. Forgiven.'

'But you will die because of it.' The maid had gone.

'Well,' Jack smiled, 'dead for love? I can think of worse causes. I am a little old to play Romeo – though Spranger Barry still does at Covent Garden and he has twenty years on me – and yet, oh, that we had that phial of poison and a dagger. We would cheat them of their show today.'

'I would not,' she said, her chin rising, only the slightest quaver to her voice, 'for I would show them how a true patriot can die.'

Death had entered their cell again, in their conversation, in the intrusion of a drum beginning to beat outside. They could hear the tread of soldiers marching into the square. The clock tolling the quarter-to.

She leaned in again, her tone softened, though there

was an urgency to it as well. 'Do you believe in a heaven, Jack?'

He hesitated. Comforting words or his own confusion? What did it matter now? But she went on. 'Because I do. I've thought of it often, these last days. Not the place commonly described. No clouds, no angels, no bands of the righteous sitting at God's right hand. I've met the righteous and they are dull company. No, my heaven is a farm, like the one where I was born in Cherry Valley. An orchard in full bloom; water meadows thick with spring grass, cows . . .'

Her voice caught and he saw the first tears come. She had stopped, was staring away, into her vision and he wanted her back with him – or to join her there. 'Isn't there a forest too? Yes, I can see it. Maple, oak, beech, hickory for the nuts in the autumn. Até will live nearby, and we will take our sons out to hunt and bring back buck and grouse for you and our daughters to cook.'

'Our daughters?' He had her again, a smile on her face, full of mock anger. '*Our* daughters will be with you on the hunt, Mr Absolute, learning as I did. On the frontier, the women must match the men in all.'

'Aye, they must,' he said, 'and ours will be as fierce and beautiful as their mother.'

'How many will we have?'

'A dozen at the least. Six of each.'

'La, sir. You will have me occupied.'

'Forever,' he said, the word bringing the silence again and with it, the world entering with the sudden cessation of the drum, with the increased hum of the crowd, with the steps in the corridor outside, pausing outside his door, moving on, halting before hers. With one bolt being thrown.

They had come for her first. Oh, God, why had they come for her first?

'Jack,' she said.

'Yes.'

He thrust his hand into the gap. She placed hers there, stretched towards his. The bricks were of no height, the gap so narrow. They struggled, pushed. Another jerked bolt sounded through the tiny hole. Then, just as they thought they would never reach, just as the final bolt of her door was shot, the tip of each forefinger touched and, in the briefest of contacts, a world went back and forth.

'It is time.' The voice of a gaoler clamoured, loud, monstrous. Fingers parted, a chair shrieked back. There was a flash of gathered green silk – *Green again. Hadn't he warned her?* – and she was gone. They left the door open as they took her out, and Jack sat and continued to stare into the air that had lately held her, staying there, staring there, as the world outside returned in sound.

The drum had started again, a single trump now, and the crowd listened to it in silence until a door was flung open. Then they roared once, and immediately fell near quiet again, only murmuring, seeing the whole of what Jack had just seen only a part – Louisa Reardon, dressed in simple perfection, in defiant green, walking, a few feet below him, from the prison door that opened directly on to the scaffold.

He could sit no more, was up, moving back and forth, wall to wall. He had sworn to Burgoyne to see Diomedes dead and that was another oath broken. Yet he would hear her die and suddenly that seemed so much worse. He thought of trying to block his ears, for each noise, how ever small, came up to echo round his cell. But as soon as he reached up his hands, he forced them down again. For she was still alive in this world, a few feet below him and his only link to her was . . . sound. Of her feet, shod in her finest, that determined walk he had heard a lifetime before on the deck of a ship when she'd come to fetch him to supper. The feet stopping, her voice then, crying out, as firm as her step, 'God Bless the Revolution!' Answering cries from a few in the crowd, silence returning . . . till the sound came of a hood being twisted over a head, a struggle as all that hair was shoved in. Sound of hands being tied, of a rope dropping from a crossbar, settling, creaking slightly in the slight wind. Silence again, just for a moment, till the clock on the square began to toll, Jack crossing the room with the first stroke, crossing back on the next, running now, touching the wall, throwing himself to touch it, pushing away, back and forth on every note.

It stopped. He stopped. And the next sounds came. Something falling through air, breath inhaled, his own, a thousand others; the snap of rope; then just the creaking of noose and bar as both took the weight and Jack's howl lost among the many, as if he were now standing outside or they were all in there with him. He fell then, on to the cot, off it, on to the floor. Darkness had come over his eyes, his hands flailed around him, smashed into walls, seemed to touch nothing. The one sense left was still his hearing, though that was now distorted, magnified, selective. Filled only with the creak of rope, the settling of timber, a breeze moving silk.

They let her sway there till the clock again struck the quarter. Then new noises came, of something heavy dropping to grunts, another gasp, more cheers, of men moving below, nails screaming as they were withdrawn from holes, hefty beams of wood being knocked down. Jack knew, despite the numbness that had taken his limbs and mind where he lay on the floor, that a scene change was underway. It was time for the final act of the play, its climax. He used the cot to raise himself, stood and began to dust the cell's leavings from his Redcoat and breeches.

When they led him on to the same scaffold, out into the grey light, he saw that he had been correct, for the simple square frame of the gallows had been disassembled, its three beams laid out one atop the other to his left, the rope carefully coiled and placed at one end. Of Louisa's body there was no sign. André had said that once her prisoner-father had been found, he would be released on grounds of compassion from the Convention Army. She would be kept for him to claim, to bury her, no doubt, in the valley of her childhood.

As the drum struck up again, as he was led to place his back against the scarred brickwork of the gaol – it had obviously been used for this purpose before – he looked around him, taking in everything, feeling nothing. Directly ahead, under louring snow clouds, what should be the fourth side of the square was open to the Delaware River, steps leading down to wharfs. These supplied the shops and warehouses lining the other two sides, split only by single archways that led out to surrounding streets. Each building had an arch, and he presumed there was one in the base of the gaol too.

He looked up. To both his left and right, balconies overhung the square and these were filled with the more fashionable of society, like boxes at Drury Lane. Indeed, it was as fine a theatre as ever he'd seen, the floor of the square the pit, the boxes above. The stage entrances were stairs off the sides of the platform. As he looked, a file of soldiers began to climb the ones to the right, moving to the steady beat of the drum. At their head was Banastre Tarleton.

The file halted on one command, on another became a line facing Jack.

'Rest your firelocks!' Tarleton bawled, and while the ten men obeyed, their officer wheeled and walked towards him. He nodded at the two men who had led Jack to the wall. Instantly, they let go his arms and moved away down the stairs.

The drum had ceased and the chatter had started again in the crowd. Tarleton had to more than whisper to be heard. 'Last blood, eh, Absolute?'

Jack, who had avoided meeting his gaze, did so now. He thought of all the wonderful sentences he could speak, full of bravado, how he would write this scene for the stage. Sheridan would have done well with it, though his bent was more toward comedy. There was a time when Jack might have appreciated the irony – about to be executed by his own army. When he'd lain in that log at Saratoga and considered all the ways he'd nearly died, could yet die, he had not considered that one. When in the forest he'd contemplated all the titles he had acquired, he had never imagined that traitor would be the one by which he would be best remembered. But humour had disappeared from the world. Louisa was dead and she had taken all the smiles away.

Tarleton expected the words, waited for the defiance. When none came, even he was somehow discomfited. Pulling a scarf from his pocket, he reached up to tie it around Jack's eyes.

'No.' It was the only word he would give him. Tarleton stared at him for a moment, then shoved the scarf away. 'Good,' he said, his momentary unease gone, 'For now you'll be able to see all your friends.' He pointed to the balcony on the right. There, sat just behind General Howe, was John André. Beside him was the Count von Schlaben.

Jack looked away, but not before he'd seen the German incline his head in acknowledgement, in triumph. It didn't matter. There was no way to convey in a look how little Jack cared.

Tarleton had walked back to his soldiers. He stopped, facing out to the crowd, took off his hat, and yelled, 'Behold the fate reserved for all traitors! God save the King!' To cheers, he turned back and on his signal, the drum began to sound.

'Raise your firelocks!' Tarleton cried.

Jack looked up into the sky above the river.

'Cock your firelocks!'

A bird flew there. It was a heron, making its ungainly way along. It made him think of that night in the forest, the one that he and Louisa had watched there. Of the other one he'd seen on the battlefield, just before Simon Fraser was shot.

'Present your firelocks!'

A strange thing happened. The heron suddenly plunged down to the far bank. Then he saw why, that another heron floated in some rushes there. The two birds now flapped together, water rising around them, reed-thin necks craning to each other.

Fighting or making love? Jack wondered. It didn't matter. It was just good to see something new, in the moment before he died.

Tarleton had paused, signalled the drum to cease, was staring at Jack intently as if he wanted to fix him for ever in his mind's eye, this enemy conquered. And in the pause, in the silence, a second strange thing happened.

An explosion came, but not of muskets. Muskets could not cause the timbers of the scaffold to be rent suddenly upwards, to bend and splinter and splay around a hole that smoke poured from, sucking three soldiers into it. Tarleton tumbled the other way, shiny boots flailing as he flew down into the crowd, as ungainly as any heron. Jack was flung against the wall, hit it hard, slid to the timber flooring.

'Rebels!' came the cry, amongst the screams, as it had at the theatre only the week before. But Jack was perhaps the first to realize that this was not true when a head thrust through the smoking hole. For it had both a scalp lock on the crown and a face he knew well.

'Come, Daganoweda,' said Até, hoisting himself half-through the gap, reaching out an arm. 'Come.'

He felt he could not move, his body still shaking from the sudden explosion. Até leaned further forward, grabbing and snagging one of Jack's feet. The pulling motion was enough and Jack now scrambled to the hole. His friend dropped away and he peered down, into a chamber filled with smoke; Até stood there with six other warriors.

Iroquois. Mohawk. Wolf.

Heavy boots were thumping towards him on the platform. Orders were being shouted, someone was taking command. There was no time to do anything but sink into the smoky space, so he did. Até and others reached up to break his fall, set him on his feet, propelled him back toward the archway under the gaol house, past two fusiliers unconscious on the ground. The arch gave on to a passage, then out on to the street beyond. Philadelphians, those who had chosen not to attend the executions, stared as they all emerged, trailing smoke. Immediately, Até and the others of his clan began to run to the left, parallel to the back wall of the gaol, helping him whenever he stumbled. They turned at the corner, ran down the side of the building towards the river, dodging around the townsfolk and soldiers fleeing the shock of the square. Someone shouted at them to stop; they ran on.

'Here!' Até pulled him right, away from the steps, through a screen of rushes. Suddenly there was ice under their feet, panes of it cracking as they went over. Then there was the shock of water, freezing water, splashing over his boot tops. Two more Mohawk appeared, pushing two canoes. The others got aboard, dragging him in after. Seizing paddles, fast strokes took them swiftly into the centre of the stream.

His ears still vibrated with the explosion, with the creak of timber and rope, the shouted commands of a firing squad. He had been so ready for his death that this sight – warriors' powerful shoulders ploughing paddles into the water, driving them away from the screams and the fury now fading on the river bank – could have come from another world, that new world Louisa had conjured for him, the one he'd wanted so to believe in.

'Até.' He said his name, as if saying it would make the vision real.

His friend turned, dripping paddle suspended above the water.

'Até,' he said again, 'she's . . . she's . . .'

'I know. I heard. We waited there below, with our barrels of powder.' Then Até, who never showed emotion, reached down and gripped Jack by the shoulder. 'I grieve for your loss. I will condole with you through the winter that lies ahead. But I could do nothing for her. She was not my blood brother. You are. I had to choose, Daganoweda. I chose you.'

He turned back, his paddle joining the others speeding the beech-bark craft through the drifting sheets of ice. In another week, less, the river would be choked with it, impassable. They had swung around downstream, were now passing the town on their left. The square had emptied of all but Redcoats, the officers among them shouting, directing. It had begun to snow hard again, slanting in from the west. No one looked through the flurries to the water.

As Jack put his face into the snow, into the wind that drove it, the vessels shot across the mouth of a little bulrush bay . . . and there were they were, two silhouettes on stilts. Startled, the herons rose, circled each other once, separated, vanished into white. All that remained of them was their harsh cries and soon even those were gone.

AUTHOR'S NOTE

'No man but a blockhead wrote except for money'
SAMUEL JOHNSON

The Malvern Festival Theatre, 10 February, 1987. Opening night of a revival of the eighteenth-century comedy, Sheridan's *The Rivals*. The actor Chris Humphreys walks on to the stage and, in reply to a question, speaks these words:

'And what did he say, on hearing I was in Bath?'

My life as Jack Absolute had begun.

I have been an actor for twenty-five years. In that time I have played over a hundred roles – from a zealot in the deserts of Tunisia at +45C to Hamlet in Calgary at −30C, in venues that range from a theatre above a pub in London to the sound stages of 20th Century Fox in Hollywood. Many I enjoyed, many I hope are never seen or spoken of again. Relatively few can I say I truly 'nailed', that I'd done the best job possible despite the obstacles presented by directors, fellow performers, the weather, the audience, a hangover, and a thousand and one other things that can come between an actor and his craft.

Jack Absolute was one of the few I did nail. I loved playing him. I have a photo of me in the role, in mid-soliloquy, pinned above my desk for writing inspiration. Posed and poised, I wear a Redcoat, gorget and sash, with a walking-stick raised at a provocative angle and a plume in my tricorn hat! I saw him as dashing, wicked, humorous, courageous, foolhardy, and, at times, plain bloody foolish. I made him a role-player, a man of masks. And I always had the feeling that the playwright,

Richard Brinsley Sheridan, if he happened to be looking down, would have approved.

The theatrical tour lasted six months. Like anyone you become close to and then lose touch with, I missed Jack when he was gone. In those days, the thought of writing novels was pure fantasy; yet even then I speculated (in the way one composes an Oscar acceptance speech) that if ever I did, he would be a wonderful character to base a novel on, with half my work already done because I knew him so well. It was a way, I dreamed, of being him again.

Then my first novel came out. My publishers asked, 'What next?' and Jack stirred inside me. They agreed on the idea but, like me, they knew that for the character to live beyond the one in Sheridan's play he would have to be rather more than the dashing army Captain and oft-unscrupulous lover. He would have to *do* something. Thus he became a spy – amongst other things.

I again worked to the principle that had guided me through my first two novels – write what you love. And as in those two books, research gave me much of the story. Since *The Rivals* was first performed at Drury Lane in 1775 and was in the repertoire thereafter, I read up on those times. Tremendous they were too, with the American War of Independence just beginning, a very suitable arena for my gallant Captain's skills and obsessions. And since, in my version, Jack became the model for the one in Sheridan's play – much to Jack's fury! – my love of theatre could be incorporated into the tale. Other passions then made their entrances – actresses in all their infuriating allure; Hamlet, the only stage role I've played to match Jack (and an obsession ever since); the use of all kinds of bladed weaponry; the Iroquois (I did so much research about them for my second novel, *Blood Ties*, that I was bloody well going to use them again!); an intriguing military campaign. These and many more, built around my memory of being Jack Absolute. This led to a sort of strange déjà vu, especially when writing the scenes from the productions of *The Rivals*. I made Jack say the lines the way I, as Jack, had said them. He reacts like me, worries, as I did, about getting laughs. And since the first play I wrote was partly autobiographical again, like 'my' Jack, I have seen my life 'acted' upon the stage. I have played opposite lovers current and past. Layers up on layers – making for some very odd writing days!

Once more I have fictionalized real people and realized fictional ones. Of the former, John Burgoyne was irresistible, an older version of my hero. Playwright, renowned ladies' man, a very capable military commander, he was also the best-dressed man on two continents – not for nothing did the American's nickname him 'Gentleman Johnny'. I have also attempted portraits of other real-life figures such as the actress Elizabeth Farren, Colonel St Leger, Sheridan, Edward Pellew, John André, Banastre Tarleton, the Mohawk Leader Joseph Brant, and Benedict Arnold. I realize that any portrait is partial, can only show an aspect. With Brant and Arnold especially, people have distinct opinions of them and their actions. I can only do what a historical novelist must – stick as closely as possible to the known facts (disputed though some of these might be) and then make a judgement call as to character. I hope not too many are offended by my choices.

Of the pure inventions I should mention Angus MacTavish, the Unintelligible Scot. He appeared after I'd read *Kidnapped*, by one of the masters, Robert Louis Stevenson, and spent much of the time resorting to the glossary of Scots-English.

As regards the history of the Saratoga campaign, and the specifics of the battles, I have drawn from a variety of sources, and most of the incidents I describe – Oriskany (both the battle and the subsequent massacre), the idiot Hans-Yost, the death of Simon Fraser, the storming of the redoubts at Saratoga, the loss of the crucial mask, to name but a few – did happen. I also had the enormous pleasure of attending, in October 2002, the 225th anniversary re-enactment of the battle of Saratoga at Fort Edward, New York, where Don Beale, 'Commander-in-Chief' of the British Army, was most hospitable and informative, along with many other fanatical re-enactors – Redcoats, Continentals, and Mohawk. Then I walked the actual field at Bemis Heights – superbly preserved – for two days. Alone in the dusk light, standing where so many brave men from both sides had fought and died, absorbing that atmosphere, was a privilege that gave me priceless detail – both the heron and the butterfly made their appearances then. The experience was like a few other, rare times in my life – such as when I was on that stage and Chris/Jack got that first laugh. My thought – at Malvern, at Saratoga – was the same: 'They pay me to do this!'

I have read a number of texts to write this novel, too many to list entirely. But certain ones were indispensable. Christopher Hibbert's *Redcoats and Rebels* gave a good overview of the war and its causes. Michael Glover's *General Burgoyne in Canada and America* was both useful and partisan on behalf of an often-derided commander. Roy Porter's *English Society in the 18th Century* was excellent on both facts and mindset as was Liza Picard's *Dr Johnson's London*. Works from the ever-wonderful Osprey Publishing gave me much background on the war, its soldiers and their uniforms, their *Saratoga 1777* by Brendan Morrissey being especially detailed and evocative. For the Mohawks, *The League of the Iroquois* by Lewis Henry Morgan was as inspiring as it had been when I wrote *Blood Ties*; and *Joseph Brant – Man of Two Worlds* by Isabel Thompson Kelsay was an excellent, sympathetic portrait of the man and his people. For the secret society, the Illuminati, I found by chance a powerful exposé, *Proofs of a Conspiracy*, written about them in 1798 by Professor John Robison, Professor of Natural Philosophy at Edinburgh University. He made them out to be as sinister and ruthless as I needed Jack's enemy to be. For spies and spying I purchased, at Saratoga, John Bakeless's *Turncoats, Traitors & Heroes*. Informative – though I will discharge him of Jack's unusual method of discovering the invisible ink, which is entirely down to my grubby mind! Jean Benedetti's life, *David Garrick* was great on theatre, its mores and questionable morals (how little we actors have changed). Of contemporary accounts, Burgoyne's own account of the campaign – published to justify his conduct – was very useful. William Hickey's *Memoirs of a Georgian Rake* makes any sin Jack commits look quite tame indeed. And Lieutenant Thomas Anburey's *With Burgoyne from Quebec* was rich in detail – and provided the antidote to snake bite. Finally, there's no escaping the influence of the playwrights on my work and, especially, dialogue – Burgoyne's *Maid of the Oaks*, Goldsmith's *She Stoops To Conquer* (in which, in 1993, I played Marlow), and, of course, Sheridan's *The Rivals*.

To these, and many other authors, I owe much gratitude. I also have some others to thank. There are the usual suspects, their importance no way diminished by still being suspected. My wife, Aletha, the first to read and comment, as always. My agent Anthea Morton-Saner. At Orion, Publishing Director, Jane Wood and especially my point man there, editor and enthusiast Jon Wood. My hands-on editor, Rachel Leyshon, whose wonderful notes challenge and inspire. My Canadian publisher, Kim McArthur.

And perhaps, finally, the man to whom this book is dedicated. For if Philip Grout had not cast me as Jack Absolute in 1987 I would not be writing this now. He has been a friend and mentor ever since. He even directed my first play here in London in 1998. It is a pleasure to collaborate with him and I always learn a lot.

C.C. Humphreys
London, May 2003